THE APPLE
IN THE DARK

THE TEXAS PAN AMERICAN SERIES

THE APPLE
IN
THE DARK

by Clarice Lispector

*Translated from the Portuguese, with an
introduction by Gregory Rabassa*

UNIVERSITY OF TEXAS PRESS
AUSTIN

International Standard Book Number 0-292-70392-9
Library of Congress Catalog Card Number 86-50619

Originally published in Portuguese as
A *Maçã no Escuro* by Livraria Francisco Alves
Copyright © 1961 by Editôra Paulo de Azevedo
Ltda.

Translation by Gregory Rabassa
Copyright © 1967 by Alfred A. Knopf, Inc.

First University of Texas Press Edition, 1986

Requests for permission to reproduce material from
this work should be sent to Permissions, University
of Texas Press, Box 7819, Austin, Texas 78713-7819.

The Texas Pan American Series is published with the
assistance of a revolving publication fund established
by the Pan American Sulphur Company.

By CREATING all things, he entered into everything. By entering into all things, he became what has form and what is formless; he became what can be defined and what cannot be defined; he became what has support and what has no support; he became what is crude and what is delicate. He became every kind of thing: that is why wise men called him the Real One.

The Vedas (the Upanishads)

✍ Contents

Introduction

CLARICE LISPECTOR was born in Checkelnik, Ukraine, in 1924, a purely incidental fact in her life, as her parents, already en route to embark for Brazil at the time, had merely paused in their journey long enough for their second daughter to be born. The family settled in Recife, and Clarice attended school there until the age of twelve, when the family moved to Rio de Janeiro. Clarice completed her secondary schooling in the capital and entered the Faculty of Law at the university there, from which she was graduated in 1944. In 1943 she had married Mauri Gurgel Valente, a fellow student who entered the foreign service of Brazil upon graduation. Her husband was posted to Naples in 1944, and Clarice spent many of the following years outside Brazil, eight of them in the United States. She did most of her writing abroad, and her two sons were born overseas. In 1959 she returned to Brazil, and she has lived in Rio de Janeiro ever since.

She had begun writing while she was still in school; and while doing editorial work to help support herself, she struck up a friendship with the novelist Lúcio Cardoso, who encouraged her and read her works. He was responsible for the title of her first novel, *Perto do Coração Selvagem* (Close to the Savage Heart), a name he had drawn from Joyce's *Portrait of the Artist as a Young Man*. This novel, published in 1943, was both a critical and a financial sucess. It was followed by two more novels. *O Lustre* (The Chandelier) in 1946 and *A Cidade Sitiada* (The Besieged City) in 1949. During these years she had also written several short stories, many of which appeared in the magazine *Senhor* and came out in book form as *Alguns Contos* (Some Stories) in 1952 and *Laços de Família* (Family Ties) in 1959. This latter collection contains her best-known story, "O Professor de Matemática," which has appeared in English in *Odyssey Review* as "The Crime of the Mathematics Professor." A *Maçã no Escuro* (Eng. tr., *The Apple in the Dark*) appeared in 1961 and was at once accepted as her finest work so far. A collection of short stories and chronicles, *A Legião Estrangeira* (The Foreign Legion), was published in 1964, the same year as her latest novel, *A Paixão segundo G. H.* (The Passion According to G. H.).

The style in all of these works is interior and hermetic. In most cases the action is seen from the point of view of the characters involved, and the description is also likely to be made through their eyes. This fact places her among the new vanguard of writers who have appeared in Brazil since the end of World War II and who have taken a further step along the path initiated by the so-called "Modernist" renovation of 1922. Because the Modernist movement was so broad as to defy exact definition, including, as it did, novelists and social scientists as well as poets like Mário de Andrade, who were most responsible for its inception, many of its effects were dissipated in the vastness of what would actually seem to be normal course of literary development in Brazil, whether a movement or not. The influence of social writers such as Gilberto Freyre led to a sort of regionalist bias in the novelist of the twenties and thirties, and even the most important of these, such as Graciliano Ramos, José Lins do Rêgo, and Jorge Amado, occupied themselves almost exclusively with their native Northeast.

The poets of the time were in many ways the real forerunners of the novelists of today. Their mythmaking tended to combine personal elements with national traits and realities. Beginning with Mário de Andrade's fantasy-novel *Macunaíma*, the story of "a hero without character," one can follow this combination through the work and styles of such poets as the protean Cassiano Ricardo—always in the vanguard—Jorge de Lima, and Manuel Bandeira down through Carlos Drummond de Andrade, in all of whom one finds introspection coupled with concrete circumstance. A second look at the novelists of the period, however, will reveal that beneath the surface of seeming regionalism there runs an extremely personal note: Lins do Rêgo's plantation boy is no stereotype; Jorge Amado, with the richness of Afro-Brazilian themes in his Bahian novels, is at work on a mythology that ultimately shows through and takes precedence over any political intent, as in *Mar Morto* (Dead Sea), easily his most Modernist and most "modern" novel; and Graciliano Ramos, as he struggles for a new expression and digs deeply into human and even genuinely canine motivations in *Vidas Sêcas* (Eng. tr., *Barren Lives*).

The most obvious heir to this mixing of intents, one who has left the thirties far behind after having been spawned in its currents, is João Guimarães Rosa, with *Grande Sertão: Veredas* (Eng. tr., *The Devil to Pay in the Backlands*) and *Sagarana*. In the second book the very title gives away his intent as he appends the Tupi suffix *-rana*, meaning "in the manner of," to the Norse word *saga*. In Guimarães Rosa we have the frankest admission of re-creation and mythmaking plus a complex and often Joycean attempt to create new linguistic forms often derived from popular speech.

With the postwar years there is something of a reshuffling of elements, and the novel loses much of its regionalism, while some poetry returns to the native soil. João Cabral de Melo Neto of Recife writes about his native Pernambuco from abroad with nostalgic feeling reminiscent of the Brazilian romantic poets in exile, while in Rio de Janeiro the novelist Nélida Piñon makes biblical themes over into modern problems with an underlay that is Freudian and universal. Her two novels *Guia-Mapa de Gabriel Arcanjo* (Map and Guide to the Archangel Gabriel) and *Madeira Feita Cruz* (Wood Made into a Cross) are exquisite models of an effort toward total expression of theme set forth with the skillful use of language that characterizes the best of current Brazilian fiction. In quite a different way Campos de Carvalho uses a shadowy Rio de Janeiro as the scene of his *Vaca de Nariz Sutil* (Thin-Nosed Cow), a Joyce-cum-Kafka-cum-Arreola antiadventure that is closest to the objective fantasies of the Cuban writer Virgilio Piñera. In all of these writers one finds this touch of the intimate, the universal, the existential, showing that many contemporary Brazilian writers are in tune with certain international currents such as the *nouveau roman* and that this has come about more naturally and less from outside influences than one might suspect. It is more a matter of the coincidences of modern society. This is where Clarice Lispector fits in, somewhere between a Guimarães Rosa and a Nélida Piñon.

The Apple in the Dark represents the high point in the development of Miss Lispector's work, the point toward which she was striving nad to which her later novel is, in a sense, a footnote. Most of the elements that go to make up the current trend in Brazilian fiction can be seen in her work. The invention is not as obvious as in Guimarães Rosa because it is less a matter of neologisms and re-creation than of certain radical departures in the use of syntactical structure, the rhythm of the phrase being created in defiance of norms, making her style more difficult to translate at times than many of Rosa's inventions. Nor is the traditional vocabulary here anywhere as rich as in the works of Nélida Piñon. It is precisely in their styles of presentation that the three writers diverge: Guimarães Rosa using the primitive resources of the language for the creation of new words in which to encase his vast and until then amorphous sensations; Piñon extracting every bit of richness from the lexicon of a very rich language without falling into archaisms or other such absurdities; and Lispector marshaling the syntax in a new way that is closer perhaps to original thought patterns than the language had ever managed to approach before. These three elements are the stylistic basis of all good contemporary Brazilian literature.

Martim, the protagonist of *The Apple in the Dark*, is a perfect antihero, almost quixotic, except that Don Quixote knows only too well—and to his detriment—where he is going, while Martim is completely without direction, negative in the sense that his motion is directed by flight rather than pursuit. He is loath to act even when action means escape, thinking that his capture will be his salvation; whereas it is obvious that there is no real salvation either way: if he escapes the law, he will go on thinking that he is morally doomed; if he turns himself in, he will go on worrying about the very motivations that made him do so, and he will be equally unfulfilled.

It is a story with no sure future, no definitive accomplishments, with everything still doubtful at the end for all the characters concerned. It is the story of three people coming together, each with an aim or a fear or a combination of the two, and what at first seems to have been a tremendous accomplishment for each one: Martim's seeming re-creation of himself and his place in the whole universe, Ermelinda's outburst into love as a defense against her fear of death, and Vitória's softening into what she had felt she should have been—all are really futile in the end as they face their mean and shapeless reality. It is in this sense that the book is quixotic. The words "hope" and "waiting" figure prominently. Don Quixote at least had the advantage of being mad, so that his view of what was around him was clear and definite to him. These people are conscious of their self-delusion, and this is what disturbs them and will be their lasting reality as they backslide out of their dreams and cogitations.

The story begins with the impression that something new will come about, that there will be a rebirth. The early symbolism is both biblical and Darwinian. It all begins in chaos as Martim flees the hotel and wanders across countryside that is described better by touch than by sight because of the darkness. It is a direction into the dark, the primitive, almost the spermatozoic, which drives him on to survive and develop. He bears a burden of guilt that seems natural to him but of which the reader has few details and which he must accept as it is. He has been expelled, in a sense, as if out of Eden, and he hopes for some kind of regeneration as he loses language, the gift that raised man above the beast. He wants language, but he also rejects the form in which he has known it. His struggle for language is one symbolic track of the futility of his rebirth and rebuilding as he goes back to what he had had before, from his own lucubrations to animal noises and pantomime with the Negro girl until he has speech again. And then he is right back where he was before.

Communion follows the same pattern as he goes from rocks to plants to vermin to cattle to children and finally to contact with other humans, whom he had abandoned before. There is a pattern of disillusionment as he climbs the evolutionary scale. Each new step up means a rejection of sorts, as he is repelled by the attitude of the little girl after he had hoped so much to make contact with her. And when he comes to the human level he had left, it becomes a shambles for him as he finds himself involved in two lives as complex as his own life had been, those of Vitória and Ermelinda. The effects of these people upon one another are transitory, a series of "happenings." Indeed, one might even classify the whole book as an extended "happening."

The trait that the three seem to have in common is a need for involvement. Vitória, so deeply involved with her sick father, has replaced him with the farm. This could well be a great tragedy (in a cheap sort of way), as she herself would like to believe, but it really is not. Her tragedy might rather be that it is not tragic at all. Ermelinda, so frightened of death and its symbols in her nitwit way, has been widowed and therefore touched by death, but her widowhood is not at issue except as a symbol. Ultimately she is a rather routine mental case. Her tragedy is even shallower than Vitória's, almost a travesty. As we examine these three levels of the "tragic soul," we come to Martim, and his situation must be seen in the light of the other two. At first it would seem that he too is involved in the mournful course of existence as it wipes out hopes and aims, but in the end he chooses to go back to where he had come from, much like Don Quixote when he recovered his senses, though at that point Don Quixote knew that he was dying, that it was all over. Martim's future is fearfully more of the same. His martyrdom (as he sees it somehow in a selfish sort of way) is represented by the shoemaker-saints in the picture on the wall of the woodshed. The patient work of a lifetime within society can end up in the cauldron. There is the prospect of ascending to heaven, but in the course of this story Martim has not thought very coherently about such things. He is still too much involved in getting back to being a normal human being with a place in society. He is still striving to be Crispin or Crispinian, the shoemarker, and must postpone the second, saintly phase.

What Unamuno calls "the tragic sense of life" must be the tragedy here, the more so because of the base circumstances— not because of the deep involvements that Martim and the others find in their own minds, but because of what the fine and peaceful human life which they have been striving for really is. We have the outside world as represented by the professor and his son. They are the ones who will give continuity to the story, and it is the professor who arranges for the authorities to pick up Martim. He is society's surrogate, the one who brings the willing martyr back to reality. This pompous and shallow man, who has ruined his son (who at best could have been only as eminent as his father, but he cannot even be that now), represents the world outside that Shangri-La *manqué*. At that point one must come to agree with Martim's futile, self-abusive feelings as he is led off. What else to do but hope for a change, any change perhaps, along with the idiotic hope that some regeneration has come about? But then we see that it will be just another introspective novel like this, and that Martim will continue on with more illusion and disillusion, Don Quixote as masochist, the human condition as gathered together to form society.

The title is a kind of symbol of all that goes to make up the final theme of the book, and what message we are left with, hopeless as it may be, is summed up in it. The second time the notion is mentioned, it comes more clearly as part of the litany recited between Martim and the image of his father, his progenitor, toward the end of the book. We understand then why Miss Lispector has stressed the motif of darkness so much, perhaps why it is an apple, the popularly accepted fruit of the tree of knowledge. The apple can be felt and grasped and recognized in the dark, but there is always the danger and the fear that we may not have a good grip on it and may drop it. In this way the story ends on what could be a hopeless note. Adam and Eve knew what it was and bit into it, becoming human, with all of the tribulations entailed. Here there is the danger that we may drop it and go on being frustrated, even though its attainment means a new frustration. In this way the story seems to be telling us that there is consolation in holding on firmly to what we can recognize around us in the darkness of our ignorance, but it also makes us wonder whether we shall be any better off for it.

Part I

HOW A MAN IS MADE

Chapter 1

THIS TALE begins in March on a night as dark as night can get when a person is asleep. The peaceful way in which time was passing could be seen in the high passage of the moon across the sky. Then later on, much deeper into night, the moon too disappeared.

There was nothing now to distinguish Martim's sleep from the slow and moonless garden. When a man slept so deeply, he came to be the same as that tree standing over there or the hop of a toad in the darkness.

Some of the trees there had grown with rooted leisure until they reached the top of their crowns and the limit of their destiny. Others had burst out of the earth in quick tufts. The flower beds had an order about them that was concentrating in a great struggle to achieve some kind of symmetry. Although this order was discernible from up on the balcony of the large hotel, a person standing at the level of the flower beds could not make it out. The driveway, detailed in small cut stones, lay between the flower beds.

Off in one turn of the drive the Ford had been parked for so long a time that it was already part of the great interwoven garden and its silence.

By day, however, the countryside was different, and the crickets, vibrating hollow and hard, left the entire expanse open, shadowless. All the while there was that dry smell of crumbling stone that daytime has in the country. Yet on that very day Martim had been standing on the balcony, uselessly obedient, so as not to miss anything that was going on. But not very much was going on. Before one's eyes reached the beginning of the road, which disappeared into the dust suspended in the sunlight, there was only the garden to be contemplated, comprehensible and symmetrical from up on the balcony, tangled and confused when one became part of it—and the man had been playing for two weeks now with what he could remember of it, carefully nurturing it, saving it for eventual use. For any other kind of attention, however, the day was untouchable, like a point designed upon the point itself. The voice of the cricket was the very body of the cricket, and it told nothing. The only advantage of daytime was that in the bright light the car was becoming a little beetle that could easily get to the highway.

But while the man was sleeping, the car was becoming enormous in the way that an idle machine is gigantic. And at night the garden was filled with the secret weaving that darkness lives on, work whose existence is suddenly made clear by fireflies. A certain dampness also betrayed the secret of the work. And night was an element in which life, by becoming strange, became recognizable.

It was on that night that the motor of the car vibrated and reached out to the empty and sleeping hotel. The darkness slowly began to move.

Instead of waking up and listening directly, Martim passed over to the other side of darkness through an even deeper sleep, and there he heard the sound the wheels made as they spat up the dry sand. Then his name was spoken, clearly and cleanly, in some way pleasant to hear. It was the German who had spoken. In his sleep Martim enjoyed the sound of his own name. And then the violent cry of a bird whose wings had been frightened into immobility, the way fright can seem to be joy.

When it became silent within the silence again, Martim was sleeping even farther away. And yet in the depths of his sleep something had echoed with difficulty, trying to organize itself. Until the sound of the car in all of its finest details was repeated in his memory, without any sense, and free from the inconvenience of having to be understood. The idea of the car alerted a soft warning that he did not immediately understand. But now a vague alarm had spread out into the world, and its center of

(4)

radiation was the man himself: "So me, then," his body thought, touched with pity. He remained lying down, remotely enjoying it.

The man had arrived at the hotel two weeks before, finding it in the middle of the night with almost no surprise. Exhaustion makes everything like that possible. It was an empty hotel, with only the German and the servant, if he was a servant. And for two weeks, while Martim was getting his strength back in almost uninterrupted sleep, the car had remained parked in one of the driveways, its wheels buried in the sand—so motionless, so resistant to the man's habit of incredulity and his care not to let himself be deceived that Martim had finally ended up feeling that it was at his disposal.

But the truth is that even on that night when he had staggered in—when he had at last let himself drop half dead onto a real bed with real sheets—even then the car had represented the security of new flight, in case the two men should seem to be too curious about the identity of the guest. And he had fallen asleep confidently as if nobody would ever be able to wrest from his firm grasp the imaginary rim of a steering wheel as he clutched the sheet in his hands.

The German, however, had not asked him anything, and the servant, if that was what he was, had scarcely glanced at him. Their reluctance to take him in had not come from any distrust but from the fact that the hotel had not been a hotel for some time—ever since it had been fruitlessly put up for sale, the German had explained to him. And so as not to cause suspicion, Martim had nodded his head, smiling. Before the new highway had been built, cars had passed by there, and the isolated big house could not have been better situated as an obligatory stopping place for the night. When the new highway had been put through thirty miles away, it detoured all the cars that used to pass, and the whole town had died. So there was no reason any more for anyone to have use for a hotel in a place that had been turned over to the winds. But in spite of the apparent indifference of the two men Martim's obstinate quest for security became tied to that car over which the spiders too had executed their perfect aerial work, which had been tranquilized by all of its varnished immobility.

That was the car that had uprooted itself with a hoarse sound in the middle of the night.

In the silence which was once more intact, the man now stared stupidly at the invisible ceiling, which in the darkness was as high as the sky. Stretched out on his back upon the bed, he tried with an effort of gratuitous pleasure to reconstruct the sound of the wheels, for he did not feel pain, but pleasure in a general way. He could not see the garden from his bed. A little mist was coming in through the open Venetian blinds, and the man could tell that it was there from the smell of damp cotton and from a certain physical yearning for happiness that fog induces. It had only been a dream, then. Skeptical, however, he got up.

In the darkness he could see nothing from the balcony, and he could not even guess the symmetry of the flower beds. A few splotches darker than the darkness itself showed the probable location of the trees. The garden remained as nothing but an effort of memory, and the man stared quietly, sleepily. Here and there a firefly made the darkness even vaster.

Having forgotten about the dream that had drawn him out onto the balcony, the man's body found that it was a pleasant feeling to sense itself in a healthy upright position. The air was in suspension, and the dark position of the leaves was little changed. He let himself stand there, then, docile, bewildered, with the succession of unoccupied rooms behind him. Those empty rooms multiplied themselves until they disappeared off to where the man could no longer see anything more. Martim sighed inside his long waking sleep. Without too much insistence he tried to grasp the notion of the rooms farthest away, as if he himself had grown too large and had spread out too much, and for some reason that he had already forgotten—for some obscure reason—it had become essential to retreat so that he could think or perhaps feel. But he could not get himself to do it, and it was very pleasant. So he stayed there, with the courteous air of a man who has been hit over the head. Until—just as when a clock stops ticking and only thus makes us aware that it had been ticking before—Martim perceived the silence and his own presence within the silence. Then by means of a very familiar lack of comprehension the man at last began to be himself in an indistinct sort of way.

Then things began to get reorganized, beginning with him: the darkness was beginning to be understood, branches were slowly taking shape under the balcony, shadows dividing up into flowers, undefined as yet. With their edges hidden by the quiet lushness of the plants, the flower beds were outlined, full and soft. The man grunted approvingly. With some difficulty he had just recognized the garden, which at intervals during those two weeks of sleep had constituted his irreducible vision.

It was at that moment that a faint moon passed out of a cloud in great silence, silently spread itself over the calm stones, and silently disappeared into the darkness. The moonlit face of the man turned then toward the drive where the Ford ought to be standing motionless.

But the car had disappeared.

The man's entire body suddenly woke up. With a sharp glance his eyes covered the whole darkness of the garden—and without a sign of warning he wheeled around toward his room with the soft leap of a monkey. Nothing was moving, however, in the cavity of the room, which had become enormous in the darkness. The man stood breathing heavily, alert and uselessly fierce, with his hands held in front of him against attack. But the silence of the hotel was the same as that of night. And without visible limits the room prolonged the darkness of the garden with the same exhalation. To wake himself up the man rubbed his eyes several times with the back of one hand while keeping the other one free for defense. His new sensibility was of no use. In the darkness his wide-open eyes could not even see the walls.

It was as if he had been set down alone in the middle of a

field. And as if he had finally remembered a long dream in which a hotel, now broken up in pieces on the empty ground, had figured, a car imagined only through desire, and—above all—as if the reason for a man to be all expectant in a place was also a form of expectancy.

All that he had left of reality was the wisdom that had made him take a leap in vague defense, the instinct that was now leading him to calculate with unexpected lucidity that if the German had gone to turn him in, it would take some time for him to get there and return with the police.

Which still left him free temporarily—unless the servant had been assigned to watch him. And in that case the servant, if that is what he was, would at this very moment be outside the door of that very room with his ear alert to the slightest movement on the part of the guest.

That is what he was thinking. And when he stopped his reasoning, which he had reached with the malleability an invertebrate uses to become smaller in order to slip away, Martim plunged into the same previous absence of reason and the same obtuse impartiality, as if nothing had anything to do with him and as if the species would take care of him. Without looking back, guided by a slippery adroitness of movement, he began to climb down the balcony by placing his unexpectedly flexible feet on the outcroppings of the bricks. In his attentive remoteness the man could smell, as if he would never forget it, the malevolent odor of the broken ivy near his face. Now only his spirit was alert, and it could not distinguish between what was and what was not important, and he gave the same scrupulous consideration to every operation.

With a soft jump that made the garden gasp as it held its breath, he found himself right in the middle of a flower bed, which ruffled up and then closed down. With his body alert the man waited for the message of his jump to be transmitted from secret echo to secret echo, until it would be transformed into distant silence. His thud would end by breaking on the side of some mountain. No one had taught the man to have that intimacy with things that happen at night, but a body knows.

He waited a while longer, until nothing was happening. Only then did he carefully feel for the glasses in his pocket. They were intact. He sighed carefully and finally looked around. The night was delicately vast and dark.

Chapter 2

THE MAN had walked for miles, leaving the big house farther and farther behind. He tried to walk in a straight line, and sometimes he would halt for a moment and grasp cautiously at the air. Since he was walking in darkness, he could not even guess in which direction he had headed when he had left the hotel behind. What guided him in the darkness was his simple intention of walking in a straight line. The man might as well have been a Negro, for all the use he got from the lightness of his skin; and the only awareness of who he was, came from the sensation he felt in himself of the movements he himself was making.

He was fleeing with the meekness of a slave. A certain gentleness had taken hold of him, modified only by the observation of his own submission and the fact that in some way he was guiding it. No thought upset his steady and now unconscious march, unless it was the hazy idea that maybe he was walking in circles, along with the disconcerting possibility that he would find himself once more alongside the walls of the hotel.

As always, along with the ground his feet were putting behind him, there was the darkness. He had already been walking for hours; this he could deduce from his feet, heavy with fatigue. Only when daylight would start to glow and dissipate the mist would he be able to tell where the horizon was. Since the darkness still seemed to stick so much to his uselessly opened eyes, he finally came to the conclusion that he had fled from the hotel not in the early morning but in the middle of the night. He had that great empty space of a blind man inside of him, and he kept on going forward.

As he had no need for eyes now, he experimented by keeping them shut as he walked, because he wanted to take the over-all precaution of trying to economize in every way he could. With his eyes closed he got the feeling that he was circling himself in some mad way, and it was not entirely disagreeable.

As the man was walking along he could feel in his nostrils that acute lack of smell so peculiar to the purest of atmospheres, and something that holds itself aloof from other fragrances that could be smelled; and he was guided by that, as if his only mission were to find the clearest depths of air. But his feet took on that age-old fear of maybe stepping on some moving thing— his feet could feel the suspicious softness of things that take advantage of the darkness as the base of their existence. His feet brought him in contact with the means of surrender and of being able to be molded, and this is where one enters the night's worst phase: its permissiveness. He could not tell where he was stepping, and only through his shoes, as they became a means of communication, did he sense the doubtfulness of earth.

There was nothing for the man to do but wait for the first glow to show him a path. Until that time he could go to sleep on the ground which, made more distant by the darkness, seemed unattainable. Danger was no longer a goad, and the sagacity born of it would now be but a shackle and had disappeared. And once more he was lulled by a soft stupefaction. The ground felt so far away that as he abandoned his body, he could feel something like a fall through a vacuum. He scarcely touched the earth, which quivered beneath his feet and then all at once became resistant to them in hard and stable folds like the roof of a horse's mouth. The man stretched out his legs and put down his head. Now that he was quiet, the air took on the sharpness and pain of its utter cleanliness. The man was no longer sleepy, but in the darkness he could not tell what to do with this great wakefulness. Besides, it made no sense.

By that time he had become used to the strange music heard at night, fashioned from the possibility that things will chirp and from the soft rub of silence against silence. It was a lament without sadness. The man was in the heart of Brazil. And the silence was enjoying itself. But if softness was the way in which the night was heard, for night the softness was its own sharp sword, one could shroud the night in all that softness. He refused to be bewitched by the joy he felt in the softness; he guessed that for miles and miles farther the darkness knew about his presence. He stayed alert, therefore, and kept nocturnal messages under his perfect control.

Several times he tried to find a more comfortable position. He took impersonal care of himself, as if he were a bundle. But underneath there was the definitive earth, and above, the only star, and the man felt he was awake because only these two things were awake in the darkness. With each of his movements his face or his hands would come upon something that, when pushed, would return to strike him softly. He felt with his wise fingers; it was a branch.

And then an instant later and all at once sleep came over him in a most unexpected position: one of his hands protected his eyes, while the other held back the harsh foliage.

The man slept wakefully for hours. Just the hours needed for the formation of a thought, whatever it was, for he could no longer reach himself except in the perception of sleep. The moment he had closed his eyes, the vast and inarticulate idea began taking shape—and everything worked so perfectly that without pause and without having to retreat for correction it filled the sleep he needed to help him think. While he was asleep, he did not use up what little he had become but drew on something such as his race as a man, something indistinct and satisfactory. Out of that thing fashioned from a grunt he drew a lot: his mouth was fat with good and nourishing saliva. So when the last step toward his future was over, Martim stirred upon the hardness of the ground. He had not opened his eyes yet; but as he felt his own sluggishness, he recognized himself and reluctantly understood that he was awake.

The great weight of day was actually bearing down upon his delicate eyelids, and he already felt the pain of it.

But with a feeling of mistrust that had no intelligible motive, he evidently found it more prudent to communicate with his situation by means of touch: with his eyes shut he slowly moved his fingers along the ground, and in a promising sign, which he did not understand but which he approved of, it

(1 2)

seemed less cold and less compact to him. With this basic assurance he finally opened his eyes.

And a brutal clearness blinded him as if he had received a salty sea-wave in the face.

Dizzy, with his mouth open, that man was sitting like a child in the middle of a wasteland that reached in all directions as far as the eye could see. It was a dry and stupid light. And he was sitting like a doll fastened down right in the midst of that thing which was beating down on him.

The place in which he found himself was much less confusing than his drowsy feet had imagined in the darkness. His body was restless and could not tell whether or not it ought to feel pleasure in that discovery. He cautiously checked the few trees scattered about in the distance. The endless ground was reddish and dry. It was not a case of brush-land, as he had imagined from the branch that had struck him in the face. He had just happened to fall asleep beside one of the rare bushes in all that open country.

Sitting there he still kept a watchful eye out; although silence may have seemed to be a natural part of darkness, he had not counted on the vehement muteness of the sun. He had always felt that the sun had voices. He did not move, therefore, so as not to startle whatever it might have been. It was a silence as if something were going to happen beyond a man's perception; but the few trees were swaying, and the bugs had already disappeared.

Keeping in mind his own limitations which gave him as much defense as a rabbit, he waited with his head lifted up, as if a position of disinterest would render him invisible. Nobody had taught him that, either. But in two weeks he had learned the way a creature does not think and does not get involved, and is still completely there. Then, with a pettiness born of prudence he began to look around, almost without moving his head, just moving it a little back, imperceptively, and so enlarged his field of vision.

And what Martim saw was an extended plain slowly rising. A long way off a gentle slope began, which from its outlines promised to descend into a yet invisible valley. And where the sun's silence stopped, there was that elevation cushioned with goldness, barely discernible among the mists or low-hanging clouds—maybe the man had not dared put on his glasses. He could not tell if it was a mountain or just a shining cloud.

Then, with the assurance that because of the distance nothing sudden would happen, the man began quickly to cast his eyes about him in a more personal way.

In the calm expanse a bush here and there stuffed with the sun's final immobility. A few rigid trees were scattered about. Every so often a large rock was sticking up perpetually.

Then the man relaxed his body: no danger. Only a peaceful and loyal extension of space that followed its own plane. And no traps—unless the short, hard shadow dug in alongside everything placed there. But there was no danger. It was really beyond imagination that this place could have a name, or for anyone to know about it. It was just great and open and inexpressive space where on their own account rocks and more rocks were sticking up. And that energetic silence which had alarmed him was nothing but the other face of silence. Even then, with open frankness, both the clearness and the silence were turning their eyes up toward the sky.

The silence of the sun was so complete that his useless hearing tried to divide it into imaginary sectors, as in a map, so that he could grasp it gradually. But then, after the first sector, the man began to roll off into the infinite, which startled him; a warning. As he became more modest, his hearing tried only to calculate where the end of the silence might be: houses? some woods? and what could that distant splotch really be—a mountain, or just the darkness created by the accumulation of distances? His body ached.

But getting on his feet the man unexpectedly regained the whole stature of his own body. This automatically gave him a certain arrogance, as if on getting up he had created the wasteland. And despite his sloping shoulders he felt that he was in control of the expanse and ready to follow it. Even so he was blinded by the light; none of his senses was of any use to him there, and that clearness confused him more than the darkness had at night. Every direction held the same empty and illuminated course, and he could not tell which path might mean advance or retreat. Actually, any spot where the man might stand would make him the center of the great circle and only the arbitrary beginning of a path.

But ever since two weeks before, when that man had felt the power of an act, he also seemed to have come to recognize the stupid liberty in which he found himself. Without any thought of response, without moving, he accepted the fact that he was the only real point of departure.

Then, as if contemplating for the last time before departure the spot where his house had been burned down, Martim looked over the great sun-filled emptiness. He could see very well. And seeing was something he could do, something he did with a certain pride, with his head erect. In two weeks he had recovered a natural pride and, like a person who did not think, he had become self-sufficient.

Soon his measured and repeated steps had formed a monotonous march. Thousands of rhythmical steps which bewildered him and carried him along forward all by themselves. Stupefied, gigantified by fatigue, he advanced now with the air of a contented idiot—to the point that if he were to stop, he would fall down. But he was going forward stronger and stronger. Meanwhile time passed, and the sun was getting rounder.

The man had wanted to head toward the sea even before happy chance had brought him to the hotel. But without map, knowledge, or compass he had been plunging inland. If only by fate some path had ended on the open coast, one which was true but difficult to reach on foot; if only he had not really had the slightest idea of going to some determined place. With the leveling continuation of days and nights—uniting himself with the continuation and clinging to it with his whole body, it had become his secret objective ever since he had fled—with the continuation of days and nights, the man had ended up forgetting the reason for wanting to reach the sea. Who knows, maybe there was no practical reason. Maybe it was only to arrive finally at the sea, in a moment of dark beauty, that would have brought him there.

Whatever his reason had been, however, he had forgotten it. And walking on without stopping he scratched his head violently with a set of stiff fingers; he got a devilish pleasure out of having forgotten. Which did not stop him even now—if in his semi-watchfulness he closed his eyes, whose moistness had already been dried up by the light—even now, while making his old desire something real. When he closed his eyes he suddenly could see green water breaking over rocks and salting his hot face. Then he passed his hand over his face and smiled mysteriously at the feeling of his hard prominent chin, which was something promising and satisfying; he smiled his mask of false modesty, and stepped up his pace a little more. He was guided by the softness animals have, that makes them walk gracefully.

But at times a deserted sea no longer spoke to that body which his steps had made mechanical and light. And finding in himself, only God knows where, a contact with a more intense desire he was able to see the high tide by the top of the masts and by the croaking of the seagulls!—seagulls croaking their salty breath from within his guts, the stormy sea of those who leave, the sea that carries them on. I love you, his glance said to a stone, because that sudden sea of shouts had disturbed his own insides down deep, and that was how he happened to look at the stone.

A mile farther on, the man had forgotten all about the shape of the sea, and the effort of its invention had really left him quite exhausted. And stumbling hurriedly on across the pebbles he thrust out his arms in a great appeal for the desire of a nocturnal sea, the sound of which would unroll at last the thickness which existed in the silence. His hollow ears were thirsty, and the primal sound of the sea would be just the thing to least compromise the cautious way in which he had become a walking man and nothing else. Because he had thrust out his arms abruptly, he lost his balance and almost fell—his heart jumped in fright several times. All during his life that man had been afraid of taking a fall on some important occasion. Well, it was going to be that moment when, as he lost the security that keeps a man on his own two feet, he risked the difficult gymnastics of flying without direction. Open-mouthed, he looked around himself, because certain gestures had become terrifying in the solitude, having a final value in themselves. When a man falls down all by himself in a field, he does not know to whom to credit his fall.

For the first time since he had started walking, he stopped. He did not even know now to whom to hold out his arms. In his heart he could feel the misery there is in taking a fall.

Then he started walking again. Limping gave dignity to his suffering.

But with the interruption he had lost an essential speed, and then he tried to compensate for it by replacing it with a kind of intimate violence. And since he had to have before him something that was waiting for him—the sea again broke furiously upon the rocks.

To reach the sea someday was, however, something he was only using now as a part of a dream. He was not even for a moment thinking of acting in any way that might turn that happy vision into a reality. Not even if he knew what path would take him to the sea would he be taking it now—it was so much that in a little while he began discarding it with the instinctive wisdom that anything in the future would keep him hobbled since the future is a two-edged knife, and the future fashions the present. With the passage of days other ideas had gradually been forming up behind too, as if as undefined time or danger became greater, the man would go on divesting himself of what was weighing on him. And especially what still might have kept him captive in his previous world.

Up until now—without any desire, lighter and lighter, as if hunger and thirst too were a voluntary disengagement of which he was slowly beginning to be proud—up until now he was advancing like a giant across the countryside, looking about himself with an independence that rose to his head with vulgar delight, and he began to fool around with it happily. "Today must be Sunday"—he even began to think with a certain glory, and Sunday would be the coronation of his freedom. "Today must be Sunday!" he thought with sudden haughtiness, as if his honor had been offended.

It was a matter of his first clear thought since leaving the hotel. Really, since he had fled, it was the first thought that had not been just a mere defensive measure. Furthermore, Martim did not even know what to do with it at first. It was only the novelty of it that bothered him, and he scratched himself voraciously without ceasing to walk. Then, applauding himself fiercely and joining a hoarse encouragement to the thought, he repeated, "Today must be Sunday."

Apparently it must have been more an indirect testimony to himself than to the day of the week, since without stopping for a second, he ended the radiant and dry glance at what he had just called "Sunday" with a listless feel through his pockets. For no reason at all, if not because of his own fatigue, he kept walking faster and faster. It was really getting harder now to keep up with himself. And excited in that competition with his own pace he looked around in innocent fascination, his head burning in the sun.

Unless he had counted the days gone by there was no reason to think it was Sunday. Martim stopped then, a little embarrassed by the need to understand from which he still had not freed himself.

But the fact is that the wasteland had a clean and foreign existence. Every single thing was in its place. Like a man who shuts the door and leaves, and it is Sunday. Besides everything else, Sunday is a man's first day. Not even woman had been created yet. Sunday was the wasteland of a man. And thirst, freeing him, gave him a power of choice that made him drunk. "Today is Sunday!" he decided categorically.

Then he sat down on a stone and, very stiff, kept on looking about. His look did not run into any obstacle, and it wandered about an intense and peaceful noontime. Nothing was stopping him from transforming his flight into a marvelous trip, and he was set to take advantage of it. He was looking.

But there is something in the expanse of the countryside that makes a man alone feel alone. Sitting on a stone, the final and irreducible fact—the fact that he was there. Then, with a sudden zeal, he carefully brushed the dust off his jacket. In an obscure and perfect way, he himself was the first thing put into that Sunday. It made him as precious as a seed; he picked a thread off his jacket. On the ground the black outline of his shadow delimited his favorable delusion to where he was. He himself was his own first frame.

The truth was that in addition to trying to clean himself up, as a mere matter of cleanliness, the man did not seem to have the least intention of doing anything with the fact of existing. There he was, sitting on the stone. Nor did he attempt to think the least bit about the sun.

All this, then, was where freedom came from. His body groaned with pleasure; his woolen suit was itchy in the heat. Limitless freedom had left him empty; each one of his gestures echoed like a distant applause: when he scratched himself, that gesture rolled directly on toward God. The most dispassionately individual thing can happen when a person finds freedom. In the beginning you are a stupid man with greater loneliness than you need. Then a man who gets a slap on the face and can still smile beatifically, because at the same time the slap has revealed to him a face he had not suspected. After a while you begin craftily to build a house and take the first lewd intimacies with freedom; The only reason you do not fly is because you do not want to, and when you sit down upon a stone it is because instead of flying you sat down. And after that?

After that, as now, what the sitting Martim experienced was a mute orgy, in which there was the virginal desire to debase everything debasable; and everything was debasable, and that debasement would be a way of loving. To be content was a way of loving; sitting down, Martim was very content.

And after that? Well, the only thing that would happen

after that is that he would say what would happen after that. For the time being, the fugitive man kept sitting on the stone, because if he had wanted to, he might not have been able to sit down on the stone. All of that gave him the eternity of a perching bird.

When that was all over, Martim stood up. And without asking himself what he was doing, he knelt down in front of a dried-up tree to examine its trunk: it did not seem that he had to give any deep thought to the problem in order to resolve it; he had disengaged himself from that too. Then he picked off a piece of half-hung bark, rolled it between his fingers with an attention that was a little affected, moving it about as if he were in front of an audience. His study was done in the peculiar fashion that comes when what is unknown becomes organized, and Martim arose as if by command, and continued on his way.

It was farther along that he stopped short in front of the first bird.

Set off against the great light there was a bird. Since Martim was free, that was the question: a bird in the light. With the minute care to which he had become accustomed, he immediately began to work on this fact greedily.

The black bird was perched on a low branch, at eye-level. And, unable to fly, paralyzed by the bestial look of the man, she moved about with less and less volition, trying to face up to what was going to happen and shifting her weight nervously from one foot to the other. There they were, the two of them, facing each other—until the man grabbed her with a heavy and powerful hand, which with the physical kindness of a heavy hand did not hurt.

In the palm of his hand the bird trembled and dared not make a peep. The man looked at her with vulgar and indiscreet curiosity, as if he had imprisoned a handful of living wings. In a little while the bird's small, dominated body stopped trembling, and she closed her minute eyes with feminine softness. Now only a faint, rapid heartbeat against the man's extremely sensitive fingers showed that the bird had not died and that the snugness had at last lulled her to rest.

(20)

How a Man Is Made

Startled by the irrevocable perfection of what was happening to him, the man snorted and looked at the little creature. The satisfaction made him laugh aloud, his head turned back, his face looking at the great sun. Then he stopped laughing, as if that had been a heresy. And deeply concerned with his task and with his hand half-closed, he let just the hard, sharp head of the bird show; the man began to walk again with greater strength, aware of his companion. The only thing he thought about was the noise his own shoes made echoing softly in his sun-fired head.

And soon, in cadence with his steps, the physical pleasure of walking once more started to take hold of him—and also a pleasure faintly sensed, as if he had taken some aphrodisiac that made him desire not a woman, but a response to the thrill of the sun. He had never been so close to the sun, and he was walking faster and faster holding the bird in front of him as if he were running to the post office with it before it closed. The vague mission was getting him drunk. The lightness born of thirst had suddenly put him into an ecstasy.

"That's it, yes!" he said aloud and without meaning, and it seemed more and more glorious, as if he were going to fall down dead.

He looked around at the perfect circle of light that the heavens were holding in an awe-inspiring horizon; an horizon which drew closer to the land, softer and softer, softer and softer, softer and softer . . . The softness upset the man with the pleasure of a tickle. "That's it, yes!" and he was free, freed by his own hands—he had suddenly realized that this was what had happened two weeks before.

Then he repeated with unexpected certainty, "That's it, yes!" Every time he said those words he was convinced that he was referring to something. He even made a gesture of generosity and largess with the hand that held the bird, and he thought magnanimously, "They don't know what I'm talking about."

Then—as if thinking had been reduced to seeing, and that the confusion of the light had quivered in him as it does on water—it occurred to him in a confused refraction that even he had forgotten what he was talking about. But he was so obstinately convinced that it was something of the greatest importance, something so vast that it was no longer conceivable even to him, that he haughtily respected his own ignorance and gave himself savage approval, "That's it, yes."

"Can't you say anything else?"

The man stopped short, surprised. As if she had been put before him, he saw again the face of that impatient woman, who once before had asked him that just because he had not answered. From the very first, the phrase had sounded like so many others—as streetcars dragged along and the radio kept right on playing without interruption and the woman listened to the radio without interruption and hope, and one day he would break the radio as streetcars dragged along, and meanwhile the radio and the woman had nothing to do with that careful rage of a man who most likely already held within himself the fact that someday he would have to begin at the exact beginning. He was now beginning with Sunday.

But this time the simple irritating phrase, ringing in the red silence of the wasteland, made him stop short, so perplexed that the bird woke up and wiggled its imprisoned wings inside his hand. Martim looked at it bewildered, frightened at having a bird in his hand. The sun's drunkenness was suddenly over.

Sober, he looked with modesty at the thing in his hand. Then he looked at the Sunday wasteland with its silent stones. He had been sound asleep as he had been walking, and for the first time he was now waking up. And as if a new wave from the sea were breaking against the rocks, clearness took over.

Calmly the man looked at the bird. Without any command his now innocent and curious fingers let themselves obey the lively movements of the bird, and passively they opened. The bird flew off in a flash of gold, as if the man had flung it. And it perched anxiously upon the highest stone. From there it looked down at the man and peeped incessantly.

Paralyzed for a moment, Martim looked up at it and then down at his own empty hands, which looked back in astonishment. Recovering, however, he ran furiously toward the bird and followed it for some time, his heart beating with anger, his impatient shoes tripping over stones, his hand grasping out in a fall that made a small stone bounce along with several dry jumps until it was quiet . . .

The silence that followed was so hollow that the man still tried to hear the last thud of the stone so he could calculate the depth of the silence into which he had knocked it.

Until a great wave of light unwound the waiting tension, and Martim could look down at his hand. It was burned, and there was a trickle of blood. He had forgotten about the chase and was very much involved with himself now; his dry lips sucked on the scratch with the loving voracity of a lonely person. At the same time thirst had awakened him and the blood in his mouth had given him a warlike attitude that quickly went away.

When the man finally lifted up his eyes the frightened bird was waiting for him, as if it had been resisting only because it had wanted to give up. Martim held out his injured hand and took it up with forceless firmness. This time the bird wiggled less, and recognizing its old shelter, snuggled up to sleep. Carrying its light weight, the man continued on his way among the stones.

"I can't say anything else," he said to the bird, trying out of a certain sense of shame not to look at it.

Only afterwards did he seem to understand what he had said, and then he looked the sun in the eye. "I have lost the speech of other people," he then repeated slowly, as if the words were more obscure than they were, and in some way more praiseworthy. He was serenely proud; his eyes clear and satisfied.

Then the man sat down upon a stone, straight, solemn, and empty—keeping the bird firmly secure within his hand. Something was happening to him, and it was something that had meaning.

Even so he had no words for what was happening.

A man was sitting down. And he had no words for anything. Therefore he was sitting down. That is how it was. The best part is that it was indisputable. And irreversible.

The truth is that what had been happening to him had a

weight that had to be borne. It was easy for him to recognize the familiar weight. It was like his own weight, even though it might be something quite the opposite something he could not seem to balance on a scale. He was vaguely aware of that. Sometimes in his old apartment, he would get that uncomfortable feeling that was a mixture of pleasure and anxiety; it had always ended up in some decision that had nothing to do with his troublesome feeling. True, he had never felt it with that final, clean feel that the wasteland gave—the wasteland where he was aided by the very shadow which unmistakably delimited him upon the ground.

That thing that he was feeling must have been, in the last analysis, himself and nothing else—the pleasure that the tongue has of being in its own mouth, and the lack of a name, like the name of pleasure the tongue has in its mouth. That is all it was, after all.

But a person was always a little aware of what was, and being aware was to be. That is how, then, that on his first Sunday, he was.

In the meantime he had become fairly intense. He moved about uncomfortably upon his stone with a physical answer to the immateriality of his own tension, the way a person does who is disturbed. And if he did that it was because, even if he had not known himself, he knew enough about himself for a reply. That was not enough, however. He looked about, like a person looking for a woman's counterpoint, but there was no synonym, unless it was a man sitting down with a bird in his hand.

Then he waited, patient and upright, for the thing to pass away without its even touching him.

The fact was that the man had always had a tendency to fall into profundity, which some day still would lead him to an abyss: that is why he wisely took the precaution to abstain. His contention, superficial and easily separated from the depth, gave him the pleasure of a contention. His had always been a difficult balance, one of not falling into the voraciousness with which every new wave awaited him. A whole past lay just a step away

(2 4)

from the caution with which that man was merely trying to keep himself alive, and nothing more—the way an animal will light up only in its eyes, keeping behind it that vast, untouched animal soul. Then, without touching it, he set himself to wait impassively until the things should go away.

Before it went away he involuntarily recognized it. That thing—that thing was a man thinking . . . Then, with infinite displeasure, physically confused, he remembered in his body what a man thinking was like. A man thinking was that thing which, when it saw something yellow, would say with dazzling élan, "Something not blue." Not that Martim had really arrived at thought—he had recognized it in the way one recognizes the possible movement in the shape of motionless legs. And he had recognized more than that: that thing had really been with him all through his flight. It had only been through neglect that just now he had almost let it spread itself out.

Then, startled, as if in alarm, he had recognized the insidious return of a vice; he had such a repugnance for the fact that he had almost been thinking that he clenched his teeth in a painful mask of hunger and abandonment—he turned around restlessly toward all sides of the wasteland, looking among the stones for a means by which he could regain his former powerful stupidity, which for him had come to be a source of pride and command.

But the man was disturbed. Why should he not be then a person able to take two free steps and not fall into the same fatal error? Because the old system of useless thinking and of even delighting in thinking had tried to return? Sitting on the stone with the bird in his hand, he felt pleasure in treating her carelessly. And if he were careless for one minute more, he would bring back in one gush his whole previous existence—when thought had been a useless act and pleasure only shameful. Unprotected, he shifted about on the hot stone; he seemed to be searching for an argument that might protect him. He needed to defend the thing that with such enormous courage he had conquered two weeks before. With this enormous courage the man had finally stopped being intelligent.

Or had he ever really been intelligent? That happy suspicion made him blink his eyes with great shrewdness, because if he could manage to prove that he had never been intelligent, then it could also be shown that his own past had been some other, and it could be shown that something in his very own depths had always been complete and firm.

"The fact is," he then thought, using great care as he tried that defensive trick, "the fact is that I was only imitating intelligence, as if I had been able to swim like a fish without actually being one!" The man moved about contentedly: "I was imitating, of course!" Well, if imitating meant having taken first place in statistics, he had taken first place in statistics! The fact is, he concluded with great interest and the essential lack of respect which is what makes a person imitate, I have only imitated intelligence. And along with him millions of men were copying with great effort the idea of what it was to be a man, along with him thousands of women were copying with great care the idea of what it was to be a woman, and along with him hundreds of people of good will were copying with superhuman effort the very face and idea of existence with the anguished concentration with which acts of good or evil are imitated, the daily fear of committing an act that is true, and therefore incomparable, and therefore inimitable, and therefore disconcerting. And all the while there was something old and rotten in some unidentifiable place in the house, and people slept restlessly—discomfort is the only warning that we copy, and we listen to ourselves attentively between the sheets. But we have been carried so far away by imitation that the thing we hear comes to us with such slight sound that it could be a vision, just as invisible as if it were in the darkness that is so deep that hands are useless. Because a person will even imitate comprehension—comprehension which never would have been invented except for the speech of others and words.

But there was still disobedience.

Then—by means of the great leap of a crime—two weeks before he had taken the risk of having no security, and he had reached a point of not understanding.

How a Man Is Made

And under the yellow sun, sitting on a stone, without the least bit of security, the man was now rejoicing, as if not understanding were a kind of creation. The caution that a person uses to transform one thing into another thing comparable and subsequently approachable; and only after that moment of security, will he look about and let himself be seen, because fortunately it is already too late not to understand—Martim had lost that precaution. And not understanding had suddenly given him the whole world.

The whole world, which to tell the truth, was completely empty. The man had rejected the speech of others and did not even have a speech of his own. And in the meantime, hollow, mute, he was rejoicing. Things were fine.

Then, just as at the beginning of the conversation, that person was sitting on a stone on Sunday.

And so the man now felt himself so far removed from the speech of others, that with a perverse pleasure and a daring that had come to him out of the same security, he attempted speech again. It puzzled him, as it puzzles a man who brushes his teeth in the morning and does not recognize the drunk of the night before. And as he fooled around now, still cautious, albeit fascinated with that dead language, as an experiment he tried to give the ancient and so familiar name of "crime" to that so very nameless thing that had happened to him.

But "Crime"? The word resounded emptily in the wasteland, nor did the voice that spoke the word belong to him. Then, finally convinced that he would not fall captive to the ancient speech, he tried to go a little further; had he perhaps felt horror after his crime? Horror? Nevertheless, that was what the language expected of him.

But horror too had come to be a word from that time before the great blind leap he had taken along with his crime. The leap had been taken. And he had jumped so far that it had ended up becoming the only event he was able to or cared to cope with. And even the motives of the crime had lost their importance.

The truth is that the man had wisely abolished the motives. And he had abolished the crime itself. Having had certain practice with guilt he knew how to live with it without discomfort. He had committed crimes before that had not been recognized by law, so that he most likely considered it just a piece of bad luck that two weeks before he had committed one that had recognition. A good upbringing and long experience in life had made him expert at being guilty without betraying himself; no ordinary torture would make his soul confess its guilt, and a great deal would be necessary to make a hero cry in the end. And when this does happen it is such a depressing and repugnant spectacle that we cannot bear it unless we feel ourselves betrayed and offended; our surrogate must be unpardonable. It so happens that by special circumstances, that the man had become a hardened hero in two weeks: he represented himself. Guilt no longer touched him.

"Crime?" No. "The great leap?" These did not sound like his words, obscure, like the entanglement of a dream. His crime had been an involuntary, vital motion, like the reflex of a knee when it is tapped: the whole organism had joined together so that the leg suddenly gave the irrepressible kick. And he had not felt any horror after the crime. What had he felt, then? Stunning victory!

That was it—he had felt victory. Astonished, he saw that the thing was working unexpectedly: that an act still had the value of an act. And furthermore with a single act he had made the enemies he had always wanted to have—other people, the others. But even further he himself had finally become incapable of being that former man, for if he returned to that self, he would be obliged to become his own enemy—and, to use the speech by which he had lived, he simply could not be friendly to a criminal. Therefore, in one fell swoop he was no longer a collaborator with other people, and in one fell swoop he had ceased to collaborate with himself. For the first time, Martim had found himself incapable of imitating.

Yes! In that moment of stunning victory the man had suddenly discovered the power of a gesture. The good thing about an act is that it reaches beyond us. In just one minute Martim had been transfigured by his own act. Because after two weeks of silence it had become quite natural for him to call his crime an "act."

It is true that the feeling of victory had lasted only a fraction of a second. There was no time after that; in an extraordinarily perfect and well-oiled rhythm there followed that deep stupefaction in which there had been such need for this, his present intelligence, to be born. And it was as crude and wily as that of a rat. Simply that, and nothing more. But for the first time it had been a tool. For the first time his intelligence had had immediate consequences. And he had come into such total possession of it that he had been able to guide it with great skill so that it would make him secure, make his life secure. So much so that he immediately knew how to flee, as if, up until then, everything he had done in his daily life had been just an indistinct attempt at action. And then that man had finally become real, a real rat, and any thought from within that new intelligence was just an act, even if it was rough like a voice that never had been used. Right now he was not very much of a rat. But even if a rat there was nothing in him that could not be utilized. The thing was fine and deep. That man had fit himself entirely within the dimensions of a rat.

Yes. All this had followed upon the crime to such a point of perfection that Martim had not even had time to think about what he was doing. But before—for a fraction of a second before the conquest. Because one day a man had had that one great rage.

He had had that rage. And for the first time, with candor, he had admired himself, like a child who discovers himself in the mirror. Apparently, with the accumulation of kindness without the act of kindness, with the thought of love without the act of love, with heroism without heroism, not to mention a certain growing imprecision about existence which had ended up as the impossible dream of existence—apparently that man had come to forget that a person is able to act. And to have discovered that he really had already acted involuntarily had suddenly given him a world so free that he was stunned at his victory.

That man had not even asked himself if there was someone

who could act by means other than a crime. What he knew in fear was only that a man had to have a great rage one day.

"I was like any one of you," he said very suddenly to the stones at that point because they looked like sitting men.

Having said that Martim sank back into complete silence, something like a meditation. He was surrounded by stones. The strong wind that blew passed over him the same way it was passing over the wasteland. Empty and peaceful he looked at the empty and peaceful light. The world was large enough for him to sit down. Inside he felt the resonant emptiness of a cathedral.

"Try to imagine," he began again suddenly, when he was sure that he had nothing more to say to them. "Try to imagine a person who has had to have an act of rage," he said to a small stone that was looking at him with the calm face of a child. "That person went on living, living, and other people too took pains to imitate him. Until it all began to get very confused with the independence of every stone in its place. And there wasn't even any way for him to flee from himself because the others had become a concrete image and gave off an impassive insistence of just what that person was; every face that person saw would bring back the peaceful nightmare of his deviation. How can I explain it to you—you who have the peace that comes with not having any future—that every face had failed, and that the failure had in itself a perversion, as if a man had gone to bed with another man, and of course there was no issue. 'The company was so boring,' as my wife used to say," the man remembered, smiling and extremely curious. There was some mistake, and it was hard to tell just where it lay. "Once I was eating in a restaurant," the man said, getting lively suddenly. "No, no, I'm changing the subject!" he discovered to his surprise—his father was the one who always had a certain tendency to change the subject; and even when he was dying he had shifted his face over to one side.

"Try to imagine a person," he continued then, "who did not have the courage to reject himself. Therefore he needed an act which would make other people reject him, and he himself would not be able to live with himself after that."

(3 0)

How a Man Is Made

The man laughed with parched lips at the way he had used the trick of hiding himself behind the name of some other person, which had seemed very good to him at the moment, a stroke of genius. Then he had that satisfaction that he always had when he had managed to trick somebody. He might have had the feeling that he was play-acting and strutting, but pretending was a new door which, as he squandered himself for the first time, he could afford the luxury of opening or closing.

"Try to imagine a person who was small and had no strength. Of course he knew very well that all of his strength, piece by piece, would only be enough to buy a single act of rage. And of course he also knew that such an act would have to be quite quick before his courage petered out, and it would even have to be hysterical. That person, then, when least expected, executed that act, and in it he invested his whole small fortune."

Quite startled at what he had just thought, the man interrupted himself with curiosity. "Is that what happened to me after all?" It was the first time it had occurred to him.

The truth is that up until then he had not even taken time to think about his crime. But coming to grips with it finally at this moment he faced it in a way that no court of law would ever recognize. Could he be describing his crime the way a man might paint a table in a picture, and no one would recognize it because he was painting it from the point of view of someone underneath the table?

What had that man done to his crime in barely two weeks time?

He still asked himself with an aftertaste of scruples, "Was that what happened to me?" But a second later it was too late; if this were not the truth, it was going to be the truth. With a certain graveness the man felt that this moment was very serious: from now on this was going to be the only truth that he would have to fight with.

What escaped him was whether he had explained his crime that way because it had really happened like that, or whether his whole being had been prepared for that type of reality. Or even whether he had been giving false reasons because he possessed the simple skill of a fugitive defending himself. But even a long period of tendentious dullness would not let him know where it was in him that his fingers could feel a sail respond as it responds when touched in the reality of a dream. And for the time being he was somebody still quite recent, so that everything he said not only sounded fine to him, but also amazed him by the very fact that he had been able to walk alone.

Actually at that moment his only direct connection with the concrete crime was a thought of extreme curiosity, "Why did it have to happen to me?" He felt himself beneath the happenings he had created with the crime. Then and there he had broken with his habits of life, with the misfortune that usually only happens to other people. And suddenly it was not just words that had happened to him. Martim was quite sincerely startled by the fact that misfortune had also caught up to him, and—more than that—that he had been, in a manner of speaking, ready for it. He had acquired a certain vanity from the fact that in the end the crime had happened to him, that until that point it had only been for other people.

The man continued to look at the table from underneath—and what was important was that he recognized it. It is true that hunger was fixing it so that any effort on his part would be difficult; the stones, meanwhile, were waiting unmoved for a continuation. Then, so as to give him a little rest, his head was wise enough to blur a little.

After that Martim began again more slowly, and tried to think with great care because the truth can be different if it is spoken with the wrong words. But if the right words are used, anybody will see that this is the table from which we eat. In any case now that Martim had lost his speech, just as if he had lost his money, he would be forced to invent what he wanted to have. He remembered his son's saying to him, "I know why God created rhinoceroses. It's because He'd never seen a rhinoceros, and He created rhinoceroses so He could see one." Martim was creating truth so he could see it.

Oh, it is quite possible that he had been lying to the stones.

The only innocence he possessed besides his tendentious habit of lying was that he was not sure where his lie was heading. And then, as he faced that ambiguity, his head began to fog up even more as a defensive measure. And with a little trick he had brought along from before the great leap, he became ingenuous.

Once recovered, he again took up his sermon to the stones:

"With an act of violence that person of whom I spoke killed an abstract world and gave it blood."

And he said that with the stoical resignation of a person who has already tried to take away the stress from lie or truth. That man had just made the definitive act of dissociating himself, after which he was more than satisfied to look. Things were getting better and better. From underneath he was beginning to recognize the table more and more.

And now, sitting on a rock with a bird in his hand, his mouth dry with thirst, his eyes burning—after his crime—that man would never again have any need for revolt. From that time forward he would have the chance to live without doing evil because it had already been done; now he was an innocent.

Who can tell whether he had thought to go so far with his unpremeditated crime. But this thought also came to him, "He had become an innocent." And, in God's name, he had never thought of coming so far, but he had freed himself from a kind of suffocating piety, now that he was no longer guilty. "If you really do understand me," he thought with deep fatuity, for he had freed himself of the great guilt by making it concrete. And now that he was at last a bandit, he was free. He was, in short, a fugitive. And that afforded him all the possibilities open to desperate people. "I have killed many birds with one stone," he said.

The stones, large and small, were waiting. Martim was very confident because his audience was no more intelligent than he, and he felt at ease. Besides, that man had never had an audience, strange as it seems. The fact is he had never remembered having organized his soul into speech, he did not believe in talking—perhaps through fear that if he talked, he himself would end up not recognizing the table he was eating from. If he was talking now it was because he did not know where he was heading or what was going to become of him, and all that put him right into the heart of freedom. Leaving out the fact that thirst was stirring in him like an ideal.

Furthermore, his improvised audience was not a cultured one, and so he was taking advantage of it just as one habitually and wisely takes advantage of an inferior and is taken advantage of by his superiors. His own lack of culture had always been an embarrassment to him; it had been his habit to make endless lists of books he meant to read, and he would try to keep them up to date but new ones were always coming out and that embarrassed him—a man who never even looked at the newspapers. He had even tried to plumb the depths of "collective psychology," since he had always dealt with numbers and had always been a man who could easily imitate intelligence; but he had never had the time—his wife would drag him off to the movies, and he would be relieved to go.

The stones were waiting. Some were round and dead like stones from the moon; they were like cross-eyed, patient, children. But the others were sun-stones and looked him straight in the eye. "Like jewels," he thought, as he had always had a general tendency to compare things to jewels. The stones were waiting for the continuation of what he had begun to think. From time to time they would have a look of fervent life which passed a painful surge of empty happiness on to the man. "I think," he thought suddenly, "that until the day I die I will be very happy."

The sun was paining his head deeply, and the man made another effort to speak because he had felt a crisp facility within himself—just as when one has something to say, and even if he does not know how, finds that minimum of inspiration gives one strength for painful groping. Even he wanted to speak, because there is no law preventing a man from speaking. And all the while what fascinated Martim was the absence of any impediments, besides which, he knew quite well that the world was so big that very soon even he would have to limit himself. The stones were waiting, having come from everywhere for the conspiracy, to which, he as a traveler, was bringing the latest news. Some stones were small and infantile, others large and pointed—all sitting in the assembly of innocence. It was an uneven audience where childhood and maturity were mixed in together.

"Childhood and maturity," he then said to them suddenly. "And yet there had been a period when the world was smooth like the skin of a fruit. We, its neighbors, did not bite into it because it was easy to bite, and there was plenty of time. Life was as yet not short in that time. And because of that the trees grew. The trees grew as if there was nothing in the world except for trees to grow, until the sun was blotted out, and people came in closer, and springs flowed, and mosquitoes emerged out of the hearts of flowers: this was growth. It was mature. It was richer and more frightening; in some way it became much more 'worthwhile.' Nights became longer, father and mother had been denied; there was a terrible thirst for love. It was the kingdom of fear. And it was no longer enough to have been born—heroism was being born. But eloquence had a bad sound to it. People ran into each other in the dark; every light confused and blinded them, and truth was good for only one day. Then all of our troubles arrived at a solution. We were lost among the solutions that had preceded us at every step. In just a few seconds an idea would become original; when we saw a photograph with light and shadows and paving stones that were wet with rain, we would exclaim, tired and unanimously, This is very original. Everything was deep and fetid, ready for birth, but the child would not be born. I'm not saying it wasn't good—it was fine! But it was just as if a person could only watch, and Saturday night would be that hell of generalized intentions if there were no poker game. In the meantime nothing ever stopped; it even kept on going at night. Power had become great; hands intelligent. Everybody was powerful, everybody was a tyrant, and I never let anyone step on my foot, my astuteness became magnificent with the help of a little practice. There were, however, those who in spite of their maturity had—had childhood gnawing at their breasts like leprosy."

The man spoke this last phrase with vanity because it seemed to him that he had put his words together with some degree of perfection. Of course, what made Martim feel such perfection was the fact that his words had in some way gone beyond what he had wanted to say. And even though he felt deceived by them he preferred what he had said to what he had really wanted to say because of the much more certain way in which things go beyond us. This also gave him, at the same time, a feeling of defeat and of resignation from the way in which he had just sold himself to a phrase that had more beauty than truth to it. The first thing he was squandering his new wealth on was an audience; but this had already forced him into an established truth, and he was disappointed, even a little curious. He had really spoken only once before; he had taken a few drinks, and had delivered an oration in a house of prostitution where the women had also looked like sitting jewels—it was getting on to dawn; work was done, and they were childlike and mature.

"Yes. It was as if there were those who had childhood in their breasts—as if our future were only in our memory," he informed the stones. "But it is also true that the moments of sweetness were very intense. And it is also true that music heard in the past can make the whole machinery come to a halt and dumbfound the world for a moment. 'A moment of silence,' my wife's radio used to say, 'for the death of the general.' There would be a terrible uneasiness for that moment; no one would look up even though the general was a stranger to us. It was unhappiness in all of its virile strength. Besides there was no other way to be adult, and people enjoyed and approved; nobody was that simple-minded. It is true that once in a while somebody would speak in a very low voice. Then everybody would come scurrying from opposite corners to listen to the low voice. But the truth is that everybody was suffering from not being able to comment and from not being called upon to either."

(3 6)

"But," said the man, a little offended by the passive naturalness with which the stones seemed to accept everything he was
telling them—he had had experience with foreigners who were
not mixed up in this and simply took pictures—"But the world
too is more than that!" he said to them patriotically. "There
were a lot of other good things besides! and it was for that reason
that, much more than for toleration, that we wanted one another
so much. Oh, how we wanted one another! even if the paint was
peeling off the walls," the man said, a little distracted, losing his
footing. "There were houses that were still unsold, and many
people who did not study languages," he said with envy for those
who had studied languages. "And just the same for one time as
another—perhaps because if the wrong door had been opened—
you understand! Which makes for the fact that sometimes again
there was nothing except trees growing, tall and peaceful. And
especially, especially there were children rising up from our fields
of battle, pure and fateful fruit of disastrous love."

In spite of being satisfied, Martim, having said what he had
to say, felt tired, as if there had been a mistake in something he
had said—as if he had been obliged to add up the infinite figures
all over again. At some unidentifiable point, that man had
become prisoner of a ring of words. "Did I forget to mention
something?" The stones were certainly going to get a bad
impression. For someone who had never seen a head of hair, a
strand of hair, it was nothing, and a fish pulled out of his water is
nothing but a shape.

For honesty's sake, he wanted to make clear to them that he
knew it was the sun that was inflating his words and making
them so overdone and so grandiloquent, and that it was the
insistent sun along with his insistent silence that made him want
to speak. But he also knew that if he were to mention fatigue
itself the stones would stop listening at once, because after all
only people in full enjoyment of their faculties have the right to
listen, which is quite proper. But since what he was saying to
them was important to him, and since he would not be able to
explain to them the fatigue that was nothing but an instrument,
Martim preferred not to touch upon the subject.

During all this he still had the uncomfortable feeling that he had forgotten to say some essential thing without which the stones would not understand anything. What? Ah. "That in the meantime time went passing by." During all of that time was fortunately passing by.

Had he forgotten anything else? He had forgotten to tell them what there was that might perhaps invalidate his right to speak: that not having had the vocation, and therefore being free from requests, he had never really specialized in any desire, had never therefore had a starting point—which surely invalidated the way he was using the stones to represent other people.

Well, he had also forgotten to tell them—but he would not tell them that because then it would be interpreted wrongly and seen in a bad light—that he had always taken advantage of what he could, since he had never been a fool. That he had told a friend that a transaction was no good; that he himself had taken over the transaction and had picked up a few pennies and had felt fine triumph in his breast, one that could not be replaced by any other pleasure, and one which makes a man love his neighbors because he has beaten them. He had forgotten to tell them that once when he was engaged to be married, he had neglected to give his fiancée his new address. But that kind of chicanery can only be understood by someone who has lived. And a person feels misunderstood, therefore, when he explains it. And so, time was fortunately passing by with dogs sniffing at the street corners.

The fact is that after the man had remembered all of that, he began to find his past life very fine, and a sort of nostalgia filled his breast. But this too can only be understood by a person who is alive. Finally, what could he say that a stone could understand? "That time is fortunately passing by," time being the hard material that stones are made of.

Time was fortunately passing by. So much so that it was like the meal one eats in the daytime, and then goes to bed and wakes up vomiting in the middle of the night. Time was fortunately passing by.

But with the passage of time, contrary to what might be

expected, he had been turning into an abstract man. Like a fingernail that somehow never manages to get dirty: the dirt is only peripheral to the nail; and if the nail is cut it does not even hurt, it grows again like a cactus. He had been turning into a huge man. Like an abstract fingernail. Which would become concrete when he would occasionally commit some base deed.

"Yes, that's what had begun to happen to a very few people." The man was startled by the thought. "The opposite of natural rot—which could be acceptable in an obscure way in a perishable organic being—his soul had become abstract, and his thought was abstract; he could think what he liked and nothing would happen. It was purity. There was a certain perversion in becoming eternal. His own body was abstract. And other people were abstract: all of them were sitting in seats in the dark movie theater watching the film. When they came out of the movies— even when they had not forgotten the soft breeze waiting for them, and which you cannot even imagine, for it has nothing to do with the stupid sun of which a stone is victim and by which it has been created—when they came out of the movies there was a man standing and begging. Then you would give him the abstract handout without looking at the man who bore the perpetual name of beggar. Then you would go home to sleep in abstract beds, held up in the air by four legs; you made love with some concentration, and you slept like a fingernail that had grown too long. We were eternal and gigantic. I, for example, had a huge neighbor."

Everything going so well! More and more purified.

But in the middle of the night you would suddenly wake up vomiting, asking yourself between one wave of nausea and another—in the middle of that fantasmagorical revolution which is a light turned on at night—what had you eaten during the day that could have made you so ill. The fingernail grew bigger and bigger; you already had trouble clenching your fists.

"Until one day then, a man materializes into the great rage," Martim said to them as if logic itself had become incarnate.

Until one day a man went out into the world "to see if it is true." Before dying a man must know if it is true. One day, finally, a man has to go out in search of the place that is common to a man. Then one day the man charters his ship. And at dawn he sails.

"Who has never wanted to sail away?" Martim asked, painfully trying to transform what he had thought into something that he himself could understand: a table that plates are put on top of.

"Try to imagine a man . . ." he said then, passing with great sensuality to the third person.

It was then, given over to the game, that he suddenly became aware of all of this with a shock of recognition. For sitting on the stone, what he had been doing was nothing except—thinking. Once more he had become a triangle in the sun, maybe a disembodied emblem for the disembodied stones, but not for the living rat he wanted to be.

With a shock the man looked at the stones, which now did not go beyond being stones, and again he did not go beyond being a thought. Unprotected for a moment, prisoner of himself, caught in the act, the man looked around him. But he had already come to such a point that he would not know how to free himself from the useless vice except with the sinful help of another thought. For a moment he was still looking for that thought, which showed to what point he was still taking refuge in the fact that he was a fingernail that made a scratch on the towel and the same fingernail that scratched out what had been inscribed.

But in the following moment he took note of the process. And since that man seemed not to want to use thought ever again, not even to combat another thought, he rebelled in physical rage now that he had finally learned the path of rage. His muscles contracted savagely against the dirty conscience that had formed itself about the fingernail. Illogically he fought primitively against his body, twisting himself into a mask of pain and hunger, and all of him made a voracious attempt at becoming just organic.

How a Man Is Made

When the hysteria of thirst had calmed down sweat was running down his face. His head was cold, the physical effort of the struggle had left him weak and dull. The sun was flashing on the stones. Weak, his stomach dry, Martim had never seen anything as brilliant as the sun when it shone. The white wasteland of light surrounded him. He vaguely recognized that light: it was the excessive light by which he had lived when he had been a man.

Tired, he breathed deeply. Still, a late spasm ran through him like a cramp. And finally the last frenetic movement stopped short, like the convulsions of a horse. When he opened his hand, which he had clenched with force he saw that the bird was dead.

The man looked at it carefully. Even its legs seemed old now and wavered lightly in the breeze. Its beak was hard. Without anxiety, the bird.

Once more the man's rage had ended up by becoming a crime. He looked attentively at the bird. He was amazed at himself. The fact was that he had become a dangerous person. In accordance with the rules of the hunt a wounded animal becomes dangerous. He looked at the bird that he had loved. "I killed it," he thought curiously.

Then, as if he had done something definitive, the man got up, seriously and tranquilly, from the rock. What had been a kind of uncontrollable delight in an act is the fact that the act had gone beyond him. With some reluctance he made himself get up, and whether he wished to or not he was forced now to go and meet the reward for what he himself had created. He got up slowly, avoiding thinking that he had killed exactly what he most loved.

And as if he had survived with the death of the bird, he compelled himself to look at the world in the part that he himself had just reduced it by.

The world was large.

In that world plants grew without sense, and famished birds flew as on a Sunday. The tree he saw was standing up—in the beauty of the silence, the tree. This was the way the man profoundly saw things. Facing it carefully, he saw that the beauty of the tree was useless. Three hundred thousand leaves trembled in the tranquil air. The air had so much grace left over that the man turned his eyes away. On the hard ground the bushes stood up stright. And the stones.

That was what was left for him.

That man standing there could not perceive what law ruled the harsh wind and the silent sparkling of the stones. But having laid down the arms of man, he was giving himself over defenseless to the immense harmony of the wasteland. He too was pure, harmonious, and he too had no sense.

What was surprising was the extraordinary peace of that hell. He had never imagined that with silence like this he could hear every one of his movements. Nor the ingenuous perseverance of a tree. Nor that enormous sun within hand's reach. Not that thing that did not need him, and with which he had ended up allying himself like just another star.

At once, having seen what a person can see, Martim put the bird down with some care under the great tree. The last thing he had to forget had died.

Then he began to walk as if he knew where he was going. He was occupied with his steps.

Chapter 3

TOWARD the beginning of the afternoon Martim began to imagine—because of the finer quality of the soil and because he had eventually come upon some fruit trees—that perhaps he was getting close to a town. He tried to eat one of the unknown fruits; but it was green and juiceless, and only irritated his avid mouth. But a fresher breeze was blowing, and it carried the smell of running water. The ground there was darker. And when he found the ferns, it gave him a feeling of dampness that sent a sensuous shiver along his dry ribs.

The silence itself had become different. Even though the man had not noticed any sound the birds were flying in a more excited way, as if they had heard what he had not. The man stopped and was attentive. There was a shifting in the air as if in some part of the world a dinosaur had slowly changed its position.

And sometimes as he kept on walking the wind would bring a vague sound to him, a more intense call. It was a call to life that disturbed the man in a soft sort of way. But it left him not knowing what to do as if a flower had blossomed and the only thing that he could do was to look at it.

Little by little Martim was figuring out his own feelings, taking care not to understand them too well and thus put a stop to his perception. The liquid call came to him as if from far away someone were whispering in his ear: that was the strange sense he had of distance, and he stopped to sniff. In the embarrassment of having recourse only to himself he seemed to be attempting to use his own defenselessness as a compass. He tried to calculate whether he was near or infinitely far away from what was happening somewhere. He had barely stopped when the silence of the sun returned and confused him.

Most likely the thing toward which the man was walking uncertainly was just the creation of his anxiety and the intensity of his desire to draw close, for alone in that countryside of light all the man seemed to want was to draw close somehow—of course his listless way of wanting to relate was nothing more than a substitute for speech. Who knows but that from now on that "wanting" might be his only means of thought. Martim kept on advancing without having any idea of what it was that was hastening his steps in the direction of nothing but the wind's suggestion.

Until unexpectedly this last, holding sway over his extreme attention, brought him back again to that unusual shrillness, as if clarity, by dint of being so insistent, had become audible. The man stopped short then, abandoning caution. And his whole face tried to capture that other quality of silence. But only the empty air was beating about his hair. His sharp sense of hearing seemed to have reached some state of invention, but just when his reception had become sharpest, there was nothing for him to listen to.

Since the breeze was blowing from the left he deliberately turned away from the direction he had been following—and with great deliberation, with the care of a craftsman, he tried to walk in such a way that he would always feel the wind full in the face. His groping face was attempting to follow that open path in the air and the promise that it held. Of what? The wind— maybe the wind. The man had not worked out any plan, and he was armed only with the fact that he was alive. Now, as the afternoon became more peaceful he fell into an empty, humble, and intense clairvoyance that put him into physical contact with the unknown. His will continued to push him forward.

Now, slowly becoming more systematic, every time the wind would start to hit him only on the side of his face, or then only on the back of his neck the man would adjust the direction of his steps patient as a donkey, until he could feel the moist breeze upon his mouth once more. And only in that way, from time to time, would the peaceful sound come over him again as if he had created it. His hard and subtle struggle gave promise of going on indefinitely.

But when that man came to the top of a rise—as if he had caught up to an illusion he had been chasing all his life and had touched it in the midst of his own intoxication, as if he had caught up suddenly in a swirl of the most delicate happiness— the air would open up into a free and whirling wind. And he found himself in the full tumult, so impossible to grasp that it could have been the sound of sunset.

He had not been wrong then! What was it? It was just the wind. What was it? No, it was the top of a mountain. His heart beat as if he had swallowed it. He, the man, had disembarked.

There was an air of jubilation, the empty and dizzy jubilation that inexplicably comes to a man on top of a mountain. He had never been so close to the promise that apparently is made to a person at birth. Stupefied, he opened his mouth several times, like a fish. He seemed to have reached that thing a person does not know how to ask for. The thing that lets him say only obscurely, I found it—as if he had aroused the depths of some imagined reality. Sometimes a person was so avid for a thing that the thing would happen; and that is the way in which the destiny of moments is shaped and the reality we hope for. His heart, anxious to beat fully, was beating fully. And the wind was singing loudly and magnificently the way it does for a pioneer who first treads strange soil.

It is hard to say with what feeling the tired man perceived it—perhaps with his acute thirst and with his previous abdication and with the nakedness of his lack of understanding—but there was jubilation in the air. A jubilation which was really just as unassimilable as that almost invented blue of the sky which, like all softest of blues, had finally made him dizzy with silly glory and with noble glory. The man's inner armor was sparkling. Unattainable, yes, but there was jubilation in the air, the same as had been promised him in processions, or in some quiet female face, or in the idea that one day he would reach what had ended with the start of his search. And it seemed to that man, who tended to exaggerate, that one could say that he had worked quite hard to reach that valuable and useless thing. It was an idiot smile, his, if only there had been a mirror to reflect it.

It was only then that Martim noticed that he had been walking across an immense plateau beside a range of hills, the first slopes of which he surely must have climbed during the night. What he thought had been the difficulty of a climb in the dark had been his own difficulty, and later on what had really been a slow approach up toward the sun had been his own fatigue. But what mattered was that he had arrived. The fervent happiness of the sky made his heart strangely heavier. There was a seriousness in being there that he himself did not understand. But he matched its unknown sense with the face a man has when wind and silence are hitting him in the face. In some way then he had not been lying! Because wobbling from fatigue he was standing there as if a man held a prophecy within himself, standing, with his tired legs rooted, with a tremulous avidity within, like a man who is learning how to read. And there was the world along the shores of his muteness. That imminent and unreachable thing. His famished heart had clumsily conquered emptiness.

It was a surprising time. Luckily the man did not even attempt to understand it. Perhaps the thing in him was only an echo of something he had heard that said, "For on the top of a mountain one reveals himself."

Except that he had not revealed anything. And if in his dullness he had clumsily recognized that moment on the mountain, it was simply because a person recognizes what he wants to. There is not even any word in speech to name the fact that by making himself gigantic he had reached the top of the mountain. Then Martim said aloud:

"Here I am," he said, "and in the heart of something."

Physically at least he made an attempt with some dignity to

maintain himself at the level of what he had found; he preened himself in keeping with the heights that he had reached. It did not take very long. And he sat down on the ground.

Sitting there on the stone the countryside seemed very pretty. A touch of sunset began to quiver with a face of quiet clarity. Harmony, an immense and senseless harmony, surrounded his empty head. The sun was trembling like the facets of a stained glass window. Now that Martin had brought about his own arrival, he did not know what to do. So the man kept on sitting, submissive, breathing. So it was true—much sooner than he could have believed it was incontravertibly true.

Then everything turned green. A transparency came peacefully over the wasteland and left no one spot clearer than the next. Then his head, which thirst had emptied, began to calm down.

"What's that light, Daddy? What's that light?" he asked in a hoarse voice.

"It's the sunset, son."

And so it was. The light had come on with great mystery.

Chapter 4

WITH the clean, new clarity of vision the man's lethargy vanished. And just as if his energy was within reach and to his measure he got up without any effort at all. He was dominated by an impersonal awareness that made him like a supple-footed tiger. Now he was real and silent.

When he came to that part of the hill where there was nothing left to do but go down, he spotted the house there below surrounded by green fields, lying at his feet, as it were, but so reduced in size that he knew how far away it really was. Then he began to go down the slope and his back felt the soft encouragement of the descent. Propelled only by the thought of how thirsty he was, the man lost track of his progress and was finally on the same level as what was there: a house in the distance; another man sitting under a distant tree, some dogs sprawled about upon the ground.

Martim could now look at the house on equal terms; it was larger than he had thought and there was a thick clump of dark trees. He could not tell how far away they were from it, but he could see that they were beyond. The dark edge of the woods blended into distance itself, and it receded and approached the way it would have looked to someone just off a ship after a voyage on the high seas.

He moved along with that lightness born of fatigue, as if he was wearing tennis shoes. An artful elegance came over him; he was preparing to meet people. And the more he advanced the more he recognized that quiet tumult of life which he had sensed hours before and to which it seemed he had given the private name of "ideal," and which now, even though it was not divided up into distinct sounds, was familiar to him—without the false joy he had felt up there on the hill which had turned into dead past and nothing more, and without any promise whatever, but sure of some place where there would be water. His ecstatic folly on the hilltop had turned into simple thirst and vague vivacity. One thing was sure. He was still a little intoxicated by the high, purple sky.

He walked along lightly. At this point his empty head was of no help to him at all. What really seemed to be guiding his steps was the fact that he was a man inserted between earth and sky. And what kept him going was the extraordinary stage of impersonality he had reached, like a rat whose only individuality was what he had inherited from other rats. The man held that impersonality in a light grip, as if he knew that it would all drain off into the ground the moment he became himself again. That most extreme individuality he had attained on the hilltop could only have been a spasm of this blind totality in which he now moved forward. Lightened by fatigue he moved along without feeling his feet touch the ground, keeping as his only point of reference the neat house which kept getting bigger, bigger, and bigger. It stood out clearly in that clearness of the air around it, and that must have been the thing, intangible as it was, that was drawing the man to that place.

As soon as he saw that the dogs, now restless, had sensed his presence, he ducked behind a tree to look things over. By pushing aside some branches he was able to take in the whole aspect of the house, now completely visible. What confused him was the fact that much larger than the house was the ant on the leaf next to his spying eye—an instantaneous and reddish equestrian statue framing his vision. Martim shook his head several times until he freed himself of the size the monstrous ant had taken on.

The upper story of the house did not correspond to the greater extension of the ground floor but stood up like a bulky tower. Martim had developed a craving for towers in his previous life and now he felt a great satisfaction. Beds of daisies about the house formed wavy yellow clouds in his tired eyes.

But if the house gained in clearness from his approach, it lost the unity it had possessed from a distance. And from behind the tree the man's eyes were incapable of uniting into one whole the lack of logic of what he was looking at: a shed with a tile roof, windows behind which lay things that simple calculation could not reveal, doors half-opened so that all he could see were the shadows made safe by distance, fences enclosing fields that would not have been fields had it not been for the arbitrary fences. It was obvious that all of this was coming out little by little, getting bigger thanks to need or fantasy. It was a poor and pretentious place. He liked it immediately.

Realizing that it would be suspect for him to be hiding behind a tree the man finally came out. Without knowing what he was doing, he held out his arms a little to show that he was unarmed. And as he advanced—greeted by the dogs, now barking furiously—he perceived that the hazy figure in the shed was moving.

Near him now, however, was the man sitting on the ground under the tree. The man was eating, and the smell of his cold lunch nauseated Martim a little because of his hunger. His face became pleading, timid, and lowly like a face that implores. The smell was strong as it reached his nostrils, and he was so overcome that he almost vomited; he needed food so much. But his body took on a new impulse; he got through the difficult steps, and soon he was standing in front of the man, looking at him with circumstantial hunger.

Without interrupting his chewing the workman looked fixedly at his own bare feet as if deliberately not seeing the stranger. With the acuteness that hunger had given his perception Martim would not let himself be cheated; a mute communication was established between them like that of two men in the arena, and the one who was not looking was waiting for his chance to jump. A slight thrill of rage together with the vague promise of a struggle, then came over Martim, but he could sustain it only for an instant. The fact that he had felt a moment of strength had brought cold sweat out on his forehead. The slight feeling of joy gave a cynical cast to his face.

"Whose place is this?" he asked, finally giving in to the powerful silence of the other.

The barefoot man did not even move. He put his plate down slowly, wiped his full mouth.

"It all belongs to her," he said slowly, nodding with his head, and Martim, following the indicated direction with his squinting eyes could now see the figure in the shed more closely. "I belong here too," the man added, coupling this information with a false yawn.

Whoever made the first false move would give the other one his opportunity. The afternoon was beautiful and clear.

"I got lost," Martim said softly.

"Lots of people get lost around here on the way out of Vila," the other man said even more softly.

"Vila?"

"Vila Baixa," the man said, nodding his head vaguely to the left, and raising his eyes for the first time with a look of frank mistrust.

Martim looked that way but on the left there was nothing but an infinite expanse of land, and the sky was lower and dirtier. Feeling himself being examined he became even milder.

"That's what happened to me," he said. "I'm on my way back to Vila Baixa. But first I'd like a little water. I want a drink of water!" he said then, taking a complete chance.

The man stared at him. During the truce he had calculated the other's thirst. There was no pity in his look but human recognition—and as if the two loyalties had met, they looked at each other with clear eyes which a moment before had been filling up with something more personal. It was not hate; it was love for one's adversary and it was irony, as if both of them had detested the same thing.

"Just inside, over there," the workman said finally.

He got up with feigned difficulty and deliberate slowness. Standing opposite each other for a moment the strangers measured each other with their eyes. Mutual rage made them look at each other with nothing to say. One allows rage in another person, however, just as enemies have mutual respect before

(5 1)

they kill each other. Weaker than the tranquil power of the other man Martim was the first to avert his eyes. The other accepted without taking advantage. Martim, feeling once more the warm contact of antipathy, began to walk toward the house, followed at a certain distance by the victor and feeling a calm menace on the back of his neck.

The dogs were growling indecisively, holding back the exultation and joy of a fight. Besides the whole afternoon had been one of long, tranquil joy. A crippled dog limped over to join the others with that afflicted expectation of the invalid. Everything was smooth yet stimulatingly dangerous. Basically no one seemed to be impressed with what was happening, and everyone was simply enjoying the same opportunity. Things revolved a little, happy—ill-timed and happy. "Good God, I never saw anything so round," the man thought, stupefied. A dog blacker than the rest sank suddenly into the afternoon as if Martim had fallen into an unsuspected hole. It was the dog that vaguely alerted him and seemed to remind him of other realities. He was feeling so light that he felt the need to tie a stone around his neck. Then he forced himself with difficulty to remember where he was. But to his own disadvantage he was feeling too well, making him lose his perception, his principal weapon of combat.

The layout of the place, or farm, was not very large if one considered only the part that was in use—a few brokendown shacks, the barnyard, the cultivated plot. But it would have been enormous if one also considered the extensive fields which in some places, to show possession and nothing more, were cut off by poorly-outlined fences. The green of the trees swayed dustily; new leaves peeped out from underneath the coat of dust.

The roots were thick and gave off a smell in the end of an afternoon; and they were arousing in Martim an inexplicable bodily fury, like an indistinct love. Famished as he was, he was excited like a hopeful dog by the smells. The ground with a promise of sweetness and submission seemed ready to be fried— and Martim, with no apparent intention except to make contact, leaned over and almost without breaking step touched the earth

(5 2)

for an instant with his fingers. His head went dizzy from the delicious contact with the dampness; he hastened along with his mouth open. Nearer the house he could see that the shed was now empty. The tile roof of the cowshed was falling apart; in some places it seemed to be held up only by the height of the invisible cattle themselves, whose movements slowly made the empty light move too.

The water from the rusty can ran down from his mouth onto his chest and wet the dust-hardened clothing. Again he could hear the sound of soft movements of the hooves in the cowshed. The sun disappeared and an infinitely delicate clarity gave everything its final calm shape. A shed nearby still had the memory of a door in a set of empty hinges. Martim wetted his face and his hair; farther on he could see the makeshift roof of the garage . . .

Having arrived at the tense threshold of the impossible Martim accepted this miracle as the only natural step left before him. There was no way for him not to accept what was happening—because man has been born for everything that can possibly happen. He did not ask himself whether the miracle was the water which had drenched him to the saturation point, or the truck under the canvas roof which was the garage, or the light that was evaporating off the ground and the illuminated mouths of the dogs. There he was like a man who has reached a goal, exhausted, with neither interest nor joy. He had aged—as if everything that could have been given to him had arrived too late.

Under the tarpaulin was the truck, old but spotless and well-cared for. What about the tires? His myopic eyes could not make out the details of the tires. This difficulty rejuvenated him, filling him with the doubt that is hope. Fascinated, he slowly put the can on the ground and with dripping eyelashes examined the truck, getting down to look at the tires, calculating their possibilities in terms of miles.

"What do you want?" a serene low voice asked him.

Without surprise or speed Martim turned himself completely around, and he was looking into the inquisitive face of a woman. He could feel the man behind him, halted in an attitude of guard. He approached the shed, slowly swaying. Hunger made his eyes light up with malice; his dark lips smiled and parted. By the side of the shed the ground was covered with purple poppies whose fallen petals had been put into piles. It was a sight that gave the man a feeling of wealth and plenty. He looked in quiet dissipation at the living flowers, some without petals, others still unopened. His eyes sparkled with greed. He saw everything at the same time as he swayed and enjoyed the clearness of his eyes, which had become the same as that of the light around him.

He did not know from where, but from somewhere a mulatto woman appeared with her hair in curlers, and she stood there laughing with her quick eyes. Martim could not tell from where she had come or when she had appeared—which made him become cautiously aware of the possibility that he was also missing other things. The dogs had come close, growling with the courage to attack. The wind and silence surrounded them. The man hitched up his belt.

"So what do you want?"

"I was just looking around," he answered guiltlessly.

And he straightened up his chest in an effort to look like a city man.

"I'm aware of that," the woman from the shed replied.

"He was thirsty; that's what he said," the man in back of Martim said, and the woman listened without taking her eyes off the stranger all the while.

"I already had a drink," he said with some candor, pointing to the empty can. "The sun was hot," he added, shifting the position of his legs.

Martim had a quality the pleasure of which he could not enjoy because that quality was himself—a quality that in determined favorable circumstances made it impossible for most women to resist him: innocence. It would awaken a certain corrupt greed in a woman, always so maternal and in search of pure things. Once purity has been given its safeguards, woman is an ogre. The woman from the shed looked at him quite coldly.

(54)

"I'm also aware that you took a drink of water."

In some way everything that was yet to happen to that woman was already happening in that instant. She noticed it in the following indirect way: she passed her hand across her head.

The overdose of water was bubbling up inside of him and it brought on a nausea mixed with an intense desire to sleep or vomit: it gave a goodness of suffering to his face, something like a halo.

"Well," Martim said then, turning around slowly, "good-bye."

Vitória seemed to come to life.

"What did you want?"

Their looks crossed and penetrated without either finding anything in the other, as if both of them had already seen many other faces. Both seemed to know from experience that this was one more of many scenes to be forgotten. And as if both of them were aware of what that capacity for neutrality entails, without knowing why, each tried to guess the age of the other. The woman had already passed fifty some time before. The man was in his forties. The mulatto woman was waiting and laughing. Part of the man's brain was still occupied fearfully in trying to determine the link he could not find: when had the mulatto woman appeared?

This made him lose sight again of another important link: little steps had approached and Martim barely had time to spot the figure of a little Negro girl before she ducked behind a hedge, like a bird.

The dogs were panting, their hot tongues showing.

"I was looking for work," Martim answered, getting ready to leave. "Is there any work here?"

"No."

They looked straight into each other's eyes without suspicion.

"The garden could use some," he said as he withdrew, his back already turned to the woman.

"Are you a gardener?"

"No." He turned around with vague expectation.

They looked at each other again. For a moment it seemed to

them that they would be confronting each other forever, so definitive was the position of each of them; and the dogs were there. Martim heard the giggle of a child or a woman. He looked at the mulatto woman, but she stood there unsmiling with hot eyes. There was some movement in the hedge where the child was hiding.

"Who sent you?" Vitória asked.

"Nobody," the man answered, and he was still able to stay on his feet, sustained by the peaceful redness of the poppies.

"What can you do?"

"A little bit of everything."

"I mean your trade," she said a little sharply.

"Oh."

There was another giggle near him. Then, quite stimulated by this applause, he hitched his belt and made ready to give a funny answer or go away. But he said nothing and stood stock still. It seemed to him, very intelligently, that the only way he could avoid collapsing on the ground was to remain motionless, and that it would be strategic to let things happen as they would.

"Well?" the woman said again with more impatience.

He looked at her without expression until little by little his eyes began to open wide in a comical sort of way.

"I am an engineer, madam."

She seemed slightly shocked. She examined him with curiosity. He bore her look without much effort. Perhaps he perceived that he had made an impression on her, because an air of insolence brought a smile to his face, one which was a little beastly and a little happy, as if he had come through a difficult moment.

"You're an engineer."

"That's what I said," the man replied with arrogance.

Vitória looked him over professionally, the way she would have inspected a horse. Shamelessly the man let himself be examined. This suddenly shocked the woman. She blushed. To her he seemed indecently masculine standing there, as if that

(56)

were his only specialty. Why hadn't he shaved? Dirty, with a growth of beard, standing upright. Finally she sighed, tired, and said without interest, "I don't have any work for an engineer."

The man turned to leave and without breaking step said again without insistence, "I can do anything."

"I have a well that needs to be finished," she said suddenly, full of mistrust and curiosity.

He stopped walking and turned around. The fact that she could make him stop or go with a single word began to irritate the woman. The man's docility seemed an affront of some sort.

"I can fix wells," he nodded.

"The cowshed is falling in!" she said with even more distrust.

"So I noticed."

"Sometimes I need somebody to hunt *seriema* birds," she challenged sharply.

"I can shoot."

"I also need some stones laid in the brook so the water will run faster," she said coldly.

"They can be laid."

"But you're an engineer; you're of no use to me," she said with faint anger.

The poppies were waving red, like good blood, and they awakened a sort of brute life in the man. He was fighting in the midst of hunger and sluggishness and happiness. Only the rich poppies were stopping him from keeling over. With some reluctance then, running his tongue over a mouth full of desire, he finally turned his back on the poppies.

"Wait," the woman said.

He stopped. They stared at each other.

"I can't pay very much."

"But you'll give me room and board?" he said in a mixture of asking and affirming.

The woman took a quick look at him, as if room and board had meant something else. Then she took her hands out of the pockets of her jacket. There were men beside whom a woman felt lowered for being a woman; there were men beside whom a woman would preen her body with quiet pride—Vitória had been insulted by the way he had smoothed his hair.

"I'll furnish that," she said very slowly at last.

"It's agreed," the man said, digging in his nails and clutching a final moment of lucidity.

"I'm the one who says whether it's agreed or not. Where are you from?"

"Rio."

"With that accent?"

He did not answer. Their eyes showed that they both agreed it was a lie. But Vitória seemed obstinately unaware of her own perspicacity. And as she tried to calm herself she asked another question.

"What other work have you done besides being an engineer?"

The man's eyes blinked, clear and almost infantile.

"I can do anything," he said.

The answer obviously did not please the woman and she made a slight show of uncontained irritation because he had not gained her confidence. This man's lack of *savoir faire* made her impatient. She put her hands back into the pockets of her jacket, holding herself back. In the meantime it would be sufficient for him simply to guarantee that he had already done some work on wells.

"But you've had some experience with wells?" she asked, indicating imperiously what she expected for an answer.

"Yes," the man said, lying as she had wanted him to.

Again she blushed at his submission. And then she looked at Francisco, trying to exchange with a look of unity against Martim. But Francisco turned his eyes away and stared down at his feet. The woman blushed even more, swallowing her rejection as if it were something hard.

It was the first time that she had sought support from him, and it had to be just that time that Francisco felt obliged to turn her down. The fact is that he did not like the way the woman was abusing the stranger. Oh, he did not like a lot of things. But

(5 8)

in the meantime he would go on accepting them—provided that she continued to be stronger than he. The farm was organized around the selfassurance of that woman whom Francisco despised as one despises something that does not flow. But all he expected from her was strength; without it there would be no reason to obey her. So he turned his eyes away in order not to see her weakness.

Martim did not understand anything that was going on, but he instinctively allied himself with Francisco and tried to exchange a sarcastic look with him.

Francisco refused this look also, ostensibly gazing at a tree. The stranger had not perceived Francisco's loyalty to the woman; he did not understand that Francisco had become accustomed to a calm hatred for Vitória, and that he would not be ordered about by a woman unless he could safeguard his own dignity through hate. And as if the woman had understood him, she had never tried to establish the slightest friendly bonds between the two of them: this had been proof to Francisco that she respected him. The moment she became kind-hearted his decline would set in. He respected in the woman the strength with which she did not let him be anything more or less than what he was.

Pretending, therefore, an interest in a tree, he also refused any alliance with the stranger. The insecurity Vitória had raised in him by looking for a support that he did not want to give was enough for one day, not only because he did not agree with the way in which she was crushing the stranger, but also because he would despise her and would come to despise himself if she needed the help of a simple farmhand.

The new arrival felt rejected without knowing why. He did not understand the rage he had provoked. What he vaguely perceived was a certain scorn in Francisco, a scorn that covered him, Martim, as well as the woman and as well as Francisco himself. And he had the curious impression of having fallen into a trap. In a dream born of his fatigue he remembered tales of travelers spending the night in houses where madness reigned.

But that disappeared directly, because if anyone was dangerous there he was obviously the one. The impression of a trap persisted all the same.

Rejected by Francisco, the woman turned with greater determination toward the stranger, whose stupid docility was desirous now. But suddenly she asked, insulted:

"What are you laughing at?"

"I'm not laughing," he said.

Then, without realizing that she was looking him over cruelly, the woman discovered with fascination that, indeed, he was not laughing. It was simply that his face had a wily physical expression, independent of anything he might have been thinking—the way a cat seems to be laughing sometimes. In spite of being peaceful and empty his features gave the impression of mockery, as a cross-eyed person, whether sad or happy, will always be seen as cross-eyed. As if she had fallen into some darkness, she slowly looked out at him. "He's no good," she could see with her alerted senses. That man had a face . . . But the face was not the man. That bothered her and aroused her curiosity. That man was not himself, she thought without trying to understand what she was thinking; that man was shamelessly sullen. And he was standing there in complete exposure of himself, silent as a standing horse.

Which suddenly made the woman retreat, as if she had gone too far.

But now she could not prevent herself from seeing what she was seeing. "How dare he!" she thought, frightened and seduced, as if he had spoken what never should be spoken. With the perversion of some sacred accepted law that man did not show himself clearly. And there was a horrible secret physical wisdom on his face, like that of a resting puma—like a man who had outraged everything in himself except his one last secret, his body. There he was, completely on the surface and completely exposed. The only thing about him that was whole, remotely recognizable by the woman in that moment of wonder, was the final barrier that the body makes.

(6 0)

She stiffened up severely. There was, in fact, a great mistake in him. Just as great as if the human race had been mistaken. "How dare he!" she repeated darkly, without understanding what she was thinking. "How dare he!" she repeated startled, suddenly offended by what there was in life that was so unintelligible. "The nerve he had to reach that point of . . . of dishonor, of . . . of joy . . . of . . . The nerve he had to come to have—to have that way of standing!" she stammered inside with rage.

She looked at him again. But the truth was really that the man did not seem to be thinking about anything, she verified then with greater calmness. On his face there remained that delicate sensibility which thought gives to a face, but he was not thinking about anything. Perhaps this was what horrified her. Or, who knows, perhaps she had been warned by the fact that he had laughed at some time past.

"I can't use you," she said forcefully, deciding unexpectedly.

But when, without the slightest protest, he was already nearing the barnyard, she shouted angrily:

"Only if you sleep in the woodshed!"

She looked at him, startled. And showing no surprise, as if she could have kept on rejecting him and calling him back indefinitely, he came over. The child, who had since come out from behind the hedge, ran back at once to her hiding place. When he was near again, the woman asked him without warning:

"Would you please tell me at least just what an engineer is doing in these parts?"

"Looking for work," he repeated, not even attempting to maker her believe him.

She opened her mouth to reply to the impertinence. But she held back. And finally she said serenely:

"Wipe your feet off before you come in."

Chapter 5

Vitória was such a strong woman that somewhere in the past she must have found a key. The door it opened had been lost many years back, of course. But when she needed to, she could bring back her old power at once. Even though she might not have said so, deep inside she called that thing she knew a key. She no longer tried so hard to retrieve what once upon a time she had known, but it was what gave her life.

It was in search of the help of everything she had ever known, therefore, that later on in the kitchen she was absorbed in looking at the plate from which the man had eaten. She also tried to imagine him putting the door on the woodshed. She had given him the door, a big strange object to give somebody. With the completely unforeseen arrival of the man that kind of orderly circle in which she moved, as if compelled by some law, had now been broken; she had to admit reluctantly—At least something had happened—even if she could not say just what. Then, a little self-consciously, she thought about her own free act and was rather curious: "It's the first time I ever gave a door to anybody." That plunged her into a feeling from which there was no escape. It was the second time the man had upset her.

Not knowing what to do with her thoughts about the door she got away from them by trying to imagine that right now the man must be having trouble setting it back on its rusty hinges. Probably still maintaining that same expression of fatigue and what could have been a laugh, and with that shameless childlike quality that giants have. Or, who could tell, maybe he was working on the installation of the door with that same remote concentration with which, morsel by morsel, he had devoured his food. It had been a long time since the woman had watched hunger, and, looking at the empty plate now, she frowned. She could not determine the exact moment when she had felt that man's cruelty. Looking at the empty plate she then had the thought that people often get about a dog: he is cruel because he eats meat. But maybe the expression of cruelty had come from the fact that when in front of the shed he was hungry and still he kept on smiling. The hunger on his face had been visible, but with a great capacity for happy cruelty, he had been smiling. Not having any love for one's self was the beginning of cruelty toward everything else. She was aware of it in herself. But she at least possessed everything she knew.

For the first time, then, with an unpleasant clarity that she could no longer hide from herself, the woman realized that the man had not attempted to give her the slightest guarantee, nor had he promised her anything. She alone had taken all the risks, just as once when she was caring for an injured dog with skillful hands—he lost consciousness. And as she felt the unexpected total weight of the animal in her lap, she lifted up her eyes, all alone and responsible for that soulless body that was entirely hers now, like a child. That man who had dropped in there with all his weight.

"You rash old fool," she said, very tired suddenly, and pushed aside the dirty plate; her lack of self-love had covered her with haughtiness.

And how could she announce the arrival of the man to Ermelinda without the latter's getting joyful? But that was a problem she could solve later. What was important right now, and with an inexplicable urgency, was trying to guess what expression the man had on his face as he was putting up the door. Without tying one fact to the other, she went over to inspect the shotgun. It needed cleaning and an oiling. The woman bent to work on the old weapon for quite a while, sitting in the kitchen with a severe and obstinate face. It was the face of a person who, out of his own abdication, has devised a weapon and an insult to be used against other people.

The worst thing still, though, would be telling Ermelinda. "Just another farmhand would be of no importance, even if he was a boarder," Vitória thought, arguing unwillingly and convincing herself after a while—because how many times have one or two men worked for a month and then gone away; just three days before two men had left. What was she hesitant about then? Perhaps because she would have to confess to Ermelinda that the man was, or said he was an engineer. But it made no difference to her, she thought moodily, and blamed him for being an engineer—as long as he did his work, and Francisco would be sure to keep an eye on him, as far as Ermelinda was concerned . . .

"I hired a man. He says he is an engineer but that he can work at anything!" she imagined herself speaking harshly in order to stifle any comment from her cousin. What comment was she afraid of? She stopped cleaning the shotgun and looked vacantly and stiffly into the air. Or just say: "Ermelinda, there's a new hand who's going to be sleeping in the woodshed, so you can't go in there anymore; it's his quarters."

None of the phrases seemed firm enough to her to stop Ermelinda's exclamation of rapture. And when she thought of her cousin's delighted face, the woman immediately put it out of her apprehensive imagination, as if she could not bear it; furiously unable to stop her heart from starting to pound with fear within her. But having transferred to Ermelinda the distaste she felt for her own stupidity, she felt blameless and free now to have a rage. From there she went on to tell herself she would not stand for the curiosity her cousin would show when she heard the news. It was not the words Ermelinda was going to use that filled her with anticipated rage—the truth was that she had never even been able to reproduce in her mind, word for word, any phrase the girl had ever used—it was the disguised expression of extreme joy that came over the girl as soon as anything happened. It was the feeling of being forced once more, having to explain the presence of the man, into intimate contact with that astute and softly insidious-looking face—as if in her cousin's misty system the means of contact with a person could never be direct because danger and waiting are also indirect. Ermelinda

(64)

always seemed to be hiding the fact that she understood. And her face would remain almost deliberately shapeless and suspended—Waiting for a confirmation?

Oh no, it was not that. What was it, then? Had it been illness in childhood that had made that girl grow up in the shadows? that sickly childhood that Ermelinda guarded as if it were her only treasure?

But none of that could explain it. Just as soon as one began to think about Ermelinda, without even seeing her, she would seem to slip off into other people's thoughts. And no sooner would Vitória accuse her of something, even just a mental accusation, than Ermelinda would suddenly appear innocent and frightened. How could one ever get to know her? Any direct contact was impossible. It was amazing how if Ermelinda was thinking about the inexplicable hatred she felt for birds, and someone asked her what she was thinking about, she would simply answer "birds." It was amazing how the only solution had to be never asking her. Ermelinda would act as if a tree were blue—but if Vitória were to ask her what color the tree was she would reply immediately, glowing like an expert, that the tree was green. What Vitória was attempting to find out was whether Ermelinda really knew that the tree was green or whether she merely knew that Vitória thought the tree was green. The wisest thing would be not to ask her anything. How could one ever get to know her? "What makes me, never committing an evil act, be evil? and Ermelinda, never committing a good act, be good?" The mystery that makes things as we know they are had left the woman quite deep in thought.

During all the time that Ermelinda had been on the farm, Vitória had not been able to interest her in the daily work or eliminate that calculated sweetness with which the other one would keep on waiting. And for all of that, Ermelinda had never once said "No." The fact that she had had "a bed-ridden childhood" seemed to have awarded her the perpetual right to wander, which she would only do with a certain touch of ritual—for only those who possess a vice are privy to its secret delights. Vitória, fascinated, would watch the other one take care of her idleness with precision and loving indolence.

Paralyzed at first by the ways of the other one Vitória had let herself be dragged along through everything the visitor had brought to the place, almost changing it over. Fear of the dark, that peaceful darkness, had taken on some shapeless power after her cousin's arrival. And the disguised allusions to death, as if it were a secret never to be admitted. And her waiting. Fear, death, waiting—a waiting that took a concrete form in her expecting things to happen, as if the unforeseen were within hand's reach. "Something might happen any moment now"—it was all of that, perhaps, that had infiltrated the farm and which had infected Vitória for a time. But then she had finally awakened with a sudden rage and had picked up her own life again.

Even so it had been impossible to get away completely from that air of sneakiness which the other one had, and to stop hearing those obscure and joyful phrases that said nothing, but hung like echoes in the air. "A horse can sense when its rider is afraid," Ermelinda would say. "A ring around the moon is a sign of rain," she would say—and the night would become broader and deeper. "A person should start to worry if a dog doesn't like him," she would say smiling, as if that was only a sample of something inexplicably expectant. Ermelinda had something of the spiritualist about her.

Although she could not make her work, Vitória at least had learned how to defend herself from her. And no sooner had the first disruption of life that the other one had brought to the farm passed, than Vitória had hastened to instruct her about the essentials regarding herself: the first thing she had to put a severe halt to in her cousin was the tendency to seek physical support and contact, rest her hand on Vitória's shoulder, look for her arm when they would be walking together, as if both of them were sharing the same delightful misfortune. After that initial physical distance had been established a kind of absence of relations developed. From the time that Ermelinda had come there after being widowed Vitória and she had never gone into the matter deeply. Until some time had passed, the way dust falls and settles; and whatever it was that might have happened had already and irremediably happened. Ermelinda had ended up by clinging to her trunks and the useless objects she had brought with her, and unable to pull Vitória along with her through her fears and waiting, she had taken refuge in laughter with the mulatto cook. From her previous life there had remained the waiting for mail from Rio, in which she would periodically receive from a candy store a small box of Jordan almonds, which she would carry about with her for days dreamily rationing them out nut by nut.

Only once on an excessively hot afternoon that held ·the threat of a storm had awareness finally exploded in Vitória, but never again. And it had calmed down when the rain started to fall, breaking branches and drenching the fields. And then, when a fine rain had turned the farm all peace and quiet, Vitória had asked herself, astonished, why had she decided so unexpectedly to reveal to Ermelinda that years before, back in Rio still, through a half-open door she had seen Ermelinda throw herself into the arms of the man she had later married.

And now, cleaning the gun with mechanical concentration, Vitória again asked herself what had possessed her to come to the point of telling her cousin. Could it have been the rain that had been threatening but had not yet begun to fall? Or maybe the insistence of that face which specialized in waiting had finally exasperated her—Ermelinda sitting and fanning herself, waiting, perspiring, and eating the almonds that had the scent of an old handkerchief about them—the rain threatening, and the smell of the almonds making the air intolerably soft, filling the room with that sweetish odor of a letter hidden deep in a brassiere, and the waiting . . . And then, as if the surface of things had to be scratched, Why? Vitória told her that "she knew quite well how it was that she, Ermelinda, had become engaged": that she had seen the man running after her around the table in a ridiculous chase, she had seen Ermelinda suddenly stop her running and throw herself into the arms of the man, who was startled and had not hoped for so much . . .

"And now that you know finally that I saw you, don't ever lie

(67)

again!" she had told her, and she herself did not know for certain what she was accusing the other one of; and she looked at her, startled.

"But I was running away from him! . . ." the other one had tried to defend herself. She had thrown herself into his arms, yes—she couldn't deny that—but it wasn't because she was in love with him.

And why had Ermelinda found it necessary to defend herself against the accusation that she was in love with him?

"And did you fall into his arms because you didn't love him?" Vitória had inquired, and it no longer occurred to her then that she had accused her cousin of having loved him since the other one had defended herself by saying that she had not loved him. And it did not occur to either of them that one did not have the right to demand justifications from the other. The heat had been getting stronger and, at the point of tears, Ermelinda had wiped away her perspiration and tried to get rid of the uncomfortable almond in her mouth. She had ended up by spitting it into her handkerchief with stingy care, and after tying a knot had put it gently into her pocket—after which, at the point of tears, she had tried to explain that "she had felt so alone with him, so unprotected with a man chasing her, that therefore she had thrown herself into his arms." It was then, perhaps inspired by the violence of the wind, which had already knocked some fruit off the trees and was blowing leaves and dust about, that Ermelinda had discovered with enchantment the word "executioner." For days after, out of sheer pleasure and vanity, she had begun to use it quite frequently, with various meanings, some of them quite forced. Gripping the box of almonds, she had tried to explain with pleasure that she had felt so alone with that man "that her executioner had to become her support and her misfortune had to be her refuge." And facing Vitória, who by then had already become drunk with her own unleashed rage, Ermelinda had stammered that "if a person came at me with an ax, I would lower my neck to him so that the one who killed me would at least not be my enemy"—she had had the courage to say all that, and it was courageous to say what simply made no sense to either one of them.

It was possible that if Ermelinda had managed to explain the absurd thing she had been trying to say, and if the other one had managed to understand, peace might have grown up between them—or at least weariness. But Vitória had answered that a bed-ridden childhood had not prevented Ermelinda from being really as strong as an ox; to which the other one, unexpectedly, had lowered her modest eyes, and that had intrigued Vitória, who after a moment of surprise, had gone back to even more serious accusations. Ermelinda, confused by the lowing of the cows frightened by the wind, had begun to talk about executioners which had brought Vitória to remark with great irony that "from what she could make out" her husband had not by any manner or means been any executioner—"that he had given her everything, that there had been nothing Ermelinda couldn't have had when the man had been alive." All of which made Ermelinda say that he had been the best of husbands, and that she would not let anyone speak ill of someone who was dead—to which Vitória had added that it had never occurred to her to say anything bad about a man who for years had tolerated his wife's calling him "my flower"; which had made Ermelinda cry in her memories. Both women had been made desperate by the unbearable wind, by the dust that had been blowing into the room as the clouds had closed in lower and had brought on a sudden darkness.

And when the storm had finally broken, the rain had made so much noise that they could not have gone on talking unless they had shouted. With a cooler and more peaceful wind, the perspiration had begun to dry off pleasantly—and a sudden peace had come about between the two of them as if they had arrived at some conclusion. Haughty, drenched with shame, Vitória had left the room. And she had started to avoid her cousin. Only a few people could have managed to do that to her: make her hate them and hate herself. Vitória had never pardoned them. People like that were in her way. Afterwards, as if everything that could happen between them had already happened, they did mot need each other anymore.

But that one direct contact had happened a long time back. And the memory she did not understand was of no help to Vitória as she sat in the kitchen in finding some way to tell Ermelinda that another hand had arrived. With a stoical expression she held onto the shotgun, bearing up under everything she knew. "With the cold key by my breast I shout from out my castle," she thought prettily, because if she did not show the world magnificence, she would be lost. She was making what she knew magnificent—but what she knew had already become so vast that it resembled ignorance more. She gave in to the latter for a moment.

"If I could only shoot up and make the rain come down," she thought for a moment when her brain failed her from fatigue.

Because out of the memory of the scene with Ermelinda, all that she had left was the vision of the blessed rain coming down. And another big rain was needed so much now, she thought with the strength she had taken on again, as if by command or as if she had again touched the key she had within. The cornfield might dry up before harvest time . . . And the pasture might dry up. Maybe not, she questioned the sky with her eyes.

But the lofty sky and the sunset's daily reluctance to turn into night promised nothing but the probability of another drought. The ground was still damp, it was true. And the vegetation was lush. But for how long? For some days now Vitória had been pretending not to have noticed that there were fewer toads around: they were already deserting . . . And that little by little the locusts had been persistently filling the evening sky. But the woman threw a challenge at the air: the birds had not left yet! That lengthened her glance on into the difficult regions of expectation, as if the authority of her faith would stop the birds from deserting. As long as they were around she would keep herself silently ready for battle.

"I suppose," she suddenly sighed dispiritedly, "the sooner I talk to Ermelinda, the better, so she doesn't find out for herself and come running up all pale to tell me 'There's a man in the woodshed!' " She would not be able to bear a stupid phrase like that. And only imagining that she had heard it her impulse now was to dismiss her cousin the way one dismisses a maid.

Passing through the living room on her way up to Ermelinda's room, however, she saw her through the window kneeling by the new rosebush. She stopped for a moment to look at her before going out on the terrace with that useless habit she had of examining people when they were not aware that they are being examined. She spied for a moment, sighed heroic once again, and as if she had been obliged to come to some conclusion, now that she had looked at her, she thought: "She's young, that's why she's still afraid. She's young, that's why she's afraid of death." "But I have a right to be afraid too!" she said to herself darkly, recovering. It was as if the other one could still be offended. And she, she never would be again.

She stopped next to Ermelinda. She knew that the other one had already seen her approaching, even if she had not even raised her eyes—as if that was the way that someone who is afraid of the dark or has been initiated into spiritualism and the secrets of a way of life ought to act.

The girl, making believe that she had only then heard the steps, finally raised a crafty face of surprise. And it was as if the sweetness of the lie had made her face take on an expression that was at the same time one of both abandonment and boon—and all of it, all of it was fake. Vitória clenched her fists inside the pockets of her slacks:

"What are you doing?" she asked calmly.

"Pruning the wild rosebush."

"Doesn't the rosebush frighten you?" she asked softly. She felt the need to wound that kneeling girl, as if she had been to blame for her own absurd action in hiring the man.

"Not this one; this one has thorns."

Vitória frowned:

"And what difference does it make if it has thorns?"

"I'm only afraid," Ermelinda said with a certain voluptuousness, "when a flower is too pretty with no thorns, just too delicate and pretty all over."

"Stop being silly," Vitória said brutally, "it's all caused by something in your body! And if you helped out with some of the work, you wouldn't have time to be frightened by pretty roses or hate this farm!"

"And are you so fond of this farm?" the other one asked smoothly.

"There's a man in the woodshed!" Vitória blurted out.

And, as she had said something that until that moment not even she herself had known how to say, she stood there with a startled and wounded look. She came to immediately.

"He says that he's an engineer. The reason he's around is that he's evidently out of work. I'm going to use him for a thousand little jobs. Francisco will keep an eye on him."

She had said it. She closed her eyes for a second with fatigue and relief. When she opened them she saw that Ermelinda had stopped with the shears in the air, and her face—her face once more had taken on an extremely sharp and tender tone, as if a face would have to be invented in order for it to attain that expression some day. "And I," Vitória thought, "I know everything, and everything I know has grown old in my hand and turned into an object." She muffled her voice as best she could.

"What's the matter? What did I say that was so extraordinary to make you stop like that?"

Ermelinda trembled.

"You didn't say anything strange. You said there's a man in the woodshed!" she obeyed quickly.

"Well, then, if you're going to prune the rosebush, which is a useless job with the drought coming on, keep on pruning!" she exclaimed without holding back. "And don't look so radiant!" And not being able to stop herself anymore she went on. "Radiant, yes!" she said with pain. "You're thinking again that today is a great day! Just a clap of the hands and you get happy; and it all scares me! He's a man who came to work. If he doesn't do a good job he leaves, and if he thinks that just because he's an engineer he's going to run things he's very much mistaken! And that's all there is to it, nothing beyond that!"

Ermelinda pretended to be so surprised that she looked at the other one with her mouth half-open—or was she really surprised; one could never tell. "I was very abrupt," Vitória thought. Ermelinda gave her a fleeting side-glance and went back to her vague work next to the rosebush—and it was if she wished to be so discreet that she would not let the other one see that she understood. Vitória caught it and blushed. A few moments passed. They remained silent, feeling the soft swirl of the breeze around them. Darkness was coming on little by little. For an instant the scent of roses gave the two women a moment of softness and meditation.

"The flowers," Ermelinda said as the half-light made her slightly anxious. "The flowers," she said.

"Do the flowers frighten the garden?" Vitória asked attentively.

"Isn't that just what it is, though," exclaimed Ermelinda, surprised and pleased. "You always say everything so well!" she said flatteringly.

Vitória was calm. She looked at her deeply, once more immune from everything that the girl was.

"I never would have said that myself. But now that we're living together I've had to learn your language."

"Why does he say that he's an engineer?" the other one asked very carefully.

"Ah, I knew it. I saw that question coming."

"But what did I say wrong now?" and an innocence that was almost real gave a childlike quality to the imploring face; but they both knew that it was all a lie.

"Ermelinda," Vitória said, closing her eyes fiercely, "for three years now you've been saying: 'I'm afraid of birds.' For three years you've been saying: 'How strange it is the way that tree sways.' For three years I've even been listening to your silences. And I can't stand any more of your bed-ridden child-

hood. That doesn't give you any rights over me. Wait a minute—let me finish. I'm quite aware that from your bed you had
lots of time to see the birds and develop a fear of them! We're
living together, fine, you had to live somewhere; I also know that
you took care of my father once, but I know too that it was only
for the three days that I needed you! I know everything. But let
me tell you quite plainly that—that I wanted peace. I wanted—
I wanted peace. If not, why do you think I didn't sell this place
when Aunty died? Answer me! Why didn't I sell it and why did
I come here without knowing anything about the place? And if I
had sold it I could have had money in my pockets and could
have kept on living in the city. That's how it would have been,"
she added in surprise. "And I would have stayed right where I
had always been living . . ." Vitória had recovered with a
sudden violence, "What I forgot to ask was whether you wanted
peace too when you came here. This place, Ermelinda, is just
right for a quiet person like me. No, don't say anything. It's all
right. You've been annoying me for three years now; I have to
tell you that. And today I'm telling you something else: I've had
enough. You've changed my life with all your—with your waiting. I can't stand it. It's been a long time since it could be called
peaceful around here. It's just as if I had rats breeding in my
house; they run around and I can't see them—but I can feel
them, you hear? I can feel their feet—their feet, Ermelinda—
making the whole house shake."

"What do you want peace for?" Ermelinda changed the tack
maliciously, trying to soothe her with a mask of grace.

"I want quiet, I want order, I want stability," and while she
was speaking it seemed more and more absurd to her to have
taken on a complete stranger as a hired hand. "And for the love
of God don't tell me that today you have a presentiment just
because the man was hired on a Thursday. You have presentiments every day. It used to be your parrot and his rasping
squawks that seemed to be scratching my throat—but luckily he
died. Your parrot, your presentiments, your gentility, your fear
of death! That's it right there! Your fear of death."

(74)

The other one twitched her nervous face:

"Do you think another drought is coming?" she cut in quickly, pale.

Vitória stopped short, thrown off balance by the interruption. "Drought?"

The poor woman looked at the softness with which night was coming on, damp and full—in that way that the world loves us at certain times. It was March and a dizzying paleness was stretching out the distances. Upset, she smelled the rotten odors coming up from the ditches. In the growing darkness the ditches looked like precipices and they resolutely drew her look away into an empty and unwillingly soft meditation. The land stretched out limitless, restful . . . And she noticed with a slight start that in the woodshed the lantern was being lit.

First the light rose up; then it almost went out. With an intensity in which there was anxiety and aspiration the woman joined in the struggle with the lantern as if it was some obscure struggle of her own. Finally, just at the point of going out, the light survived. Tremulous at first, dim. The darkness all around had become total.

"Drought?" the woman repeated, looking at the woodshed as if she was not seeing it. "Maybe not," she said, absorbed. "What has to be is very powerful."

Chapter 6

WHILE all that was happening, Martim felt almost as big as the woodshed itself as he held the lantern over his head. Damp wood was piled up next to the cot, and he looked at the bed with such sensuality that one would have thought he had not slept for years.

The clarity into which he had forced himself in order to answer Vitória's questions had already disappeared, and the agility he had needed to hang the door had vanished from his hands. Wobbling and stumbling with the abrupt swaying of the light against the walls, he inhaled deeply the woodshed's smell of wet leather and shook his head hard in an effort not to go under. Even though he did not need himself for anything, he was aware of an internal struggle against submergence. The menacing feeling that he was losing important connections was making him force himself to be aware of everything. When the smoky light of the lantern passed over the cot, he noticed the useless detail of the strap hanging motionless on a rusty spike and the frameless cardboard picture.

With a face drugged from sleep the man brought his lantern submissively over to the picture. Beneath the engraving in huge and femininely designed letters, as if it were the work of fine embroidery, was written "St. Crispin and St. Crispinian." The man's bloodshot eyes regarded the two saints at their shoe-maker's trade. He liked the picture very much. The hands of the saints were suspended for a moment over the sandals in the perfect silence the artist had chanced to create. Above the haloes of the saints and inside a smoky circle (a conventional way of showing the distant future time of an event) were the same St. Crispin and St. Crispinian, this time being boiled in a cauldron. "Jesus," the man grunted, "I wonder what their crime was?"

But underneath the cauldron, outside the smoky future of the cauldron, the saints were green, blue, and yellow (colors which, instead of violence, gave the picture the great spaciousness that can fill a church). The saints had the look of peaceful concentration that repairing sandals calls for, as if Man's task were sandals.

In his dull stupidity, which showed itself in a smile of submission, the man insisted on bringing the lantern close again. Still wound up by the need for care that his flight had given him, it seemed to him that there was something that was eluding him. And so with timid fingers he touched the cardboard faces of the martyrs like one who furtively approaches something that possibly might get enraged. Then, listlessly, he put on his glasses. But the truth is that the thing still eluded him, and his eyes, strengthened by the glasses, could see only what they had seen before without understanding. Inside the smoky circle was the boiling cauldron. Beneath it were the shoes calmly being repaired. The man had not managed to advance one single step. The mute scene of the picture gave the shed perspective, however, and the woodshed itself had a shoemaker smell about it.

If that man still remembered what the world was like, in that picture there was something to which he certainly would have responded if he still had been a man. That thing the man had learned and had not completely forgotten still bothered him; it was difficult to forget. Symbolic things had always bothered him a great deal. But he was just as sluggish as the food that was lying heavy in his stomach. When he blew out the lantern the darkness was filled by the breeze that was coming through the window. And as if shadows were meeting other shadows, with some pity, fatigue dropped him into sleep.

At last a pale dawn began to move about. And the breeze blew the first frail life into that shed that had been warmed by breathing, leather, and intestines. Without yet knowing what he was doing the man sat on the cot. Then, person of strong habits that he was, he stood up.

It was a very pretty dawn; the time when there is still no

light, and the only light is the air, and one does not know whether he is breathing or seeing. From far off there came to him the smell of cows, which always fills a person with delight: the smell of waking cows came mingled with the great distance he could see. Martim, with eyes heavy-lidded from the long night looked out with surprise at the empty plot which the half-light of sleep revealed to him through the window in the back of the woodshed. He had apparently forgotten that he had gone to sleep in the country. Here, in these surroundings he looked through the low fog at a dry and dirty land hardened by the dawn with a childish curiosity. The man had expected nothing and he saw what he saw, as if he had not been made to draw conclusions but just to look.

One more second of that real freedom and his head was also touched by the incomprehensibility of what he saw. And in a deception which he certainly needed, a deception as certain as the certain fall of an apple, he had a sense of empathy: it seemed to him that in the great silence he was being greeted by a landscape out of the Tertiary Period when the world and its dawns had nothing to do with a person, and when all that a person could do was look. Which is what he was doing.

It is true that it was hard for his eyes to understand the thing that was, was doing nothing but happening. That it was only happening. That it was just happening. The man was "opening the curtains."

The plot had probably been an attempt at a garden or a nursery that had been ultimately abandoned. One could see the remains of work and of a will. Certainly at some time there had been an attempt to establish an intelligible order. Afterwards nature, previously banished by the scheme of that order, had surreptitiously returned and installed herself there. But on her own terms.

Because, whatever its period of glory and lushness might have been, the plot now had the silence of a person wrapped up in himself. There were some hard, ash-gray stones, a piece of fallen trunk. The exposed roots of a tree that had been cut down long ago; for no moisture now oozed out of its oblique cut. Weeds were growing straight up; some had reached such a height that now they were waving, sensitive to the compelling breeze of dawn. Others crept out very close to the ground, and only death would get them away from it. Thick earth lay crumbled alongside an ant hill; it was a peaceful disorder.

The man kept on looking until the life which had been put into the plot began to awaken. Mosquitoes shimmering as if they were bringing in the first cargo of light. The cautious bird among the dried leaves. Rats and mice crossing from one stone to another. But in the brotherhood-producing silence, as in a working spindle, one movement was indistinguishable from another. That was the restful confusion into which Martim had fallen.

It was only with a stupid effort that the man was able to bear the intense light of the countryside during the confusing days that followed (all ties eluding him, his first orders from Vitória dully received, Ermelinda examined from a distance, and hearing the mulatto woman's repressed laughter) as if he were not yet ready to understand clarity—

But day by day, having finished the arduous work that he would not have known enough to do if Vitória had not told him, he would come down from the high and open light of the countryside. And he came blind with incomprehension. Guided by the stubbornness of a sleepwalker, as if the uncertain tremble of a compass needle were calling him, he would finally go to that Tertiary plot where life was only fundamental—on a par with his own. And with the sigh of someone regaining consciousness, he would find the wavering shadow, the movement of the rats, the thick plants. In that vegetative pit, which the light at best made hazy, the man would take refuge, silent and brutish, as if the thing he was could find its place only in the crudest beginnings of the world—in that pit, that crawling plot of land, the harmony made up of so few elements did not transcend him, not even its silence. The silence of the plants was his own diapason and he grunted approvingly—he who did not have a word to say and who never wanted to talk again; he who had gone on strike against being a person. Sitting there in his plot he was enjoying his own vast emptiness. That way of not understanding was the primeval mystery and he was an inextricable part of it.

The Tertiary plot had great perfection about it. Not even when the light came close did it change the atmosphere of silence. There clarity, coming after ages and ages of silence, became reduced to mere visibility, which is all eyes need. Much more had always been given to that man than he had needed— at least that was how it seemed to him now sitting in his territory which satisfied him so much—and if visibility did reach the plot of ground, it revealed dead leaves rotting, sparrows blended into the earth as if they had been made of dirt, and little black mice that had made their nests in that rudimentary world.

Since Martim had never known anything about plants or animals he found there plants and animals of new and rare species. A rat was a large creature of a rare and hairy species, with a long tail. A plant had a mouth sticking to the ground. A bird flying low warned the man that he, too, followed with his mouth open. And no one told anyone where to go. The plant all dirty with dust understood well enough how to twine itself. There, there was the dark air from which living things live. Martim was surrounded by something he understood: flies were laying eggs, and the meaning of laying eggs was the primative meaning of man; it was there, just as if there was a plan of which he was ignorant, but which a plant would join on to with its mouth and which he himself had joined quite obviously by sitting on the stone—sitting on a stone was becoming his most intelligible and most active position.

And the thing was so perfect that even the perspective of distance became a part of that world without God. For when the man lifted up his eyes the distant trees were as tall, as tall as a thing of beauty; the man grunted approvingly. The more stupid he was the more face to face with things he was.

So it was that after a while Martim's strength was coming back.

Even though he had wanted nothing from the farm except

bed, food and the use of the truck at the most favorable moment, the days began to become more occupied than he had expected. And they followed one another with rhythmical and certain hammer-blows, as if the days were the very links that were escaping him. The mornings were cool, the trees leafy, the jobs followed one upon the other. The mulatto woman would look at him and laugh, the Negro child spent all her time hiding so that she could spy on him. But he had grown used to it. And he moved slowly like a man sowing a field. His great silence was not apathy. It was a deep and watchful sleepiness, and an almost metaphysical meditation upon his own body, in which he seemed to be carefully imitating the plants of his plot.

His strength was slowly coming back, and that was how he spent the first week, the most important of all those he spent on the place. At the end of the first week it was as if Vitória had ruled him harshly for months, as if the man had been sweating for months in an arduous apprenticeship. And in such a way had whatever thing it was happened that week, and in such a way had the invisible links come together, that after seven days the thing that one becomes aware of unexpectedly had come about: a past. And at the end of one week there was restlessness and indistinct noise in the place, as happens when everything has stayed without evolving for a long time, and everything wants to change.

Martim had also become accustomed, without resistance, to Vitória's constant commands. She seemed to have discovered an incessant and impatient game: watching over him and inventing work for him to do.

"I have an English Arabian that needs currying!"

"Yes."

"Really," she said then very attentively, "the last thing I needed was an engineer."

But the woman doubted that he had heard or understood her.

"I said," she repeated, examining him with surprise, "that the last thing I really needed was an engineer!"

"If you had needed one it wouldn't have been so easy," the man finally answered without seeming bothered in the least.

Meanwhile his peaceful face gave the impatient woman the idea that he was permanently amused or occupied with something that escaped other people.

"All of this," she concluded, "all of this is nonsense."

The country air had left him raw and weather-beaten but his eyes were clearer. He moved slowly about through the great expanse, unhampered in the end because he had no thoughts. But if his *compact* absence of thought was a dullness it was the dullness of a plant. For like a plant he was aware of himself and of the world—with that same delicate tension with which a weed is a plant down to its last extremities, with that delicate tension with which a blind plant can feel the air in which its hard leaves are imbedded. The man had reduced his whole self to that kind of vigilance. What was happening to him was one of those periods of time about which one says after it has passed. Nothing happened.

Chapter 7

IT WAS the warm and inexpressive face of a man—and one afternoon Ermelinda looked at Martim, startled to see him so definite in the midst of the vagueness of the countryside.

Experiencing that vast surprise she never knew how to use, she then became startled at the coincidence of the man's being right there on that place, and she was startled at the curious coincidence that she too was on the place. "But," she thought, making herself become a bit modest, "one fact is always linked to another, and things always have a great coincidence about them."

Immediately, in the first week Ermelinda fell passionately in love with Martim. Primarily because he was a man and she, in a manner of speaking, had never fallen in love—except some other times that did not count. And then because Martim, without knowing it, was a man beside whom a woman did not feel humiliated. He had no shame.

She was sitting in the afternoon hulling corn. The fact that she had taken on the job was already perhaps a beginning of the need to be alone and to let herself become absorbed. Being absorbed was the usual manner of doing what Ermelinda called "thinking."

On that afternoon, from where Ermelinda was looking at him, the man in the distance appeared to be a black dot, like a single point of reference in the countryside, which the girl regarded fixedly until brightness clouded her vision and thousands of black and luminous dots forced her to close her eyes, shattering the man to pieces.

When she opened her now-dimmed eyes again, the countryside was empty once more. Martim had disappeared. What was

left for her to see were the hated birds flying calmly about, and
the weeds, tall and ghostly, trembling at the slightest hesitation
of the breeze. Once more everything had become an antenna
sensitive to what never came to be spoken. As if in a visitation,
with the anxiety of waiting, Ermelinda was looking. She was
very thoughtful.

It was at that moment that Martim reappeared in her field
of vision. He, the concrete man who seemed to stop things from
flying off. For Ermelinda's way of looking at things usually left
everything as unstable and light as herself. He, the man, reappeared ensuring reality. And that coarse body counter-
balanced the softness of the cornfield, the softness of the women
and the flowers. With the ingenuous stability that a man has,
and which is his strength, he was counterbalancing the nauseating delicacy of death—that innocent stability that even Ermelinda's husband had possessed, even Francisco, even all the other
men who had worked on the place temporarily. With a stolidity
that was unaware of its own value, Martim's commonplace body
seemed to guarantee that death, most gentle death, would never
conquer. And the man's strength justified the fact that she,
Ermelinda, was soft and the softness that without a man was as
gratuitous as a flower. Like a flower it seemed to lead to nothing,
and nothingness was death so subtley diffused that it even gave
the appearance of being life.

Ermelinda was not thinking about anything. She was absorbed.

Her head down, she hulled the corn automatically. Something different from Martim's hammer-blows—which she was
listening to one by one, waiting in sweet torture for the next
one—very carefully, with the inception of a feeling of exasperating pleasure that she feared she would destroy if she made it
stronger, she said to herself: "but who's talking about death,
girl? I'm so very much alive." She said it as if she was enjoying a
fainting spell or the heat. The man's hammer was beating like a
heart in the countryside. Her eyes, looking at the corn, did not
see Martim. But with each blow he gave body to the open

countryside, and he gave body to the ever so vague body of that girl. Ermelinda felt a shameful weakness against which, for no reason, she was struggling, lifting up her head in a kind of spirited way. It was true that the challenge could not last for very long, and in a while her heavy head hung low again in meditation. Her mechanical fingers kept on working.

But at times she made a slight movement with her head, very calm and pretty, as if she was avoiding a fly. Meditation was staring into space. The girl was meditating.

It was then that she lifted up her head and stared out with some intensity. Some soft and insidious thing had become mixed in with her blood; and she remembered how she used to speak of love as a poison, and she agreed submissively. It was something sweet and filled with a feeling of malaise. And joining in, she recognized it with painful softness, the way a woman recognizes with pride and clenched teeth the first sign that the baby is going to be born. With joy and impassive resignation she recognized the ritual that was taking place inside of her. Then she sighed: it was the seriousness she had been waiting for all her life.

Then, the way a woman becomes confused in moments of crisis, she clutched the raw ear of corn with greater force; several kernels fell. The whinny of a horse sounded across the fields, and Francisco called "whoa"; several kernels fell into the pail. It was something that might be love or might not be. It would be up to her, during a few thousand seconds, to give it just that slight emphasis love needs to come into existence.

Ermelinda paused with the ear in her hand; her head turned a little, satisfied, vexed. Because in one second lost among thousands of others in the vastness of the countryside, subject to the law of that single cell which fertilizes among the ones that perish, she had known, as if she had made a choice, that she loved him. Not directly, for she was not a courageous girl. "I am alive," she thought: in this way she had chosen to know that she loved him. And at the thought "I am alive," she had become aware for the first time that before then she had been thinking about death, and that she had also been thinking about the man. Ignorance of her own thought processes gave her an innocent surprise. And only then did she perceive that now it was too late, that now all she could do was love him. Painfully, haughtily, she had lost forever the possibility of resolving the problem. She was relieved, as one always is when it is too late. A second before it might still have been possible for her not to love him. But now, softly, proudly: nevermore. In the same instant she felt a sense of tragedy.

And now it was too late—whatever feeling had brought it on it had evaporated forever. It was too late. The pain had remained in her body just as when the bee is already far away. The pain, so recognizable, had remained. But we were created to bear just that.

A little startled, she then became enveloped in the afternoon heat, restless and heavy. Nothing had changed in the country-side, still hot from the motionless sun. For an instant, however, the girl did not recognize it, neither did she recognize herself; and if she had looked into the mirror she would have seen large eyes looking back at her, but not herself. With the keenness that wonder brings on, she noticed a vein in her own hand that she had not noticed for years, and she saw that her fingers were thin and short; and she saw a skirt covering her knees. And beneath everything that she was, she felt something: her own attention. She looked around a little worried. From some obscure need for self-preservation she was trying to recover from the countryside that same moment when she had boldly admitted to loving the man. She was trying to recover that moment in order to destroy it. Perhaps she was amazed that the need to destroy love was love itself because love is also a struggle against love. If she knew that, it was because a person knows. Desperate and offended she tried to find that moment which already now she would never know again, to learn whether it had been fateful to the point of ruling her completely—or whether in that minute she herself had been so extremely free that she had picked it out with a

(86)

gratuitousness that was already sin, and would have to be paid for later on.

She tried to recover the instant in order to destroy it, but it was painful and useless—because everything had happened all too rapidly. And the girl was left with only the following: with a pail of corn, without even anything to fight against.

She was so very abandoned and so very alone as if everything that might happen in the future had nothing to do with that solitary minute of glory which a long ago had been lost forever among the hammer-blows—those hammer-blows which the girl, recovered and frightened now, was hearing stronger and closer, fateful, fateful, fateful. Her strange freedom: she had chosen to go out and meet fate. It was the dignity she had been waiting for all her life. A sense of tragedy again enveloped her. And it was strange that within it she was just anonymous.

Then she looked at the flies on the rosebush. The grace of being alive filled her with Christian modesty, and she humbly sought moral support from the flies, who were blue inside. But what she saw was only blue flies and a rose trembling from the fly that had left it trembling. Although the entire world had become her accomplice for an instant, the girl had been dragged off by her own volition.

Then she lowered her head and started to work again. The kernels of corn rhythmically fell into the pail, hard drop by hard drop. The sun suddenly lengthened into a great light and the warm wind blew. But something had certainly happened, because the shout of the mulatto woman made the girl twist her face as if she had been wounded.

Uncomfortable inside the unexpected grandeur that her life had taken on, the girl pretended not to notice anything. Then, revolted and taking refuge in consoling pettiness where at least she was herself, she said to herself as a challenge, "If I don't take care of myself, no one else will! I'm going to drink more milk to build up my strength; I'm no fool!" she said brutally. But she lowered her head, completely distracted by what she had said,

(87)

breathing heavily, breathing. Then she wiped away the perspiration.

"The fence hasn't been fixed yet!" Vitória said to Martim at that moment.

Ermelinda shivered, startled at the fact that someone was speaking to the man. She could not have imagined it—and at that moment! She resented the stranger's intrusion, as if he had meddled in the love which had just been born.

"The fence is falling apart," Vitória added demandingly.

Martim never seemed to get annoyed at having to interrupt the job he had just begun and start on another one. He would begin the new task with the same concentrated indifference with which he had been so perfect at in the previous job.

"Don't you want to finish what you're doing first?" Vitória finally suggested, having to supply herself the argument that he had not offered.

But he did not seem to be surprised at anything Vitória might say to him. At first the obedience with which he listened gave Vitória a dark rage in her breast. In her fantasies Vitória would get the impression that if she were to tell the man, "At night I sleep under my bed," he would reply, "Of course, ma'am." The fact that he would accept anything at all from her, even the most contradictory orders, offended her—and worse yet, all of that was surreptitiously removing one of the supports of that vague heroism by which she lived, the motives of which had already been lost. But after a while she was becoming involved in his way of accepting everything in her or in himself. It was as if he said, "I see nothing good or bad in sleeping under the bed." A little uncomfortable, she could not even discover what was wrong with sleeping under a bed. The woman blinked her eyes, upset. The man's stolidity and calm did not transmit any stolidity or calm to her; they only irritated her.

As for the man, his muscles worked with exactitude, slowness, and certainty. And nothing bothered him, as if he were carrying in himself the great silence of the plants in his Tertiary plot as a defense that could not be transferred to others. Where he would return every afternoon, the way a man returns home. And where he would remain sitting on a stone.

And it was good there. There no plant knew who he was; and he did not know who he was; and he did not know who the plants were; and the plants did not know who they were. And all of them in the meantime were just as alive as it is possible to be alive. This was probably that man's great meditation. Just as the sun shines, and just as the rat is only a step beyond the thick flat leaf of that plant—this was his meditation.

Martim had blue eyes and heavy brows; his hands and feet were large. It was a question of a heavy man with an idea in his head. He had a lively, attentive look, as if he would only answer when he had heard all sides. That was his real side and also his external side, visible to other people. Inside—much more difficult to reach than his exterior form that had preceded it—inside he was a man of slow comprehension, which was basically a kind of patience, a man with a confused way of thinking, who sometimes with the embarrassed smile of a child would feel himself intimidated by his own stupidity, as if he had not deserved so much. It was true that inside he was also wise, always ready to take advantage of a possibility. In the past this had led him to ignore certain scruples and do certain things that would have been sinful had he been a person of importance. But he was one of those people who die without really knowing what happened to them.

As he sat on the stone in his realm his thoughts, so to speak, reduced him to nothing more than a man with big feet sitting on a stone. What he had not noticed is that he was already beginning to take some care in being exactly just what he was. Sometimes a thought would glisten in him in his alert torpor the way the chip off a rock would. "This region is dry," he thought profoundly. "You can still see charcoal around," he seemed to think, sitting upright on the stone. The statement had a dull virility about it. It was like a man sitting on a stone knowing how to hope, of course! If a man sitting on a stone knew how to hope, then the humidity would help the roots, nuts, fruit, and seeds to rot. That obscure piece of logic seemed to suffice him perfectly.

Sitting on the stone, he also felt satisfied at the fact that he now knew how to work so well in the country. His knowledge was slight but his hands had gained a wisdom. "A man is slow, and it takes him a long time to understand his hands," he thought looking at them. His thoughts were almost voluntarily enigmatic, and in his plot he felt the pleasure that one gets from certain empty moments, as if everything in truth had been created out of pleasure. The plant, for example, was nothing but pleasure.

It was true that sometimes the intense stillness of the plants now seemed to bother him in a dull sort of way, and to bring on the beginnings of unrest. Then he would patiently change the position of his legs without understanding. He did not realize that there he was slowly making his first arrow and sharpening his first spear.

Nor did he realize that he was now completely different from that man who had looked out at the plot at dawn. Nor did he realize that by changing the position of his legs so many times he was becoming impatient for the first time, looking out upon a world that was ready to be hunted. He was dimly upset as he began to feel himself superior to the plants, and to feel himself in some way a man in relationship to them—because only a man could be impatient. Then he changed the position of his legs again. And furthermore—only a man was proud of his own impatience. Changing the position of his legs once more he was proud. It was that generalized vanity which sometimes came over him and which had no trouble existing side by side with the prudence of not risking himself beyond that reassuring somnolence of the plot by the woodshed. Reassuring but no longer sufficient. The man was growing and he was uncomfortable.

But that restlessness, which was almost only physical, would only happen for moments at a time. And it was still happening so far away from him that it had not yet affected the wholeness of the world in which he moved. And soon, with the great pleasure that there is in the restraint of one's own energy, he put himself once more into a state of "not knowing very much." Because that was the condition essential to his plot. In not knowing the man had an unsmiling happiness, just the way the plant grows thick.

Sometimes that man, who was always missing important links, would grab the land like a person who owned land. And he would sit with the fistful of earth in his hand. Crude, with the earth in his hand; the best way to be. What were that man's thoughts? Satisfactory and substantial they were thoughts that were scarcely profound. One afternoon he came to the point of thinking along these lines:

"Extinct animals are legion."

That was the kind of thought that had no possible answer. And on that very same day he thought like this:

"Once, more than a billion years ago." Martim did not know exactly how much time there was behind him, but since there was no one there to stop him from making a mistake, he puffed up, impassive and great. And he continued making statements of greater importance. Another time, for example, this was his thought: "Maybe there is the head of a mastodon somewhere here under six feet of rubble." Thinking had now become transformed into a method of scratching on the ground. And then one afternoon, with the most legitimate pleasure that comes from meditation, he remembered nothing more except that "buffaloes exist." That gave the plot great space, because buffalo move slowly and in the distance.

Anyone who might have looked at him, so satisfied and dominating, would have shaken his head in envy at his good fortune in having been born when the global ice caps had already melted. He was enjoying a favorable land. Sometimes, for example, he would get the desire to eat—and he would note it with approval. Now he had all of the senses of a rat and one more by which he verified what was happening—thought. This was the least corrupt way to use it. He was letting himself be cured by that complete thing there is in plants. With a feeling of relief he placed his singed portions into the coolness that existed. It was damned fine not to lie. Well, sitting on the stone, that was exactly what he was doing: he was not lying.

For example, Martim was not sad—Martim who was finally to be free of the whole moral duty of tenderness. That man had come from a city where the air was filled with the sacrifices of people who were unhappy and therefore searched for an ideal.

"I'll bust in the face anybody who messes with me!" he said aloud, making use of his soul and perhaps trying to provoke a rage in himself which in some way would put him in tune with that quiet energy around him.

Then he stood and looking up at the sky he calmly urinated. High up the clouds were passing by. He stood there, stupid, modest, haloed. His unity seemed to be a unity.

"This region is dry," he thought again. And it gave him a very satisfactory pleasure. He looked up at the dry sky. The sky was there—high up. And he was underneath. It was impossible to imagine greater perfection.

When he slept, he slept. When he worked, he worked. Vitória gave him orders, he gave orders to his own body. And something was growing with a shapeless sound.

Chapter 8

THEN during those first days there was the feeling that there was a man on the place. And moreover one could guess that the person in charge was a woman; for despite the threat of drought and the fundamental necessities of that poor attempt at a farm, what suddenly was worrying Vitória most was the appearance of the place. It was as if she had not noticed the neglect of the fields until his arrival. Now she was trying furiously to transform them. She appeared to be facing some set date for a festival, before which everything had to be in readiness. A feverish precision took control of her. And the minutiae to which she had descended had the air of a fly in motion. There she was in the middle of the morning, pointing at the twisted fence. And the man's calm strength straightened the fence. Off in the distance Francisco, distrustful and skeptical, watched the woman pointing at the disorder of the few flower beds and smiling, he watched in silence as Martim dug, cleaned, and pruned. Between Martim and Vitória a mute relationship had been established that was already mechanized and in full swing. Its basis was the coincidence of the facts that the woman wanted to command and that he acquiesced in obeying. The woman was avidly the mistress. And something in her had become intensified: the happy severity with which she now stood on what was hers, disguising the glory of possession with a challenging look at the passing clouds.

"And what about the cowshed?" she asked attentively one day. "You never did clean up the cowshed!" she said impatiently with that blinking her eyes the way one does who no longer knows what she wants; but time was pressing.

Thus it was that Martim—as if he had been imitating in his

(93)

task of becoming concrete a fateful evolution whose traces he felt groping—thus it was that his new and confused steps led him one morning out of his realm in the plot into the half-light of the cowshed, where cows were more difficult than plants.

His contact with the cows was a painful effort. The light of the cowshed was different from the light outside, to the point that at the door some vague threshold was established. The man stopped there. Used to figures, he recoiled at the disorder. Inside there was an atmosphere of entrails and a difficult dream, full of flies. Only God does not feel disgust. He stopped at the entrance and did not want to go in.

Mist rose from the animals and slowly enveloped them. He looked deeper inside. In the dim filth there was the sense of a workshop and of concentration, as if from out of that shapeless entanglement little by little one more form were taking shape. The crude smell was one of wasted raw materials. Cows were made there. Out of disgust the man had suddenly become abstract again like a fingernail tried to retreat; he wiped his dry mouth with the back of his hand like a doctor facing his first wound. Nevertheless, on the threshold of the stable he seemed to recognize the dim fog that came out of the animals' snouts. That man had seen that vapor before rising from sewers in certain cold dawns. And he had seen it emanating from warm garbage. He had also seen it like a halo around the love of two dogs; and his own breath was that same light. Profound cows were made there. A man of little courage would have vomited at the foul smell, and seeing the attraction that open sore had for the flies, a clean person would have felt ill watching the tranquillity with which the cows stood heavily wetting the ground. Martim was that person of little courage who had never before put his hands on the intimate parts of a stable. Nevertheless, even though he turned his eyes away, he seemed to realize with reluctance that things had been so arranged that once in a stable a child had been born. That great smell of matter was right. Only Martim was not ready for such a spiritual step. More than fear, it was a kind of delicacy. And he hesitated at the door, pale and offended, like a child to whom the root of life has suddenly been revealed.

Then he disguised his cowardice in sudden rebellion. He resented Vitória's having pulled him away from the silence of the plants to that place. There with disgust and curiosity he suddenly remembered that there had been a dead era in which reptiles had wings. There a person could not escape certain thoughts. In that place he could not escape feeling with an objective horror and joy that things are always fulfilled.

Could it have been that realization, by chance, that had turned his stomach, or was it just the warm stench? He did not know. However, all that was needed was a step backwards, and he would have found himself in the full fragrance of morning, morning—a thing already perfected in the smallest leaves and smallest stones, a finished work without fault at which a person can look without any danger because there is no place to enter and lose one's self. A step backwards would have been all he needed.

But he took a step forward. And he halted, confused. At first, as when one enters a cave, he did not see anything. But the cows, used to the darkness, were aware of the stranger. And he felt in his whole body that his very substance was being tested by the cows. They began slowly to moo and moved their feet without even looking at him—with that ability that animals have of knowing without seeing, as if they had already transcended their own subjectivity and had reached the other side: that perfect objectivity that no longer need be shown; while he in the cowshed had been reduced to weak man—that dubious thing that could never transcend anything.

With a resigned sigh the slow man understood that "not looking" might also be the only way to enter into contact with the beasts. Imitating the cows with an almost calculated mimicry, he stood there not looking at anything, in fact making an effort not to look at anything. And with an intelligence brought on by the very inferiority of his situation, he let himself remain submissive and attentive. Then, sacrificing his own identifica-

(95)

tion, he almost took on the form of one of the animals. And by doing just that he suddenly seemed to understand, with surprise, what it was like to be a cow.

Quite motionless and somehow understanding, he allowed himself with profound insight to accept the cows' recognition. Without the exchange of a single glance he gritted his teeth and allowed the cows to recognize him with an intolerable slowness. It was as if hands were exploring his secret. Uneasily he felt that the cows saw in him only that part of him which was like a cow; just as a thief would see in him that part which was avid for theft, and as a woman would want of him what a child would not even understand. Except that the cows chose something in him that he himself did not understand—but which was growing little by little.

This had been a great effort on the man's part. Never until that moment had he become such a being. To make himself like the cows had been a great work of intense concentration. The fingernail finally hurt.

For a moment in which faith had deserted him, the man had had the certain feeling that he would lose and never attain the admission to the cowshed. He was confronted by one long look after another, followed by a long moo from a heavy raised head; he was rejected. In the midst of the intense smell of the cowshed, the cows had sensed the acid human smell about him.

But it was also true that in that moment *joie de vivre* had already come over him, the delicate joy that sometimes comes over us in the midst of our own lives, as if a same musical note had been intensified. That joy took hold of him and guided him instinctively into battle. Martim no longer knew if he were merely obeying that indefinable ability with which cows, having it, can force a cowboy to look and act in a certain way. Or whether, really, it was he himself who was trying with a painful, spiritual effort, to free himself finally from the realm of rats and plants and rise to the mysterious breathing of higher animals.

He barely understood—since he had just now acquired the intelligence essential to a cow—a simple law. He must not

(96)

offend their inherent rhythm. He must give them time, their own time, their time that was completely dark, while they chewed their cud. Little by little, moreover, this became the man's rhythm. Indolently, slowly, immeasurable by the calendar; that is how a cow crosses a field.

Then, since things tend to come to an end and to rest in a phase, the cowshed at last became peaceful. The warmth of the man and the warmth of the cows mingled in a single ammoniated warmth. The man's silence had naturally changed. And the cows, pacified by Martim's apology, had stopped worrying about him.

With trembling joy he felt that something had happened finally—but then it gave him an intense loneliness, as when one is happy and there is nothing to use the happiness on, as when he looks around and there is no way to share the instant of happiness—which until now he had usually felt on Saturday night.

Something had happened. And though something else still escaped him, he at last had something in his hand, and his chest filled up with subtle victory. Martim took a deep breath. Now he belonged to the cowshed.

And at last he could look at it in the way a cow would see it.

The cowshed was a warm and good place which pulsated like the beating of a heart. This is why men and beasts have offspring. Martim sighed, exhausted at the enormous effort: he had just found himself. This is why a large animal crosses a stream and splashes sparkling water. The man had seen that. However he had had only a slight concept of the beauty which now was rested on a deeper understanding. This is why mountains are far away and high. This is why cows wet the ground so loudly. Because of a cowshed time is indefinably replaced by time. This is why birds migrate from cold regions to warm. This—this cowshed was a warm place and it was pulsating.

Perhaps he felt all this, because, satisfied, he spat on the ground. After which, with a sad determination and hiding his emotion, he put out his hand and gave the dry cow a few pats. A great and peaceful empathy had sprung up between him and the animals.

"You have to cultivate the corn!" Vitória said to him irritatedly.

Then—he went to cultivate the corn. But the cows were waiting for him, and he knew it.

Chapter 9

OUTSIDE of the orders and the execution of those orders there was little to be said. And what was not being said began to be missed. Ermelinda was surrounding him without coming close; just barely looking, he guessed. And Vitória rode out through the fields.

To her Martim still had the air of one who was ready to laugh from one moment to the next, like the inexpressive face of a clown looking at a dirty picture; Vitória was restless. And she was exasperated with Martim's silence. The stupidity of the man suffocated her, but she had nothing to complain about for his work, in spite of being slow, was perfect. Vitória was restless. Her own strength was growing in a certain way; the woman seemed to be developing more and more and becoming more sure of herself.

And in the afternoon, as the heat lessened, she would stand on the porch and look out at the things that little by little were changing into what she wanted them to be. Then her ambition would grow without any objective like a heat-wave. And the desire would arise in her to invent new orders to be given, just to find out what would happen; she was the disturbed owner of all of that, and she was getting disturbed. She would become enraged because nights would intervene and during that time there would be no progress in the work; the man's sleeping in the woodshed seemed to her such an insolence that she tolerated it because there was nothing else that she could do. In the daytime too, at a certain time, she would get irritated knowing that the man was in the cowshed taking endless care of the cows, complying with an excess of docility to an order she had only thrown at him once. And then again night would come on with its exasperating interruption. She could barely wait for the following day, and her feeling of power was already so great that it had become uncomfortable and useless.

That was the dull way in which the work was progressing little by little. At the sound of the plow Vitória would close her eyes, her breast would become agitated. Under a heat that was becoming stronger and stronger the work was progressing. But it seemed to be going too slowly for her: the woman standing on the porch would unbutton the neck of her blouse because she could not breathe. Coming out of nowhere the menace of a drought was approaching, surrounding them with brilliant heat. Every day it was becoming more difficult for the sun to die. It was an agony that the woman would bear standing all alone. Even after the sun had disappeared, the farm would keep on reverberating for an indeterminate and unquieting time. During the day it was that sparkling, those hammer-blows, sweat. But night—she knew it well—would be no truce. Night during a drought always hid in its belly a bright profundity which was like a light imprisoned in the hard shell of a nut.

The woman on the porch bit her hand distractedly until she looked at her own injured hand with suddenly severe eyes. That night she stayed up late on the porch, and apprehensively examined the thousands of stars that the strange cleanness of the dark would let be seen. Restlessly she checked her hearing, and it was true; every night there were fewer toads to be heard, they were deserting . . .

At least while she was on the porch, fighting with the stars and scrutinizing the vibrant dryness of the night, she was still powerful because she was working, working coldly, and calculating. But when it was time to go to sleep she would be overcome by misery, a proud misery that asked for nothing. And no matter how strong she might have been during the day she lessened then, quiet and unfathomable. Poverty came over her like a meditation. The small woman was stretched out on her bed, calm, looking at the ceiling. And since no one would be able to understand her, she was calculating in vengeance, with her eyes open, wounded—calculating, wounded like a prisoner in his cell.

And every night her step went farther, every night her obscure menace went out to watch over the indecent sleep of the happy man.

With the vigor of the morning her feeling of discomfort in relation to the man would disappear as soon as she discovered another field of action: an ant hill that had to be destroyed, the open well that did not seem to be deep enough and beside which she tapped her foot impatiently. And then she would not seem to know for sure what order she wanted to give; she felt that she had at her disposition that silent man who sparkled in the sun, silent, with his eyes wide open. Then her own power would weigh on her, and she would gallop from one side of the field to the other giving more orders, staring in an authoritative and questioning way at the mysterious and dried-out horizon—she who could not give herself the luxury of not being powerful—spreading her severe efficiency about between gallops. And there was no solution; her blouse clung to her sweating body, and she feared that the more powerful she became the more she would someday have to see herself free of her own power. But was there no way to escape the situation into which things had fallen and to escape before she would bear down excessively upon the passive man and the malleable farm—before the man would suddenly laugh, or the ground on the place would suddenly break out in arid cracks? Then rage would take hold of her: someday she would find out what the man had come to do upon the place.

In that interim the farm was becoming beautiful.

The farm was becoming beautiful, and with the heat the tension grew with excessive happiness; the days followed each other clear and long. There the only sign of danger was the agreement under which they all seemed to be living—and happiness. Vitória had never been so happy, and the one who suffered was the horse she whipped those mouth hung open in surprise. It was when he was spurred that the horse kicked and ran away—the woman, taken by surprise, lost her balance and fiercely clutched the horse's neck. A chill ran up the woman's sides, and she panted in terror. Without the courage to let go of that heavy neck her legs trembled; she stayed motionless; and with her eyes closed she gave the bay free rein to take her to his food and let him lower his unconquered head to eat. The woman's whole body humbly accompanied the head of the horse down to the hay and with her eyes closed she could feel him eating; it was a strange peace, being led by the disorientation of the horse. The farm was becoming beautiful, the wind was blowing, tears of rage ran down Vitória's face.

"How long are you going to stay around?" she asked the man then, ready to discharge him without knowing why.

"I don't know," he replied, continuing to dig.

"What do you mean, you don't know?" she asked rigidly.

Having forgotten that she had been ready to send him away, she looked at him insulted. It was an insult, that man's playing with time and bringing doubt into the mechanical passage of days, bringing a frightening freedom to them as if on each day he might suddenly say yes or no. Bringing indecision to her, when if he had been asked how long he was going to stay there, and had replied "I don't know," meaning unlimited time, time beyond her control—and not, as it was for him, a short time.

Yes, a short time. Without tying one idea to the other Vitória now seemed to want the man to work fast and twice as hard, and the well, the digging of which she had obliged him to interrupt so he could start working on the line fences, should be started up again at once.

"But why doesn't he know if he's going to stay or not?" Ermelinda asked in surprise.

Ermelinda was nervous with headaches and palpitations. "Why doesn't he know if he's going to stay or not?" And as if they had eliminated the possibility of waiting for a more favorable time and a natural ripening, the girl felt herself trapped, forced to define herself before the man left, and have that fruit, even if it was green, even if it was still incomprehensible. Whatever the obscure stages of love might be they would have to go along more rapidly now. Trying not to stumble over shame,

Ermelinda had already forgotten what she had wanted from the man. She was only trying to bring back that instant in which love, beside the pail of corn, had been fateful and grand—there had only been that instant in an afternoon lost now forever. But in that instant death too had seemed to her to be a ritual of life—there had been that instant in which she had faced death with the same grandeur as one looking from a distance.

But it was useless: with that lost instant she had lost contact with fatality. And again she only saw trickery and meanness in death. And she too became mean again to the point of fearing death; and she was avaricious and crafty, and she tricked because she felt that she was being tricked.

In the meantime something told her that no one could die without first resolving his own death. She looked around, afflicted. The bee in some way had resolved it: she saw the bee fly off. And Francisco too, in the same way, standing mute in the concentration of watering the mule as if watering the mule in that silent way were some signal of preparedness. Ermelinda looked at him with envy. But she, she was mean: she did not forgive death. She would never know how to tell what she wanted from Martim. Obscurely, she wanted her life to take on a destiny through him. She was confused; she knew only that she had to hurry for time was growing short.

And false, calculating, she tried to project herself in some way into a crisis of love, until finally, from so much looking at the man and so much pushing herself and demanding so much of herself, she began to feel that uneasiness once more. Then, radiant, weakened by the effort, she loved him. The countryside seemed empty to her, ashen. She looked at the sick grass beside the hen-house, and she looked at the dirty flock, the chickens running weakly and rapidly about, cackling; the dissonance of the wheels of the plow bothered her: it was love, yes. So much so that if the man were to appear in the distance with his hoe— then—then it happened: there he was!

There he was, wrapped up in the power he had over her, and which she herself had conferred upon him.

Until finally Ermelinda reached the point where she no longer asked whether she loved him. She was no longer ashamed of watching him as she hid behind the wall, and she rediscovered every feature of the man's face with an exclamation of recognition and surprise. And when, untiring, she discovered for the thousandth time that the man's eyes were blue she was surprised that so much could be given to her, a woman. His mouth was thin, and he had that extraordinary beauty that only a man could have and which had left her mute with a desire to flee—which made her spy on him in a bloodthirsty way. She trembled with the fear that she would stop loving him. She had never got close to him; between the two of them there had always been a distance. But after a while the girl had spiritualized the distance and had ended up by turning it into a perfect means of communication, up to the point at which now only distance was able to provide sufficient space for her to unfold her love and reach the man; near him she felt herself inconvenienced by him, and she did not know how to give him all her love.

Which had not stopped the girl from becoming very active; she carefully calculated the steps she would have to take, feeding what she felt with the foresight of a murderer. She bathed with scented herbs, she took better care of her underwear, she ate a lot so she would put on some weight, she tried to feel emotion at the sunset, she intensively petted the dogs on the farm, she cleaned her teeth with charcoal, she protected herself against the sun so she would be quite fair, she was worried over how much times love would assault her unexpectedly, as when, shuffling too herself to see if she was right, "I want to be the shoe he wears, I want to be the axe he has in his hand" and then she waited very attentively; and she was so right that she lowered her modest eyes with emotion, confused, hiding a smile as best she could.

But Ermelinda did not always have to arouse herself. Sometimes love would assault her unexpectedly, as when, shuffling through Vitória's writing desk in search of a pair of shears, she came upon the list of tools Martim had ordered for the mistress of the place. Even before she thought about it she was sure it was his writing. Because her heart was beating as if she had been reading the very secret of the man; "one shovel, two scythes," she went on reading. And what he had written gave her such a feeling of ripeness that she felt ill. The words seemed full and painful, heavy with themselves. It was heartbreaking to feel the strength of the man in his words, a quiet and contained strength —and in the meantime, all of it right there in front of her, a fruit that could only shrivel up after that. Since Ermelinda was quick-witted the vague idea of a fruit brought her to the idea of "the harvest of death," for she had read that somewhere, and she had even seen pictures to that respect. "Oh, my love," she thought then, but her heavy heart did not know how to express itself. The hands that had written "those very simple words" were large and ugly, and they saddened her. "Oh, my love," she said in a final touch of resignation, and while she was asking herself if perhaps she could give and receive life in love, she stole the list the man had made and kept it in her room. "My way of loving is so pretty!" she thought. She had never been so happy. In fact, she had never even come to the point of asking that he love her. In the selfishness of her happiness she thought like this; "a pity that he doesn't feel what I feel, he doesn't know what he's missing."

On Friday, since he was nearby, she finally said the following to him: "I'm dying with this heat." And her eyes filled with tears because she had said nothing, as it were. Then later on she said humbly to Vitória: "This heat is bitter."

But Vitória replied with: "Cold is what they call bitter, not heat."

Chapter 10

As for Martim, he had time. In fact, he seemed to have discovered time.

At the end of the day he would leave his work and go to the cowshed, with that same serene avidity with which he had formerly gone to the plot by the woodshed. And, free at last from the imminence of an order from Vitória, free from Ermelinda's increasingly besieging presence—each day the man would again pick up in the cowshed the instant interrupted on the day before putting into one theme all the scattered instants that he had had with the cows, and creating from it all the only sequence, "As I had been feeling . . ." he would seem to think as he entered the barn—he would go on with what had been interrupted.

The dark heat of the cows filled the barn. And as if there had been something which no person and no consciousness could have given him, there in the barn, it was given to him; he received it. The suffocating smell was that of the slow blood that flowed in the bodies of the animals. It was no longer the intense sleep of the plants, no longer the mean prudence of survival that existed in the suspicious rats.

But the cows had already begun to upset him a little. One day, for example, he woke up and opened the door of the woodshed to let in the first light. And since the day seemed to have been given to him, he received it. But—but now he wanted, for the first time, to do something on his own. It was at the door of the shed for the first time he was in need of a deeper experience —even if he could never share it with the cows. Restless, he was separating himself from them. It was a risk and an initial audacity. Then seeing that the countryside was large and full of light he—took the risk of having a deeper experience. He blinked several times, quietly.

That was how that man was growing, the way a rolling thing takes on volume. He was growing calmly, emptily, indirectly, patiently advancing.

He had never looked directly at the mulatto woman. But she would laugh. And a peaceful strength had come awake in him. It was a power—he still remembered well. Alert, without any plan, he waited day after day for the moment when he might make the mulatto woman stop laughing. Both the woman and the child would observe him in pretense from a distance, never coming close. As for the child, Martim avoided her, confused, evasive.

But the woman laughed a lot. One might really say that she laughed too much. Without thinking about it he knew what her laughter meant. And sometimes it was as if her laughter were a moo: then he would lift his head, stunned, summoned, powerful. But he waited. As if patience had become a part of desire he waited without hurrying.

The mulatto had an open nature, as open as her laughter; she would laugh before she knew what she was laughing at. Life had arranged itself in her in some dark, sweet way, and she laughed at anything; perhaps she had pleasure from it. Even if sometimes that same thing would stir inside of her in rage the way a dog will snarl. She was a person who could err without sinning. The slaps she gave her child were almost filled with joy, and they reinvigorated her all over. The man observed that the usual thing would be for her to start out singing and end up beating the child. The girl would duck away from the slaps, learning without resentment that this is how it was, and that her mother was that force that laughed out loud and beat her without a sense of vengeance; and to be a daughter was to belong to that mother in whom vigor was laughter. The man pretended to be interested in his work as a cover-up. The fact was that a person could come to understand himself completely in the mulatto woman. The man found in her a past which if it was not his own could serve just as well. What she brought out in a man was what he was. Martim had only to take a look at her and he knew that she was there. You could deal man to man with her, except that when you came right down to it, she was a woman.

Two days later, instead of going to the cowshed, he finally went over to the woman, who was washing clothes. And he stood there without looking at her.

And without looking at him, she laughed. He meticulously crumbled a piece of kindling-wood he had in his hand, and without looking at her, he knew that she was young. Her hair had long, hard curls. Since Martim was a person who immediately liked what he needed right away he found that she was pretty. Finally he threw the stick of wood away and looked straight at her; either he would let her alone or he would grab her. He grabbed her slowly, the way one day he had grabbed a bird.

"You're strong as a bull," the woman laughed. He was concentrating. Grasping her shoulder the man could feel her small bones and higher up the tendons and threads beneath her soft skin; she was a young creature, he could calculate her age as he felt her. He could feel the warmth coming out of her, and that is the way it should be: body to body, in tune with the most intimate pulse of the unknown.

It was already dark when his movements woke up the girl. The man lit the lantern in the woodshed and she gave a short shout of rage. Whatever it was she had it had curled up into anger. He looked at her curiously. She was trembling with rage, God only knows why.

And he was all alone by the door of the woodshed.

Martim was very surprised because in the past he had been used to knowing everything. And now—like a fact that was somehow much more concrete—he did not know about anything. He who had grown up to be a clear man and around whom everything had been customarily visible. He had been a person who had known all the answers; formerly he had been a person who had lived without pain. The clarity with which he had lived had made him capable of working with figures with a never-changing patience; and naked within, his clothes had fit him well. Expert and elegant. But now that the layer of words had been removed from things, now that he had lost speech, he was finally standing in the calm depths of the mystery. By the door of the woodshed then, revitalized by his great ignorance, he kept on standing in the darkness. It was almost night already. He had just learned all of that with that woman: how to keep on standing when one has a body.

Then the days began to pass.

But if at one time his tongue had grown too thick in his mouth for him to give expression, and if in his head there was not enough circulation of air for his thoughts to be more than anxiety, now behind every clearness there was darkness. And it was from her that the dark flame of his life had come. If a man were to touch darkness once, offering it his own darkness in exchange—and he had touched it—then his acts would lose their error, and perhaps he would be able to go back to the city one day and sit down in a restaurant in perfect harmony; or brush his teeth without compromising himself. A man had only one time when he could surrender. And only then would he be able to live, as he was now living, in the latency of others.

And then, perhaps because one day followed upon another, something began to happen slowly, enveloping, great, in spite of the links that were escaping him. It was as if, living there, he no longer counted his life in terms of days or years but in spirals that were so large that he would never get to see them, just as he would never see the long line of the curvature of the earth. There was something that was a gradual essence not to be eaten all at once.

Thus it was that Martim's life began to reach beyond him: the days were broad and beautiful, and his life was much broader than he. And he himself, after a while, became more than just a man alone. There had been a wearing away of his previous knowledge, and as for words, he only knew them as a person who had once suffered from them—as if he had been cured. "At last his crime was only as big as a fact"—and what he had meant to say by that, he did not know.

He began to understand women again too. He did not understand them in a personal way, as if he were master of his own name; but he seemed to understand why women are born when a person is a man, and it was a strong and tranquil blood that rhythmically entered and left his chest. Dealing with the cows, he realized the desire to have a woman had been reborn with calm. He recognized it then; it was a kind of solitude, as if his own body was not enough for himself. It was desire; yes, he remembered well. He remembered that a woman is more than the friend of a man; that a woman was the very body of man. Then, with a smile that was a little painful, he carressed the feminine hide of the cow and looked around him; the world was masculine and feminine. That way of seeing things gave him a deep physical contentment, the restful and contained physical excitement that he got every time he "drew back the curtains." A person has very high spiritual pleasures that no one suspects, the life of others always seems empty, but a person has his own pleasures.

It is true that he did not yet understand individual lives: the two cousins seemed to him to be both shallow and abstract at the same time, and he did not suspect what meaning there was in the lives of those two women, nor had it occurred to him that to understand them would be a means of contact.

He did not understand individual lives. But now he looked at them all together; the mulatto woman who had unfortunately been his and was now filling the pail with water while she sang, Francisco sawing wood, Vitória courageous, Ermelinda spying, and the smoke rising high out of the kitchen chimney. When it was together he seemed to understand. And it was as if a heat were evaporating off the efforts of them all, and it was as if he was finally learning that night falls and day is reborn and then night comes again. And that is how it was. His body was in good shape during that understanding without the need for the mistake that would be evil. Just as the cows quietly relied on the existence of other cows the man became wrapped up in the indirect heat of other people. And furthermore, it even seemed sometimes, as he looked out, that he was owner of a great factory and that the bustle and the smoke were the sign of a progressive advance. In what direction? The man did not ask himself, even though he might have felt—with the same vague unrest with which the drought was gradually approaching—that he was not too far away from the question, unripe as it was.

During all this time the drought was approaching in the tassels of the corn.

"The days have been beautiful," Vitória said apprehensively, shading her eyes with her hand.

They were large and clear days, and while they lasted, menacingly infinite.

"They're beautiful!" Ermelinda exclaimed, "I even had to take a tranquilizer!"

The lizards, attracted by the promise of glare and glory, were appearing in greater numbers, coming from nobody knows where. They burst out of the dry land and crackled. Vitória looked at the arid bodies multiplying, she closely examined some leaves that had already begun to curl at the edges; she lifted her inquisitive face up to a pure and deserted sky. In the fields the sun was full of dusty butterflies.

"Pretty days like this come before a drought."

"Oh!" Ermelinda put her hand over her heart, "They're so pretty you don't know what to do with them."

And Martim? The smell of the earth was breaking up under Martim's hoe—the smell of crumbling clods; the smell of hay in the light; the smell of certain secret herbs brought to exhalation by the heat, confused herbs providing with their twining shadow some realm that was darker than the one that could be seen. Martim was working; his hoe went up and down, up and down. A branch in the shade suddenly became disentangled from another branch frightening the bee, and making it fly off until it was lost in the distance of the clarity. Its flight made one sense of a world that was made up of distances and repercussions— that deep world which seemed to be enough for the chiaroscuro of a cow and enough for a man raising and lowering a hoe. Sweat was one of the best things that had happened to him: Martim raised and lowered the hoe. That nameless thing which is the smell of earth, which upsets with its warmth and insistently reminds us (who knows why?) that one is born to love, and then it is not understood. It was when the illuminated bee flew off. It made the man stop working and slowly wipe away his sweat, squinting his eyes at the clarity—at the clarity that was slowly becoming his too. His effort to understand was crude and shy:

Then, he said "The countryside looks like a jewel," and blushed violently.

He looked around as if someone had seen him do a dirty thing. He looked like a man who had unwillingly wanted to give someone a flower and had stood there with the flower in his hand.

"The countryside doesn't look like a jewel at all!" he said furiously. Then the bee got tangled up in the grass as it would have in a head of hair, the ants marched in a long and wavy line—and all of this began to belong to Martim. That was the bottomless pit into which he had thrown himself in his passage from the plants to the longer future of that black work-horse that just then passed by in the distance pulling the plow. And Francisco was sitting upright on the plow with his silent effort at attentiveness. All of that was beginning to belong to Martim because a person looks and sees. The cows were drooling; the bee, smaller and smaller, annoyed the air as closer and closer it approached an imaginary center. And Francisco's shout suddenly gave dimension to the distance.

"I have to talk to you," Ermelinda said to him at that moment.

The man did not interrupt the movement of his hoe upon the ground.

"You might ask Vitória to plant some everlasting," she went on with a spruced-up smile.

"Ask Dona Vitória," the man answered without looking at her.

"That's the trouble; I'm afraid of her. Besides," she suddenly said intimately, "you have to be careful too. Don't get me wrong; she's very good, but she's so strict. She's very nervous."

As the man's face was still bent over the furrow, the girl leaned over too and, looking up, tried to figure out his expression. "Just imagine!" she said, from below now and speaking louder, since she was not sure that he had been aware of her presence. "Just imagine!" she said almost bellowing. "She humiliated me once, you know?" Without stopping his work, he took a quick look at her.

"Then she said she hadn't meant to," Ermelinda added in a lower tone, now that she was sure the man had noticed her. Then she added, hesitant whether she should continue the lie, since he had finally looked at her, "Maybe she didn't mean to."

"I said that she said she didn't mean to!" she repeated when she saw that he was not paying attention to her anymore, "But I don't think that's true! She really did humiliate me!" she shouted at him attently, watching to see how her words would make the man's face react.

But her fruitless attempts had not discouraged Ermelinda. "That's just how it was," she thought, because "time wasn't ripe yet." When time would be ripe she could not say. Perhaps when she had been a child she had heard tell that it was when the moon was full. Perhaps too she might have known how animals need a minimum of security when put together so that at least they will have that primary guarantee of not being interrupted. Maybe she had heard more tales than she had been able to understand—and what had been left with her, disquietingly incomplete, was the notion of a time that was ripe. Oh, her plans were vague, very vague. She did not even have a plan; her plans were so vague that, embarrassed, she closed her eyes a little and smiled. If perchance her plans could have become just a little clearer for a moment she would have felt offended and sincerely startled. The fact was she was so very susceptible.

When had Martim finally begun to individualize her? She was almost ugly even though she was cute. Her short and dark lashes outlined eyes that could be perceived even from a distance in the midst of the brightness of a skin in which not even her mouth had any color. Her eyes were alway blinking, knowing or maybe afflicted, as if the girl was always calculating the distance between herself and other things. Her eyes were the only positive thing about her. Her other features were so indistinct that one could imagine how they could lose their shape and come together in some new combination which would be just as undefined as the first one. She was an aging adolescent and if there had been troubles they had not been the kind that had given her wrinkles or hardness, but the kind that had smoothed and squelched her. The scattered rapid moments in which the man had looked upon her face had been useless for he had not found support for any point he could remember, whether ugly or pretty. Even in the certain moments when she had been unprotected there had appeared to him a certain expectant frankness on her face, which gave her the kind of beauty which one saw on the patient face of a dog. Then her face could be seen in all its nakedness, like the face of a blind man.

It was that weak face, expectant and trusting, without the lies of expression that the girl had used so much to beautify herself, that the man finally came to see. And he went on "not to think about her," as a way of thinking.

"When I was married I had everything. There wasn't anything I ever lacked!" she came back to say the following day, persevering in her encirclement of him and opening up the basket of hard-boiled eggs to have a picnic while he worked.

Speaking without cease the girl saw again that face with its hard lines; and again she was touched by the stability of the man and it seemed in vain for the wind to try to wear him down. And, who can tell, if she were to cling to him maybe the wind would not shake her either. Then the girl was so filled with a strong and malignant hope that without stopping talking she took a tranquilizer out of the basket and gulped the dry pill down with a little bit of trouble.

"How long are you going to stay here?" she asked him.

And when he said he did not know, and the empty and painful sense of speed whirled about her, time was short—time was short; she did not know why it was, she only knew she had to hurry. Then she began to talk with such volubility that the man felt his work become easy as if his strokes now had some kind of counterpoint, and the girl was the repercussion of a man filling up the distance. Martim then looked up at the sun and spat far with pride. Ermelinda lowered her eyes in shame.

Chapter 11

ON THAT AFTERNOON when Martim and Vitória rode out so that the mistress of the farm could show him where the irrigation ditches should be dug—on that afternoon when they rode up the same slope down which the man had come alone—then he stood out MATURE from the darkness of the cows.

High up on the crest the woman was looking over the ground. Then suddenly, innocent and unwarned, he rocognized the landscape that he had seen when he had first come to the farm—that first time, when drunk with flight and exhausted, he had relied upon that vague thing which is the promise made to a baby at birth.

On horseback, with a flash of incomprehension worthy of a genius, he saw the countryside. Stupefied and attentive he saw that at the top of the rise there was that same freedom as if something had been unfurled in the wind. And like that first time the glory of the open air brought something to him that hit him hard on the chest and pained him with the extreme upset of happiness that one sometimes feels.

But with a new and unexpected hunger he wanted to give it a name this time.

The idea of wanting something more than just a feeling seemed to afflict Martim; that confused sign of a transition toward the unknown bothered him, and his unrest was passed along to the horse who kicked up as if he had been touched somehow and had that dazzled look that horses have.

As he faced that enormous extension of empty land Martim made a suffocated effort at painful approach. With the difficulty of someone who is never going to arrive he was approaching something that a man on foot might humbly call the desire of a man, but which a man on horseback could not resist the temptation to call the mission of a man. And the birth of that strange anxiety was now provoked by the vision of an enormous world which seemed to be asking a question, as it had been when he first walked upon the slope. And which seemed to be asking for a new god, who, as far as could be understood, would in that way complete the work of the other God. Confused there on a jumpy horse, jumpy himself, in just that second necessary for a glance, Martim had emerged totally and was a man.

In the same moment he had also felt himself completely unrewarded.

As his face was beaten by the wind which then went off to symbolize something Martim looked down below at the animals loose in the pasture. As he had come to understand the cows, now for the first time he found himself higher up on the slope. And this too was beating in his breast. With the beating of his heart, Martim remembered then and unexpectedly what a man normally is: it was what he was being now! With an agonizing sensation he felt himself a person.

Martim was humble in some way, if being humble was that involuntary and triumphant way he rode astride the horse—the way which gave him height and fright and determination and a longer vision. With that unexpected humility he seemed to recognize another sign that he was coming out of it—because only animals are proud and by the same token a man is humble. He also wanted to give a name to that defenseless and at the same time audacious thing, but he had none.

In some way it was good that he had none as he was unable to find a name that had imperceptively increased the restlessness he was now enjoying. The fact was that even though he was intimidated he was deriving something from his own restlessness, as if the tension in which he found himself had been the measure of his own resistance, and he had been making use of the first fruits of the difficulty just the way a man's muscles become more intense as he starts to lift a weight. He, he was his own weight—which means that, that man had made himself.

Meanwhile the impatience of the horses was hard to hold, and it increased Martim's instability and pulled him toward a decision of which he was still not aware. The wind was bringing Vitória's outlined figure close to his; the pure air made the horses blacker and larger. The air was so light that the man could not suck it all in at once. After breathing it a while, after being alive for a while, he was breathless because he could not take in more air. And meanwhile "not being able" intensified his happiness; the enormous vastness surrounded him, and he could not dominate it; his heart beat large, generous, restless; the horses moved their feet with nobility and skill. The constant wind had ended up by giving the woman's face a physical rapture that did not match the words she spoke about the opening of the trenches, and there was an agreement between their solitary bodies, the way bodies will agree on the same ultimate destiny. That his man's heart beat large and confused, recognizing things. To be a person was to be all of that.

It was then that it occurred to him that the promise which had been made to him was his own mission, even if he could not understand why it is incumbent upon us to fulfill a promise that had been made to us somewhere.

It was particularly good to be alive at that moment because there was also that clean afternoon air. And at that moment the mounted woman suddenly laughed because her horse had drawn back and startled her. With certain surprise he heard the laugh from that woman who never laughed. Everything was probably opening up for Martim; just as flowers open up in some determined moment, and we are never close enough to see. But he was. For the first time he was present when something that was happening was happening. And he! he was that man who for the first time had come to a realization not just from having heard tell, but at first hand, and that upset him. He was precisely that man. He was puzzled, therefore, at the impulsive way in which he had recognized himself. He had simply decided to be not just anyone, but that man.

And more than that he himself had suddenly become the

sense of the land and the woman; he himself was the goad for everything he saw. That was what he felt, even if the only thing he was receiving from his thought was just the throb. And as he held back, aroused, he remembered that this is a commonplace on which a man can finally tread: the wish to give a destiny to an enormous emptiness that evidently only a destiny can fill.

Then, with an impulse like the urge to want to name something, he tried to remember what gesture was used to express that instant of wind and mention of the unknown. He tried to remember what he had done one day when he had been up on Corcovado with a girl he loved. But even if he could remember, there was no way to express it. In that first impotence of his, for an instant, Martim felt the anguish of restriction.

But to feel the anguish of restriction was being a person too; he could still remember that well! Oh how well he could remember! With anguish he remembered that it was the anguish of being a person, and up on Corcovado he had kissed the girl he loved with the ferocity of love. He remembered just in time that there had never been a way to express the joy; and therefore he had built a house, or had taken a trip, or had loved. With the apprehensive air of someone who can make a mistake; he too was mounted on a horse, and he was attentively trying to copy for reality the being that he was, and in that birth he was creating his life. The thing was done in such an impossible way—for in impossibility there was the harsh claw of beauty. They are moments that cannot be narrated; they happen between trains that pass or in the air that wakes up our face and gives us our final shape, and then for an instant we are the fourth dimension of what exists; they are moments that do not count. But who knows whether it is the anxiety that a fish has with his open mouth, the one a drowning man has before he dies? They say that before going under forever a man can see his whole life pass before his eyes—if in just an instant one is born, and if in just an instant one dies, an instant is enough for a whole lifetime.

The man finally remembered then what he had done with his girl friend in the winds of Corcovado. In order to express himself, perhaps he would have to overpower Vitória; now that he was a man again, she had become a woman. But not just the fact that she was indocile for that would make it a gratuitous act and it would not have the perfect weight of fatality that desire for the body gives. He remained silent, embarrassed, not knowing what to do with that whole thing into which he had suddenly become transformed. Then it was that, out of nowhere, out of pure recklessness, he wanted to be "good" as a way of solution. He wanted to be good so much that once more he began to feel a kind of impotence.

It was true that the fugitive thought he had got about the woman had not become completely lost in the air. The woman felt the remains of it, obscurely offended the way cats on the roof are offended. Vitória turned toward him, and while she talked about the trenches she faced him; and there was no doubt but that he was that man: in him she saw him. And that was unexpected. With the curiosity of one in whom an artery has burst and unsuspected blood comes gushing out she looked at him, with repugnance and great pride—and he was that man, never any other, but he himself, and it made her avert her eyes severely. She remembered how one night she had passed by the woodshed and had heard the man snoring. The memory of that had made him undeniable. The reasonable possibility that he did not know that he was snoring had turned him over to her again with all his unconscious weight, the way an unconscious dog had once before belonged to her.

Until—until another wave of breeze extinguished everything. Leaving as reality only the man and the woman on horseback.

Out of everything the man had only the somewhat useless feeling of having finally emerged with the heart of a living person which, small as it was, gave him great power; as a person he was capable of everything. That was what he felt, perhaps. And just to show him to what point everything was converging toward a fertilization, as when grace exists, Vitória at that moment stretched out her arm to point out a mountain in the distance, the slopes of which took on a certain softness from the impossibility of being touched. Then Martim had a kind of certainty that this was the gesture that he had been looking for, just as distances seemed to need someone to determine with a gesture what they were. And therefore the man decided to conclude that it was this human gesture which is used for purposes of allusion—pointing.

Nor did it make any difference to him that the woman had done it unconsciously. Nor even that it had been she and not he who had done it. In the mute potency in which he found himself anything that was spoken would have been considered by him as his own voice, and anything that moved would be his own movement; and maybe he would be able to say "the greatest moment of my life was when Napoleon's troops marched into Paris," and he might have said "the greatest moment of my life was when a man said, 'Give bread to those who are hungry' "; and once more his work had become most difficult and most dazzling. The growth of trees, the width of the world grew painfully wide in his chest. And if that was the way it was, it was because since he had created himself he had come to need much, much more than he was. So that when the woman pointed her outstretched hand at that distant mountain it no longer mattered to the man whether it was she or a stone or a bird who had done it. What mattered was that the gesture had been made. He admitted that without reluctance—except that as a vindication he wanted to pick up the job at the point where the woman had left it, and he demanded that from now on the determination should fall upon his shoulders. And in that instant it was as if a whole future was being sketched out up there, and he could only come to know the details as he went along creating them. Martim had begun to belong to his own steps. He belonged to himself.

What had happened in that interim was just that the woman was looking around for good land where the trenches could be dug without much trouble. And to bring truth down to pure reality—what was happening to Martim?

What had really happened to Martim had simply been a

most acute physical consciousness that had been heightened on both sides by the horses, and with an even more acute perception he had felt the horses loose in the air. And this had given him a vague feeling of beauty, the way one gets that restless feeling of beauty where something seems to say something and there is that obscure encounter with a meaning. As far as real perception was concerned, one might honestly say that Martim had not perceived anything. So while the horses whinnied, they simply turned toward each other, and without there even having been a single moment of interruption in the dialogue about the trenches the woman went on to talk about the drought; and he listened to her and agreed. And just as if there had been a reincarnation of the spirit after death and the law ordained that there be no memory of having lived the moment of contact that Martim had had with "that which is" had passed by, unperceived by him. The only clear thing that remained was the thought that it was a place where he could well spend more time. Martim was very satisfied with himself.

And it turned the satisfaction, even if it was no longer enough for him, into some kind of hard tenacity which, like the first universal step, was becoming his measured attitude toward the slow descent down the hill. They were erect; the horses were twitching their flanks.

Part II

THE BIRTH OF
THE HERO

Chapter 1

BUT THAT VERY NIGHT, walking back and forth in the narrow confines of the woodshed, Martim found it difficult to restrain himself because of what he had gained. It was joy. As if he had just heard some news and there was no one to pass it on to, he did not know what to do with himself. He was very happy to be a person; that was one of the great pleasures in life. At the same time it seemed to him, unconsolable, that he would never get his reward.

And for the first time since he had fled he felt the need to communicate with somebody. He sat down on the edge of the bed and put his happy head in his hands. He did not know where to start thinking. Then he remembered his son, who had said at meal-time one day, "I don't want to eat this!" His mother had retorted, "What do you want to eat, then?" The child had ended up saying, painfully afraid of being found out, "Nothing!"

Then he, Martim, had said to him, "It's quite simple. If you're not hungry you don't have to eat anything."

But the child had begun to cry, "I'm not hungry, I'm not hungry . . ."

And as the radio was turned on the man had shouted, "I already told you that if you're not hungry you don't have to eat anything! What are you crying about?"

And the child had replied, "I'm crying because I'm not hungry."

"I can promise you that you'll be hungry by tomorrow. I can promise you that!" Martim had told him, upset, using love to enter into the truth of a child.

Sitting on the bed with his head in his hands Martim closed his eyes and laughed, filled with emotion. It was joy. His joy came from the fact that he was hungry, and when a man is hungry he gets happy. In the last analysis a man is measured by his hunger; there is no other way of figuring things out. And the truth was that on the hill the great lack had been reborn in him. It was strange that he had not had anything to eat and that he was rejoicing in his hunger. With his heart beating from his great hunger Martim lay down. He heard his heart pleading, and he laughed aloud, bestially, unprotected.

Ermelinda returned on the following day, and she was getting more and more systematic. "You may think I'm crazy," she said to him in that persistent way one sees in blind people— "but there's a place inside of me where I go when I want to sleep! Oh, I know it's all very queer, but just the same—if that place were nearby I could say that it's in the left side of my head—I sleep on my left side," she explained to him in passing, licking her lips—"but that place is so much farther away, it's as if it were way beyond where I leave off—and yet, it's inside of me. I'm still myself, you understand?"

Since particular details of her body, her eyes, hers and no one else's, were being turned toward him she made an effort, as she described her special traits, to prove to the man that she was herself alone. Since Martim had not looked at her she went a step farther, "It's a place that exists out there after my death," she said finally, and she suddenly became so pale that her unexpected silence made him look; he stopped smiling, without knowing why.

But Ermelinda knew quite well that it was still too early for her to stop lying and stop enticing him. She knew that it was too early to show herself to him and that he might chase her away if she was real; people are so afraid of the truth about others. She could only do it indirectly. The idea that if she did not amuse him she might drive him away filled her with fear for now she had progressed so far that she had got him to listen to her, even if he did not look at her! Then, suspicious that she might have gone too far and might have frightened him, she started to laugh a lot, and said, as if it was a joke, "I know that in order to get to

that place I go when I'm asleep I turn to the left. Just think—
that's how I fall asleep. Sometimes, so I won't be nervous, I try
to bring something into sleep with me, something from the day
that has just passed—understand?—a handkerchief I can twist
in my hand or the missal, just to give myself some assurance so I
won't be alone. I'm really silly, aren't I?" she said with tenderness directed at herself. "But you can't take anything with you
or you won't be able to go. It seems to be a place where you go
just to sleep or to think. Of course I'm not one who wants to go
back there! But"—she said helplessly—"but after you've been
there once, you get the habit. Believe me," she added greedily,
"believe me, I haven't been able to stop thinking what I think."
But she did not tell him what she was thinking, and she felt the
pleasure of one who confesses when there is no one to listen, as
if her confession had been stolen from her while she slept. "Did
you ever manage not to think about what you're thinking about?
It's what they call an obsession! A real obsession!" she said very
playfully, not forgetting for a moment that she always had to
take patient and perfect pains to flatter the man.

But she did not forget that she was in a hurry. It occurred to
her, while she was speaking to him, that she might unwillingly
let out what she was; and then the man would see how much
she needed him, and therefore he would no longer want her—as
happens with people. Ermelinda gave a lonely shiver at the
simple possibility of his never getting to like her, and she looked
at the flying birds. Her work on the man was always so delicate
and called for so much precision that she would not have been
able to do it had it only been a simple decision, or if she had
been ordered to do it. It was work that called for infinite
caution; where one step too far and the man would never love
her, where one step too far and she herself might stop loving
him: she was protecting both of them against the truth.

"It's like an obsession! Do you think I'm crazy?" she asked
him, because she knew that she was living off an idea and that
was not "normal."

"No."

"But other people don't seem to think that death—" Erme-linda quickly covered the revealing words with an ostentatious smile. "You don't think so?" she added coquettishly. "I'm not crazy then? I'm so silly you have no way of knowing!" she told him, as if she were promising a whole future of attractive silli-ness which he would only lose if he wanted to.

"You're crazy because you talk so much," he finally said heavily.

"Aha!" she said with the wise air of someone who will not let herself be tricked. "I see it all, then; you do think I'm crazy! I see it all now; you can't fool me!" she said, all smiles, inten-tionally addressing him in the familiar form—but his open eyes were thinking about something else.

Martim was remembering a man he had known who had traveled all alone through the interior for a long time and when returning he had lived talking about trees and snakes and birds, to the absolute boredom and incomprehension of everybody; until the man realized that a person did not talk about trees and birds and snakes, and he stopped talking.

"No," he said, looking at her with the first softness of curiosity in his voice and using the familiar form. "You're not crazy. You live a very isolated life, and you no longer know what should be told to other people and what should not." He stopped and looked at her, perplexed at having talked so much.

He had never talked so much, and the girl's heart began to beat. "I guess so," she said in a spritely way.

With an instinctive wisdom Ermelinda did not let on that she had spotted his first step in her direction, just as one does not give a shout of joy when a child begins to walk because he might get startled and not do it again for months.

As for him, he did not spot anything. As for him, he was waiting with patient anxiety for the time when his work would be through, for the time when he could go—not to the plot where the plants were nor to the cows in the cowshed—but to the hill again to recapture every day with the uncertain deter-mination of living jelly the moment of his formation on the day before. There he would remain standing; all he needed was to be standing without knowing what to do. The need a person has to climb a mountain—and look. That was the first symbol he had touched since he had left home: "climbing a mountain." And with that obscure act he was fertilizing himself. That place was an old symbol that had never been formulated, as if his father's father had breathed it in, and as if that reality had been born out of the invention of an ancient legend. That place had already happened to him before, it did not matter when, if only in a promise and in an invention.

And only God knows that Martim did not know what he went to do up on the hill. But it was so much of a fact that something objective must have been happening to him there that, now that he had formed the habit of re-evaluating his own nature by means of the final argument of the nature of animals, it was enough for him to recall how a bull stands on the top of a hill. Looking! That objective thing which is like an act: looking. Sometimes a dog looks too, even though rapidly, and he immediately becomes restless—because a dog has no time; he needs lots of love and he is nervous, and he has an afflicted feeling of the time that passes by, and in his eyes he has the weight of an intransmissible soul: only love can cure a dog. But it so happened that, that man, by circumstance of fate, was closer to the nature of a bull, and he was looking. If it was true that if someone had asked him why, he would not have been able to answer, it was also true that if a person only does what he understands, he will never take a single step forward.

Oh, maybe nothing had happened when he was up on the hill, and even he had still not demanded that something should happen. It seemed enough for him to have the extended light of the afternoon or the naked air or the empty space. Even a word that did not go beyond being thought would have scuttled the air. He abstained. Up there, existing had now become an emphasis, as if it were audacious and a step forward for a person to be standing in the clearness. It was as if Martim had become the symbol of himself, as if he had at last become incarnated in himself. The birds, avoiding the light, kept inside the darkness of the heavy branches. The clearness was resting, solitary, blue, delicate. It was afternoon. And Martim was looking, as if looking meant being a man. He was enjoying his state. It was a generous gift the world was giving him. He received it without shyness because he no longer felt any shame—it was difficult to tell why.

Until one day, as he faced the inhospitable clarity without any emotion, he finally thought, a little anxious but moving forward, "My God, if we did not create a world, then this world which is only divine would not receive us." It had begun to get dark. Dogs appeared in the distance, attentive. Birds came out of the foliage, and each one took a little greater chance. After a while the air became thick, and his feelings finally began to show their nature, which was not very divine, a deeply confused desire to be loved which was mixed in with the human smell of the night. A slow sweat began to sppear on him, spreading that good and bad smell he had of earth and cows and rat and armpits and darkness—that furtive way we have of noticing the earth after a while: we have finally created a world and given it our will. The maximum of clarity had given way to our habitual darkness: was that what Martim was waiting for perhaps as he stood there? As if with that submission to the clarity he had been shown just how the harmonious union is made harmonious—not intelligible, not with any finality, but harmonious—as if in that submission of the light before the darkness there had finally come about the union of the plants, of the cows, and of the man that he had begun to be. Each time that day turned into night the man's dominion would become renewed and a step forward would be taken, blindly—blindly in the end, like the advance of a person who desired something.

Martim was not able to discover why it was that on the hill he could complement himself so well, be harmonious himself—unintelligible but harmonious—while he looked out at the immortality of the countryside. For the time being that was all he needed. A man who has walked far has the right to an inexplicable pleasure, a harmony even if he does not understand it, does not understand it for the time being. Because with tranquil presumption he said to himself, "It's still early." It was not however just presumption. It was that now he had learned to rely upon the ripening of time, just like the tactics that cows use to live by. He seemed to understand now that one could not brutalize time and that its broad movement could not be replaced by any voluntary movement.

Thus, each day, when he was free from Vitória's orders he would go up on the hill to wait for the return of that instant when, stupefied, he had approached the farm for the first time, and for the first time had been alerted. And it would come back again and again. Repetition seemed essential to him. Every time it was repeated, something seemed to have been added. So much so that Martim was already starting to get upset—he was a man, but something worrisome remained: what does a man do?

Chapter 2

To THE POINT at which, that afternoon up on the hill, Martim began to judge himself. The unpleasant time for explanations had arrived.

There, before he went any farther, he had to be innocent or guilty. There, he had to know whether his mother, who would never have understood him if she had been alive, would love him without understanding him. There, he had to know whether his father's ghost would hold out his hand to him without fright. There, he would judge himself—this time using the speech of other people. Now he would have to call what he had done a crime. The man was trembled, afraid he would touch himself on the wrong spot; he was still covered with wounds.

But because he knew deep down that he would even resort to farce so as to emerge whole from his own judgment—that if he was not cleared, he would remain perplexed, with a crime on his hands—the fact that *he knew that* he would not let himself emerge unless he came out whole gave him the courage to face up to it and, if necessary, be horrified.

And furthermore: because he would only let himself win, because at the point at which he found himself he had a fierce need for himself, he had already thought in advance that after the necessary judgment he would have his great task ahead of him. Because it would be then that he would have to remember what a man wants.

It occurred to him that he was reversing the order of what had happened, that he had not committed a crime in order to give himself the opportunity to find out what a man wants, but that the opportunity had been born casually along with the crime. He tried to ignore the uncomfortable feeling of mystification; he needed that mistake to go forward, he needed it as an instrument. Willingly he put his confusion off in the distance and finally made an attempt to come to grips with things. With a sigh, he came to grips in clear terms, and he thought along these lines—He had not committed an ordinary crime.

He thought that with that crime he had executed his first act as a man. Yes! Courageously, he had done what every man has to do once in his life: destroy life in order to rebuild it on his own terms.

"Had that been what he had wanted out of the crime, then?" His heart beat heavily, irreducibly, illuminated with peace. Yes, in order to rebuild it on his own terms.

And if he could not succeed in rebuilding it? Because in his rage he had broken what had existed into pieces that were too small. What if he could not succeed in rebuilding it? He looked out at the perfect emptiness of the clarity, and the strange possibility that he might never succeed in rebuilding it came to him. But even if he did not succeed it did not matter. He had felt the courage to take a big gamble. A man must risk everything one day. Yes, he had done just that.

And proud of his crime, he saw the world in ruins. Ruined by him and at his feet—the world tumbled down by a crime. And only he, because he had made himself the great perpetrator of it, could put it together again, give it meaning, and raise it back up.

But on his own terms.

That was what it was, then. And Martim asked himself with intensity and pain, "could that be all it was?" Because his truths did not seem to be able to bear attention for a long time before they became deformed. And for an instant the truth might just as well be one thing as another; only the countryside was immutable. It was at the cost of a certain control, then, that Martim stuck to one truth only and with difficulty erased all others. (Without his realizing it, his reconstruction had already begun to gasp.)

It made no difference to him that the source of his present

strength had been a criminal act. What mattered was that from it he had received the impulse toward a great revindication.

That was how it was, then, that Martim emerged whole from the judgment—a little tired from the effort.

Well, now it would be a matter of remembering what a man wants. That was the real judgment—and Martim lowered his head, confused, in penance.

Oh Lord, it was not easy for that man to express what he wanted. He wanted this: to rebuild. But it was like an order that one receives and does not know how to fulfill. Free as he might be, a person was used to being commanded, even if it was only by what other people were commanded. And now Martim was on his own.

One had to have a lot of patience with him; he was slow. What did he want? Whatever it was that he wanted had been born far away inside of him, and it was not easy to bring the stammering murmur to the surface. And it happened that what he wanted was also strangely mixed up with what he already was—what, in the meantime, he had never attained.

His obscure task would have been easier if he had allowed himself the use of words that had already been created. But his reconstruction had to begin with his own words because words were the voice of a man—not to mention the fact that Martim possessed a sense of caution that was merely practical. The moment he accepted alien words he would automatically be accepting the word "crime," and he would become nothing but a common criminal in flight. It was still too early for him to give himself a name—and give a name to what he wanted. One step further and he would know. But it was still too early.

Then Martim went back down the hill to tell Vitória that the following morning he would start digging the trenches. He went to the porch and waited for Vitória to finish talking to Francisco.

The fact that he had finally managed to think had not given him any plan. But he had accepted his crime, in his way; and he felt himself a whole man, tall and serene. Standing on the porch, not in any hurry, he listened to Vitória's harsh voice and Francisco's agreement as it blended into the rhythm of the woman's voice. Then, almost without being aware of it, he began to hear the words too.

". . . you have to pick the tomatoes too. And this time do a better job of packing them, Francisco. Better and quicker—this time the German will get to the Vila sooner."

Martim was listening and waiting patiently. And then he understood what he had heard.

So she was going to meet a German. The German. So she was going to see the German. Stupefied, attentive, Martim turned the phrase over in his head to see if he could make it lose its meaning. But any way that he repeated it, it was always the same, "the woman was going to see the German." She was probably going to sell him some of the produce from the place! he thought, suddenly recovering that old voracious intelligence he had had in his flight. And every moment he became dominated by an expert power of reason that went beyond his normal ability, as if now he was capable of shedding his bodily weight, sinking low, and losing himself among the shadows on the wall. His memory took on a catlike sharpness and he instantly recalled seeing Francisco cleaning the truck.

"To go to Vila Baixa or just for the sake of cleaning it?" He remembered that he had already heard Vitória talking about the German—but when? when! Or hadn't he ever heard? No, he had never heard her—And Francisco had already cleaned the truck! But the trip would not be today. Would it be the next day maybe? Then she will see the German, he thought with the care of one who might have been handling something treacherous that could suddenly rebel within his fingers and take on a life of its own. Then she will see the German, he thought carefully. But the thought, even though it was quite clear, did not take him anywhere or lead him on to another thought. Trapped, he moved his head fiercely from one side to the other to calculate the distance of a leap off the porch. "She will see the German," he repeated rapidly and meanly, like a rat, and even his head seemed hairier to Vitória who looked at him for an instant without interrupting her orders to Francisco. "He looks like a filthy beast," the woman concluded as she kept on talking to Francisco.

But soon the intimate darkness that had enveloped Martim and in which he was already beginning to move with some skill began to dissipate. His head was coming back into place little by little. And when Francisco left and Vitória began to talk to him and give him orders Martim forgot that he had come to tell her about the ditches, and he looked intensely into her eyes. And he tried to guess, with the help of that rare element that was composed of dark eyes, whether Vitória was the kind of woman who would chatter on about what was happening on her own place—about a new worker, a stranger in the region. Even if she did not mention him directly she might make some casual reference about him, and the German would guess that he was the one who had fled in the night from the hotel.

"I wonder how well she knows the German?" Martim tried to guess, probing avidly with his eyes. But he found no answer at all in that face which had one day become tired and had shut itself off forever. "Maybe she wasn't the kind of woman who chattered—but maybe the German himself would talk about that night when the guest had run away—and then she would know!" Martim became enraged with himself for never having paid attention to that woman whom he did not know and whose acts, therefore, he was incapable of predicting. Out of practical necessity he examined her for the first time. Hers was a hard and thin face, the bones of which seemed to speak more than the flesh. Hers was a lofty head. More than that he could not tell.

And when would she leave? How much time did he have left to run away? "She can't be leaving too soon!" he thought, suddenly more lucid, "because Francisco won't have had time to pick the tomatoes and pack them! The tomatoes still have to be picked because just now Vitória told Francisco to do it!" he remembered with a fury of joy. "Or have they been?"—suddenly he became confused.

"When are you going to Vila?" he asked, unable to stand the

doubt any longer; and the question that he had not planned but had wanted to be casual sounded brusk and imperative, suspect to his own ears.

Vitória interrupted herself, her mouth opened with surprise. It was the first time the man had said a word to her without being prompted.

"I don't know," she said finally, frowning.

Then Martim, with the same sudden perspicacity which was reaching beyond him and beyond logic, realized that Vitória had found him out. He lowered his shoulders and let the tension unwind, and as if the first instant of certainty had given him only the relief of not doubting, a calm took control of him. He looked at the woman with contempt.

Her face blushed nakedly under that undisguised and peaceful look. Stared at so openly her face contracted into a quick attempt at an expression, and finally resolved itself into an impassive look which the determination had only increased the blushing.

Then the man understood even more, from the moment he had set foot on the farm she had decided to send him away. The only new element that he could see on top of that was that she had finally found the way.

Why had he not seen before what was now so clear? he thought, surprised. Why had he not noticed that day after day the woman had been fighting to make a decision, and that the accumulation of it all had brought it out. The man quickly remembered certain looks the woman had given him while he had been working, and which he had scarcely noticed; he remembered the tone of voice in which so many times she had asked him how long he was going to stay on the farm. But why had she asked him that question? Was it that each time she was suggesting the idea of his voluntary departure, giving him a chance to flee, and in that way freeing herself from the difficult decision? He understood now that she had guessed his need from the moment he had set foot on the farm. She had guessed everything as far as one can guess without knowing anything.

There was just one thing he could not understand yet, and he looked at her with curiosity: she still had not turned him in. Vitória could not bear the simple stare of the man and she averted her eyes.

"That was her last reply, then," he thought. "And therefore there wasn't much time left," he determined next.

Chapter 3

At NIGHT, sitting erect on his bed and not having lighted the lantern, Martim finally understood what he had meant when he had said that there was not much time.

Frightened, he realized that he had not really thought about the time that was left for him to plan his flight. From the moment he had spoken to Vitória on the porch he had acted as if it were obvious that the flight would have to come that very night, before Vitória used the truck—if he wanted to, he could be far away by the time she met the German. But as if the darkness of the woodshed had led him into his own darkness, he finally understood: it was not because of his flight that there was not much time. He had been so busy planning his escape that he had not realized that he was not thinking about running away.

"He had to possess everything before the end and he had to live a whole life before the end." That was why time had become short. With a dazzled fright—because the fact was that up to that moment he still had not become serious or even been aware of how far he had gone toward accepting the seriousness. Startled, he saw now that he had not been fooling—saw with dazzled fright that it was not because of his flight that there was not much time. His courage then made him mistrustful. He was suspicious of himself.

And that was not all that the man perceived with surprise. With the suddenness of the present ultimatum, Martim realized that the idea that he had no time to lose had been with him constantly, even before the ultimatum, masquerading as daily work, patiently lying under the sleep in which a person slowly moves. Then suddenly very excited and walking back and forth in the dark limits of the woodshed, Martim became aware that now he was only the guardian of a small amount of time that did not belong to him. And that his task was greater than the time left to him.

Now that he had emerged far enough to reach the point of the man on the hill, now that he had emerged enough to understand his crime and know what he wanted—or enough to invent what was happening to him and know what he wanted? what did he care whether truth already existed or whether it had been invented, because even if only invented, it still had value as the act of a man—now that he had come to judge himself, he had to continue. And as he faced the approaching end, continue toward the—the rebuilding of the world.

Yes. Rebuilding the world. The fact is that the man had just completely lost all shame. He did not even feel ashamed at going back to using words out of his adolescence; he had to use them because the last time he had possessed speech of his own had been in adolescence; adolescence was risking everything— and now he was risking everything.

He had little time and he had to begin right then, in a manner of speaking. "From the rebuilding of the world within himself he would proceed to the rebuilding of the City, which was a form of life and which he had repudiated with a murder; that was why time was short." "I don't think I'm the least bit stupid!" he thought, fascinated.

Having come to understand himself finally, he was dominated by an enormous calm. He was not even startled by the wild enormity of his plans. Once he had destroyed the order he had nothing more to lose, and he was not selling out to any compromise. He could go out and face a new order. Then, startled, he asked himself if ever any man had been as free as he was now—after which he calmed down. Not that he was really calm. In fact, his body was trembling. But from now on, starting with this very instant, he would have to be calm and unbelievably astute in order to succeed in keeping up with himself and with the rapidity with which he would have to act. He had to be calm—now that he had found his own greatness up on the mountain, the greatness with which he was being born.

(140)

The Birth of the Hero

That greatness—oh, just the measure of a man—that had been buried as a shameful and useless weapon. To be a man was to be something without trying hard. But he finally needed greatness as an instrument. Martim needed himself deeply for the first time. As if finally—finally—he had been summoned . . . Which left him flustered in the darkness. And since in the darkness not even the walls could see his face, Martim took great relief in making a face of pain, and then one of shame for the joy that he felt, and then one of pain.

Finally he sat down on his bed. And on a cold and calculating level he decided that his first battle would be with himself.

Because if he wanted to rebuild the world, he himself was not fit for it . . . If as the end result of his work he wanted to reach other men he would first have to stop the complete destruction of his former way of being. In order for the beggar at the door of the movies not to be a perpetual and abstract person Martim would have to begin from far off and from the very beginning. It was true that there was little left to be destroyed for by his crime he had already destroyed a great deal. But not everything. There was still—there was still himself, which was a constant temptation. And his thought, as it existed, was only able to provide a predetermined and inevitable result, just as a scythe can only cut a predetermined swath. If he had managed the first and primitive destruction with his act of rage the more delicate task was still to be accomplished. And the delicate task was this: being objective.

But how? in what way is one objective? Because if a person did not want to make a mistake—and Martim never wanted to make a mistake again—he would end up prudently adopting the following approach, "There is nothing as white as white," "there is nothing as full of water as something full of water," "a yellow thing is yellow in color." Which would not be just prudence, it would be an exactitude of calculation and a rigorous sobriety of mind. But where would it lead him? because we are not scientists in the end.

The task was this: being objective. And it could well be the

(141)

strangest experience a man can have. As far as Martim could remember he had never heard anyone talk about an objective man. No, no—he was a little tired, and he was becoming confused—there had been men like that; men already had existed, yes, whose souls had come to exist through acts and to whom other men had not been gigantic fingernails; there had been men like that—he no longer could remember who, and he was a little fatigued, a little lonely. In fact it would have been so easy for his plan to escape his own perception, which was so frail in the midst of all his merely brutish strength, that he feared lest instinct should not come to his aid, and that as a desperate measure he would become intelligent. And he, in the meantime, had not got beyond being a vague thing that wanted to question, question, and question—until little by little the world would take the shape of an answer.

Martim hesitated, tired; he looked around him; he recovered a little. He advanced backwards, with apparent freedom. What sometimes gave him support and an overall desire to continue was the memory of his successful pleasure with women. But then immediately the fact that he had never had a bicycle would paralyze him; he might be wrong, then. All through his life, like a dripping faucet, he had wanted that bicycle. Again his plan seemed too fragile to him, and that breathing thing that he was there in the darkness seemed very small to him, like the start of a conversation. Martim became all mixed up, as if he had more fingers than he needed, and as if he himself was getting his own road confused. Then he got the desire for a child to start crying so that he could comfort it. The fact was that he was unsheltered and he felt the necessity for giving, which is the form an unskilled person uses to ask for something. His ambition was great and unprotected, he would have liked to hold the hand of a child; he was a little tired.

"Why do I want so much?" and it was brought on by that habit which once more would end up making an abstraction out of the hunger of others, the same habit which is the fear a man has. "And what if I were not to take myself seriously?" he thought astutely, since that had been the age-old solution, and of many people. "Because if we were suddenly to give importance to what really is important to us—we would have our whole life lost." But it was also said that he who loses his life shall gain his life.

When the restful discouragement had passed Martim moved about restlessly; he would have to control himself every time the habit returned. Because from now on he would no longer even be permitted to interrupt himself with the question—"what do I want so much for"—any interruption could be fatal, and he ran the risk of losing not only his speed, but his balance as well. Growth is full of tricks and self-derision and fraud; only a few people have the requisite dishonesty not to become nauseated. With the fierceness of self-preservation Martim could no longer permit himself the luxury of decency or interrupt himself with sincerity.

Chapter 4

Dᴜʀɪɴɢ ᴛʜᴀᴛ ɪɴᴛᴇʀᴠᴀʟ ᴅᴀᴡɴ ʙʀᴏᴋᴇ.

And while he was opening the first trench in the morning light, at the same time that his thick hands were obeying him, Martim had already begun to apply himself to a task of infinite exactitude and vigilance. Was it that of monopolizing himself and along with himself the world? Was it precisely that he was doing? But did it really make so much difference to know what he was doing? He was constructing a dream—which was the only way in which truth could come to him and he could make it live. Was it indispensable, then, to understand perfectly what was happening to him? If we understand it deeply, do we also have to understand it superficially? If we recognize our own taking on shape through its slow movement—just as one recognizes a place where he has been only once before—is it necessary to translate it into words that compromise us?

Groping, then, and having only his intention for a compass, Martim seemed to be trying to start at the exact beginning. And rebuild from the very first stone, until he would come to the moment when the great deviation had taken place—what had been his impalpable mistake as a man? Until by stirring up the vast and useless spread of the world he could once more reach the instant when the great mistake had been made. And when little by little he had rebuilt the path already followed and he came to the point where the mistake had taken place he would go off in a direction opposite to the deviation. In the morning light it seemed as simple as that; once the world had been rebuilt within him, then we would know how to act. And his action would not be the abstract action that comes from thought, but the real kind.

What kind? "Whatever it turns out to be," he said with

(1 4 4)

quiet insolence. And if the time were too short, if Vitória turned him in before he was ready and he did not have any freedom for the action, he at least would have come to know what the action of a man is. And that too was a maximum. (Oh, he knew quite well that if it was explained, no one would understand, because explaining how one foot follows the other cannot give anyone an idea of what walking is like.) Oh, there was little time, yes, he knew that. He could almost hear the enormous silence with which the hands of the clock advanced. But he did not feel upset at being the guardian of so little time; the time of a whole lifetime can also be little. That man had already accepted the great contingency.

On the first day, then, all he asked of himself was objectivity, which became a source of worries and deceptions. For example, a bird was singing. But from the moment in which Martim tried to make it concrete, the bird stopped being a symbol and suddenly was nothing more than what can be called a bird. In compensation the chickens, in his tired eyes, had become day itself; they ran white and hurriedly about through the mist—if Martim was not quick, he would lose the morning sun—the roosters ran around, sometimes they would flap their wings; the hens who were not busy with their eggs were free. All of that was morning itself, and a person who was not quick would lose it— objectivity was a dizzying glance. Martim then discovered the business of rhythm. When his eyes tried to do more than just describe things the result of his effort would be the empty shape of a rooster. Besides, in his task of constructing reality, Martim had in his disfavor the novelty of things not being obvious anymore; he was bumping into things at every moment. Against him too was the feeling of precious time. Although Martim did have one great advantage: if life was short, the days were long. Still in his favor was the fact that he knew he should walk in a straight line because it would not be very practical to lose the thread of the maze. In his disfavor there was a danger he was on the lookout for: the fact that there were pleasure and beauty in a person's losing himself. In his disfavor there was also the fact that he did not understand very much. But especially in his favor was the fact that not understanding was his clean, new starting point.

All right. That was a first attempt at reconstruction and with a fresh starting point.

But—but could he have started too far back at the beginning?

Then he looked about the empty countryside and it seemed to him that he had gone back to the creation of the world. In his leap backwards, through an error in calculation, he had gone back too far—and it seemed to him that through an error in calculation he had put himself uncomfortably facing a monkey's first perplexity. As a monkey, at least he would have been endowed with the wisdom that would make him scratch himself and by which the countryside would gradually become within reach of his leaps. But he did not have the resources of a monkey.

Had he begun too far back at the beginning? And then, in spite of his heroism, there was a practical question: he did not have sufficient material time to start so far back. There was already so little time left for him to cover what had taken him almost forty years to cover; and not just cover the old road in a new way, but also to do what he had not been able to do until that time, reach comprehension and go beyond it by using it. There was little time for all of that now. Especially because he was starting, in a manner of speaking, from scratch! And yet, if he wanted to be faithful to his own necessity, he could not deceive it. He had to start at the very beginning.

Which, as he dug away, suddenly seemed easy again. Because each minute might be the whole time—if a person were free enough to be aware of that minute. Martim knew all about that because once, in one minute already lost, he had accepted rage, and in one minute a path had opened up like a destiny. And later on, in one minute, he had not been afraid to be great; and without shame, in one minute, he had accepted the role of a man as his own.

That was what it was then; having already lost his first

modesty on the mountain, Martim, without feeling it, was losing his last bonds, so that now it was no longer monstrous for a person to take on the function of a person and to "rebuild"— which seemed most easy to him. Until today everything that he had seen was so that he would not see, everything that he had done was so that he would not do, everything he had felt was so that he would not feel. His eyes would see today even if they exploded. He who had never faced anything head-on. Few people had probably ever had the chance to rebuild existence on their own terms. "À *nous deux*," he suddenly said, interrupting his work and looking. Because it was just a question of beginning.

But as if he had had a childish dream, he looked again at the bird that was singing and said to himself, "What can I make out of him?"

Because in this first vision there was no longer any room for a bird. Everything had been given to him, yes. But taken apart and in pieces. And he, with pieces left over in his hand, did not seem to know how to put the thing back together again. Everything belonged to him to do with as he wanted. In the meantime his very freedom left him helpless, as if God had listened too well to his plea and had given him everything. But it was possible that He had withdrawn at the same time. The whole countryside belonged to Martim, and also a bird that was singing. And in that short time it was the whole of life for him too. And no one or nothing could help him. It had been exactly that which he had prepared with care, and he had prepared it even with a crime. But even if he had begun astutely with the easiest thing— what is simpler than a bird singing? He asked himself embarrassedly then, "What do I do with a singing bird?"

Then he looked sharply at the bird. But he, he could not deduce anything. The fact was that by concentrating and brimming with good will he managed to attain from the effort of staring at the bird a maximum tension that was like a feeling of beauty. But only that. Nothing else. Was watching the bird sing the limit of his intuition? Is "two and two are four" the great leap that a man can take?

As could be seen, that first day of objectivity was like walking in his sleep. If he had tried to go from the spirit of geometry to that of finesse things obstinately would not have any finesse that could be reached by his large mouth or his rather unskilled hands. His was a great spiritual effort, then—and a little dull and cheap. What helped him was that he had the fearlessness of those who, since they are not foresighted enough to spot the difficulty, fail to see any obstacles. What also helped him was the fact that having become accustomed to the fact that he was not brilliant, he thought once again that the difficulty was only his own; so he made an effort. Until he reached a point of anxious responsibility at which it seemed to him that if he was not conscious of the fact that flowers were growing, flowers would not grow.

In the meantime—in the meantime, on that very day there were moments when the effort of applying himself in an attempt to understand was like beating with a stick on the dry ground and feeling that there was water there. It was also true that his talent did not go beyond that.

It was at night that Martim had a thought more or less like this: whether the story of a person was not always the story of his failure. By means of which . . . what? By means of which, period. Right away, unwilling to use that thought, he took refuge in thinking about his son. Because his love for his son was one of the truths he liked best.

Chapter 5

WITH the passage of days the woman became more aware of his presence and took for stability that sluggish air Martim had assumed and which had arisen from the fact that moment by moment, with the stupid face of a man who is thinking, with the patience of the shoemakers in the picture, he was practicing a way to open up his path. Certain then that she would finally get her tranquilizing answer, with the assurance a mother uses to establish domains where she can fit in with her children, Ermelinda asked him, "How long are you going to stay?"

"I don't know," he replied.

Ermelinda was startled again. And as if her shudder had been impalpably communicated to Vitória, both of them, more active, began to act as if the time were coming to a close; Vitória grew impatient about the ditches with which he was not making much headway, she watched over him on horseback. And a new rhythm could be felt on the place.

And Martim? Martim worked. He looked and he worked, making a fair copy of the world. His rudimentary thoughts were meanwhile still stubbornly anchored in what he considered most basic—from where he would gradually go on to an understanding of everything, from a woman who for years had asked him "what time is it" to the sun that rose every day and people would get out of bed then, to an understanding of the patience of other people, understanding why a child is our investment and the arrow we shoot off in the air. Could that be what he wanted? it was really hard to say. In the meantime he was molding himself, and that always takes time; he was giving shape to what he was. Life in the making is difficult, like art in the making.

It was becoming difficult to see all of that. The most easily recognizable truth was that the man was confused. As has been pointed out, it was only persistent ambition that kept him from seeing any obstacles in his path, and thanks to his stupidity it was easy. His grandiloquence, in the meantime, had taken on some humility. Because he had already come to accept the fact that each moment had no strength in itself he had begun to rely on the cumulative strength of time—"the passage of many moments would take him to where he wanted to go." And so his humility became an instrument of patience. He worked without cease; the trenches were getting deep.

The small group on the place would look up at the sky, scrutinize, and keep on working. Everything was quivering in a heat that was gradually growing without anyone's feeling the transitions. The branches trembled; the heat was duplicating everything in a refracted glow. From the depths of his own mystery Martim looked at the plants in their innocent lushness that still did not seem to feel the menace being sparkled out by the red sun; drought. He looked. Now that he had courage everything belonged to him, which was not at all easy. He looked, for example, at the fields which had become his field of battle, and there was no breach through which anything could invade what belonged to him. What was all that he saw? That everything was a soft prolongation of everything; what existed joined with what existed; the curves became full, harmonious; the wind devoured the sands, beat uselessly against the stones. It was quite true that in some strange way, when something was not understood, everything became obvious and harmonious; the thing was rather explicit. In the meantime, looking, he had trouble understanding that evidence of meaning, as if he were trying to observe a light within another light.

And that was how from time to time Martim would lose sight of his objectives. Had there really been a planned finality, or was he only following an uncertain necessity? Up to what point was he determining things? Martim was probably quite capable of arriving at a conclusion quite quickly, but when you have been purified, the road is longer. And if the road is long, the person can forget where he was going and stand in the middle of the road and look amazed at a stone or lick with pity the feet that have been wounded by the walking or sit down for just an instant to wait a little while. The road was hard and beautiful; beauty was the temptation.

And the meaning of it is that in that interval something had happened.

Something insidious had begun to gnaw away at the master beam. And it was something that Martim had not counted on. He was beginning to love what he saw.

Free, free for the first time, what did Martim do? He did what imprisoned people do: he loved the harsh wind; he loved his work on the trenches, like a man who had marked out the great meeting point of his life and never arrived because he was injured and had become distracted examining green leaves. That was how he loved and lost himself. And the worst was that he loved without having any concrete reason to. Just because a person who was born would love and not know why. Now that he had created with his own hands the opportunity not to be a victim or a torturer any more, to be outside of the world and not have to worry himself any more with pity or love, not to have to punish or be punished any more love for the world was suddenly being born. And the danger in it was that if he was not careful, he would stop advancing.

Because something else had also happened just as important and serious and real as sadness or pain or anger: he was content.

Martim was content. He had not foreseen this additional obstacle, the struggle against pleasure. He was enjoying the petty chores in the cowshed too much. To his surprise, he was becoming satisfied with so little, doing jobs . . . It was more than enough for him to be simply a person who wakes up in the morning. The not quite dark sky was enough for him—and the mist-covered earth and the fresh trees, and he had learned how to milk the cows, who lowed apathetically in the dawn. So it was. "I am a man who milks cows." The flow of grace was strong in the morning, and it was enough to possess a living body. If he was not careful he would feel that he was the owner of it all. If he was not careful a tree taller than the others might make him feel complete; and when he was hungry he would be bought by a plate of food, and he would join his enemies who had been bought by food and beauty. Restless, he would feel guilty if he did not transform, in his mind at least, the world in which he lived. Martim was losing himself. "Could there really be a finality?" He was starting to have an astonishing and benevolent vanity about his "escapades," and he would see himself as a great horse we have at home, who would sometimes take wild runs about the place, free with impunity, guided by the beauty of his restraining spirit, the same as the way our bodies do not come to pieces. Exercises in living. Martim was finding pleasure in himself. Miserably, nothing more than that. As is evident, he could not have been happier.

It was with superhuman effort that every day Martim tried to overcome the sense of vanity of belonging to a countryside so vast that it grew without sense; it was with austerity that he overcame the pleasure he found in the empty harmony. With effort he reached beyond himself obliging himself, in the face of the current that was dragging him along in all its grace, not to betray his crime. As if by means of contentment, he was plunging a knife into his own revolt. Then he would get the strength to force himself not to forget his compromise. And once again he would assume a spiritual state of work, a kind of trance into which he had learned to fall when necessary.

His state of work consisted in taking an animal-like attitude of purity and vulnerability. He had learned the technique of how to be vulnerable and alert with the face of an idiot. It was nothing easy, in fact it was quite difficult. Until—until he could reach that certain imbecility he needed. As a starting point he would create an attitude of astonishment for himself, he would become defenseless, without any weapon in his hand; he did not want to use any instruments at all; he wanted to be his own instrument, and with empty hands. Because after all he had committed a crime just so that he could be openly exposed.

But if that attempt at innocence made him reach objectivity, it was the objectivity of a cow: no words. And he was a man who needed words. Then he would patiently correct the exaggerations in his imbecility. "It is also necessary not to make myself any more of a jackass than I already am." Because there were not so many advantages in being an imbecile either, it was necessary not to forget too that the world did not belong only to imbeciles. Then he would take on a new way of working, the opposite direction, and a resolute attitude that made one think of a challenge. That attitude was not difficult to take on. But he could not get beyond it, and with everything in readiness, like a' man preparing for a mile race who finds out that he only has to run six feet, he deflated in disappointment. It became obvious that the pose of letting himself go into imbecility had been a task beyond his real capacity to let it be what it was.

It was true that when it occurred to him that the end was not far off he no longer needed to harass himself or create techniques to get on with his monstrous task. When it occurred to him that he suddenly had to have everything, and "revelation" as well his haste would once again become perfect, tranquil, and concentrated, like that of the two shoemakers underneath the cauldron. And his own contentment seemed to be a necessary part of the slow work of craftsmen.

Oh, he was quite unprotected. He simply did not know how to approach what he wanted. He had lost that stage in which he had taken on the dimensions of an animal and in which comprehension was silent, like a hand that grabs something. And he had also lost that moment up on the hill when all that he had needed was the use of words. All had been so perfect and so almost human that he had said to himself, "Speak!" and all that had been lacking was the words. What point had he reached now? The point at which he had been before the crime. As before, now he was something that might perhaps have meaning if seen from a distance that would give it the proportions of a leaf on a tree. Seen too closely, he would either be too big or people would stop looking. He was nothing, basically, and it took some effort for him to assume a bit of importance. Because he really was quite important: he was only alive once.

And the fact was that now it was too late. Despite his contentment he would have to continue on. Not only because of the obligation to preserve his crime. Because even in retreat he felt that he was going forward.

He felt that—that's it—that he was almost beginning to understand. It was true that by a mistake in calculation he had started too close to the beginning; it was true that the green of the weeds was so strong that his eyes could not translate it; it was true that it occurred to the man that he had destroyed the world so completely that he would never receive it whole again, not even for one single moment, as one receives extreme unction. All of that was true, yes. But the fact was that sometimes the resistance seemed ready to give way . . .

There was a peaceful resistance in everything. An immaterial resistance, like trying to remember and not managing to. But just as the memory would be on the tip of one's tongue so the resistance was ready to give way. So it was that on the following morning, as he opened the door of the woodshed to the coolness of the morning, he felt the resistance giving way. The clean air of the morning trembled among the bushes, the coffee in the cracked cup joined him to the mistless morning, the leaves of the palm trees showed darkly; peoples' faces were red from the wind, as if a new race was walking through the countryside; everybody working without haste and without cease; the yellow smoke rising up from the bottom of the wall. And, in God's name, that had to be more than great beauty. That had to be being. Then as his resistance began to give way, even with some scruples, he almost understood. With scruples, as if he did not have the right to use certain processes, as if he had been understanding something entirely incomprehensible like the Holy Trinity. And he hesitated, hesitated because he knew that after understanding all would be irremediable in some way. Understanding could become a pact with solitude.

But how to escape the temptation to understand? Without

managing to overcome a certain feeling of sensuality he understood. Not to become completely compromised, he turned enigmatic, so that he would be able to retreat as soon as it became more dangerous. Then, careful and crafty, he understood it in this way: "How can one fail to understand, if a person knows so well when a thing is there!" and the thing was there. He knew it; the thing was there. "Yes, that's how it was, and there was the future." The long future that had started with the beginning of the centuries and from which it is useless to flee, for we are part of it, and "it is useless to flee because it will be something," the man thought, rather confused. "And when it is"—oh, how could he explain it to himself in such an innocent morning?—"and when it is, then it will be," he said, humiliated by the little he was saying. And when it is, the man who is born will be astounded that before . . . "But who knows if it isn't already?" —it occurred to Martim with great acumen. "I think maybe it already is," he concluded with the dignity of a thought. Then, satisfied in some way, he took on an official pose of meditation. He meditated as he looked out at the morning in the country. And who will ever have to explain why butterflies in a field can stretch out a man's sight into an obscure comprehension?

In this way, by means of half-excuses, Martim finally reached a state, jumping over himself like a hero. And in this way, by means impossible to retell, he finally freed himself of the beginning of beginnings where by ineptness he had been trapped for so long. A phase had come to a close, the most difficult one.

Chapter 6

THERE WERE SILENCE AND INTENSITY beneath the sun on the farm.

There was probably no way for Martim's mute vigilance to be communicated to the others because he kept on working calmly with the same face that did not speak and in his eyes there was an expression that eyes take on when the mouth is gagged. However, a date beyond which everything would be impossible seemed to have been established. Maybe his intensity had been communicated by his strongest hammer-blow, or maybe by his thick-booted walk, or by his sudden disappearances. They would look for him and not find him, but before his absence would upset them he would appear peacefully, as if out of nowhere.

"And where have you been?" Vitória would ask inconsiderately.

The man's answer gave her no sense of relief. The man's stability did not fool her; that was all going to end, she knew it. Vitória gave him new jobs, she invented petty chores, and she never let him out of her sight. Since the time was limited the woman had assumed a wisdom that was instinctive, and she did so much that in it all that one essential thing might have escaped her grasp without her wanting it to.

But if Vitória did not seem to know what she wanted, Ermelinda knew. And she kept circling the man closer and closer. "Look at that fern!" she said one afternoon. "Look how uselessly it grows! It's so pretty it's becoming drab."

But the man did not understand what she was hinting at; he was too foggy. And nothing was happening. If the emotion brought on by his feelings had given him a pretty little ignorance it was not very efficient. And if Ermelinda bathed herself in the surf of what she was attempting and became entranced with the beauty of her plans no one understood. And why should they? When she had been a girl, out of a pure tendency toward subtlety and weakness, she had said to a boy she liked, "I'm going to give you a stone I found in the garden"—and he had understood that she liked him and had given her in exchange a matchbox with a cookie inside. And then, following her vocation for subtlety along that torturous road of delicacy which had saved her from becoming offended with the truth—truth to Ermelinda may have seemed an inferior form, primary and "styleless," so to speak—then she would thank her husband for having given her a new dress by telling him, "It's a nice day today, isn't it?" Because of some mystery in her process of realization she always avoided being completely understood.

In the meantime there was no exclamation of horror as she brought herself to face the simple crudity with which she wanted that man. Perhaps that delicateness of hers, incomprehensible to other people, came from the very delicateness of her reasons for wanting him. Her reasons for wanting him were those of a woman who wanted love—which seemed terribly subtle to her. And as if that reason was not enough, she had woven in a still more subtle reason: saving herself—which is a certain stage that love can sometimes reach. It was all of that, then, that had turned her into someone who could not be understood. It did not really make her suffer, because it was part of the order of things. Since she did not understand other people it was not for her to be understood either.

She did have a practical problem however that was quite intense: the way she lived did not give her just anything that she wanted. And the result was that, against her wishes, she seemed to be pure without really wanting to be—just to avoid the vulgarity of becoming clear. For example, she had never confessed to a priest that she was afraid of dying; instead of that she had told him with all sorts of hints and allusions: "I think a stone is so much prettier than a bird." Perhaps by that she had meant to say, who knows, that to her a stone seemed closer to life than a bird which in its flight reminded her of death, or that it naturally meant she was afraid of dying. The priest had not understood her and she had gone away without having confessed, frightened at not having got an answer. For so many years that girl had never had the satisfaction of success.

"Look at that fern!" she may have said to the man because a person cannot say "I love you."

The man's face was warm and red, covered with grime. She looked at the warm face of the man, and the strength she had was the frail strength of a woman; but she had talked about ferns and the man had not understood her, and his face had kept on being simple and unreachable. The girl began to despair because she had already begun to convince herself that one did not summon a man by talking about ferns. She did not know how to summon him and she wondered about the empty urgency the man was communicating to her as he pounded.

Then, on the following morning—as soon as Vitória had mounted her horse and before the dust from its hooves had settled back onto the ground—Martim noticed Ermelinda by the cowshed where he was washing the cows, standing there like a schoolgirl.

She was standing there not saying anything. In a desperate way the girl was trying to be simple for the first time: not saying anything. Martim put on a curious mask that he himself probably could not have interpreted. The fact was, without really knowing how, he had just understood. Maybe because Ermelinda's mute face had the intensity of what she was not saying. When Martim understood, he became happy. She was funny, with that fragile air and her audacity of not speaking; her tremulous courage of just standing there so that he would know.

"When is Dona Vitória coming back?" he finally asked.

The girl tried to answer, but her voice failed her. Her emotion at being understood was strong, as if someone had finally crowned that only way she had of expressing herself. At that moment she was at last getting recognition for her way of life. The instants had gone by, but her heart, as it calmed down, had not been able to give her back her voice. But from the experience of past failures she knew that if she did not fling herself forward with her eyes closed everything would be lost again and she would have to go back and exhaust the talk about ferns. Then, bracing herself against what she would have liked to have been, much more obscure and pretty and not so blunt, she answered aloud, closing her eyes, and made a bridge of herself.

"Vitória will be away a long time. Because Francisco isn't going to meet her in the cornfield until noon, she won't be back until two o'clock for lunch—I heard her say so myself!"

She stopped, amazed. For the first time in her life she had said something straight out. Her heart retreated into her breast, as if to avoid the touch of a disaster.

The man looked at her, curious, attentive, patient. It was true that "not thinking about her" had really been a way of thinking. But until that moment he had managed to keep her inside of him, surrounded by a clear and neutral element, while he himself kept busy at other things. And even if he was not really surprised when the girl proved herself as now, he looked at her with a certain coldness. He seemed to be accusing her of not knowing enough to wait until he himself would summon her to be the focus of his attention. Once more he was being pushed before it was time, just as when Vitória had sent him to the cowshed.

He put the pail of water down on the ground to say something. And Martim's way of telling her that he had understood did not compromise him completely.

"I'll be back from the hill at noon."

But at eleven o'clock Ermelinda was already standing in the sun, serious, her heart beating, the birds flying, and the large tree swaying.

She had finally reached a certain point. What seemed to alarm her was that now there was no question of turning back—too late finally, and it left her heroic. And besides that there was that excited and happy uneasiness, a certain pernicious

(159)

happiness, that secret she held against the world: nobody knew what was happening to her, what a secret.

More than anything else, however, with her heart all dry and painful, she—she, she was playing for high stakes.

If she failed she would come back torn to shreds, holding her shoes in her hands. That was the picture Ermelinda had of how a person failed, even if she did not know what failure was, for she was fighting against immaterial things—she had fallen into the habit of considering as immaterial "things of the spirit" and she did not have a very clear idea of what the spirit was, and it seemed to her that something was happening to her now that was more or less of the spirit and in things like that a person never knew for sure whether he would fail or not; it was a matter of thinking one way or another. But at the same time that she saw herself with her shoes in her hands, she had that intimate warning that she would not fail; that with a sure hand she was going to touch life in one of its vulnerable spots, even if the hand was trembling. The trembling that came from the importance of that moment which was after all—after all—impossible to be substituted by any other. Few times in her life had she had the opportunity to come face to face with what cannot be replaced. "At last I am going to live," she said to herself. But the truth was that it seemed more like a threat.

That did not mean that she was not mistress of herself. Because, even if she was looking neutrally at the importance of that happening, she had time to assume various poses that seemed to reflect that importance. She arranged her hair, as if having it a certain way were indispensable; she made her mouth small and her eyes large, a sketch of an innocent and beloved woman; and she re-created great love affairs with much emotion. All the while she grew perplexed and weak inside. The fact was that she knew she was risking much more than it seemed on the surface; she was gambling with what later on would be a past that would be forever impenetrable.

In order to distract herself, she quickly went over what she would say to him. What, exactly, would she say to him? Something like this, "Fate is a very funny thing." She would say that to him. Not because she was an artificial creature, but because of an experience that could no longer be broken down into facts, she had ended up by knowing that "at least in her case" naturalness did not always hit the mark. When she relied on naturalness, truth was not what came out. Naturalness was for someone who had unlimited time which would give certain words a chance to be spoken eventually. But a person who had just the space of one lifetime would have to condense herself by means of artfulness and tricks. That girl was dying of the fear that she would spend her whole life without ever having had the chance to say certain things that no longer seemed important to her, but they still carried the obstinate idea that one day she would utter them.

After going over what she would say about fate she could not escape returning to the idea that she was playing with what later on would be a past that would be closed to her understanding. Having had some experience, she knew that at the moment things seemed certain and that afterwards they would no longer seem so. And she was already vaguely asking herself—while her restless heart was beating all across the field and her look seemed to share its apprehension and go along—she was vaguely asking herself if later on, when she would have returned to the common days that judge us, if later on she would be capable of understanding herself and would have to pardon herself perhaps. Even now she was already asking herself what her future and inscrutable memories would be like. Because she knew that she was petty: she was not a person who could forgive easily.

Yes, all of that would happen. But she had to risk everything. Since time was short that fearful girl had to know whether love can save, as if she had to tell somebody afterwards. Martim—as Vitória had said in a moment of rage—did not seem to have anything to lose. But—Ermelinda guessed as she suddenly found out in herself—there was no such thing as having nothing to lose. What there was, was risking everything; because underneath the nothingness and the nothingness and the nothingness there we are, and for some reason we cannot lose that. She discovered that right there as she was standing. How that man had managed to push her into the problem of playing for high stakes and risking what we are Ermelinda was fated never to know. Perhaps the very sight of him, for eyes know much more than we do. All that Ermelinda knew was that as a last chance she had to take a gamble. It was then she thought, with a feeling of great uneasiness, that the world is malignant. It gave, yes, but at the same time it said, "Don't come to me afterwards and say that I never gave you anything." What was given was not given through friendship but through hostility.

Standing there startled at eleven o'clock on April 17, she was receiving just as if there had been no kindness in the way the offer had been thrown at her. She who had worked so hard to receive what now she herself did not seem ready to understand. But nothing more depended on her now. She was experiencing that rare instant in which "it still hasn't happened," "it's still going to happen," "it's almost happened already" and which she called, with an effort at understanding, "the instant before the man appears." By giving it a name, she was attempting to appease the world.

The girl passed her hand over her head, her heart all clogged up. From what she was feeling she gathered that her face must be ugly and red; she was deeply sorry that she was not beautiful enough to correspond to the instant when she would belong to a man. "That's not my face!" she rebelled—"that isn't I." In the despair that perhaps she would not be accepted by a man who was so much more elegant than she and so much more of a person than she, she tried once more to make her eyes larger and her mouth heart-shaped. In her opinion they did not make an "ideal couple," and not only was she unable to get that idea out of her head, but she was bothered by it to the point at which she had to hold back her tears; it seemed to her that nature did not approve of them. The day was so beautiful that it just increased her unhappiness.

Oh, if she only had more time. "Nothing should be as quick

as that!" she thought in desolation, shaking her head. She might even have sent for some material from Vila to make a new dress. But how long was that man going to stay on the place? And death? No, she had no time; time was short. The birds flying in the distance seemed to be waiting unhurriedly for her to join them. They were not in any hurry; they were sure. And they flew about, waiting. Waiting for her to join their serene and disturbing freedom . . .

The girl, her feet tight in their shoes, was trembling with fear of herself. She was afraid that she would purify herself so much that she would never need anything else. How do you think about a person who does not need anything? It was monstrous. "I don't want progress," she said fearfully, remembering the phrase of a spiritualist who was all in favor of progress. But what would be left of her if progress were taken away? There would be a whole body; there would be desires—and so much dust. What would her liberated soul do without a body to exist in? She would wail at the windows until living people would say, "What a windy day." And at night she would be the uneasiness of nights imprisoned in the gardens.

It was then, standing there among the thousands of unperceived beats of a heart that did its proper function so well, that she heard that deeper throb which she knew the way one knows a person; a deep and empty throb, as if her heart had tumbled into an abyss. And as always she asked herself, "But is it sickness or life?" Among a thousand butterfly palpitations that tragic throb . . . "I'm going to see a doctor," she decided with the desire of a glutton—"I'm going to see a doctor." The cold within the sun had chilled her.

Oh, just the same, up until now life had not been serious— since she possessed a body that complained it all went to her heart; she had monthly cramps, she had a body in which she was happening. But afterwards? After? The spiritualistic girl was not sure that she was pure enough to just shake off her leaves and be nothing but a thought that someone could sense in the air and,

(163)

according to her, would call it inspiration. It would not be enough for her in her liberation to peer impatiently at the dawn and take sneaky and crafty advantage of that materialization of light—and be. Nor would it be enough for her to look up at the dry sky for days on end hoping to become one with the rain so that she would be able to cry. She had become too accustomed to life; she was used to certain minimal comforts; she needed some place where she could hurt, could bleed if she cut her finger. "Oh dear God, why did you pick me to be a medium and understand and know?" she thought burdened by the weight of her calling. "I'm only human; don't give me tasks that are beyond my capacity." And death was clearly beyond her capacity.

Oh, and if it was just to be a ghost—if they expected her to be one, and she did not know for certain what they expected of her—then she would need a whole house at least and more than one story, she calculated with detail. And with doors that would open to her lack of hand, with halls that would sound beneath her lack of feet—but—but would all that just be set in action by memory? How difficult it would be for her memory. "How in the world did I ever play the piano when I was alive? How in the world?" she would ask herself. So much money spent on lessons and she ended up playing with just one anguished finger. And would her audience be just one living woman possibly frightened by her own imagination?

No, no, she could not think of frightening a woman with her difficult memories. Really—she reflected with that mania of worrying beforehand about details—really, she might be content to find someone's body in which she could sleep. And some flesh where she could explain herself. Because what would hurt most of all would be her own absence. For example, there would be the water in the river just as now—except that she simply would have no more need to drink, the way an amputated leg will bother, even though it has no more need to walk. Would she still have the function of the leg but have no leg? Then—then all that would remain would be to contemplate the water. But would she be her eyes or the countryside itself? And—and what about hearing? Would she not be the sound herself? And little by little, more and more free, could she at least think? Because thought is nothing but the child of things, and she would not have any more things. She would finally be free.

Just as horribly free as the hated countryside. So free that perhaps she would no longer even be able to be that thing which in the meantime was so free and was a bird. Because even a bird was covered with warm feathers and was dirty with all of its intimate blood.

Most of all—just as one day when she was a girl she had turned into a young woman—most of all, one day she would get her first feelings of revulsion like a sign of terrible perfection, like a sign of progress. In the first place, she would probably begin by avoiding warm things so as not to defile herself. She would keep away from everything she needed so that she could exist, be in the world for even just one second. Until she would end up being what would make a person feeling it say, "I am an empty man. I am an empty man."

"Foolishness," she said suddenly, freezing. "When the time comes, I'll figure it out; who knows even if that's the way it happens." But that thought did not ease her mind. "What I need is confidence in myself, that's my trouble." She knew that when the time came she would not figure anything out.

"Oh, what am I thinking about?" Then she became startled. How could she have been able to go so far in the freedom of her thought? And—it occurred to her—that freedom, could it be just the start of another freedom? . . . Because thinking was always the kind of adventure that gave no guarantee . . . Then Ermelinda began to perspire, fully awake now from her daydream, feeling herself standing in the middle of the countryside. The birds were all that was left, the only real proof of her dream. She looked at the birds, wondering, as it all she had left out of a whole dream was a feather in her hand, and she did not know where the feather had come from. She looked at the simple birds and did not understand what was happening to her, like one who wakes up with anxiety and cannot remember the nightmare that brought it on.

Suddenly she did not know about anything. And she asked herself with a start whether the man had really said "noon." And if he really had been speaking about today. And if Martim had really understood her. Or perhaps she had been the one who had not understood him? But, feeling her feet tight inside her shoes, she remembered with relief that when she had put them on she had been sure of the reality that was happening to her. And then she courageously resolved to trust more in her previous certainty than in her present doubt. "Everything is true," she said firmly to herself. "Everything is true," she said now, anchoring herself in that feeling of sin she seemed to have been pursuing all her life. "Evil is being done," she thought strongly, and her eyes darkened with pleasure and vengeance; the sun was burning her—evil, the symbol of being alive. The birds were flying, gliding about in the bright light. She looked out at them as if she were shaking her fist at them. They were the opposite of evil; they were death and beauty and progress.

The sun was making an inferno inside of her head; the flowers were crackling with light and heat. And inside her high-heeled shoes she cursed the day she took them out of the trunk; her tired feet were sweating. All Sundayed-up and unhappy, she waited. To tell the truth, she no longer knew very well what she was waiting for. If a certain point had been reached, she no longer knew very well which point. "But if I were to go away now tomorrow I would suddenly understand it all, and I could not come back again." Then, resigned, she bore it, a little startled. After all, she was a small person put into a big situation. She had wanted the situation to be big, as big as she could stand. And it gave her a feeling of punishment and irretrievable advance. And, as can happen in moments of great importance, the moment itself did not seem to have any importance. She was so much in contact with the moment that she could not even see it. This was the basis that made dreaming superior to reality: when she dreamed she knew quite well what was going on. And still in this terribly real moment the real feeling came from her shoes. And in a mistake of reason that was so common to her, she asked herself if it had been worth so much trouble dreaming for it to end up this way: taking her shoes out of the trunk. She felt like taking them off so she could rest her feet. But she knew, as if it was the result of a great experiment, that if she took them off, her feet, relieved for a minute, would never again fit into the shoes. And, by analogy, if for an instant she were to get out of the situation into which "they had put her," she would never fit into it again. The bones in her toes were sore.

That moment was noon. The flowers were illuminated from within and the red roses were a trumpet-blare; from far off Martim saw the girl as a dark patch in the air.

The garden was lengthened by two or three cutting shadows that the clothesline laid upon the ground. The motionless sun left the plants heavy, in a watchful silence where anything could happen. Martim kept coming closer, with the axe in his hand. The things were waiting, deserted. But the honeysuckle was quivering the way a lizard does before he dies.

Then—looking at the bright, motionless roses and walking toward them, as if looking and walking were the same perfect act, looking at them and what there was red about them—a wave of power and calmness and listening passed through the man's muscles. And a man walking in the sun is a man with a power that only one who is alive can come to know.

From afar he saw her standing in the sun, a woman's face hardened by lights and shadows, with splotches of light on her dress. With interested eyes he asked himself how can it be that a person can put so much into another person. And he thought that because, while he had been working, it seemed that in a short time he had transformed the simple girl into something vague and enormous. Only when he got closer did he discover to his surprise that the girl's face was really cold and colorless. In some way that discovery reconciled him to the fact that she was just herself and not the repository of some great hope. And it seemed to him that the murmur of the cold water among the rocks also ran inside of her. Not that he was in love with her. But it could have been because of love. Attentive, he drew near and looked at her, so snuffed out among the mischievous flowers. Without any disillusion then he saw her exactly as she was.

And she, she looked at the stranger. Before that the girl had had within her a kind of silent heat of communication from her to him, put together from begging, softness, and a kind of confidence. But face to face with him, to her surprise, love itself seemed to have ceased. And thrown into the situation that she had created, feeling herself all alone and intense, she was held there only by determination. The way she had spent a whole exacting week getting ready for a dance, and just as then, left waiting, had taken a taxi and gone to the dance: exactly what she had wanted. Ermelinda was sad and surprised. And just when he was finally right in front of her, she looked at him with resentment, as if he was not the one she had been expecting, and she had been sent an emissary with message: "The other fellow could not come."

Martim had not thought about his own timidity, and he was ill at ease. So there was nothing Olympian between them. It was quite difficult to create the solemn situation that Ermelinda had wanted all her life, and into which the man, without any feeling of it, had hopelessly joined himself. The girl lowered her eyes with a sigh; she was not up to the level of great love affairs. In just that moment when she wanted most to be herself, her whole personality collapsed as if it was not real, and just the same it was, because that invented personality would come to be the maximum of herself. And what she now felt was only a base anxiety that had taken on the form of the ideal she could not reach by at last taking off her shoes. And in a disheartening but yet disconsolate softness she hid behind a smile in which there was no glory; she had wanted so much to have a lover! But now it seemed that she did not want to any more. And even to the truthful point where the question of dying or not had lost all importance, it suddenly seemed to her a faraway and softly uncomfortable thing.

(168)

Why did she not tell the man the truth, then, and go away immediately? She felt the truth as a weight upon her heart, and she did not know what it was—even though she had been thinking more and more, as if all of her was the sleeping heart itself. Why then, if she was to open her mouth, would this one truth not come out in words? Ermelinda did not even part her lips. Not wanting to lie, she would say to him, "I don't love you." But she seemed to know something else: that she did love him, she did love him. It was only that it seemed as if the things in this world were not made for us, it was only that it seemed as if in the meantime we had to compromise with the thing we are born for, it was only that it suddenly seemed as if love was the desperate, clumsy shape that living and dying take on just as if even in that very moment the absolute were abandoning us. And the truth, still untransmittable in her heart, was the weight with which we love and do not love. And yet, the solution for all of that was precisely love. "Don't offend me," she thought, looking at him, less to protect herself than to save what they both had created almost outside of themselves and which they were offering each other at that moment.

So Ermelinda only realized that she loved him when he took a step and she thought he was going away. With a start, she stretched out a hand to hold him back. And she knew that if he went away, she would not be able to bear it. She saw then that the truth was that she loved him; she resigned herself to not understanding. Then she smiled at him, fawning, hopeless.

Intimidated, the man sensed that he had to do something. Then he took her hand. The woman's hand was freezing cold.

"Are you afraid of me?" He was sincerely startled, because after all, the girl was the one who had offered herself to him.

"Yes," she said as her voice cracked, abandoning pretenses. "But don't get upset over my fear," she said wearily, calming him down. "I'm not upset, you see," she said as if she were the mother of both of them, or pardoning nature.

"Afraid of what?" he asked, very curious, prepared for something trivial.

"I don't know," she said confused. "I don't know, afraid because—because you're made a different way from me, I don't know . . ."

"What?"

"Oh," she said desperately, "but it has to be just like that! Of course! Otherwise how could it be?"

"Be what?" the man asked stupefied.

"Oh, Lord!" she said crying, "I mean that you're a man and I'm not a man, and that's just it!" she exclaimed, making a great effort at conciliation.

"Oh," he said, puzzled.

Martim's curiosity, increased now by ignorance, was growing blindly, instinctively. He had let go of her hand when he had felt it so cold, but this time he took it again without effort. And the little hand was light between his hands hardened by those calluses of which he was proud and which were there like a stigma. His pride in himself filled him with emotion then. And with pride he was able to take that hand with assurance.

When a man and a woman are close, and the woman feels that she is a woman and the man feels that he is a man—is that love? The sun, ninety million miles away, was burning both their heads. "Oh, free me from my mystery!" she implored him inside herself. And as if everything were entering into the same serene and violent harmony, life became so beautiful that they looked into each other's eyes with the tension of a question, the incomprehensible eyes of a man and a woman. Sometimes people feel like that when they are all alone and with the question. But it does not hurt—or if it does hurt, that is the way in which things are alive. "If you knew how much I love you," the girl looked at him, "and it's for ever." She, who at least once in her life wanted to be able to say "for ever."

And Martim? When they went into the woodshed, after going through hedge after hedge as through so many doors, what he loved in her had already become mixed in with the freshness there was among the shining flowers, mixed in with the smell of rotting wood, the good smell of the damp earth that comes from logs—as if he had been thrown into his first human love. In the woodshed the incandescent flowers lost their sway. There it was like a stable, and people became slower and larger, like animals who do not accuse or pardon themselves. He looked at her, and she seemed to have been storing her body in a cool, dark place, like a fruit that must get through an adverse season without damage. There were golden hairs on her arms and that gave her the value of golden things.

But it was certain that in the disorder of a first encounter there was a moment in which they both finally forgot what they were painfully trying to copy for reality; the moment had not been prepared for either of them. It was a gift of nature in which both needed to know why the other one was the other one, and they forgot to say "please"; it was a moment in which, without abuse, they both took for themselves what was owed them, not stealing anything from the other one. That was more than they would have dared to imagine; that was love with all its selfishness, and without which there would have been no giving. One gave to the other the need to be loved, and if there was a certain sadness in submitting to the law of the world, that submission was also their dignity. It was selfishness which gave itself entirely. And although the girl's desire to give was greater than what she had to give she did not know what to give him. She remembered mothers giving to their children but she did not feel maternal toward that man. With the great strength of the irrational she wanted to give him something, simply so that ultimately she could go beyond what one can do and in the end break the great mystery of being only one. She gave him her completely empty thought within which her whole self was contained. In the wanting to give, rather than in the giving itself, something had been accomplished. She had gained the minimum destiny that the brief insect also needs.

It was with an obedient and thankful air, like that of a woman, that she told Martim she was going to mend his clothes. Stubborn above all, what she wanted was to project herself into the safe environment that the man had ultimately created by living in the woodshed—spurs on the floor, the scythe, muddy boots, a world that could be touched. As she calmly picked up the clothes to be mended, she felt a happiness much too minute for her capacity to feel, but it was a question of what she wanted to be: concrete. Then she looked at him. Thank you for being real, her open eyes said.

The man did not understand, but he puffed out his chest a little. As for her, now she could use the word love without lying, and with ingenuous hope, as if she did not know what it was. Because in one perfect moment, the world had become whole again, even with its ancient mystery—except that this time, before the enigma had closed, Ermelinda had put herself inside of it, just as enigmatic as the enigma. Then the girl got up, as if giving the man an order to go away and leave her alone.

"I belong to you," was what was being said in the proud and mute way in which she stood, serene and without any humility.

He seemed to understand; he did not want to have anybody belong to him, and he whistled as a cover-up, then he looked down at his own shoes. A woman was always more brazen than a man; he became embarrassed. She was noble. "She got what she wanted," Martim thought, offended in his own chastity, and covering up again with a listless whistle. "I belong to you," was being said tyrannically in the way she was standing; he grunted in agreement, uncomfortable, wanting to be free of her. Her shoulders were slender and fragile; her skin was like a child's, and as if he had shattered the girl's present, there was something of the past in her. She was soft around the waist. "My God," the man said to himself—"she's a ghost." He was comically embarrassed at her fragility. "Delicate, but a virago like the rest of them," he thought with malice, but he did not think that what he had said was funny, not even fun; what he really felt was a kind of pride in her—he admired her. Women always stretched things out longer than necessary and right away would start raising a family. And he was proud to be her victim: that was the constrained homage that the man succeeded in paying her.

"Thank you for my liking you," the girl's look also said; but that the man did not understand, and he only blinked his eyes. Then, as if he had had time to sense it better, he nodded in agreement, now that for one instant she had taken charge of both their destinies.

And perhaps because his submission to her was the way in which he had made her submit, Martim became powerful and alive as he left the woodshed, with a touch of insolence.

Chapter 7

MARTIM SIGHED DEEPLY, as if until now he had been wearing a gag. It was sweet and powerful for a man to go out and for a woman to stay behind. That was no doubt the way things should be. Going down to the water of the river to wet his face he felt pride and calmness. Now that he had had a woman it seemed natural to him that everything should become understandable and within reach. The meadow was broad: a multitude of brilliant points against an obscure and uncertain background. Within his reach was the water, which the sun had turned into a hard mirror, and that was how it should be. He approved of the way the land was. Without modesty, like a man who is naked, he knew that he was an initiate. Facing the water, which was cutting him down with its scythe-like brilliance, everything was his, and a stupid happiness filled his head; in his arms he could still feel the weight that a submissive woman has. Initiated as a man who is alive. Even if he did not have time to be anything more than a man who is alive. It was a rare instant, and with no feeling of vanity he recognized it as such; before it vanished he touched it with all his soul so that his soul might at least have touched the enormous reality.

"I wonder what the woman is doing all alone in the woodshed?" he thought, and he wondered what she wanted of him. The lucidity that was exaggerated by happiness made him understand that she was waiting for a word from him, and that she was tied to him by the last hope. And who was she? That had suddenly become important, who was she? Because if he had been locked in a cell with just a blade of grass in his hand, that blade of grass was everything that a whole field could tell him. And if he had taken a woman who was ugly and ignored, a woman among thousands of women, the whole world was in her, hoping for hope in him. But what could he give her except mercy? It was at that instant that uncertain and badly orchestrated, there crept into him for the first time the ancient word "mercy." But he had not heard it clearly.

Because when he was thinking about Ermelinda he had begun to think about his own wife, listening to the radio as time slipped away, and receiving presents with a sigh. "Never look a gift horse in the mouth," she had said with a sigh. And thinking about his wife he thought about his son, about whom he had never wanted to think directly. He thought about his son with that first and happy pain, as if having Ermelinda in his arms had finally given him his son. That son he had produced with such care, and who had turned out so handsome, and who was quite tall for his age. And he thought of going to the mulatto woman's daughter the first time he spotted her spying on him, he needed a child so much.

And with his son a love for the world had assaulted him. He now became quite moved by the richness of what existed; he became moved with tenderness toward himself. How very much alive and powerful he was! How kind he was! Strong and muscular! "I am one of those people who understand and pardon!" that was exactly what he was, yes, wrought up, missing his son. The sun had halted and was getting deeper and deeper into him; love for himself gave him a grandeur he could no longer contain and which stripped him of the remains of his modesty. Next to the sparkling water, nothing seemed impossible to him. Now that he had taken the first step and through his son had reached that point at which pain was mixed with fierce joy, and joy was painful because that rapid point must have been the goad of life and his meeting with himself—then, just the way a dog's soul barks, irrepressible, he said: Ah! to the water.

Ah! he said with love and anguish and ferocity and pity and admiration and sadness, and all of that was his joy.

But why was it not enough for him, then? Why was it not enough just to exclaim? Because it happened that he wanted the word. As long as he was who he was he would be prisoner of his

(175)

own breathing, waiting for the word to carry him to the image of the world, waiting for it to join him to himself, living with that word on the tip of his tongue, with understanding about to be revealed, in that tension which ends up becoming confused with life, and which really is life itself; it happened that he wanted the word.

And now that he knew the oscillation of a human love; he had never been as close to it. The weeds trembled it. The water sparkled it. The black sun expressed it in its own way. And the meadow became more tense under the man's gaze.

Why did he not say the word, then? The sun had halted. The water was cloudy. Martim was facing it. Why did he not say it? The fact was that everything was perfect and he was not needed. The hard glass of the water looked at him and he was looking. And everything was so splendid and motionless, so complete in itself, that the man did not wet his face; he did not dare touch the water and interrupt the great stasis with a gesture. Everything was bursting with silence. With the smell of warm grass that the wind brought from far off he breathed in the revelation, uselessly trying to think about it. But the word, the word, he still did not have it. The foot, the foot with which a man takes a step, he did not have it. He knew that it had been done. But he lacked the knowledge of what it is that a man does. If not, what good would he get from the freedom he had attained?

The twisted sun was burning his head, leaving him tranquil and mad. It was then, under the truth of the sun, that he was finally not embarrassed to want the maximum. And through his love for his son, he decided that the maximum could be reached through mercy.

Could that be the word? If it was, he did not understand it. Could that be the word? His heart beat furiously, dispirited.

Not mercy transformed into kindness, but the deep mercy transformed into action. Because just as God wrote directly by means of crooked lines, in the same way great pity and love flowed through the lines of mistakes in action. Once a person had that strange capacity: that of having pity for another man, as if he himself were of a separate species. Because at that point he did not seem to want to rebuild only for himself alone. He wanted to rebuild for other people.

Martim had just "drawn back the curtains."

Had he just discovered gunpowder? It makes no difference; every man is his own opportunity.

But through what action would love flow? From monstrous thought to monstrous thought, he calculated with lucidity that if he could obtain a new way of loving the world, he would transform it in some way. The most important thing that could happen in a world made up of people—would it not be the birth of a new way of loving, the birth of an understanding? It was. Everything for Martim was unexpectedly coming into harmony . . .

Then, intoxicated with himself, dragged along by the madness to which logical thought can lead, he calmly thought the following: if he could reach that method of understanding he would change men. Yes, he was not ashamed of that thought because he had already risked everything. "Would it change men even if it took a few centuries?" he thought without understanding himself. "Am I a preacher?" he thought, half-fascinated. The fact was that in the meantime, however, he really had nothing to preach—which embarrassed him for an instant. But just for an instant, because a moment afterwards he was again so full of himself that it was a pleasure to see.

Then he dropped the rest of his prudence, and without any shame at all he thought more or less the following: even if he spoke about his "drawing back the curtains" to just one person, that person would tell another, as in a "chain of good will." Or then—he thought boldly—that person, transformed by the knowledge, would be observed by another, and that one by another, and so on. And in a while there would be surreptitious news in the air, the way fashion spreads without anyone's being obliged to follow it. Because what are people if not the consequence of a way of understanding and loving that belongs to someone already lost in time? "That was the way he lived." One person would tell another, as if it were the password he had been waiting for. "That was the way he lived," the rumor would pass around.

Martim had finally made a pronouncement—except that he was constrained a little by the sudden ease with which it had come. But who could tell if that was not the way it was: that after it has been spoken, truth is easy? The obscure plan then seemed perfect to him, like a perfect crime.

And full of himself, bursting with sun like a toad, the task seemed grand and simple to him—as now he mixed water and cement, preparing mortar for the well. The cauldron of the saints might be burning over his head, but he was concentrating on the sandals. His urgency was tranquil. Not an urgency that would make him want to skip stages, but an urgency like that of nature: without the loss of one instant, when a pause is in itself an advance. He mixed the cement with exactitude, with an uninterrupted urgency, just as the thousand shudders make up the vastness of the silence and the silence goes along. "The thing is progressing," he thought.

He found that thought of his fine and his feelings fine too. He became emotional and serious; he stopped working for an instant. "I offer this thing I feel in homage to my mother," he thought vaguely, already a little absentminded. Then, having come by chance into closer contact with what he had thought, he found it "silly." But then he was very sorry that he had found it silly and said to himself, offended, "Let's not turn into such a beast that we think everything is foolishness." Since foolishness was a very long word which quickly lost its meaning he was finally left with nothing but a taste of nothingness in his mouth. That alerted him to how necessary it was to be careful not to be vague, which was a legitimate temptation—but if a person did not specialize, as they say about doctors, he would never get anywhere. It was very difficult to be global and at the same time try to maintain a shape. He could not afford to lose sight of himself.

(1 7 8)

As he began to concentrate, a certain plan began to take shape; the cement was taking on consistency. He applied himself with perfection to his work, peaceful hours passed.

And the first cooler breeze finally blew.

So when Ermelinda pushed open the door of the woodshed, afternoon had arrived. Like a continuation of the shadows of the room the whole afternoon had fallen apart and could be smelled in the quivering shadow of roots with ants upon them. The girl's eyes were broad, tranquil, avenged. She had managed to absorb the security of the man to use against the countryside, and armed with her talisman she looked out with a serene challenge; the countryside was nothing but a larger woodshed where a thousand trees had room to lose themselves in the distance. The world was a place—only that and nothing more. And the countryside had lost is lack of limits. Without any effort she passed across the multitude of grasses; the flowers had now been tamed. There were no wrinkles showing on her face. She looked like an Indian woman carrying a jug on her head, balancing herself so she could balance the jug. Nothing contradicted her. There are moments like that too.

Chapter 8

THAT NIGHT Martim had an excellent idea that would end up being just the opposite. What really happened was that later on the man had occasion to compare the excellence of his idea and its subsequent disillusionment with a round fruit that he had once eaten—a pomegranate—and which had proven hollow to his teeth. And as the only reward it gave him, an instant of absorbed meditation and a contact with experience.

On that night, then, he lit the lantern, put on his glasses, took a sheet of paper, a pencil; and like a schoolboy he sat down on the bed. He had had the very sensible idea of putting his thoughts in order, summing up the results that he had reached that afternoon—there had been a time that afternoon when he had finally understood what he wanted. And now, just as he had learned to calculate with numbers, he got ready to calculate with words. The exaltation that had come to him with the afternoon sun had already left him now. Now he was a slow man who applied himself, the slow face a woman has when she threads a needle. His face concentrated on the trouble at hand.

It came to him with some surprise that his thought proved to be as crude as the thick fingers gripping the pencil. As a start of the conversation, the pencil seemed too slim for his resolution, because that was too fat with decision. He did not know that in order to write he had to start by abdicating strength and heading into the chore as one who has nothing to wish for. The dark smoke rose up from the lantern and enveloped the picture of St. Crispin and St. Chrispinian. Every so often the sound of the piano reached the woodshed and the silence made it far away. Ermelinda was playing. Time was passing.

But in the near darkness of the woodshed, without the advantage of the afternoon's intoxication, the man seemed to be disappointed because he had lost the meaning of what he had wished to write. And he hesitated and bit the end of the pencil, like a farmhand who was embarrassed because he had to translate the growth of wheat into figures. He twisted the pencil again and he kept on doubting, captured by an unexpected respect for the written word. He thought that what he would put down on the piece of paper would become something definitive, he did not have the nerve to scribble the first word. His defensive feeling was that as soon as he wrote the first word it would be too late—so treacherous was the power of the simplest word over the broadest thought. Actually, the only thing about that man's thought was that it was broad, and that did not make it very useful. At the same time he seemed to feel a curious repulsion toward making it concrete, a little offended even, as if something dubious had been proposed to him.

And he bravely made ready to get started and wet the point of the pencil with his tongue.

And deflated, with his glasses on, he found that everything that had seemed ready to be said had evaporated now that he wanted to say it. What had filled his days with reality had turned into nothing face to face with the order to describe it. It was obvious that the man could not accomplish anything and that, like so many others, all he could feel was the intention, and Hell is paved with intentions. But when it came to writing he was as naked as if they had not let him bring anything along. Not even his own experience. And that man with his glasses on suddenly just felt humiliated as he faced the blank piece of paper, as if the chore was not just jotting down what already existed, but was the creation of something that would exist.

Had there been something wrong in the way he had sat down on the bed, or maybe in the way he held the pencil; some mistake that had placed him face to face with a greater difficulty than he had deserved or had aspired to? He seemed to be waiting more for something to be given him than for something to come out of himself, and so he kept on waiting painfully. He shifted his position on the edge of the bed a bit and took austere care to reduce himself to just a man who was sitting down and was about to take some notes on what he had been thinking.

(1 8 1)

And he became surprised once more; there was no denying that he did not know how to write. He smiled self-consciously. Like a docile illiterate, there he was in the situation of asking someone: write a letter to my mother and tell her what I am thinking about. "What the devil is happening to me?" He suddenly became upset. He had picked up the pencil with the modest intention of jotting down his thoughts so they might become clearer. That was all he had meant to do! he claimed in irritation, and there was no reason why he should be having so much trouble.

But just as in the fables in which the distracted prince happens to touch the one forbidden rose in the garden and to his astonishment has disenchanted the whole garden, so Martim had carelessly executed among a thousand innocuous gestures some familiar act that involuntarily had brought him face to face with something greater. The lantern was giving off a thread of black smoke. He looked at the woodshed as it wavered in the dim light. The walls were hesitating. The wind was beating at the door. And around him there blew the emptiness in which a man finds himself when he is about to create. Desolate, he had brought on that great solitude.

And like an old man who had never learned to read he measured the distance that was separating him from the word and the distance that was suddenly separating him from himself. Between the man and his own nakedness was there some possible step that could be taken? But if it was possible there was still the strange resistance that he was offering. Because there had just been awakened in him that inner fright of which a person is made.

Because he did not believe in what could not be explained he creased his brows as if that would help to thread the needle. What was he waiting for with his hand at the ready? Well, he had an experience, he had a pencil and a piece of paper, he had the intention and the desire—no one ever had more than that. And still it was the loneliest thing he had ever done. And he could not do it that way, and not being able to do it had taken on the grandeur of a Prohibition.

And only when he thought about breaking the Prohibition did he retreat, opposing again the immaterial resistance to a hard instinct, cautious again, as if there was a word that said what a man is. . . . That missing word which sustained him nonetheless. That nonetheless was he. That nonetheless was the thing that would die only because the man had died. That nonetheless was his own energy and the way he breathed. The word that was the action and intention of a man. And which he not only could not babble, but somewhere in himself did not even want to . . . With vital prudence he kept it safe inside himself. And by only imagining that he could say it he closed himself up in austerity, insurmountable, as if he had already risked himself too far. Susceptible all of a sudden he had fallen into that sacred zone a man will not let a woman touch, but where two men at dusk will sometimes sit in silence on the stoop. Within that solitary zone the choice would be to let himself be touched by humility and debasement—or shelter the integrity of a man who does not speak or act. He had fallen into the thirst that had always made something personal out of his life. And which had made the act of "doing," giving himself perhaps, the one impossible action. A coward before his own greatness, he balked.

With no word to write Martim meanwhile resisted the temptation of imagining what would happen to him if his strength might be stronger than his prudence. "And if I suddenly had the strength?" he asked himself. But he could not fool himself; whatever he wrote would only be something he had written because he could not write "the other thing." Even within his own ability what he would say would simply come from the impossibility of saying something else. The Prohibition was that much deeper . . . Martim had surprised himself.

Obviously that man had ended up by falling into a depth that he had always sensibly avoided.

And the choice became deeper yet; either keep the sacred zone intact and live off it, or betray it by what he certainly would come to do, and it would be simply this: the unreachable, like one who could not drink the water of the river except by filling up the hollow of his own hands—but it would not be the silent waters of a river; it would not be the frigid movement, or the delicate greed with which water tortures stones; nor would it be the thing a man is in the afternoon beside the river after he has had a woman. It would be the hollow of his own hands. He would rather have the silence intact then. Because little can be drunk; and one lives off what is left abandoned.

So from painful approach to painful approach—because Martim had in his progress a feeling of suffering and conquest—he ended up wondering if all that he had finally come to think, when he had been thinking, might not also have come simply from his incapacity to think about something else; we overuse allusions as the end point of objectivity. And maybe his whole life had been nothing but an allusion. Could that be the end point of our making things concrete: trying to allude to what we silently know? Martim thought about all of that, and he did a lot of thinking.

And there he was. What he had just meant to do was take some notes, nothing else. And the unsuspected difficulty of it all was that he had had the presumption to try to put into words the blink with which two insects can copulate in flight. But who can tell—he asked himself then in the absolute darkness of the absurd—who can tell if that is not the ultimate expression, the way we describe insects coming to glory in the air. Who can tell whether the high point of that description is only and precisely in the wanting of it . . . (And so he was saving the value of his intention, the intention he had not known how to transform into action.) Who can tell whether our objective was the fact that we are the process itself? Then the absurdity of that truth enveloped him. And if that is how it is, oh God—the great resignation one must have in order to accept the fact that our greatest beauty escapes us, if we are only the process.

In that way then, sitting there quietly, Martim had failed. The paper was blank. His brow was furrowed and attentive.

But who knows what happens in a person? Because he was failing and he could not call his failure suffering, even if the disillusion and the offense he had received had flowered right under his nose, the flesh allows so few feelings? But how can one call suffering the fact that he was passing through the truth of the Prohibition as through the eye of a needle? How could he even revolt against the truth? He was his own impossibility. He was he. He had arrived at that point of great and tranquil anguish: that man was his own Prohibition.

Suffering? He thought as his face was irremediably offended opposite the blank paper. But how was it possible not to love the Prohibition itself since he had driven it as far as he could go, since he had pushed it even to that last resistance, where . . . where the only irrational solution was the great love? When a man is cornered, the great love is the only thing that occurs to him. Suffering? A man can know only by being unable. A man is measured by his lacks, after all. And to touch the great lack was perhaps a person's aspiration. Would touching the lack be an art? That man enjoyed his impotence in the way a man recognizes himself. He was taking frightful advantage of what he was. Because for the first time in his life he knew how much he was. And it pained him like the root of a tooth.

A great sweetness enveloped him, the way it does when one suffers. He could not face the blank paper without feeling pain. Where had his action failed?

But had it really failed? Because compensation was also predestined. He could not get over the admiration he had for the perfection of the Prohibition. Because, in a perfect balance, it happened that if he did not have the words, he did have the silence. And if he did not have the action, he did have the great love. A man was not meant to know anything; but he knew which way to turn, toward the sunset, for example. A man had the great resource of position. If only he was not afraid of being silent.

Oh, not suffering. Because in the impossibility of his creating he had not been through the worst; he had not been plundered. In everything else, that man had been mistaken or had been swindled; they had robbed him or expertly he had done the

robbing. But in his passage through the great emptiness, for the
first time in his life, he had not tricked or been tricked. The
thing was clean. Because it was a question of a person the neat
result had been the completion of the experience of not being
able. It even seemed to him that there were few people who had
the honor not to have been able. Then, with a feeling of genius,
born out of his pain perhaps, he knew that the most accurate
result was to fail. "Suffering?" he thought with an offended face.
But how can we not love the Prohibition since its fulfillment is
our task? The involuntary writer reflected on this painfully.

Martim had now begun to get enmeshed in a curious feeling
that he had attained something extraordinary. He had passed
through the mystery of wanting. It was as if he had touched the
pulse of life. He was startled at the spontaneous miracle of his
body's being enough body to want a woman, and his body's
being enough body to want food—now he had touched the
source of all that, and of life. He had wanted . . . In a deep
and general way, he had wanted.

In a way that was a little too deep, to his disadvantage.
Because there he was, confused, not understanding why he had
the feeling of having fulfilled himself without having taken a
step outside his own personal terrain. He looked at the empty
paper. Kindness then came over Martim as it comes over one
who suffers. In his abandonment he felt the temptation to call
upon God. But as he did not have the habit or the belief, he
feared provoking so great a presence, more careful now not to
touch the forbidden rose in the garden.

"I don't know how to write," he said thereupon.

He had stopped. He had the impression that he had escaped
by just a trice. His relief was great that he had escaped un-
scathed out of the empty darkness, even if he also felt that none
of his future thoughts would be untouched by this real cowardice of his, which had only been revealed just now. No heroic act
of his would be completely free of that experience, which had
immediately become old, like wisdom.

He took off his glasses, he rubbed his tired eyes; he put his glasses back on. And relieved, finally abandoning what his spirit had refused to give him, he felt ready for a humbler task. Modest, applied, near-sighted, he simply made a note of: "Things I must do."

Writing that phrase he was not the same person who had faced up to possibility and its frightening promise. He was someone who had withdrawn from the truth—and which one could it have been? never more now! oh, he would never know again!—and he had dedicated himself to a truth that was so small that already it had found its limits in talent; but it was the only truth within his reach, the only action within his reach. Humble, knowing with remote surprise that he had been "near," but that he had managed to escape, the man became even more humble. So that even a phrase as modest as "Things I must do" seemed too ambitious to him. And with an act of contrition he took the risk. He wrote further: "Things I must try to learn: Number 1."

Then it happened that Martim came to know what the first thing was that he must try to learn, but he could not give it a name. He even thought that he would only get to know the name the instant when he would obtain the thing, as if a person found out what he was looking for only when he found it.

Good, the much simpler reality is that it had taken effort for that man to try to keep himself at the level he had reached that afternoon beside the river. Now he was reduced to his own proportions and without the help of the greatness of the sun. He had lost the faith and the motive. And he looked at the poor woodshed as if it were something strange. Even then he insisted on continuing, and next to "Number 1" to try to learn, he wrote "That," because what he was managing to do was to allude. And he read the phrase over again.

And then it was—then it was he had his first great emotional pleasure, the kind that fate brings on when it makes one love what he has done. The phrase was still wet and had the grace of a truth. And he liked it with the excitement of creation. He recognized in it everything that he had wanted to say! Besides, he found the phrase to be perfect in the resistance it offered him. "That is as far as I can go!" And it seemed to him that the phrase had touched his very insides, he felt its resistance with ecstasy. It was true that a second later, with a glance, Martim saw to his distaste the great mistake of a writer: it had been his own limitations that had reduced the phrase to what it was, and perhaps the resistance that it offered was the resistance of his own incapacity. But as he was a difficult person to defeat he thought the following, "It doesn't matter, because if at least with that phrase I just suggested that the thing is much greater than I could say, then I really accomplished a lot. I made an allusion!" And then Martim was happy the way an artist is. The word "That" contained in itself everything he had not managed to say!

Then he wrote: "Number 2: how to link 'that' which I may know with the social state of things."

And that was what he wrote. Having lost the practice of thinking, and having lost the vocabulary, he could not come up with any other expression that would show what he wanted to say except this, "social state of things," It seemed quite good and clear to him, and it had an erudite touch about it that Martim had always wanted to have. Erudition, being external, became mixed up with the basic idea he had had of objectivity, and it always gave him a feeling of satisfaction to hit the nail on the head.

When the man reread his work, his eyes blinking from sleepiness now, reality made him make an about-face, and he came upon a piece of paper that had the physical and humble concretization of a thought, and he gave a long and empty laugh—where for the first time, a sense of the ridiculous appeared, and it undermined his grandeur for the first time. That man who had been trying to build up his grandeur and the grandeur of others. Then in a painful defense he began to laugh, a little against his will and showing his own self a little, and a little out of masochism, and a little to show that he was a martyr who was making believe that he was not suffering but was

(188)

waiting for God to guess with remorse and pity that his son was suffering and he was only laughing out of heroism, a little so that God would repent as he offered him his disguised suffering as a slap, in the way of one who says he does not hurt but hurts and who is sanctified in his pain. Then Martim ran into a reality less flattering and less possible to dramatize. He ran into the fact that he was just a confused person who had forgotten the books that he had read; but out of them there had remained many doubtful images that he was pursuing, their terminology was outmoded, and he had stayed with his first readings. He really was a man of slow comprehension and not very intelligent. Why not admit it?—a man with a stumbling way of thinking, an ill-informed person and one who did not know what to do with the little information he had, and who, now unprotected, was obliged to rely on himself. This made him go on living by rediscovering gunpowder, as if a person had only one way out: himself. "At least that's the way it is today," and then he was laughing, which was foolish, because not even God was offended at the mistake of having created what he, Martim, was. Because God made up for it with more efficient results.

Out of pure self-martyrdom he laughed again. And as he had not laughed for a long time he began to cough; he gagged. Then he stopped laughing because the trail of saliva had gone up into his nose and had given him the disagreeable suggestion of a physical mistake: it was as if his body was failing too. He blew out the lantern and lay down.

But sleep had disappeared with the laughter. And he was restless in the dark. The rose that he had inadvertently touched in the garden had left him stamping like a horse whose gallop was being reined in. At that point things had lost their material size in some way. No one could ever have faced for even one second the emptiness from which things come without being caught forever in the restlessness of want. Goaded by the desire to get close, he was indomitable and daring. "What's wrong with me?" He was puzzled, alert, sniffing things out. A minute later he recognized that the state he was in was one of action or of love. It so happened that he could do neither. "I'm not used to fighting without getting hurt." He avoided the creative act; and the night was empty, without a woman's love. "I've got insomnia," he said then to his wife in a complaining and accusing tone.

Martim did not know what to do with his desire or how to apply it. From one thought to another—most of them were getting away from him—he reflected that even if he had failed in the creation of the future, he still had the past that was already created. With an intense desire he finally wanted to have something in his hand. And that seemed to him to be the easiest and least sensitive part of disillusion: the clay out of which it had already happened was at least a material from which one could begin. Then, with the same attitude of severe good will with which he had tried to create his plan of action for the future, he went back to his memory. "Oh, remember that trees exist and there are children and that bodies and tables exist," the man said to himself, trying to reach a maximum of objectivity.

And he really did become objective and clear. But what had he succeeded in doing? Pebbles—he looked curiously at the pebbles of facts, centennial, hard pebbles, unswallowable, irre-ducible, imperceptible. He was drowning in a sea of pebbles. Not only reality but memory too belongs to God. The man rolled over in the dark. He had been held prisoner within the structure of his own past. He had never left the world, he had never entered the world. It was always the same pebbles; the roulette wheel had always been spun, and improvisation was impossible! Those were the elements—the ones already there—and all at once they had closed the door, and nothing could come in or go out. And if he wanted to make a new construction for the future he would have to destroy the first one so that he would have some pebbles to use, because nothing more could come into the game and nothing else could leave. The material of his life was precisely that. But, he thought, "what infinite variations! All with the same pebbles." One could go to a fortune-teller; she would shuffle the pebbles, a pebble would pop out, and she would say mysteriously behind her glasses and her wig, before she died of cancer, "I'm looking at a pebble."

"But the fact is," he reflected with an intense desire to stop thinking about the future—"the fact is that there is at least something definitely organized about those pebbles. And that is where we fit in. True, sometimes we fit in with an arm that was paralyzed in the building or with an eye closed by the hardened mortar that dried too quickly; but something is at least definitively organized. And even if we just barely fit into it, the fact is that we do fit. What shall we do? Use the same pebbles to build another definitive organization, demolishing the earlier one first? Or shall we sensibly make up our minds to fit into the first one? It is true that in order to fit into the first we shall have to eat less. Because if we get fat we will not fit, and if we grow we will not fit; and we will be left there with pants that are too short, staring meditatively at our exposed feet. But we will be careful. It is a question of being careful. Oh, how good it is that we are very careful. Until we forget how much we have grown and got fat lately, and we give an absent-minded yawn, and the construction is too short. That is what is called being upset."

It was what that man called being upset. Had that man committed a crime because he had grown too fat? Martim rolled over with a cramp in his stomach; he did not fit. At that point his thought had begun to echo inside a church and that gave him a respect that was made of love and respect in its true meaning. And just as every time our feet make noise and for some reason we instinctively try to walk quietly the man now tried to advance on tiptoe. His thoughts had taken on the echoing grandeur of a nightmare, and he suddenly struggled against his old distaste for thought. Oh, would he never reach beyond just being a creator of truths?

Until, fortunately, he perceived that the creation of the world was giving him a stomach ache. Then, happy with the fact that finally he could give in to a pain, he lay down on his belly and, with the warmth of that contact, began to fall asleep.

But that night had many lessons. One must be patient; sometimes a night can be long.

The fact was that in the shadows the birds had perceived the acidity of dawn, and long before it broke through for a person, they were breathing it in; and they had begun to wake up. There was one bird especially that drove Martim almost crazy. It was one who would call for its mate in the dark. Patiently and calmly it called and it called, until things reached the point at which Martim jumped up and shoved open the window. At the open window he was met with the sudden silence of the bird. More with his nostrils than with his eyes he perceived that the darkness was unstable and that the bird was already living in a dawn that for him, Martim, was still in the future. And in a vague way it seemed somewhat symbolic and satisfactory to him. He turned around and lay down again, and the patient bird began once more. The calm song of summons drove the man into a paroxysm; he covered his ears.

After covering his ears he could not hear the bird.

It was only then that the man realized that he was really burning to hear it. It seems that so many times people love a thing so much that they try to deny it, so to speak, and so many times it is the belovéd face that makes us so ill at ease. And it occurred to Martim, who was trying so hard to find explanations for his crime, that he might have fled from the world because of a love which he had not been able to bear.

Now defeated and weak, he took his hands away from his ears, suddenly accepting the beauty of the pebbles, accepting the maddening song of the bird, accepting the fact that dawn preceded the perception of dawn. The man began to listen sentimentally to the plaintive bird. And more than that: with a little timidity, Martim was also plaintive. He smiled in the dark, amused and hurt, because Ermelinda was not a name that one went about shouting, nor would his manliness allow him to perch up in a tree. And still, if he were to call her, she was quite capable of coming. But he did not love her to the point that he wanted her to come. Martim smiled again, quite sad. Since his stomach ache had returned he rolled over on his belly again, and this time he fell asleep.

That night had been a great experience, one of those that cannot be explained in a court of law because words are lacking and a man could be constrained because, in the end, he has the obligation of being responsible for what he says, of knowing what he is talking about, and of understanding what is happening to him.

The truth is that he did not give up entirely. In his agitated sleep, that stubborn man tried to build in his dreams another house with the same stones, since now there were no others to be used. In every piece of the construction that he attempted he would forget something outside or then put something too far inside, and the construction would collapse. And then, for the first time, the man seemed to see some advantage in the fact that the stones were harder than our imagination, that they were immutable and intransigent with that human nature that stones have; the nature that is our own nature. For the first time he was relieved that the creation of the world was not his task. In his construction he suddenly saw himself as a man who had built a room without a door and was a prisoner inside.

In his agitated sleep he sat up in bed once or twice. But his haste was the useless haste of a man on a train that he is not running. Sitting on the bed he was devoured by a thought that had not been so strong during the day: that the time was near when Vitória would go to Vila and see the German. Time was passing, time was passing, time was passing; and the future was ripening in a way that could be defined.

Chapter 9

ONLY WHEN Vitória went again with Francisco to the cornfield did Ermelinda have a chance to put in an appearance with a basket of food.

"For a picnic in the woodshed," she said, waiting for him to give a sign of joy at the surprise.

But he murmured dully something about the mania women have for picnics, and for an instant she shriveled up in disappointment. Just for an instant she had to make the vague effort of pretending that "everything was all right." Because even though she ate all the sandwiches herself she recovered rapidly, and now she was talking volubly, intoxicated with the joy that "whether they wanted it or not," it was a picnic. Without blinking, Martim cynically received several spurts of saliva on his face. For some reason, he tried to be ironical and keep himself above the situation.

But it was really a relief to him to have that woman who gave herself so easily, as if having her at his disposal were a milestone he had already reached. He had been in command up to that point. The more foolish she was, the more she belonged to him. She compensated for the difficulty that Martim was having with himself. And with a relief that he realized must have been the one man had felt when woman had finally been created, a relief that at last brought him freedom and had at last made it impossible for him to be formidable, he smiled and scarcely listened to her. The girl was one of those women who do not take offense at the absence of a man, and he was being absent as naturally as if they had been married. And soon, absent and smiling, he was flattered by the foolishness that flowed sweetly out of her and lulled him into peace. The girl had the smell of powder about her, and that made him a little nauseous.

"Wouldn't you like to take a bath?" he had said to her one day with great delicacy. "I really can't take the smell," he said, ill at ease.

"But it's only powder!" she said, surprised.

"Well, I can't take it."

"All right," she said thoughtfully. And she never smelled of powder again.

Now she was caressing his hair attentively, insinuating, distracted, small. "Do you believe in another life?" she asked him then, immediately becoming more tense as she smoothed his hair, as if she were blowing on a cut so that it would not hurt so much. For an instant he was surprised as if, with the look of a bird who pecks with its beak, she were capable of a thrust. But it was only an instant of mistrust—his mistrust. And he smiled, grabbing her, foolish and soft as she was, and so curious in the way a woman is curious, and it made him remember his wife. "No, I don't believe in it," he said.

"Stupid!" she said laughing. Because people have the habit of insulting each other in intimacy; insulting one another could be a form of intimacy, and therefore they felt very close. With a certain amount of speed they had already gone beyond the cowardice of simply tolerating love, and they had entered into familiarity; and with relief had lost the larger size of things.

There, familiar at last and all of her revealed to him, the man examined her. She would be pretty only if a person was in love with her. But she had the beauty that can be seen when one is in love with what he sees. "All mothers of ugly daughters should promise them that they will be pretty when the wisdom of love enlightens a man," he thought. Around Ermelinda's dark eyes, for example, Martim saw a slightly amber circle, which he would have missed had he not been in love. He noticed also that the beginning of the hair on the nape of her neck was soft and that those strands which were too short to be wound up into a braid were a light that fluttered in the air. The light hair on her arms gilded the girl as if she was not to be touched. Once she had been loved, she had a rare delicacy and beauty. He looked at her curiously, fondly. She was capable of making a man happy; but for some reason, it had been necessary for her to trick him with wiles before she could make him happy—only then had she showed him that she had not tricked him and that the happiness she was giving him was real.

The man vaguely noticed all of that, and he looked at her, feeling the gentle energy that emanated from her and which he himself had aroused in her, the gentle energy that she herself had obliged him to arouse in her—so that in return, as now, she could give him back that gentle energy. In the whole web that Ermelinda had woven until she had captured him, she had used dubious, false, and unpleasant methods; as if life had been revealed by means of some kind of dirty trick. He owed the love of both of them to her and to the wise lack of scruples of the girl who, having got what she wanted, was there, made completely innocent by her own prize. All of this the man considered with tranquillity and wisdom because they had stopped embracing, and, completely engrossed though they were, he felt meditative and tranquil.

Then she asked, with her face showing the innocence of very curious people, "Have you ever enjoyed another woman like this?"

And he, within the cloudiness that feminine repose was giving him, with his eyes half-closed and almost not having heard her, continued along in his own thoughts about the other woman and said this: "She came to me, not because I was who I was or because she was who she was. She came to me out of her own laziness. She was very lazy," he said with the pleasure of remembering. "And she would interrupt me to tell me that she'd gone to the dentist. She spent her whole life asking me what time it was. Every so often she would ask me—'What time is it?' "

"Oh, I'm just as lazy!" Ermelinda said. "I'm a lazy one. I only want to be happy but I don't want to have all the horrible work that goes into being happy. I'm such a different person!

(196)

I'm very lazy, but I want things. What are you thinking about?" she asked him then, with sudden anguish—because there he was, lying down, suddenly inaccessible, as if surrounded by an inch of isolation. "What are you thinking about?" she implored, accusingly.

"Nothing," he said simply.

She sighed softly, pacified and dreamy at the same time; and she isolated herself immediately, secure within her own circumference. "I always wanted something for forever, so to speak," she said.

In comparison to other people he was very sensible, and he used an offensive adult tone when he said, "That's absurd."

"Of course it is," she said, agreeing only so that she would not be alone—because when she spoke the truth she always came upon the defensive wall of other people. "It's absurd," she agreed, telling a sensible lie.

They had not asked themselves what they meant by the word "absurd," nor had they realized that they had put untouched, to one side, the very thing they had been talking about. That is how the conversation about "forever" went—they would think about it later on, when each one again would have the assurance of being alone.

"Was she pretty?" Ermelinda suddenly asked, greedily.

A little frightened and half-offended, because a man's wife must never be touched by a man's mistress, he came to slightly and looked at her.

"I don't know," he said mistrustfully, trying to guess whether Ermelinda was defiling something sacred. "I don't know," he said, and then he became relaxed and the lucidity of sleep returned. "I don't know, we haven't seen each other for a long time. We were already talking directly to one another as if all we had were a soul—What time is it, she would ask me. She would say: what time is it? I went to the dentist today. That's what she talked to me about—I went to the dentist today."

"I haven't been to the dentist for a long time. Thank God I

have good teeth! But I like to go because I can take advantage of it and spend a few days in Vila; I take advantage of it and do some shopping and go to the movies. I miss the movies terribly."

"She had good teeth too," he said, a little annoyed.

"Well, I didn't mean she didn't. I was only talking about myself, because after all, I don't know who 'she' is," she said, trying to offend him with her sudden formality.

As the sweet and monotonous tone of the girl filled the woodshed from the depths of the half-light where he was hovering, he said to her, "Try to think of a person who needs an act of violence—an act which will make people reject him, simply because he did not have the courage to reject himself—a cowardly person, perhaps?" He stopped in anguish and sat down on the bed.

"Lie down," Ermelinda said with worried authority because she had never had him at her disposal for so long, and there was still so much she had to tell him.

He looked at her suspiciously for a moment; but then he laughed, at ease again.

"There's no danger in what I've been telling you," he said, enjoying the fact that she did not understand him—"because I'm telling you what I am, and no one can denounce what other people are. No one can even make any mental use of what other people are." Martin found it so funny to use the ancient word "mental" that he laughed; it was a strange and empty word, and he was a little off course. "After I stop talking, you won't know me any more. That's the way it always happens. When people reveal themselves, the others stop knowing us."

"What?" she asked, intrigued, interrupting her own thoughts for an instant.

He perceived then that he had said too much—to the point of getting her interested—and he looked away quickly. But either she had not heard or she was not interested. Then, stimulated by her unimportant presence, he said, "Try to think of a person," and he repeated everything.

Then, like a rooster who had proudly crowed alone in the

yard, he grunted with pleasure and nodded his head in agreement several times.

"But when I do get to Vila," she said, "I have so many things to buy that there isn't much time. I'd love to spend a whole week in Vila, but Vitória wouldn't like it."

"You don't like women very much, do you?" he said with curiosity.

"Well," she said reluctantly, concentrating—"on a desert island I'd rather be with a man."

Only after she had spoken was she aware of the implicit hint, and she smiled, excited and modest about her own capacity. He chuckled a little too, and examined her with a fondness that also came from cold curiosity. At that moment Ermelinda was peacefully swallowing a pill she had taken out of the picnic basket.

"Why do you take so many tranquilizers?" he asked her, smiling.

"Oh," she said simply, "it's this way. Let's say somebody was shouting and then somebody else put a pillow over her mouth so they wouldn't hear the shout. Well, when I take a tranquilizer I can't hear my own shouting. I know that I'm shouting, but I can't hear it—that's why," she said, smoothing her skirt.

Embarrassed at the painful confidence she had shared painlessly with him, he laughed. Ermelinda suddenly noticed his look; she stopped herself, she became aware of herself—"I'm somebody who can make another person look at me"—and she put on a falsely animated face, playing the role that he certainly expected of her. But unexpectedly, as if that time she had heard her own shout, she said to him, intense, hard, hopelessly:

"I love you."

"Yes," he said, after a pause.

Both of them remained silent for an instant waiting for the echo of what she had said to die out.

Then, as she bent over for a moment, some apple peels fell out of her blouse. And before he could even understand, in some way it confirmed the sweetness of that girl. He smiled, picking

(199)

up the peels, rolling them around between his fingers, and then he began not to understand: there was no doubt, they actually were apple peels. Without stopping her babbling, she looked at him with the peels in his hand and she said, "Perfume is so expensive."

"But these peels are all dried out," he said, scrutinizing her attentively.

"So soon?" she was surprised and examined the peels with great curiosity. "Look at them. I'll put some fresh ones in today."

She was simple and a woman, and he could laugh at her—and as another way of laughing, he caressed her face for the first time. With great tenderness he pushed aside the strands of hair that framed her thin face. And the face that appeared, naked and strong, made him suddenly withdraw his hands, as if he had stepped on the tail of an animal.

Up to what point had she been lying? Up to what point had she been pretending to be woman? Because the jaws of that girl were much broader than he had supposed, and they gave her a harsh look of beauty that he had not wanted in her. Had she feigned being weak? Because with her jaws showing, like those of a beast of prey, she gave a picture of herself as if she were supreme and on the scent. He began to be frightened in his depths, like a child who is startled when he touches something moving and it looks at him, accusing him.

Having withdrawn his hands in his fright, however—the locks immediately fell back into place, and a face that once more was indecisive denied the involuntary vision he had had. And now, without the strength of the chin, her eyes lost the horribly victorious expression that had come to confirm certain vague thoughts Martim had, subsequently rejected, that the girl was using him for some end—which irritated him. He had created the freedom to be alone and flee entanglements, but more and more the invisible circle was tightening around him. How we devour each other! Vitória more attentive, her strange way of demanding something from him; Ermelinda with her ambitious fangs revealed for an instant. And facing those strong women, he felt himself abjectly innocent; the fright seemed to make him the purest of them all. And he slipped away so as not to be contaminated; everybody's lives began to become obscurely intertwined with his. But himself? Himself, disguising his anxiety? How many times had he tried to find the mulatto woman's daughter, without even knowing why he wanted the contact with a child so much, as if she were the only one as pure as he? Had the former man returned? The former man who seemed to need a pureness he would not know what to do with? Had he strayed from his path again, at some undetermined point, and had he become the former man again?

"What do you like about me?" Martim asked demandingly.

"Oh," said Ermelinda voluptuously, as if at last he had touched on the main point at issue, and her whole attitude now became that of one who was finally going to have a good conversation between women. "I just don't know!" she said intimately, and the man had the unpleasant feeling that she was not speaking to him but was talking about the two of them to a third person. "It began," she said, "with a kind of curiosity, and then it kept growing and growing, and when I saw that it was not curiosity, it wasn't anything any more. It was you and me!"

"But," he said, a little irritated, "what did you like about me?"

Ermelinda looked at him a little startled, almost resentful. Something immediately closed up tight inside of her, and she looked at him without any love at all. Into her head came the temptation to offend him with the truth that he was dangerously seeking, as if the truth was that she did not love him. But she knew quite well that she did love him, and she laughed with relief, as if the subject had been changed.

"I had a kind of tremendous fascination with what you are!" she said as if she had made up a story, because she had chosen a different truth that was just as true except that she could join in this one without lying. "I really don't know what you are, but I'm terribly fascinated by it. It happened little by little, in a short time. I can't tell you what I like about you; I can't separate you into pieces. I think you're a whole person," she said very precisely.

"But how did you happen to like me?" he asked, as if the girl had left him shapeless.

"I don't know—certain little things—I don't know. Little things, I don't know what they are any more."

The demanding stare of the man made her retreat, and because she was wounded by the lack of care with which he asked such a dangerous question the girl suddenly became in-solent and ironical. "If I fall in love again, I'll make a note every day of what I felt so that I can give a report! But one thing I'm sure of," she said with a generalized disdain for people—"when I take a look at my notes, I'll just have a handful of dust."

Because a handful of dust was what she had right now. And what the girl had right now was a past so full of disillusion that it made her ironic.

But in the afternoon, her body being more knowing than she, she got a headache which expressed it all perfectly. In the afternoon, lying down in her room, fighting at last with a good, solid, satisfactory headache, like someone who has had a good nutritious meal.

Things did not always turn out the same way. Because the next time they were together, they were enveloped in perfection. There in the dirty woodshed, Ermelinda was irradiating. Vitória was far away; the countryside was completely cut off by the closed door of the shed. And the girl was the way she wanted to be: having forgotten about her fear, crackling with happiness, talking without cease. Everything seemed so secure to her on that afternoon that she was able to enjoy daydreams. Imprisoned and concrete at last she was no longer afraid of going too far and not having any place to come back to. She was anchored; and she was finally taking a chance at freedom, without any fear of the possibility of going beyond the almost non-existent dividing line between her and the countryside. So secure, in a word, that she could even lie. And if she just wanted to she could do what she was doing now—inventing some type which, even though it did not symbolize her, did please her as a choice. In this way, she talked to Martim, leaning her head back, which gave her an air that was somewhere in the neighborhood of daring, ambitious, and cruel. She really did not have any of those three attributes, nor did she want to have them.

Or she would pretend to be absent and thoughtful, even though in fact she was as attentive to her task of pretending as a seamstress is to the details of her sewing. Living with Vitória, who knew her too well, was horribly restricting. Vitória knew too well how to cope with her. While Martim did not know her and with him she could invent a new life. And above all, an engineer, "an educated man"—who knows, before he left he might even say the word that would take away her fear forever. She had hope in him because she had known several educated men who did not believe in God and did not believe that one lives after death.

Oh, he would leave. Yes! But she would not care. As long as he left the word behind with her, perhaps one of disbelief, which would forever give her the same security that his presence gave her. That man would have to leave behind him there the living part of his life, that thing that makes a person exist in the eyes of another. Ermelinda looked at him avidly, one might have said that she hated him, but it was only ambition and hunger. A little paler then, because the time was short and now was the moment to ask him for the word—a little paler and taking care not to be too clear and reveal herself—she said with a sharp and disagreeable laugh, "For example, I don't understand what infinity is! Just think of that!"

Through the peal of laughter she was using to disguise herself she looked at him intensely, as if through a keyhole, and her heart was pounding.

Martim was nailing up some loose boards on the wall of the woodshed that afternoon and he looked over his shoulder at her, amused.

"I'll bet," she said, very ostentatiously shaking her finger

(2 0 3)

close to his face—"I'll bet that an engineer knows about things like that!"

Martim slowly pushed the uncomfortable finger away from his face and kept on working.

"How is it," she went on, struggling to maintain her coquettishness, trying to remove the expression of urgency from her face and the call for help from her eyes—"How is it that the world, for example, never ends? And never begins, for example . . . That's horrible! don't you think?"

The girl's voice trembled a little and he, who was smiling, flattered by the fact that she was ignorant, looked at her quickly. Suddenly she was so imploring and emotional that it occurred illogically to him that she had come with her bothersome picnic basket through all the labyrinths just to ask that question: "How is it that the world never ended and never began?" Martim was intrigued and he laughed again.

"The idea really is monstrous," he conceded.

She was hanging on the lips of the man with such complete attention and for the first time she was paying so little attention to herself that her whole face was exposed; and Martim saw a pale face, neither ugly nor pretty, with features that seemed to have been put together for just one expression—that of expectation.

"What's monstrous?" she asked, startled, as if instead of giving her his hand to lift her up he had pushed her down deeper.

"The idea of a world that never has any beginning and never has any end," he said, a little bothered by the fact that the girl had placed him in the situation of saying something that neither he nor she understood.

"So?" she said, with her head to one side—all of her in wait.

He did not understand what she was waiting for, and asked, "So what?"

"So?" she repeated, as if insistence would be clarifying by itself.

(2 0 4)

He shrugged his shoulders, put another nail in the board, and said, "Well, so try to imagine the opposite: a world that began one day and will end one day. That idea is just as monstrous."

Ermelinda continued waiting, cocking a deaf ear like a person who was hard of hearing. But suddenly realizing that she felt very serious and that men don't like that, she gave a laugh, which trailed off too quickly, however. Then her mouth seemed to suffer, and she twisted it several times involuntarily:

"I'm going," she said slowly, getting up and shaking the crumbs out of her lap.

On the following day, as soon as Vitória had disappeared, Ermelinda, continuing her careful work, spoke to Martim about the death of a turkey, and about what was happening now to the turkey that had been eaten. And she guided Martim along so well that he ended up saying, inspired perhaps by the expression that a turkey dies the day before, "The thing is so well done," he said—"because no one dies one day too soon. He dies exactly at the instant of his own death, not a minute before. The thing is perfect," he said.

But it was precisely that perfection that she was afraid of! Ermelinda looked at him stiffly. Martim became a little embarrassed. But guided by an intuition that came from the sweet way he always treated her, he. said illogically, probing and feeling generous without knowing in relation to what, "We don't know where we came from and we don't know where we're going; but we just experience things, we experience! And that's what we have, Ermelinda. "That's what we have!"

Martim did not know how to interpret the blank look in the girl's eyes, whose pupils suddenly looked just like any other inexpressive feature of the face and not something to see with. It was as if she had just turned off in herself the possibility of thinking. And it made Martim shuffle about uncomfortably. He did not know how much what he had just said was worth—either to her or to himself. "Now we're starting to tell ourselves things that keep on swimming in the air." he thought, as if that was the sign of an inescapable transition and the delicate way in

(205)

which things become corrupted, without our being able to do anything about it. Martim had noted that both of them were already "conversing."

But on the following day, as soon as Vitória went away, Ermelinda came back and, with the haughtiness of someone who no longer had much to lose or keep, she asked the man what fate was like.

This time, however, without her understanding why the engineer was so angry all morning—perhaps because he was already tired of her?—this time instead of answering, he repeated in a dumbfounded way: "Fate? What is fate like?!" he repeated with a surprise that left Ermelinda mortified. Then because it was impossible for him to express his own anger the man's face took on for an instant an appalled look that Ermelinda rejoicingly interpreted as participation—until she discovered that the repetition of the question was only fury and fatigue. Whatever the next word would be it would come like a punch in the face. She waited, intimidated.

"Fate, oh for God's sake!" he finally said, furious.

The girl did not cry. She immediately passed on to things that might flatter him, telling him that the place had changed so much since he had come, that everything now looked so well cared for and new, "that now it was something different." And if that did not succeed in changing the man's glowering expression, at least it calmed him down and pleased him. And the girl quickly calculated as she blinked her eyes that she still had the right to come back to the woodshed sometimes. Only a few times, because time was passing . . . her face drew itself up tight in anticipation. With a hope that tried to be stronger than her disbelief, she promised herself, "Who can tell, maybe the next time . . ." She did not interrupt herself even for an instant to ask herself honestly what it was she expected from Martim.

Part III

THE APPLE
IN THE DARK

Chapter 1

AND so the day arrived when Vitória left for Vila Baixa with the truck loaded up with tomatoes and ears of corn, and the truck looked like a harvest festival. They all came out with smiles and anxiety to watch it leave, because everything they all had worked for had finally come to the end of its term. And since it had been exactly that for which they had worked so hard it was with smiles and anxiety that they watched the truck, garlanded with yellow ears. Vitória, feigning seriousness, looked at them for an instant, alone with the product of her effort. Ill at ease, they waved good-bye to her.

Martim stood there watching her go away, until the last bit of dust had settled to the ground and until the noise of the wheels had disappeared even from his memory and the country-side was restored to silence and the wind.

The time had come to an end.

Without Vitória's presence, a sudden lull came over the farm, which was in a state of emergency just as when someone is about to die or go away, and then the sun shone and then the plants waved their leaves—that was how the birds flew about, attentively.

And that was how it was on the farm, where the people seemed to have worked in vain, and yet it was not true. From wherever Martim looked he seemed to see the place from the distance of years and years already gone by. The place seemed unpopulated; he felt the breeze blowing. And because something important was going to happen in such a near future—Vitória's meeting with the German—the farm was relegated to the past, the standing flowers to the wind, the sparkling dry tile roof to the sun.

There was a silence as when drums are beating.

As for Ermelinda, she was quite wounded because he did not love her any more. For he did not love her any more. The great attraction that had justified a whole lifetime had passed. She was wounded and melancholy. It was a dead pain. There is the water—and I don't need to drink any more. There's the sun— and I don't need it any more. There's the man—and I don't love him. Her body had lost its feeling. And she, who had concentrated her entire self in anticipation of the day Vitória would leave for Vila and leave her the man all to herself, without hiding places at last, without precautions at last, she only sought him out once, when she told him sadly, honestly, indirectly:

"I loved a man once. Then I stopped loving him. I don't know why I loved him, I don't know why I stopped loving him."

Martim, worried about the German, did not know what to say in return, and then he asked, "And did you become his friend afterwards?"

And he asked a question like that because he was unprotected and he needed friendship.

"No," she said, looking at him slowly. "No. Friendship is very nice by itself. But love is better. I couldn't be friends with a man I had loved."

"And afterwards?" he asked, with an anguish of whose origin he himself was unaware.

"Afterwards," she said, "afterwards I cried sadly, even though it was painless. I begged; 'Make me suffer from love!' But nothing happened, I was free again."

"And wasn't it good to be free?"

"It was as if the years had passed and I saw in a face that before had been everything for me, I saw in that face the thing that love is made of: ourselves. And it was as if the most genuine love had been made out of a dream. If that's being free, then I was free."

Since Ermelinda had never told him that she had loved him up to the point of making it a life Martim did not know that he himself was the man not loved now, nor did he understand that she had stopped loving him. But as if she were imploring him for a truth more merciful than reality, he pleaded desperately for the cause of someone else:

"But what stopped you from becoming his friend?" he asked.

"I was all alone," she said.

The man became dark, sad, heavy. Nothing had been said that would be remembered afterwards. But the two of them looked at each other with a smile worse than death, silently submissive to the powers of nature. Scratching the ground with his foot, keeping his hands in his pockets, Martim said inside, quiet, intense, "Please!" He did not know really what he was asking for, and he said "Please." But it was as if a man dying of hunger had politely said: please. The back that Ermelinda turned on him to go away had no face, it was a narrow and fragile back. Nevertheless, with bitter vigor it said to the man: "No."

And the drums kept on beating.

The whole countryside now belonged to Martim to make or think of it what he pleased. But the expectation of what was going to happen had cut off communication between him and what now had become a desert. And the truth was that the man did not want it otherwise. He did not even know what it was that he had wanted so much. Since love had died in Ermelinda, so the lack of desire gave silence to the man's heart. He sought out his own hunger; but it was the silence that answered him. He was experiencing what was worst of all: not wanting any more. The first moment was quite terrible; he figured out right away that not wanting was so often the most desperate form of wanting.

And at certain moments, with an imponderable change in the weather, even the farm would change and show a closer face, and impose its living fields. And then for an instant the man and the farm would vibrate again on the same level of the present moment. And once more, as he looked at the world, once more the man would feel that promising tension which seems to be the maximum a person can attain, just as one becomes aware of a stone because it resists the fingers. More than tension? He tried to go forward in himself; but no, that seemed to be the limit. If he were to try to go beyond the resistance of the stone, suddenly nothing would happen. Challenged for an instant Martim still tried to pick up the interrupted thread of his slow construction and suffer at least. But the time had really come to an end.

Vitória returned on Saturday, covered with dust and looking older, with an empty truck. She had fought so hard—and perplexed, she had got what she wanted; growing old, she had got what she wanted; Martim did not understand her. While the woman was talking about selling the produce he avidly tried to read her eyes and guess through them whether she had talked to the German. But all he managed to learn, which she told him without enthusiasm, as if fatigue had removed all interest from the wonderful bit of news, was that it was already raining four miles away from Vila Baixa.

Had she seen the German? Using minor pretexts Martim patrolled the house, uselessly looking for Vitória; she was the only element he could use to calculate with.

Until when, downcast, he stopped trying to find her and he saw her again. But it was as if he had seen a stranger. She was coming down the hallway against the light. He did not really see her body, just her walk, as if he only saw the spirit of her body. Little by little, closer to the light now, she took on shape until she became opaque—and the man blinked, looking at her with a start. Her hair was loose and wet from her bath and she was no longer wearing the tight and dusty slacks that had already become a part of her in Martim's imagination. He saw her for the first time in a woman's dress and she was a stranger. There was no harshness that could hold up against the damp tresses on the shoulders. When he looked at her for the first time in terms of a body she gained a body in his eyes. Which was no longer energetic, as he had always seen it, and whose strength had given the man a reason for fighting somehow against that strength. It was a body that was so much more docile than the face. Scandalized, mournful, Martim looked at her. It was indecent how the feminine clothing made her naked, just as if an old woman had revealed an anxious desire to be a girl. He looked away with shame. Just as Ermelinda had refused, Vitória—who had served him previously as a firm landmark—now refused to present him with a form, and she left him free. On the face between the hanging hair there was the same tired look with which the woman had returned from Vila Baixa and which he had tried to interpret in vain. It was the first time that he had seen her tired. The woman's eyes, as if they no longer wanted to contradict, were black on the surface. Martim tried to goad her so that she would be stronger than he. But she replied: "No, we'll let the ditches go tomorrow. The professor and his son are coming."

Their looks met and nothing was transmitted or said. Or one would have had to be a god to understand what they had said to each other. Perhaps they had said; "We are in nothingness and we touch each other in our silence." Because for a fraction of a second they had looked at each other in the eyes.

When was it that Martim had first heard the professor mentioned? It must have been during his first days on the farm, when his dull eyes could barely tell Vitória from Ermelinda. "As good as the professor"—had he heard that phrase? And if he had heard it, which one of the women had said it? Martim suddenly remembered another phrase: "It's the last Sunday of the month, but the professor can't come, he's ill."

Who had said it? Martim cursed himself for not having paid attention to everything now that he needed every detail so that he could understand. He had had only the impression of links escaping him—but which ones? Could the professor be the same person as the German? And in that case the son—would the son be the one he had thought was the German's servant? No, because Vitória had referred to him as the "German," but she called tomorrow's visitor the "professor" . . .

And suddenly Martim managed to find no danger in the visit. The professor, as far as he could make out, was accustomed to visiting them on the last Sunday of the month, except that through coincidence he had not been able to make it until now. And the following day was precisely the last Sunday of the month! There was no reason to suspect, then. It was just a visit . . .

The only thing to suspect was the unexpected break in Vitória's way of life; she had stopped giving orders, and the only time she had spoken to him she had withdrawn like a timid woman.

At the same time Martim could not be sure whether the change in Viótria was real or whether she seemed different only because she was wearing feminine clothes and had let her hair down, as if it were the first time she had had those graying hairs. Yes, it must have been just a superficial transformation in appearance. But then it wisely occurred to Martim; "And why has Vitória suddenly changed her way of dressing? what's the reason?" Since he could find no logical explanation he became suspicious again.

On that Saturday, with no work being done on the farm— "Why had Vitória wanted to stop it? Oh, maybe just because in her dry way she wanted to celebrate the sale of the produce?"— with no work being done the farm became even vaster. As if it were already a Sunday, a soft wind was running along without hindrance across the fields. Martim walked around, turned loose, the sequence of the days suddenly cut off. It was raining close to Vila, and the news that the drought was going to end had left them all calm and idle. On the silent Saturday the afternoon came on rapidly and tamely. Martim did not even see Erme-linda. And that worried him too. They had given him a sudden freedom. He felt a lack of the encirclement by women which had previously hemmed him in. The mulatto woman no longer seemed to leave the kitchen. No one was looking for him. Martim wandered through the countryside not knowing from which direction the danger would come.

It was then, with his heart pounding, that he saw the child playing near the cowshed. The drums had suddenly stopped.

His first avid impulse was to run over and grab her before she too could slip away. But he reined himself in so as not to startle her. He could barely contain the suspicion that she too would refuse him. With a casual walk, his heart pounding with thirst, he approached. And next to her, out of fear and softness of feeling, he did not look at her.

But the girl, the girl lifted up her eyes from the bricks she was playing with. She looked at him—and smiled. The man's heart contracted with an affliction of joy: she was not afraid of him!

"Perhaps she never had been!" he then thought. For an instant a suspicion crossed his mind. Had he been imagining all that time the danger in Vitória's meeting with the German and had he invented that emptiness on the farm—just as it was now clearly proved that he had only been imagining that this child was afraid of him? Because the girl was smiling at him, and now she was pointing her small finger at the unstable structure she had managed with the bricks . . .

In the meantime there was another possibility: that the child really had been afraid of him and only had stopped because she had become used to his presence around there. If that last hypothesis were true, and if he had not just imagined the fear or the rebuff of the girl, then the danger of the German too could still be a reality! Fearing that he would get the proof that he had been right, he looked at the girl without daring to speak to her.

The girl was peacefully piling up bricks. And standing there, he soon began to be moved by the charming indifference with which she had admitted him, pleased that she was treating him as an equal in that same obvious way that children have when playing with one another.

"In this funny house," the girl said suddenly, pointing at the bricks—"a funny man lives. His name is Funny because he's funny."

"Oh, please forgive me," the man said muttering to himself, timid, happy. A child is the arrow we shoot off, a child is our investment—he needed her so, that he took care not to look at her. He remained still, his heart pounding because it had received human kindness. He was big and clumsy, and feeling himself abandoned did not help his awkward situation. He remained still, afraid he would make a mistake. He wanted so much to be right, and he did not want to spoil the first thing that was being given to him. "Oh God, I've already ruined so much; I've already understood so little, I've already refused so much. I spoke when I should have kept quiet; I've ruined so much already." He, for the first time, was experiencing the worst kind of loneliness, the one in which there is no vanity; and then he wanted the girl. But he had ruined everything that had been given to him! To him, who once had again been given the first Sunday of a man. And out of all that, what remained after a while was a crime.

Martim did not know what word to say to the child without its breaking in his heavy hand. The child was silent. Who knows but that it too was silence she expected of him. But what sort of silence did she want to share with him? Ready to stop being entirely what he himself wanted, he just wanted to be what the girl wanted him to be. A child was the common denominator of a man; he wanted to join in with her.

But the silence of the busy girl was different from the silence he had shared with the cows, and it was different from the high cold of a hilltop. He remained silent. As his first donation he then stopped thinking, and thus he came close to the natural heart of a little girl. In a little while the silence between the two of them became a silence that would fit into a matchbox, where children keep buttons and little wheels. Both of them therefore remained in a secret calm. Except that he was afraid because he had already ruined so much.

Then she said; "One day I went to Vila and I went into a drugstore," and she knew just how to speak without breaking that silence in which they both understood each other and which he, since his heart was soft now, loved. "When I went into the drugstore I ran and I didn't even fall down. Then I weighed myself on the scale in the drugstore with Mommy."

She adjusted the bricks and she added in an educated way, "You know what? I don't weigh anything. Even Mommy said so. She said I didn't weigh anything. Then I ran and I didn't even fall down, and I almost crossed the street all by myself but I'm too smart because of the cars. Mommy doesn't like for me to sleep in her bed and she stays there looking at magazines, looking at magazines, looking at magazines. Then in the night time she'd go out with her high heels on, but I didn't cry: I slept and I slept and I slept. The next morning when I woke up I stubbed my toe here on the edge of the bed. Do you think it hurt?" she asked and stared expectantly at him with her calm and yellow eyes.

When the man finally managed to speak, he said with effort, "I don't know, child, I don't know."

"Well it didn't," she told him with impersonal sweetness.

She was almost black and she had little teeth. She started putting one brick on top of another again and another one on top of that—for the tall man who was standing there. They looked at each other. The man's heart gave way with difficulty; he could not swallow his saliva, an extremely painful sweetness weakened him. "Oh God, then it's not with thought a person loves! It's not with thought that we build other people! And a little girl escapes my strength, and what do you do with a bird that sings?"

The girl looked at him attentively.

"Will you give me something? Will you give me something?" she said, attent and expectant; and her little face was that of a prostitute.

Then the man tried not to look at the girl. He stared stoically at a tree.

"Will you, huh? Anything!" she said very intimately.

"I will," he said hoarsely.

Suddenly satisfied, pacified, her face again became childlike and extremely shiny. "Did you know that José's grandmother died one day?" she said in thanks.

"No, I didn't."

"I swear by the Holy Virgin," she said without insisting. "I was even there when she died."

She arranged the bricks better, socially, carefully, maternally. But a slight restlessness passed across her face. She lifted up her blinking eyes at him, and once more a false flattery appeared on her features, which were mature, sweet, corrupt.

"You will give me something? A present? It doesn't have to be today," she conceded greedily. "Maybe tomorrow? Yes, to-morrow?"

"Tomorrow?" he said, lost. "Tomorrow?" he said with horror.

"Yes, tomorrow!" she repeated authoritatively, laughing. "Tomorrow, silly, it's what comes after I fall asleep!"

The man drew back horrified. He could not leave right away. But when he did manage to get out of the greedy claws of the child, he almost ran—and as he looked behind in disbelief, he saw to his still greater horror that the little girl was laughing, laughing, laughing. As if he had been horrified with himself, he almost ran. The water—the water was polluted. The girl had not wanted to be the symbol of childhood for him. For the first time, then, he thought that he was a criminal, and he got all mixed up because, even though he was a criminal, he had at the same time a great horror of the impure. And what confused him even more was that that child with her sharp little teeth that could bite and with her yellowish, expectant and dirty eyes full of hope was also pure—delicate and pardoned eyes like those of an animal. He almost ran. What did he need so much that he froze up when they asked him for it? He saw Vitória again with her graying hair, which now seemed luxuriant and lascivious to him. He felt in his heart the hardness with which Ermelinda had fallen out of love. "Are we terrible?" he asked himself perplexed, as if he had never lived. "What a dark thing is it that we need; what an avid thing is this existence which makes our hand scratch like a claw? And yet this avid desire is our strength. Our children are born astute and unprotected out of our darkness, and they inherit it; and the beauty is in that dirty wanting,

wanting, wanting. Oh, body and soul, how can we judge you if we love you? Are we terrible?"—that had never occurred to him except as an abstraction. "Are we terrible?" he asked himself, he who had not committed a crime out of evil. Not even his own crime had ever given him the idea of decay and anxiety and pardon and the irreparable way the innocence of the Negro girl had.

Now it was nighttime and everything was peaceful. He spent the whole night waiting. The drums had been beating all the while. He had not been able to lie down. Then he sat down on the bed and waited the whole night through.

Chapter 2

ON THE LIMPID SUNDAY that seemed to have dawned before its time the man had the impression that he had only invented the danger. In the round sky the angels were on guard across the clouds—that was how he had the idea of inoffensive peace.

Later on, when he saw Ermelinda with her hair curled, it became clear to him that she had disappeared the day before to curl her hair: it had been only that, then! And—why not? The doldrums had only meant the eve of the last Sunday of the month; for Martim now understood what a revolution took place for the visit of the professor and his son. In the happy morning two chickens had been snatched up out of their squawking and had turned up dead in the kitchen. Jam to stuff a cake with had appeared out of the pantry.

And at eleven o'clock, from behind the woodshed door, he finally saw an old car approaching. The short fat man who got out did not look anything like the German! And the boy who was with him, looked timidly at Ermelinda and Vitória waiting there well-dressed on the porch unsure of himself. Then the visitors disappeared inside the house . . .

So everything had been in his own imagination! Almost laughing, passing his trembling hand across the dryness of his mouth. With relief Martim heard for an indeterminate time the sound of conversation coming from the house and the sound of dishes. The noises were familiar, innocent, reassuring. Free of tension at last, he fell onto the bed and into a deep sleep.

When he woke up, the afternoon had become broad and tranquil. And a while later Vitória appeared. She still looked tired and defeated, erect in the woodshed door.

"Since you are an engineer," she said to him, "and he is a teacher, the two of you should have lots to talk about."

When Martim did not answer she added with even more fatigue, "The professor is very intelligent, he makes wonderful puns."

There was an empty pause.

"We're expecting you; all right?"

Martim ran his hand across his rough face, which he had not shaved for days. She noticed the gesture and made one of her own that showed an inexplicable despondency.

"It doesn't matter," she said, "the professor doesn't worry about things like that."

She was already going away when she stopped short. She seemed to make a resolution and she explained to him. "He isn't the headmaster, but he really runs the whole school because he has a strong personality. His puns are excellent. He's quite smart and brilliant."

The sleep had left Martim feeling calm and well-fed; and now that there was no danger, he looked at her expectantly.

"The professor is strict, but he's like a father to his students. His theory is that a teacher deserves to be on a higher level than the students."

He did not ask any questions, and he looked at her serenely. She was pretty and she was tired. He had never seen her so well-groomed. She was still waiting, and for the first time they were talking about something that did not have to do with work. It was then that Martim, sensing the novelty, looked her over with mistrust.

"He's quite strict with his students," she went on monotonously, and she did not seem to be paying much attention to what she was saying. "One day a student was whispering in class, and at the end of the period, in front of them all, he called the student up—and such a speech he made, calling him son and asking him to lift his feelings up to God. The boy was so sorry that all he could do was cry. No one laughs at the professor; he won't tolerate that. The students laugh at other teachers, but not at him."

"Yes," Martim said, the way a doctor would to a patient.

"The student cried so hard," the exhausted woman said— "that they had to give him a drink of water. He became a regular slave to the professor. The professor is quite well-educated. The boy became a regular slave; he's quite well-educated."

For the first time, Vitória did not seem to get impatient with Martim's silence. And standing there, with her features puckered up from fatigue, as if she had nothing else to do and did not want to leave, she kept on reciting; "Just today the professor used the boy as an example. The boy now has an angelic look; he's become paler, he looks like a saint. The professor was so pleased with what he had accomplished—such a moral victory—that he even put on some weight," she said, exhausted.

"He put on some weight," Martim repeated cautiously, as if he were afraid to wake her up.

"He put on some weight," she said, waking up a little surprised. "But he did suffer!" she added quickly, as if Martim had made an accusation against the professor. "He's a good man. He suffers just like anyone in a position of command!" she said in reaction. "He has a heart of gold!" she said, looking at him with a kind of anger. "He suffers other people's sufferings, the suffering that other people have in their hearts!" she added with sudden ardor.

And as if she knew that Martim had not understood anything, she looked at him with rancor.

The professor was occupying the best easy-chair in the living room, and from the way the table was set Martim understood with a glance what role the man played within the small group. Ermelinda had just sat down at the piano with her very curly hair, with a tense and absentminded air. The mahogany furniture had been dusted. Martim stopped in the doorway and no one seemed to have noticed him. Perhaps only the professor, who with a signal of finger to mouth asking for silence, seemed to address himself especially to the newcomer. The son was chewing on his fingernails and looking down. Vitória had her attention fixed on some embroidery in a hunched-over and feminine position—Martim could not see her face and he looked for it, searching in it the severity that was what he loved about her eyes. Martim sat down near the door.

Ermelinda was playing without looking at the keyboard.

"I managed to make some variations," she said very softly. "Sentiments," she then added, for herself.

The sentiments flowed from her fingers easily, and she seemed to draw some pride from that, thinking that perhaps it was a sign of perfection.

"I can already play without even paying attention," she announced again, turning her head around a bit.

"Don't talk!" the professor said suddenly, as if he were in pain. "Music should not be interrupted with words!" he said, suffering from the fact that he himself had been obliged to speak.

Martim was surprised at his rudeness.

"The professor is a spiritualist," Vitória said suddenly to Martim, as if that explained it all.

Without looking at the keyboard and without having to pay any more attention, Ermelinda's music emerged mechanically and lightly into the Sunday truce. The piano was just enough out of tune to have the crystal sound of a clavichord, and the notes seemed to be played singly, with the precise impersonality of a player-piano. The sound in some way seemed to come out pure, as when one hears something and does not know who is playing. Even Ermelinda finally seemed to have become enraptured; the music had apparently begun to tell her so many and such confused things—perhaps of love, judging by the expression of anxiety and sad desire on her face—that she stopped playing and abruptly spun around on the stool with a surprised air that said nothing to the rest of them.

"Music is spirit itself," the professor said with great assurance.

"I," the son suddenly said—"I like opera. As far as I'm concerned, that's the best there is."

(2 2 3)

The professor flushed and looked down at the floor.

"I've explained to you already," he said in a very low and soft voice, "that you're wrong."

"Opera's what counts," the boy repeated with courageous obstinacy; his face was pale and ugly.

"You're wrong!" the professor exploded. "I've already told you that you're wrong!" The professor shouted, his eyes closed with tolerance and rage. "I've already told you that nowadays opera is considered second-rate music! You're the only one who won't pay any attention! I explained it to you already!"

"Maybe," the boy said with painful pride—"but as far as I'm concerned, opera is the thing."

The professor looked at him with bulging eyes. The vein in his neck was throbbing. The boy lost his strength then; he lowered his head and went back to biting his fingernails.

"The professor is very high-strung," Vitória said simply, for Martim's benefit.

With those words of Vitória's, the professor seemed suddenly to calm down; the paleness returned to his fat face, and as if he had suddenly decided to forget about the problem of his son, he turned resolutely and tranquilly toward Martim:

"Well," he said with extreme attention, "what do you think about our Vitória?"

Vitória lowered her head toward her embroidery and a flush came over her face.

"So much dryness," the professor said—"covers up—if you'll excuse the beauty of the words—a heart that is bursting for love."

Vitória tried to protest weakly, blushing:

"The professor," she said with a confused and imploring voice, and Martim did not know whether what she was saying was praise or an excuse, "the professor ought to write a novel!"

"I couldn't!" the teacher burst out. "It's as simple as that! I couldn't," he exclaimed wearily. "I couldn't, because I have all the answers! I already know how everything will come out! I've never been able to get out of this impasse! I have an answer," he said, spreading out his arms in perplexity. "I have an answer for everything!"

No one seemed to understand very well what he had meant to say, or what it had to do with the fact that he could not write novels. As if he himself had perceived that nobody understood, he seemed to abandon the problem again, leaving it unfinished; and he turned toward Martim, calmer now, cooled off.

Feeling the professor's intent eyes upon him Martim lowered his own, and in an attempt to control himself he reached for the piece of half-cured cowhide in the corner of the room. When he had calmed down he noticed that he had also picked up the mallet and was now pounding the hide to cure it. Vitória looked at him startled, as if he had gone too far, and restlessly scrutinized the teacher. Swallowing the challenge with difficulty, he closed his eyes for an instant and his face seemed to be asking God to give him humility. When he opened them he had a real smile on his face, understanding and ironical, and he was able to look impassively upon that man, himself, who without saying a word was pounding on a piece of leather.

"Ever since this morning," Ermelinda said, unable to bear the silence any more—"ever since this morning I've been so thirsty! Thirsty as a bear, as they say."

"I don't think that's quite what they say, if you'll permit me," the professor said smoothly, but with the swiftness of an eagle. "Hungry as a bear is what they say, if you'll permit me," he repeated with dignity, somewhere between ceremonious and displeased.

"But what I am is thirsty . . ." she dared to say very timidly.

Vitória destroyed her with her eyes. The other one averted her eyes and crossed her hands.

Vitória had gone back to her embroidery. Martim was softly pounding. The afternoon had softly spread itself about; it came into the room and imposed silence. Nothing could have made the afternoon more evident than the rhythmical beating of the mallet. With each thump the distance became greater, the branches more leafy; what had been lost more lost; a chicken cackled in the shadows. And a vague desire seemed to have been born, as when one is dreaming. The son, immersed in himself, was chewing on his nails with a melancholy voracity. Vitória kept her darkened face over the embroidery. Ermelinda, sitting on the stool with her back to the open piano, faced them all with an intense and immobile smile, as if her face were glowing on its own, without the aid of thought. Martim, head lowered, was applying himself in cadence to the cowhide. The smell of the leather and the mallet-beats drew the total immobility away from the scene and gave it a progressive march. Little by little the stronger smell and the mallet-beats brought the situation to an end. Vitória lifted up her widened eyes from the embroidery; the professor's son coughed and, startled at himself, looked at his father, Ermelinda let her smile fade a little, her dry lip lightly held by a tooth. Martim, the unconscious author of the destiny of moments, kept on pounding. The teacher kept his eyes half-closed, a little dark, where a subtle point was being thought. With restlessness Vitória noticed him and took the lead:

"I had a dream," she said aloud—"that I was surrounded by boats."

"Lighted up or dark?" Ermelinda immediately asked, waking up.

"What difference does it make?" Vitória exploded.

Ermelinda lowered her head.

"It would be prettier if they were lighted up," Martim said, looking softly at Ermelinda.

Quickly Vitória turned towards him, offended. The professor immediately examined him, squinting his eyes even more; it was the first time Martim had spoken.

After a second of surprise had passed, Ermelinda laughed heartily. "Prettier if they were lighted up, that's right! It's happier when things are lighted up," she repeated with pleasure.

"On the outside, my dear girl," the professor said very coldly. "On the outside a ship is much more whole than on the inside," he said with a bitter smile that he was testing.

(2 2 6)

Again nobody understood, and nobody seemed to be changed by not understanding. Noticing that, the professor blinked his eyes several times. Night had fallen. Vitória got up slowly and lit the lamps.

The professor was speaking calmly now, sunk back into the easy-chair, which made his fat belly stick out all the more. Martim did not know whether they were waiting for him to leave or to stay.

"Let us divide the path of humanity into periods," the professor was saying.

The hammering had stopped, the frogs were croaking. The professor was talking and playing with his key-ring; he threw it into the air and bit at it with his hand without catching it. That was when the keys fell.

Martim automatically leaned over to pick them up. But the professor, with no apparent hurry, was more agile than Martim, and he picked them up. And as if he had calmly showed what he was capable of doing, he laughed at the other one. With the motion still outlined in his hands, Martim looked at him with surprise. He could not have imagined that this small fat man could be capable of such a nimble motion. Then the professor, understanding, laughed even more and began to twirl the keys again.

The man was showing something off—Martim's mouth was dry, he could not take his eyes off the keys. Vitória, with fascinated eyes, was also watching the twirling motion of the teacher's little hand.

"Dividing the path of humanity into periods, we can come to the conclusion that today we are in the period of perplexity. We might say that modern man is a man who no longer finds anything to learn in the age-old lesson of the ancients. I would say, therefore . . ."

Vitória was listening, upright, somnambulist, looking at the keys. Finally the professor stopped, looked at the clock. He held in his breath for an instant and finally spoke:

"My game is the human charade," he said, clearing his

(2 2 7)

throat. "You don't answer me?" he suddenly asked. "You, an engineer?"

As if something had finally happened, Vitória, startled, moved in her chair. Dulled by his long immobility, Martim changed the position of his legs.

"Yes, yes," he said.

"Everything that is human interests me, you won't give me an answer?"

"No . . ."

"I," the professor said with pleasure, "am a born mystifier."

Vitória became agitated. Martin passed his glance from the professor to Vitória and from her back to the professor, remotely trying to grasp what was going on. An incomprehensible web was closing in on him, he was upset without knowing why.

"Precisely because the human charade—which with an English kind of humor I like to call the human mystery—precisely because the human charade, as I was saying, interests me is why I am curious about the following fact: What is an engineer, a man, let us say, such a high calling, doing here?"

Swell! So that's why they had called for him.

"Let us ask what it is that makes a man leave a place like São Paulo—because your accent shows, sir, that your place of origin is not Rio de Janeiro as you have affirmed. As I was saying, what is it that makes a man abandon his exalted calling, which might be the building of a city, which, *par excellence*, is that of an engineer? What makes him, as we were saying, end up in the neighborhood of Vila Baixa, where the only resources are those of the spirit? And furthermore: you, sir, did not even know where you were, as was stated by a man as ignorant and unlettered as Francisco, who does not have the gifts of acumen that spiritual evolution endows a man with, but, *quand même*, he did have enough instinct to probe. As we were saying, what has a man done, or what has he been thinking, to bring him to these parts? What did he do, I ask with all reason, now that you, sir, have agreed that my game is the human charade?"

(2 2 8)

"Try to guess," Martim said, trying to smile through his dry lips.

The professor had no doubts. He opened his eyes and looked at him nakedly. Martim gave a pale smile.

"I will try to guess," the professor said abruptly.

He got up as he looked at the clock.

Behind a candle, while the others were saying good-bye on the porch, Martim tried in vain to make out everybody's face in the dark, but all he got was a general spirit of good-bye. He quickly tried to analyze each dark face and perceive some further indication, even though the very haste with which he was trying made such a search difficult. The yellowish light that trickled weakly out from inside the house was not sufficient for him to distinguish anything more than shapes, and the throbbing of the blood in his own ears prevented him from making out words. At the same time, his inner disorder had left him acute and lost, as if alert in a vacuum. Nothing seemed very real to him, and he was upset by the very strange fact that the professor, even though he had not been the German, had still . . .

The car finally left, the two women slowly went up onto the porch and disappeared inside the house.

Chapter 3

THE DOOR of the main house closed and left him isolated outside. Shortly after, a light went on on the second floor. And Martim was all alone, pitching about in the dark.

"All right," he said suddenly with false assurance and a pleasant disposition to which he added a little irony. "And now," he went on pleasantly and sensibly— "let's go to bed." He felt that in some way he was acting stronger than he was, and self-pity took over. "Well, all right," he repeated with sarcasm.

At the same time that he was deciding to shut himself up in the woodshed and calm his heated head as a first step, confused and distracted he went off in the opposite direction. At first the lack of understanding of what he himself proposed to do made him stagger, and he went forward almost as if he were going backwards. Then the direction of his flight became something more than an obscure impulse—and when he suddenly understood, panic came over him and he almost ran. "All right," he still said, like a man who has time to tuck in his shirt before he falls down dead. It was then that he really began to run, run for all he was worth in the direction of the river, and his foggy objective was the woods, the dark woods. Dominated by the sound of his own panic, he passed through the cold water. Slipping on the rocks, his legs terrified by the icy black water, he ran very frightened, and he went into the woods—but the edge of the woods was not enough for him. With the avidity of a shout, what he wanted was the black heart of the forest; he could not run freely because of the branches, but he ran along getting scratched and breaking branches like a wild horse.

Until he suddenly felt that he had arrived where he wanted to be and he stopped, panting, his chest heaving, his eyes wide open in the dark. And God is witness that he did not know what he had come to look for in the woods. But there he was, still breathless, and the mere possibility of not being there frightened him. The heavy air was close against his face, as if the darkness were filled with the panting of a dog.

The man remained there, tall and getting back his wind; his eyes were open and evil. He felt that he was basically protected by the darkness, despite the fact that it was the darkness itself that frightened him most. No thought occurred to him; his hungry soul was feeding on the total blindness of the dark, and he was breathing crudely and astutely; he listened, hungry, to his own breathing, which had become his most basic guarantee. As long as he breathed, he would be a great expert. He moved his head from one side to the other, ready to take a leap, and, if he took it, he would give a ferocious shout at the same time. The feeling that he had the ability to make that shout also calmed him. But none of those guarantees stopped his body from trembling or his teeth from chattering.

He passed his hand across his mouth several times; and with fright he noticed that he was laughing. Without being able to remove the idiotic laugh from his mouth, he then looked in the dark at the hand that had touched the smile, as if it might have come away covered with blood. His teeth were chattering lightly and precisely, without Martim's having control over them. And as if they had just told him that he was afraid, he laughed.

It was a fear that had nothing to do with the equations he had prepared before the professor's arrival, as if the fear had been happening to someone else. Except that, that someone else was, frighteningly, himself. Who was he? Martim had fallen so deep into himself that he could not recognize himself. As if up till now he had just been playing. Who was he? He had the intuitive certainty that we are nothing, that we think we are and that we are what he was being now. One day after we are born we invent ourselves—but we are what he was now. Martim had fallen into truth the way a person falls into madness, and then his teeth were chattering. The truth would become chaotic only when he tried to understand it. But in itself it was absolutely perfect. And he—he was the one whose teeth were chattering. His teeth were chattering from a fear that made him forget that he had taken on the task of a superman. He was frightened as if he had finally fallen into the trap—into that trap which he had denied as long as he could. And yet he would feel frustrated if he did not fall into it—Martim, who had been created to fall. But he kept on denying it; and his fear was base, as if he had stolen something—not the lofty and punishable fear of someone who has committed murder, but the fear of a thief.

In a little while the darkness calmed him down. But then, it immediately began to terrorize him and his eyes shone until the impassiveness of the dark, which had just terrified him, calmed him down once more with that very quality of impassive permanence, and he stopped trembling just as quickly as he had started.

At once, taking that as a sign that the crisis had passed and that everything had not gone beyond being merely a crisis, Martim said to himself mechanically: "Well, all right!" And he began to recover as quickly as possible, striving to put himself mentally into the past which had been interrupted by the professor's threat. To his surprise, he could not do it. Then he passed his hand over his mouth that was still smiling. But he simply could not do it. An instant of real fear made him come to his senses. And the man was being hurled about with no support from any of the thoughts that just a few days before had begun to make of him the man that he had invented himself to be. Right now! Right when he had begun to feel that the sandals were almost completed, close now to the domination of the smoky circle where the cauldron was boiling—right now it was the end of the journey! But what had he attained at the end of the journey? Fear . . .

Sobbing with rage and fear he clenched his teeth and punched the tree several times, and the more his hands hurt the more he felt compensated, and the more the rage grew the more fear closed up his still so unknown heart. At the point where he was, it was as if no step had ever been taken! As if all of his steps had been useless. "Oh, stupid, stupid!" he said to himself as he wept. He had had everything at his disposal but— "I don't know how to figure things out!" he said as he punched the tree. "A bird doesn't even have a place in the plan, much less me!"

After which, as if he had said something so great that it had been incomprehensible even to him, he quieted down, grumbling. "Stupidity," he said then, passing his hand over his unshaven face and feeling by the touch that the laugh was no longer coming out of his face. He blew his nose with precise care.

As if no step had been taken. Because in the dark he was now merely that shapeless thing with one single primary feeling. With one single jump backwards he had once more merely removed himself from the territory of the word—he who had begun to be able to do more than just babble. And as if no step had been taken, he was now indistinguishable from a frightened horse in the dark. But the truth was that Martim at that moment no longer even wanted one of the minimal things that he had once proudly wanted and he was even surprised at having wanted them; he was puzzled by them the way a man at the hour of death is frightened at having been worried because the tailor was late. Now all he miserably wanted was the immediate and urgent solution to his fear, and he craved to make any bargain.

The worst was that there was not even any glory in that punishment, not even martyrdom. That thing who, with frightened eyes had one day suddenly ascended to the point of a crime and then to the top of a mountain, that thing who was Martim could no longer be distinguished from an animal that had had the courage to escape its trap. Both of them would have the same indiscriminate punishment, the fear that reduced them suddenly to the same grave fate.

Suddenly it even seemed to Martim that until now he had been traveling along roads that had been superimposed, and that his real and invisible journey had been made underneath the reality of the road that he had thought he was trudging along, that the real journey was now suddenly coming out into the light, as if from a tunnel. And the real journey had been this: one day he had left his house of a man and his city of a man in search, for the adventure of precisely the thing that he was now experiencing in the dark, in search of the great humiliation; and along with himself, with ferocious pleasure, he was humiliating the whole human race. Fear humiliated him and then he blew his nose violently.

If he had undertaken the task of a man, it now seemed to him that he had meddled in things that should not be touched. He had touched illusion too closely. And he had tried to understand more than was permitted and to love more than was possible. A monk renounced life to take on life—he did not act. Had acting been his mistake? He had committed a total act, but he was not total; he was afraid just as one loves one woman and not all women, he was afraid just as if he had his own hunger and not that of the others; he was only himself, and his fear had its own particular size.

Then in the dark, not knowing for certain what he was afraid of, he became afraid of the great crime he had committed.

Face to face with the word crime he began to tremble again and feel cold, without being able to erase the laugh that had returned. And the criminal was so afraid that for the first time he completely understood his inexpressible feeling, which meant salvation.

Salvation? His heart pounded strongly then, as if the barriers had fallen away. Because, who knows, maybe that was the great bargain that he could make—salvation. Then everything that was individual in Martim ceased. Now he only wanted to join those who had been saved and who belong—fear had brought him to that. To salvation. And with his heart wounded by surprise and joy, it seemed to him for an instant that he had just found the word. Had it been in search of the word that he had left home? Or once more would it be only the remains of an ancient word? Salvation—what a strange and contrived word, and the darkness surrounded him.

Salvation? He was startled. And if that was the word—had it happened then? Had he had to live everything that he had lived, then, in order to experience what could have been stated in just one word? If that word could be spoken he still had not said it. Had he walked all over the land just because it was more difficult to take the one and only step? If that step could ever be taken!

Absurdity enveloped the man, logical, magnificent, horrible, perfect—darkness enveloped him. In the meantime, from what little he could understand, he seemed to feel the perfection there had been in his obscure path until he had reached the woods. There was an impersonal perfection in his steps, and it was as if the time of one life had been the time rigorously calculated for the ripening of a fruit, not a minute more, not a minute less—if the fruit were to ripen! Because it seemed to him that fear had established a harmony, the frightful harmony—"I tell you, God, I understand you!"—and once more he had just fallen into the trap of harmony, as if groping along twisted paths. Out of pure obedience he had traced a perfect fateful circle until he found himself again, as he found himself now, at the very starting point which was the final point itself. At the very base of his fear, and as if the path that was just a circle had ended up by rendering useless all the steps he had taken, the man suddenly seemed to agree with that path, with pain and with fear, he seemed to admit that his unknown nature was more powerful than his freedom. Because what good has freedom been to me? he shouted to himself. He had got nothing from it . . .

What good had he got out of a freedom that was deep but powerless? He had tried to invent a new way of seeing and understanding and organizing, and he had wanted that way to be as perfect as that of reality. But what he had experienced had only been the freedom of a toothless dog; the freedom of going off in search of the promise that surrounded him, the man thought, trembling. And so vast was the promise that if a person lost sight of it for a second he would then lose himself in an empty and complete world that seemed to have no need for an extra man. He lost himself until, exhaustively and born out of nothing, hope arose. And then again, just as for a toothless dog, the world would become able to be walked through, touched. But only touchable. Then the one who shouted loudest or howled most melodiously would be the king of dogs. Or the one who kneeled down most deeply—because kneeling down was still a way of not losing sight of the promise from one instant to another. Or then the one who would revolt. His strike!

His strike, which was the only thing that up until today he could take some pride in.

Until the desire of a toothless dog would be born again? Yes, that was it. And all of that just to die some day? Well, he was dying. In his fear the man saw that he was dying. And if it was not the pain—which is our reply—that is all it could have been. Would he die some day?

But not so simple as all that! The man shouted to himself, horrified, because in the dark he seemed to have the great intuition that one dies with the same intense and impalpable energy with which one lives, with the same kind of offering that one makes of one's self, and with that same mute ardor; that one would die strangely happy in spite of all, submissive to the perfection that makes use of us—to that perfection which makes us, right up to the last instant of life, sniff out the dry world with intensity, sniff out with joy and acceptance . . . Yes, fated through love, accepting with a strange accommodation, accepting . . .

Only that? Practically nothing! The man was still rebelling, but, my God, that's practically nothing.

No, that's a lot. Because, through God, there was much more than this. For every man there was probably a certain unidentifiable moment in which he would have more than he could sense, in which the illusion would be so much greater that he would reach the intimate veracity of the dream, where the stones would open up their hearts of stone, and the animals would reveal their secret of the flesh; and men would not be "the others"—they would be "us." Where the world would be a hint that is as recognized as if it had been dreamed about. Might there not be for every man that unidentifiable moment in which even the monstrous patience of God would be accepted?—that patience which for centuries permitted men to annihilate other men with the same stubborn mistake, the monstrous kindness of God which is not in any hurry, that certainty of His that made Him let a man commit murder because He knew that one day that man would be afraid and in an instant of fear, be finally captured, unable to avoid looking himself in his own face. That man would say "yes" to the harmony made up of beauty and horror and perfection and beauty and perfection and horror, the perfection that makes use of us.

And that man, with great respect for his fear, would say "yes," even knowing with shame that this would perhaps be his greatest crime because there was an essential lack of rightness in finding all of that beautiful and inevitable, there was an essential lack of rightness in a man's joining himself to the divinity. Up to what point did a man have the right to be divine and say "yes"? At least not until he had put his affairs in order!

But no. Even without knowing how to put his affairs in order, the man would end up by committing the crime of saying yes. Because having touched upon the incomprehensible knot of the dream he accepted the great absurdity that mystery is salvation.

"Oh God!" Martim then said in calm despair. "Oh God!" he said. "Our parents are now dead and it is useless to ask them 'What's that light?' It is no longer they, it is ourselves. Our parents are dead. When will we finally face up to that? Oh God!" he said then. He looked at the darkness around him and since every other person was at last in his own house and there was no one in the world would guide him in his jaundiced flesh he then invented God. It was enough to invent Him so that out of the depths of centuries of fear and abandonment a new force would become gigantic in a place where nothing had existed before. A man in the dark is a creator. The great bargains are made in the dark. It was by saying "Oh God" that Martim felt the first weight of relief in his chest. He breathed slowly and carefully: growing hurts, becoming hurts. He breathed very slowly and carefully. Becoming hurts. The man had the painful impression that he had gone too far.

Perhaps. But at least for one instant of truce he was no longer afraid. It was only that he felt an unexpected loneliness, the loneliness of a person who creates instead of being created. Standing there in the dark, he succumbed to the loneliness of a complete man, the loneliness of the great possibility of choice. The loneliness of having to make his own tools. The loneliness of having already chosen. And then having chosen the irreparable: God.

At last, all alone before his own greatness, Martim could not bear it any longer. He knew that he would have to shrink before what he had created so that he could belong to the world, and shrink until he became the son of the God he had created because only in that way would he receive tenderness. "I am nothing," and thn one fits inside the mystery.

And with a frightened look, with a reborn fear, he now wanted only one thing from this world: to belong. But how? The wind filled his mouth with dust, the wind that he had noticed only now and that suddenly frightened him. He began to tremble again; he passed his hand across his dry and avid mouth. The fear of never reaching the kindness of God overtook him. He had called on the strength of God, but he still did not know how to incite His kindness. It was then that he suddenly said inside of himself, "I killed, I killed." He finally confessed.

Was it because of this, perhaps, that they were waiting for him to free him from his fear? He offered his crime as a pawn.

But—he rebelled immediately then, justifying himself to God—someone had to sacrifice himself and bring unconsoled suffering to its ultimate term and then become the symbol of suffering! Someone had to sacrifice himself. "I wanted to symbolize my own suffering! I sacrificed myself! I wanted the symbol

(2 3 8)

because the symbol is the true reality and our life is symbolic of the symbol, just as we ape our own nature and try to copy ourselves! Now I understand the imitation. It's a sacrifice! I sacrificed myself!" he said to God, reminding Him that even He had sacrificed a son and that we also had the right to imitate Him. We had to renew the mystery because reality is getting lost! "Oh God," he said in justification—"don't you even respect our indignation? My hatred always saved my life. I did not want to be sad. If it were not for my rage I would be all softness and sadness; but anger is born out of my purest joy, and out of my hope. And You want me to give up the best part of my wrath. You who had Your own," he accused. "That's what they told me, and if they told me they were not lying because they must have sensed Your wrath in their flesh," he accused.

Then, what happened was that Martim was afraid of his own wrath as one is afraid of his own strength. Darkness surrounded him, and the silence that enveloped him replied that this was not the way to the world, this was not the way to free himself from himself. And he—he wanted to belong. But how? It would really be so simple. If animals were nature itself, we are the beings to whom things are given. It would be so simple just to receive them. It was enough to receive, just that! So simple.

But a person does not know how.

"How? How is it done?" he asked himself. The wind left his mouth dry with dust. A total fear, greater than the fear that the professor would turn him in to the police, finally made him want to give in. He no longer really knew whether he wanted to accept because there was no other way out, or because accepting was accepting a great and obscure meaning that came from meeting with the unknown creature that he was. It no longer even mattered to him if, in the act of accepting, he felt that he was betraying the most worthy thing about himself; his revolt —not only his own revolt alone but also the revolt of other people. He who had made himself the repository of the wrath of others, he who had needed a great crime to prove something knew that he was betraying his own sacrifice. Even then, he wanted it.

(239)

Even though, aware of his betrayal, he would become a very old man. He could never again be understood by an adolescent. Never again, never again would he be understood—not even by himself. More than that he knew, just as if he had taken a blood oath, that no thought of his would ever be free of the limits of the cowardice now revealed, the cowardice that is the necessary submission and the experience of a man. He realized that never again would he be able to begin to be free without remembering the fear that he felt now.

He knew. But, in the darkness of the woods, all he wanted to do was set himself free. How? With no training, he did not know how to accept—as if there were some kind of ritual he did not comprehend which not only symbolized submission, but also brought it about. Oh, it did not even matter that after his acceptance a new lack of sense would immediately take shape in the kaleidoscope, a harmonious and intangible lack of sense in a system closed off again, where he would again be unable to enter. What was really important was becoming part of a system and freeing himself from his own nature, which suddenly made him tremble all over from head to toe. Oh, it did not matter, because he had already gone too far. And being afraid was already too late; it already meant belonging to salvation, whatever that might mean. What did it matter if it were the word or not? We who make allusions only make allusions.

At night, in the woods his enormous fatigue made the man lose his lucidity, and instinctively his blind thought made him want to look for the most remote source. He guessed that in that dark source everything would be possible, because in that source law was so primary and vast that within it the great confusion of a man would also fit. Except that before being admitted into the first law a man would humbly have to lose his own name. That was the condition. A castaway has to choose between losing his heavy riches or sinking with them into the sea. To be admitted into the vast source (of natural law), the man knew that he had to believe only in light and dark. That was the condition. After that step he would become a defeated part of what he did not know and what he loved.

The wind was blowing stronger through the trees. In the dark the loosened leaves swatted his face. With a soft and wounded chest, he breathed in the humidity that was approaching. He wondered, curious, whether it would rain that night. Because he did not have the courage to leave the festival of the forest he knew that the rain would come and find him there, defenseless. And with that thought he again began to tremble with fear of the dark and the rain. He too trembled, just like the others—because he had been told that it even happened to the strongest, and sailors knew all about it.

One day in a rage he had brought his strength to fruition— just like other people. And in his regret, he had brought his sweetness up to the limits of honey, until, transfigured by his own nature, he said nothing and saw nothing in the dark. But to be blind is to have a continuous vision. Could that be the message perhaps?

But first rage and repentance. Until in extreme unction a man would come, and in order to be saved, he would implore you with a menacing face and a shout of summing up with which we try to understand what belongs to us: "Say yes! Just once! Now! Right now! Say yes once before you die! Don't die in damnation, don't die in rage! The miracle of blindness is nothing but this—saying yes!"

Was that what they wanted him to do then? To say "Yes?" In exchange for everything he knew, what did they demand of a man? In exchange they asked a man—to believe, to eat mud until he bursts with it, but to believe. The man himself might have stolen the bread of others but they ask him, horrified with him, to believe. He may have never done an act of kindness—but they ask him to believe. He may have forgotten to answer his woman's letter, begging for money for her sick child—but they ask him to believe.

And he believes. "I believe," Martim said, terrified with

himself. "I believe, I believe! I don't know what truth is, but I know that I would be able to recognize it!" He justified himself. "Give me a chance to know what I believe!"

But it was not given. And then, because he did not know what truth was, he said to himself in the woods: "I believe in truth. I believe—just as I see in this darkness. I believe—just as I do not understand. I believe—just as we murder. I believe—just as I never gave bread to someone who was hungry. I believe that we are what we are; I believe in the spirit; I believe in life, I believe in hunger; I believe in death!" he said, using words that were no longer his. And because they were not his, they had the value of a ritual which was only waiting to free him from fear, words passed on to him: "I believe."

The man sniffed, ashamed. A new and painful dimension had opened up in him, that which "God" must have silently foreseen in His strange vision of us. The man really seemed to have lost his relativity for an instant, just as a horse sometimes becomes completely abandoned. Could that have been what God had patiently waited for him to understand? That was what he had promised him. But even if God could have spoken He would have told him nothing, because if it had been told it would not have been understood. Even now the man did not understand.

Humiliated, the man sniffed, wiping away his tears—a little intimidated. The first flash of lightning broke across the sky. The tall main house lit up and turned dark again. After a moment of silence the dry thunderclap rolled across the mountains in reply, until it unwound, in the grumbling murmur of silence. Sniffing, the man thought that this was harmony.

Then the wind began to blow stronger, making the windows bang. And Vitória sat up in her bed.

No thought had occurred to that lady yet, but her heart had certainly heard the thunder. It was rain that was coming. It was rain that was coming! She recognized it in the stifling air and in the wrath of the imprisoned wind. It was rain that was coming.

Her heart became ferociously happy. Triumph, her triumph, she had known how to wait.

Only then did she understand with a certain remoteness that she was awake. It was cold and yet she felt stifled, with her heart all puffed up in her breast, perhaps because no drop had fallen yet.

Then, sitting in the dark as if there had been no interruption, she once again recaptured the thought she had had when she had seen Martim for the first time by the porch: a man standing, his face showing the gross beatification of having satisfied his thirst—but even then she could not tell whether she had found it beautiful or ugly. And as if it were quite natural to be thinking about the man in the middle of the night, the lady once more seemed intrigued with that indifference of his face whose physical traces were at the same time those of pure malice. But it was like a tiger who seems to be laughing and then it becomes obvious with a sense of relief that it is only the cut of his mouth. Which did not pacify her, however, because physical things also have their intention. What softened the danger in the man was the contradictory duality of his physical face and an expression that did not conform to it. From malignant curiosity the woman imagined that along with the maleficent features, the expression had also become malicious, then—then she must have seen the face of laughter and of evil. Then she trembled with pleasure.

The pleasure startled her and she drew back in fright. Perhaps her fright had come from being awake in the middle of the night or from thinking about the man. She immediately smoothed the sheets, preparing herself severely to go back to sleep.

She knew, however, that it was a lie and that she was not getting ready for sleep. Therefore, then, she remained quiet in the dark. The compact darkness permitted everything because her face could not be seen even by the walls. And, as happens, the night seemed to whisper to her that she could think any thought at all, as if the animals had been turned loose in the black field before the storm broke and the lady could take advantage of the wind to mingle furtively among them. "I love you," she tried with care giving a first cautious show of herself in the darkness to see if it was true that nothing would happen to her. And nothing happened. The lady seemed disappointed, as if she had really hoped that after the audacious phrase the darkness would turn into day, or that it would finally start to rain, or that she would suddenly be transformed into a different person.

Then the phrase echoed and echoed in the temporarily docile wind.

Nothing had happened. A tranquil sadness filled the room. It was love that lady felt in her body warm with sleep. It was love, that sadness of a beast mixed with rage in the dark; the darkness was her love. It could not be love, that thing, as if she were the only person alive in the dark. She had never heard love spoken about like that. But the wind was blowing . . . And uncertain she looked for love the way the darkness looks for darkness, the way the flame of a candle seems to go out, finally conquered by what is so much greater than the small flame of a candle. If it was not love the man owed that to her before he left; the lady had suddenly become stubborn the way one does when plunged into the middle of the night.

The window was open to the opaque night, that opaqueness which would become a trembling transparency when the darkness finally would get wet. And the lady, trying to calm down, said to herself that she would certainly go to sleep when it began to rain. "That's the only reason I couldn't sleep." All the while, as sharply as her eyes pierced the dark, they found nothing and there was no obstacle to stop them from going on forward. She was looking for an impediment out of habit; until now obstacles had served her as a great support. But surrounded by love now, by wind in the trees, by permission, it could no longer be the embrace that had symbolized that woman's love. Sitting there she had already come to the point of using her soul, which was the darkest part of her body, and the saddest part. "I love you," she tried again, with a hard and haughty voice. But love could not be that. Loving like that was melancholy. "The animals are loose," she thought then, soft, soft, melancholy.

"What animals?" she was startled when she realized what she had thought, and the little flame of the candle tried to give a last justification before it succumbed. "What animals?" she asked herself, forcing herself austerely into a logic that would make her be "puzzled," and being puzzled would be defending herself. But she herself replied with the stubbornness of pleasure; "The animals out of which the dark is made."

After which the woman painfully tried to recuperate; she had to keep herself as lucid and clear as she was in the daytime. Had she not finally managed to live peacefully on her farm, busy with her duties? Had she not finally managed to free herself from that menace which was the anxiety of living? And free herself from that hard and empty ardor which would have carried her God knows where?

"I managed!" she answered herself painfully, feeling her great loss. And had she not managed God with a great deal of effort? "I managed," she answered, frightened. She did not know exactly what she meant by God. But she had managed. Then what she should logically do was lie down and go to sleep.

She had managed, yes. But just as in the case of a former addict who could no longer resist temptation—there had appeared a man, who by his temporary stay seemed to require an ultimatum that she manage again and renew the decision. Why should a person have to decide every day and every night? What freedom was it that the woman had not even asked for? And as if she had not already chosen with such great effort, she had to choose over and over again; as if she had not already chosen. The shortness of the man's stay on the place recalled with an obscure echo another transitory time and another urgency—which one?—and it gave her a last opportunity. Opportunity for what? And her heavy soul, which had desisted with such great pride, felt itself obliged to choose between continuing the struggle and giving in. Giving in to what? No sooner had she seen the man for the first time by the porch than with rage she had guessed that she would have to decide again.

"Which does not mean that I have not resisted!" she shouted to herself in justification, angrily demanding the right to receive mercy—she, who out of caution had betrayed the man to the professor. And was that not a sign of resistance? It was. So now that she had done her duty, now that she had turned him in, she could sleep peacefully.

But she kept on sitting. "I love you," she experimented carefully. As if loving was somehow the way of reaching one's own limits and the way of giving one's self to the dark world that was calling her. "Because I'm unhappy," she thought with the tranquillity of one who was looking way off into the distance. At least if what she was feeling was happiness. Because it resembled it so much. She remained quiet, sitting, listening to the frogs, quiet, with her love-wound, and all alone to resolve, without the resources of comprehension, the fact that she had reported the man. The calm expectancy of the night confined her, just as silence obliges one to speak.

Suddenly Vitória came back to her senses. "After all," she thought with authority, "after all, I have my rights and duties, and there's no reason to be awake in the dark. After all, I'm not lost in Africa!"

But she was. The frogs were croaking as if they were in the room; the black wind came in through the window. The woman shivered. "That dark and good and welcome thing which is evil." The only word that she had left over from her unknown thought and which came out with another shiver was: "evil." Evil? why use that terrible word? Still it was what she was feeling in the dark, all surrounded and welcomed and received. What stages had she missed to arrive at the point at which the dark received her? Could she feel only the cruelty in love? In love what there was of a diluted feeling for life all came together in one single instant of fright, and the rage by which she lived had become transformed before the concrete man into a mortal hatred of love, as if the spread-out green of all the trees had

(2 4 6)

come together into one single black color. In love what there was of a vague foreboding of life came together in one single instant of horror.

And yet—yet one might say that she loved that fright and that darkness, and that was where the terrible joy that the woman felt in the dark came from. Her ambition for rough fingers had come back. Touched by what one does not know how to call except love—so different from what one hoped love and softness and goodness would mean—her ambition had returned, canceling out the bright and busy days on the farm. In the darkness of the room, obscure ambition, obscure violence, the obscure fear that makes one attack, she who out of fear had turned the man in.

The night was made for sleeping. So that a person is never present at what happens in the dark. For that reason, with eyes blinded by the darkness, sitting and quiet, that lady seemed even more to be spying, since her body was functioning inside: she herself was the dark stomach with its nausea, the lungs with their tranquil bellows, the warmth of the tongue, the heart which unfortunately never had been heart-shaped, the intestines in their delicate labyrinth—those things which do not stop while one sleeps, and at night they enlarge, and now they were she. Sitting with her body, so much body suddenly. At midnight Cinderella would be the rags she really was, the coach would turn back into a pumpkin, and the horses into mice—that is how it was invented and they had not been lying. At midnight one entered the dominion of God, which was such a broad domain that a person, unable to cross it, was lost in God's means without understanding their clear ends. Because there was that lady face to face with her own body, which was a means, and where she suddenly had become bound without being able to get away. And the means of God were such a heavy force of enveloping darkness—the animals came out from their curfew one by one, protected by the soft animal possibility of the night. "It's dark," the lady said, as if it were the awaited password that would initiate her into hell, because the ways of God resembled a hell most of all. And the hell was the way in which one worshipped the ways of God. Absorbed, quiet, she listened to the frogs. To be a frog was the humble and ugly way of being a creature of God. And as if purity and beauty were no longer possible ways to serve Him, the lady too seemed to be a frog on the bed, with that primal joy of the devil which things take on in the dark—so rolled up as they are, and themselves so dark. Like a green animal, then, sitting on the bed.

The night was made for sleeping because otherwise one understands what was meant when they talked about hell, and everything a woman does not believe in during the day she will understand at night. And so, in the dark of the room, with the heavy weight of pleasure, she seemed to understand why they said "hell" and why people wanted hell. She seemed to understand what the figure of a black monk in children's stories meant and what there was gloomy about the flight of a large butterfly. And if she were to see a dark dog now, it would be useless to know that the soul of the devil was not in it: because now perhaps she knew what they had meant when they invented the tale that a black dog is inhabited by evil. Something is being said in a black dog. And motionless, without committing any sin, she too knew what evil and sin were. And if bats did not exist, they would still end up coming through the window at nightfall: only in order to say what we know with the shape of their wings. "Everything I know is occult," she felt, and she was sitting on the bed captured by what she knew. But it was also true that when she was not in the dark, her heart did not recognize the truth.

Her eyes were soft, constrained, intense. Perhaps she too was understanding why it is that God, in His infinite wisdom, gave and ordained only certain determined words to be thought—and only them. It was so that one would live by them and only them. Perhaps she had understood, because she remembered from out of nowhere that the professor had said that there had been a period in which it was considered heresy for liturgical music to contain more than one melodic strain; yes, the professor had said that it was considered the work of the devil. More than one melodic strain and one was in the bonds of luxury. The foolish woman remembered stories that had been told to her about peaceful men who had gone wrong from having once experienced nocturnal life, and then had abandoned wife and children; and then had taken to drink in order to forget what they had felt or to maintain the nocturnal feeling.

Suddenly, having been dragged along the course of her feelings, she passed her hand across her face, trying to wake up. It had been an involuntary mistake, hers, waking up during the night that is made for sleeping, as if against her will she had opened the forbidden door to the secret and had seen the livid wives of Bluebeard. It had been an involuntary and pardonable mistake. But it was already more than a simple error, her not having closed the door and having yielded to the temptation of gaining power in that silence where, because she had refused to limit herself only to the use of His comprehensible words, God had left her alone. Probably she had counted on a God stronger than her mistake and stronger than her will to make mistakes. But the silence was enveloping her. And the lady, facing her greed, was sitting there. "My God, I pardon Thee," she said, closing her eyes before continuing on irrepressibly along her joy.

And all of that was love. That was how it happened, then. With that darkness and that silence and that wind and the waving trees. "But I pardon Thee even if it is just because I want it to be that way."

All alone with the misery of her lust, which was not even lust for love. It was more serious. It was a lust to be alive. The frogs were enormous now, with their open mouths near the window. The legs that came forth out of those neckless heads, those split mouths croaking out an ancient noise, the small monsters of the earth. And for an instant, in a torture of joy, the woman too seemed to have claws there on the bed because something happens in the dark of night. In the midst of her suffering, now at its high point, only a minimum of consciousness stopped her from going to join the frogs beside the window. A minimum of consciousness within her waking nightmare stopped what was darkness in her from joining in the orgy of the frogs. Half-awake, she made that effort not to be an animal, because we do have their ears and we also have their innocent faces. A minimum of consciousness was stopping her, favored in it all by the growing dampness, from following the pattern of lament and howling which exists inside a person and which the darkness of the countryside temptingly promised to bless.

Feeling that perhaps she no longer was afraid, she dared ask herself; "Why did I turn him in?"

But even in the inviting darkness, remorse turned her blood to acid. And the worst thing about remorse was not understanding the usefulness of its vengeance. "Why did I turn him in? why that bit of cruelty, why?" Then, as a balm, she remembered a phrase from a children's book: "The lion is not a cruel animal. He kills only in order to eat." The lion is not a cruel animal, he kills only in order to eat, the lion is not a cruel animal—was it her fault that she was so hungry? But would she ever be able to eat all that she had killed, she who had killed so much already, she who had killed so much already? Sitting on the bed, she had killed more than she could eat. That was her great sin. Her infantile fright was that once she had betrayed the man to the professor, the man remained betrayed.

If the lady had thought that in the dark she would not feel remorse for what she had done, she had been mistaken. Even in the dark the inexplicable point was hurting. And humiliated, she could not bear the weight of her petty crime. The will to burn in Hell, for which all are called and so few are damned. She did not have the strength of evil, the flesh is weak: she was good. And the devil was as difficult as sainthood.

She had told on him, and the man would of course end up being arrested. "Oh God," she said then, proud and not imploring, "have mercy on a weak heart." Because she, she did not have any. She only felt revulsion for the meanness of her crime, and did not even want consolation. Consolation seemed petty compared to the depths of the dark light that suffering was and where she again seemed happy and startled.

But a minimum of consciousness made her know that at any

moment she would finally have the strength to free herself from her evil delight in the darkness. At any moment the lady would finally have the strength to get out of that rejoicing state into which she had dangerously fallen, just as one falls into a hole while searching for a path. She had gone so far that she could only bring herself to understand what was happening to her if she called it a nightmare. Because it must have been a nightmare to be all alone with that warm feeling of living that no one can use. God, who out of pure kindness had deemed that feeling to be a sin. So that no one would dare and no one would suffer the truth. All alone with the warm feeling of living. Like a rose whose grace cannot be appreciated. Like a river that exists only to have its murmur heard. A warm feeling that the woman could not translate into any movement or thought. Useless but alive. Imponderable, but alive, like a drop of blood on the bed. There she was, like a drop of blood in the dark. And just like a dead person who arose and walked, the warmth of her life suddenly made her rise up slowly, and it brought her, serious and blind, to search out her equals in the night.

When it finally began to rain, the lady had reached a point of silence at which it seemed to her that the rain was the word. Surprised with the sweet and unexpected meeting, she gave herself over to the water without resistance, feeling in her body that the plants were drinking, that the frogs were drinking, that the animals on the place were listening to the noise on the roof—the news had spread out foggily and was soaking the whole farm: it was raining, it was raining, it was raining. "Let it rain," she said. "Because I love you that way too," she thought before she fell asleep; the darkness was also kindness, we were kindness too.

It was a little while later that Vitória woke up as if she had been asleep for hours. And, finally free of the nightmare, she was startled to find the night at the same point where she had left it.

What had happened was that she had slept so deeply for a few minutes that her body was heavy with hours of sleep. When she went to the bathroom she saw a calm and puffy face in the mirror. Thirst alerted her a little, the noise of the rain among the hollow leaves made her even thirstier. She went down to the kitchen and picked a big mango from among the fruit. She carefully hit it against the wall, vaguely trying not to awaken Ermelinda with the mushy noise of the mango against the brick wall—until, absorbed, she felt that the fruit was soft inside its skin, full of its own juice. Meditating, Vitória bit off the top of the hull, spat it out, and sucked up all the juice through the opening. Then she tore the skin with her teeth, ate the yellow pulp until she came to the pit.

Only when she was standing over the wash-basin brushing her teeth did the sobs come into her chest. Then, hiding her face in the crook of her arm against the wall, she waited patiently for the tears to pass—after which she wiped her eyes and looked at her teeth in the mirror.

Then she went out on the porch. While she had been in the bathroom the rain had slackened. The night was peaceful and calm; small, indeterminate sounds cuddled in the darkness. Trembling from the good cold, she could guess from the porch at the path that would take her to the woodshed and, in the secret confusion of the bushes, she could almost guess where the door was. She went down the steps.

She breathed slowly until she felt her lungs full of the black wet air. Pushing back branches, she managed to reach the little clearing which told where the door was. She could almost hear the silence coming from the woodshed. It was hard for her to imagine that someone living existed in that darkness besides herself, who was breathing softly; her head was to one side, listening, listening. Where could the man be? She remembered once when she had heard him snoring. If it were not such an absurd idea, it would have occurred to her that the woodshed was empty; she had always been able to sense when a place was empty.

It started to rain again. The drops ran down the branches,

beat delicately against the leaves and scattered into the vastness of the countryside. A green flash of lightning suddenly revealed the unsuspected height of the sky. Another flash of light suddenly placed a previously invisible tree within her reach. And the thunderclaps rolled over into the abyss. "I"—said the old woman—"I am Queen of Nature."

Tightening her bathrobe across her breast, she then came close enough to get the smell of the wet wood of the door and, from a little deeper inside, the smell, the rotting smell that came from the logs in the woodshed. Her hands ran slowly and lively across the door. It gave way without any noise. She pushed it slowly, and as she opened an unknown door, the woman seemed more restless than the similar cautious figure in the dark which the man would become out of fright when she woke him up. She stood motionless, neither inside nor out of the woodshed, with her face attentive and wet.

But the kind of instinctive stubbornness of will that had guided her that far seemed to have become extinguished. Even before the act was done, the inspiration that had fed it had ended. And as if on that night the woman had been enveloped by innumerable layers of nightmare and each time had freed herself from one of them, she would think mistakenly that she had come to the last one—only now had she wakened completely from the dream. She passed her hand across her face where the water freely flowed. Even her trip to the kitchen and the mango she had eaten had been a nebulous part of a dream and of a strength. Why had she gone to the woodshed? she asked herself, curious.

Then she remembered that in some no longer indentifiable instant she had planned to tell the man that she had betrayed him to the professor. It had been that, then, that she had come to do in the woodshed. But although until she realized that, she had seemed so determined to the point of not even questioning it now she suddenly did not know what step to take next. She was reduced to being a woman by a door on a rainy night. Was it that if someone saw her, he would say "Look at the old woman out in the rain"? she asked herself, meditating. "I am the queen of the beasts," the lady said.

Nobody in the world knew that she was there. And nobody would ever know—because now she already seemed certain that she would not talk to Martim, and that she would go back to bed, going along the path through the rain again. "Nobody in the world would ever know"—which suddenly stretched out the great darkness of the countryside, and the woman remained lost in it, she, tremulous queen of nature. That thought which was so secret that only the rain partook of it gave her a pleasure, as if she had finally done something beyond human strength. She trembled with joy. The night beat hard upon her face with the wet wind; the lady accepted the unknown pact with delight.

It was with the same previous care, but without the same emotion, that she turned to go away. In a little while she reached the porch, slipping on the wet steps and the moss; in a little while she was going through the living room and the hallway, without making any sound, leaving behind her the wet footprints of a biped. But when she reached the landing of the stairs, her caution became useless: her foot had stepped on something that rolled and rolled and rolled. With her back flat up against the wall, holding in her breath, she bore with horror the object that was rolling down step by step, pausing like the minutes of a clock. Perhaps it was the spool of thread that she had lost. And she had heard, or had she only thought that she had heard, the creaking of the bed in Ermelinda's room. The silence closed in again in a little while; the shadows went back to their places.

Only when she got to her room did her heart begin to pound violently. She stood there in the darkness, and while she trembled from the daring of what she had done—now she could not tell whether the daring had been her trip to the woodshed or her betrayal to the professor—while she was trembling all over at what she had done, she began to smile in triumph. She did not turn on the switch because she was afraid that she would not like the weak and yellowish light they had on the farm, to which she had never become accustomed. Every time that she put on the light, it seemed to her that she was only gilding the darkness. Without turning on the light, without making any noise that would wake up Ermelinda, who slept like a bird, Vitória turned down the spread, carefully tucked in the sheets, and carefully got into bed; she covered herself up to her chin and stayed there with her eyes wide open in the dark, enjoying the still-tremulous comfort of a dog who goes off by himself to lick his wounds, with the human look that animals have.

It was only then that it also occurred to her that there had been no act . . . That she had gone as far as the door of the woodshed and returned; just that. Just that? Her eyes opened wider in the dark. With surprise—with pain? No, with relief— with surprise, her life on the place was completely intact. Everything became clear then:by turning in the stranger she had only been defending that life. So that in the clearness of the next day a thousand little chores awaited her. She had managed one thing at least: she had cried. She cried. "And," she thought illogically, "since the man had not gone away yet, I still have time." Another indistinct sound from Ermelinda's room made the lady try in some way to not even think: she immobilized herself even more, looking for the sleep that would deny everything.

As for Ermelinda, she too was taking a little time to realize that she was awake. Lying there she looked peacefully at the darkness of the ceiling. Then she went on to distinguish the crickets that were separated from the silence. And then the noise of the calm frogs began to come to life in her ears. Her attention then searched for a certain rhythmical sound that she heard no more now; a sound within the house itself or within her sleep, something that was strangely related to the steps of a staircase. She remembered that she had dreamed that she was going down them one by one. And she had dreamed that a mouse had rolled down the stairs. The house was peaceful in the rain.

But when she finally realized that she was awake, she asked herself with a sudden start how long she had been awake. She rolled over quickly, really began to listen, close to the window, to the hoarse frogs, and she heard the noise of the wind in the leaves. Everything that had been faintly in the background took on the hard shape of reality. "It's now," she thought, with cold hands.

She did not even have to think about what "now" meant, because her heart had already beaten as it knew. She knew that if she stayed all alone in the dark one instant too long, she would end up feeling once more the expanse of the countryside in the dark and the little flowers that continued to exist even at night with their soft laughter—by the same process that had made the frogs and the wind real.

As if she had been bitten, in less than a second the girl was standing up, in less than a second she wrapped herself up in the sheet and was running through the hall with her slippers in her hand. Without asking herself why, she had found the door to the porch unexpectedly open; she went through it with a wind of sheets and hair. And only when she reached the clearing by the woodshed—after covering in one single instant of an almost audible fear the distance that separated her from the man—did she realize with a hollow exclamation that she had found the porch door inexplicably open . . . The door of the woodshed was also open . . .

This was the final sign that perhaps that thing which cannot be known until it happens had already happened: between life and death there was no longer any barrier, the doors were all open.

The girl then became motionless in the clearing, with her wet sheet, rigid, not taking another step. Her terror was peaceful in the falling rain. And standing there, she seemed relieved. She had been captured without warning. Captured by her religion and by the abyss of her faith and by the consciousness of a soul and by a respect for what is not understood and which ends up being worshipped, captured by what in Africa makes the drums beat, by what makes a dance a danger, and by what makes the jungle a person's fear. Incapable of moving, with respect and

(256)

terror for her own thought, which was flying away from her, and the rain seemed to be flying up from the ground the way smoke rises up from ruins. But it was not the ruins that the girl was afraid of, it was the smoke. And it was not death that she feared. What she respected, with the veneration one had for a jungle, was the other life. Standing there, looking at the empty fields through which one day she would stroll free of her body. With that indirect way of walking which her soul would have: backward and forward and to both sides all at the same time. So all alone after being dead. Completely alone. Finally given over to the dream that was dragging her along through life, she, who had understood the miracle of the spirit so poorly.

The girl stayed quiet in her sheets then, like a great white butterfly. And she could offer nothing as sacrifice in exchange for death. She had nothing that was needed as a gift of martyrdom. There was no possible bargain. The thought of death was the last point that her thinking had managed to reach and also the one from which her thought could not even retreat. To go back would be to find, as in a persecution nightmare, the broad fields of that land, the inflated and empty clouds in the sky, the flowers—everything that on earth is already as soft as the other life. The small and perfect flowers waving in clusters in the field . . . did they not have the serene madness and delicacy of the "other life"? When she was obliged to face up to her fear, the very soft smell of the flowers would pursue her like a bird that was circling about her head. That delicate girl preferred a rat, the body of a steer, the pain and the continuous work of living, she who had so little skill for living—but she preferred all of that to the horrible and tranquil little cold joy of the flowers, and to the birds. Because on earth they were also the nauseating sign of the after life. Their presence, an innocent reminder, took away the assurance of terrestrial life itself. And it was then that even houses with their lives inside seemed to her to be built too fragile, with no feeling of the danger there was in not being more deeply rooted in the ground. Yet only the girl seemed to see what others did not see, and what the solid houses did not even suspect: that they had been built without caution, just as a person in the dark will fall asleep in a cemetery and not know it. Houses and people were merely perching upon the earth, just as temporary as a circus tent. That succession of temporary things on an earth that did not even have frontiers marking off where a person lived in life and where he lived in death—that earth which perhaps was the very place a soul would someday stroll about in lost, sweet and free.

But if the girl did manage to see, coming from afar where one day she herself would go, if she did manage to see the birds—what? What were the other "signs"? How could one distinguish them in their disguise? Sometimes she could distinguish. Sometimes she could suddenly perceive in a solid tree the soft suspicion. But how, how could one distinguish the other signs? Even if the wind did blow sometimes.

All of the work of that girl, who once had fallen into the mystery of thinking, was to search uselessly for proofs that death would be the total peaceful end. And that would be salvation and she would earn her life. But with her tendency toward details, what she managed was a contrary indication. A chicken that flew higher than usual—had that naturalness of the supernatural. Hairs that always grew so quickly would make her so thoughtful. And a snake. "But it was there a minute ago, I swear! and it isn't there any more!"—the rapidity with which things would disappear, the rapidity with which she lost handkerchiefs and did not know where she had left the shears, the rapidity with which things turned into other things, the automatic evolution of a bud as it mechanically opened up into a flower—or the head of a horse that she suddenly would discover on the horse, the added head, like a frightful mask on that solid body—all of that was in some way an indication that after death immeasurable life began. For that had been the way that Ermelinda had come to take note of beauty: by its eternal side. And if thousands of ways of seeing things exist, the girl had fastened herself forever to one of them.

Oh, but not this time!

(2 5 8)

There in the clearing, suddenly, and in an unexpected movement of liberation, she unstuck her feet from the soaked ground —and as in flight, she crossed the threshold, throwing herself forward in search of the man with the despair of a caged bird. And when her body struck his, she was not even surprised to find Martim standing up and dressed and soaked to the skin, as if he too had just come into the woodshed.

And the stupefied man, seeing her with her hair hanging down, wild as a chrysanthemum, only realized what was happening when he finally recognized the shape of the girl. And he could not tell whether she had run to him or whether he himself had thrown himself at her—so much had one startled the other, and so much was one the very solution for the other's not becoming terrified at the fact that they were so unexpectedly together. She was glued to him in the dark, that big, wet man with the smell of verdigris about him, and it was strange and voracious to be embraced without seeing him, merely trusting in the avid sense of a desperate touch, the rough, concrete clothes, he seemed to be a lion with a wet mane—would he be the executioner or the companion? But in the dark she had to trust, and she closed her eyes tightly, giving herself completely over to what there was that was entirely unknown in that stranger, beside the minimum that was known, that was his living body—she clung to that dirty man in terror of him, they clutched each other as if it were an impossible love. It did not even matter if he were a murderer or a thief, it did not matter for what reason he had ended up on the farm; there is one instant at least in which two strangers can devour each other, and how could she help liking him if she was in love with him again? and when his voice sounded as a grunt in the dark the girl felt that she was saved, and they loved one another the way parents do when they have lost a child.

And now the pair of them were embracing on the bed like two monkeys in the zoo, and not even death can separate two monkeys who love each other. Now he was a stranger, yes. No longer because she did not know him, but in the way she had of recognizing the particular and untransferable existence of another person, she accepted the stranger in him with the reverence of love. At that moment she could have said, "I recognize you in you." And if the funniness of it lit up the man beyond the fear of wondering, she would also be the great wonderment for him at last and he would say to her, "And I recognize in you, you." And that is how it would be, and it would be everything, for that was most likely love.

The girl grasped his hand and feeling it warm and still wet, she sighed deeply and gave a little laugh. The fact was that she scarcely believed in her own skill: that night she had conquered fear. And even bemused by sleep, she had known enough to run to be close to a man because a man did not have the softness of women, a man denied the other life for an instant. Lying there pensive, Ermelinda understood what a frightened girl friend of hers had said one day, "I want to get married because it's very sad for a person to be all alone." Ermelinda gave the phrase a very special sense of warning, because her friend too was a person who, for example, was afraid of the dark. And it was true, Ermelinda reflected very sensibly. Because when she had been married, her husband had had schedules and habits, which had done so much to take away the breadth of the world. And even when they had lived in the city it had been different: in shops and stores life was smaller, it fit within her without fear and not like in the damned country. She should have stayed in the city and got married again; that was it, yes, that was what she should have done. And tomorrow, tomorrow she would tell Vitória that she was leaving, because right now she was getting the proof that that was what she ought to do, now that she was snuggling up against Martim, and a man takes away that freedom which a person all alone feels as the foretaste of a greater freedom.

It was then, with a smile of sleep upon her face, well-armed with what she might tell Vitória on the following day, that the girl left the woodshed, still befuddled, stepping on the wood chips and the mud, walking carefully in the dark so that she would not fall.

(2 6 0)

And it was then that, as if her eyes had been looking straight at herself, that she had the idea of herself as if she were looking at herself; and what she saw was a girl all alone in that dripping world, with one shoulder uncovered by the sheet she had trouble wrapping up in, her hair hanging loose, and that face on whose facile indecision had now been painted the joy of living.

And seeing herself, she stopped so suddenly that her feet slipped in a puddle of water and her helpless hands grabbed for the tree which had been thrown up in front of her in the dark. And as if she herself were a lost stranger who suddenly had seen that girl all alone in the rain, she shivered all over. She was alive and she glowed with horror. Could she have been alive in that life or in the other one? Perhaps she had gone beyond the vague horizon, like the birds who go and come back . . . She thought that maybe she had died in the arms of the man without knowing it because she had given her body to him, and her soul was there, white and vacillating, with that sweet joy which the girl was not aware could also come from the body.

Perhaps because, having tripped, she was almost kneeling and did not have to be audacious to do what her heart asked of her; perhaps because, being out of the house at night for the first time, she had broken some law of possibility—now she did not have to be brave in order to complete the half-gesture of a fall, and then she knelt down by the trunk of the tree that had hurt her, and without any shame asked God that she might be eternal. "I am I!" she begged Him, not as a privilege, but to make it easier for Him to grant the tremendous exception. "Oh God, let me always have a body!" The tears were running down her still happy face which, startled, had not had time to change its expression. "My God," she finally confessed, feeling that with it she was confessing a great sin—"I never want to see You!" She felt horror for God and His sweetness and His stability and His perfume; she felt horror for the birds that He had sent as messengers of peace. "I don't want to die because I don't understand death!" the girl said to God. "Please don't judge me so superior to the point that You will send me death! I don't

deserve it! Sneer at me because I am inferior, any life is enough
for me! And I'm not intelligent, I was always backward in
school, why give me so much importance now, then? It's enough
to put me aside and forget about me, who am I to die! Only
privileged people should die! Whom are You asking the truth
from! You can give it to anyone who asks for it!"

She leaned her face against the trunk as against another
wrinkled face, and she smelled the odor of dirty mud that is so
reassuring and simple, the smell of her own life on earth; then
she leaned with desire and love against the dirty tree trunk,
where her mouth was glued in supplication. And out of pity for
herself, it was as if God were telling her:

"That's the way it is. People live and people die."

Had that not been what she had felt that afternoon when
she had been hulling corn? Whoever accepted the mystery of
love accepted the mystery of death; whoever accepted the fact
that a body that is not yet known fulfills its own destiny, accepted then the fact that our fate goes beyond us, we die, that is.
And we die impersonally—and with that we go beyond what we
know about ourselves. There was something impersonal in the
fulfilling to which the girl simply said amen—and a person only
shouted when he was taken by a pain or by surprise and it
became personal. The girl was confused and tired, leaning
against the tree trunk. Underneath it all she understood herself
and she understood. Her way of understanding was what had
become so difficult through the mystery of words.

It was more or less that which she felt in her state of sleepiness and love, embracing the good trunk of the tree for the love
of which we are so well created, clinging to the tree, liking so
much its good, hard knots, hoping that for many, many, many
years she would be able to smell the odor of things, happy
birthday. The unnatural position was breaking her in two. But
she could not manage to say good-bye to the warm perfume
which was coming out of her sleepiness and fatigue, the smell a
body makes as it lives; and once more she breathed in the
freshness of the wet leaves, that smell of rain which is like the

bitter taste of nuts, and her blind hands felt the rough tree which was made for our fingers, and the wet ground on her knees. All of that is our joy, all of that which gives us so much pleasure, and if we are so well created for that, then—then Ermelinda, so tired now, had the wish to give in at last and to follow her calling at last, which was to die some day.

Chapter 4

WHEN MONDAY DAWNED, the sun was so strong that the water in the puddles was gasping with the heat and the bees were already making their rounds among the wounded flowers, and it was as if there had been a party and the decorations had not been taken down yet. In a short while a new heat had taken over, made up of green woollen leaves and body dampness, an unpetaled heat, and already by nine o'clock its soul was rotting among swarms of mosquitoes. A few greenish pieces of fruit had been squashed on the ground for the curiosity of the ants; on the surface of the puddles the dusty threads of fallen spider webs were strung out. But a few diligent spiders had already built new shiny links in the air. With attention brought on by unconscious hope one's glance would accompany the silk threads they moved rapidly from one tree to another, filling in again the space that the rain had caused. At nine o'clock only the spider threads were delicate in the light. Everything else had the exhaustion of satisfaction, the wetness of felt which is difficult to dry, and the weight of its own weight. It had rained everywhere.

With renewed strength, the mulatto woman was singing in the hot kitchen. The rain of the night appeared to have been in everyone's imagination, what happens at night has no use in the daytime. Martim's eyes were red from lack of sleep. His fatigue was worse than he had calculated, and his mouth had the taste of sleep that had not been slept. "I was in the woods last night," he thought, obstinately reducing what had happened to him to this: he had been in the woods and when he had come back Ermelinda had come to the woodshed. "A fresh girl," he thought, fatigued and without malice, looking at her from the distance and seeing her with her hair parted sensibly again as if nothing had happened. Sunday night seemed like an absurdity to the man, and he could not really remember the details very well; being in the woods, which "did not mean anything after all"—and that was why he spat into the plate from which he had just eaten. "Later. I'll think about it later," he said to himself. "There's still time." It would be quite easy to take the truck at nightfall, and when they heard the noise of the motor he would be far away. He still had some time, relatively speaking, being still just a charade for the professor. "Later," he thought.

The mulatto woman was singing and Ermelinda said to her as she drank her coffee, "Last night I had such a fear of dying that you can't imagine! I thought the whole world was going to collapse!"

"No such luck, Dona Ermelinda!" the other one said happily.

They both laughed. But they grew silent like accomplices when they heard Vitória's steps coming through the living room. In the old black slacks again and her blouse open at the neck, with her hair in a bun, Vitória was coming in from the fields. She did not know what time it had been when she had had her coffee; she had waked up so active, as if she had lost time that she had to make up with the rain.

"Today's the day," the mulatto murmured, nodding at Vitória. "Today's the day we're going to catch it"—and Ermelinda agreed in silence.

But Vitória did not even look at them as she passed through the kitchen. She was worried about other problems—she had decided, for example, that they would finally have to cut down the old apple tree because it bore fruit only rarely and even then the fruit was sour, and especially because it was taking up good land. But now the moment of decision had come because a bolt of lightning or a gust of wind had broken off some branches, which were hanging down like rags across the crotch.

Martim rebelled a little; he thought that it was a shame to destroy the beautiful tree. Vitória insisted, and she turned red as she insisted. He looked at her, listened to her argue, and offered a mute resistance. The woman became more and more insistent that the tree come down, as if the repugnance that the man showed for the chore was inciting her.

So, after a few orders had been given to Francisco and other matters had been decided, Vitória followed Martim and his axe, and she stationed herself near the tree to watch—and she was resolute, as if the chopping down would be a question of minutes. One of her feet was resting determinedly on a rock.

Martim sluggishly began to cut the first round notches. She, as if prepared to witness a violent and quick destruction, became restless with the man's slowness, and she could barely control her face that was being taunted by the sun.

"Faster," she finally whispered rapidly and softly, unable to restrain herself any more.

He did not turn around or even break the slow rhythm of his strokes.

"How long before it will fall?" the restless woman asked.

"That all depends."

"Maybe you'd like me to get Francisco to help you? Maybe you can't do it alone?" she suggested, impatient for a reply.

"That won't be necessary," he said at the same time as another hard blow rang out. "Slow but sure."

"But I don't want it to be slow," she thought, kicking with her boot at the gnarled roots that were scattered about, protruding far from the old black tree that in its strength was barely trembling under the blows of the axe. They remained silent, the sun was getting higher and becoming stronger. It was a restless silence, full of flies. The chopping was taking on a regulated rhythm—small chips flew away, damp and white, showing how young the tree still was inside. The woman sat down on one of the outcroppings of the roots, and the man, without stopping his work, took a quick look at her. The silence continued, the flies were shining, dirty and blue; the restless dogs were smelling each other. A whistle was heard far off, a fall was heard far off; the flies were shining black.

The woman's heart began to pound rapidly when she finally

asked with a calm face, but so upset that she did not hear her own voice:

"Why did you come here?"

She heard nothing in reply. Only the axe-blows were making any sound, deepening the circle around the trunk. And with great relief she came to believe that she had not spoken and that she had only heard her own thoughts. Her ears, which had been prepared for an answer, could only hear the gurgling of the river. But he replied:

"I separated from my wife and I went away."

Without even noticing that she had just learned that he was married, she said:

"But why did you come here precisely?"

"It might as well have been here as well as any other place."

She realized that he had said that he was married.

"The first impression I had of you was that you were a fugitive!" she said then very harshly.

"In a manner of speaking," he said.

And having said it, he slowly interrupted his work. He threw the axe aside. He turned around and faced her.

The woman became a little pale. A slight tic made her mouth and her left eye contract simultaneously, and it gave her the innocent air of someone caught in the act.

"You," Martin stated without anger—"you only want me to chop down this tree so you can keep me in one place and ask me questions."

"Me? Of course not!" she answered, and the truth had been revealed so suddenly that the woman felt innocent before it.

"I already told you. I separated from my wife and I went away."

"But you seemed to be running away . . ." she could not help saying, full of curiosity.

"People run away from things like that too," he replied with extreme care, not turning his cold eyes away from her face for a second.

They remained there looking at each other; both of their

(2 6 7)

faces were raw in the open air and red from the sun. There was not a wrinkle on the woman's face that was not showing, but since she did not know it she lifted up her head suddenly with a good deal of haughtiness.

Then, even though the thick tree was barely wounded, Martim turned to go away as if the job had been done.

"Stay here," she said hurriedly and harshly. "I want to talk!"

"I already told you," he repeated even more harshly. "I separated from my wife and I went away. Does the professor have to know any more than that?" he added, calm and cruel.

She did not seem to have heard, but she grew pale:

"That's not what I want to talk about!" she cut in quickly, surprised at herself.

Martim assumed a stiff air of strict expectation, as if he meant to go away as soon as she said what she had to say.

"I want—I want to talk about Ermelinda," she suddenly invented.

He lifted his eyebrows with sincere surprise, and his eyelids, open wider for a minute, left his blue eyes suddenly naked in a sign of mistrust. The woman did not go on right away, as if she were sure that she could hold him better with silence than with unlikely words.

"So?" he asked, looking at her defensively askance.

"It's like this," she said slowly, as if she was no longer in a hurry now that he was the one who inexplicably seemed to have a hasty curiosity. "It's like this," she repeated as if she still did not know what she was going to say.

Pushed then by the now authoritarian expectation of the man, she repeated, "It's like this: Ermelinda is a very impressionable person, you might even say sensitive."

They remained there looking at each other.

"Anything can impress Ermelinda; anything can make her lose her composure. She," Vitória said, licking her lips—"she can lose her balance over anything. She's very impressionable, even very sensitive. When she came to live with me after her husband died, I knew very well what sort of person I was going to have in the house because, I don't know whether you're aware of it, she spent her entire childhood in bed. But she had to live somewhere and she didn't have any money, so she came here. Since Ermelinda is so sensitive I feel a little responsible for her, you understand? I watch what she does very closely, you understand? Oh, please believe me; she's not unbalanced, not in the least: I never knew anyone who was less at a loss. But what happens is that she, since she's so kindhearted and giving she doesn't take spiritualism as just something symbolic. She doesn't really know what spiritualism is and she mixes it up a little with Catholicism, you understand; and then she becomes a little removed from us. Please understand that I don't mean that she loses her head. Quite the opposite. But she can give herself the privilege of being silly without really being silly," Vitória said with a sudden wave of admiration, and her face contracted in envy and bitterness.

The man was intrigued and nodded yes. He stood there in vague suspense, waiting for her to go on, his face already looking a little malicious in its expectancy.

"So," Vitória said after a pause and running her tongue over her lips again, "so, since I am responsible for Ermelinda . . ."

She paused again, and this time she looked at him indecisively without knowing what else to say. But he, beyond appeal, was waiting.

"What I mean," the woman began again in a strong tone, as if she were talking about something entirely different, "what I mean is that perhaps it would be good if you were a little careful. I mean: I know perfectly well that it's a lot to ask, but I wonder if you couldn't be careful so that one day she wouldn't, let's say, get interested in you . . . Oh, nothing serious," she said subtly as if the answer had occurred to her. "Nothing very serious!" she repeated with a sudden assurance at having had the opportunity of interrupting him with her spiritual penetration. "Ermelinda isn't capable of that! But if you could only watch out . . . The fact is you can't trust her. She loses her composure over anything, and when she gets excited a little she blushes and squeaks.

. . . For example, she's not a heavy eater, but if she's encouraged in a friendly way she thinks that she has to match the friendship by eating a lot, eating like a servant girl . . ."

She stopped suddenly. The fact was that if the man had been waiting with surprise in his eyes before, now the desire to laugh was plain to see on his face.

"I know," she continued impassively, wiping the perspiration from her forehead with difficulty, "I know that it isn't up to you; I understand that quite well. You don't have any argument with me. I know very well that one person can, let's say, get interested in another without the other one's, let's say, having the least notion of it . . ."

Could the horrible malice in the man only be that peculiar expression of his, or was it a genuine expression already? Her uneasiness was holding her back; she flicked the fly away from her chin.

"But the fact is," she then said nobly, "since we can't count on Ermelinda's good sense, as I said before; and the fact that she might get interested in you, I can only tell you then that you yourself have to help!" she concluded with relief, as if she had just finished a great piece of logic. There was the tremble of a slight triumph in her voice; she had never thought she would ever be able to get out from under the weight of the words.

The man seemed to be quite content. And he looked at her; she was so immaculate and satisfied!

"You're afraid that she'll go to bed with me some day?" he asked with great pleasure. "Is that what you're afraid of? But how could that happen! And besides there's no time left; you said that, didn't you, you and the professor? But what bothers me is that a conscience as clean as yours could stoop so low as to imagine such a thing! You really amaze me!"

The woman was quiet, her mouth half-open . . . The man looked at her with careful attention, filled with delight.

"What I meant to say," she answered quickly, skipping over his rudeness—"what I meant to say is that—let's say the world is too much for Ermelinda because she's very sensitive," she said, putting on drawing room manners. And without realizing it, she brought her hand up to her blouse and closed the neck a little. "The world," she concluded, frightened, without paying the least attention to what she was saying, "is too much for Ermlelinda; she can't take it," she added foolishly.

"She can take it," the man said unexpectedly in a sluggish tone, without looking at her but without running away.

The woman's heart contracted not from what he had said and what she had barely heard but perhaps because she had not expected any reply. Only then did she realize that there they were standing and talking to each other; only then did she see that she had not been talking to herself. And, for the love of God, had she not also been the one who had brought about that undeniable wound on the trunk of the tree, and had she not also after all brought on that feeling of soft offense that the man had offered her; or brought on that sun that was blotting out everything in front of her eyes. Only then had she fully realized that she was not alone. And the feeling she got filled her with the tremulous excitement she would get after having carried a heavy load; she finally saw with amazement that she had carried it. She had gone farther than she had thought she could go and now it was too late to turn back. Even if nothing else happened, she would never be able to deny what had already happened . . . She had gone so far that she could not go back, and her skin pimpled out like a chicken's. Everything around her then seemed to be infected with the possibility of her becoming real, a possibility which was suddenly very revealing—the tree, almost intact, but doomed to fall nonetheless; today's sun which was nothing but yesterday's rain, everything that was solid and still ready to fall. And even in the man's eyes the woman could almost guess at the gentle spot there is in a person's eyes, the vulnerable spot in the coldest of eyes: possibility.

"And if I really did say something?" it occurred to her. Did the man understand? Or didn't he? And for an instant—facing all the unequal things that were receiving the same sun nevertheless—for an instant there was not even any contradiction in the fact that he understood her and that he did not understand her at the same time, as if that was the only way it could have been. But had she not spoken? How could she guess as to what point it had all been understood by that fearful body the man had. And even deeper, even more inexplicable—how was she to know up to what point her own words were those she had spoken or those she had kept quiet?

Once she had been initiated into the delights of communication, all obstacles seemed insurmountable, as if she had been turned over to the miracle of the sap that feeds plants and it was saying, "It can't be done." She did not know that certain things are done all by themselves or else they never would be done. Used to the strength of her own determination, she had ended up by thinking that she walked because she wanted to and slept because she had decided to. And now she was thinking that before she spoke, it was essential to know how speaking is done. With a slight feeling of despair for happiness, she looked at the countryside and the plants and the flies; and all of that had been made all by itself, everything knew how to live. But she—she did not know how to do it. "Because I am unhappy," she said peacefully to herself then. But could that imminence for which everything suddenly seemed laid out, the great risk that a person runs, be unhappiness? And as if that were precisely our happiness. "I think that that is being happy," she thought with curiosity. Because if both of them were there conversing . . . because if the river was running full and slowly . . . because if, raising up her eyes to the thick crown of the tree, she was illuminated . . . because if the beetles burst into the air . . . because if moments are never repeated, and if knowing that we have this delicate thirst . . . what other happiness could she want except that? She wanted to be assured that the thing she felt was so real that it was on the point of happening. She wanted—she wanted everything she knew to be less mysterious.

"You missed my meaning," she said, swallowing her saliva in the severity of her joy. "I don't mean that Ermelinda can't take it. Ermelinda would be able to respond, let's say, even to love, but she wouldn't resist. Ermelinda has a sickness of the soul, as the . . . as is said . . ."—she was going to add "as the professor says," but she caught herself in time.

The man did not answer. Vitória felt that not only had she not convinced him, but also that perhaps he thought she had said too much. And if that was what he thought, it was because, having lost the habit of speaking, she herself had the painful impression that she had been prattling on with great pleasure. Here she was, accused of talking too much! She was pricked with pride mixed with pain.

"Everything in Ermelinda is held together by a delicate thread!" she shouted as if in a final order.

"And in you?" he asked very calmly.

Before she even felt the question as a small shock, in what it implied as a personal offense, Vitória relaxed all over; it was sweet to hear him talk about her. "You, you, you." The respectful and sweet word finally untied some knot in her breast, she who had always been afraid of not being respected.

"Not me," she replied without vanity. "I'm strong."

An instant later it occurred to her that she had really only said to the man that she was strong to the point of being able to stand love. Had she simply offered herself to him? Her eyes blinked several times as if that thought had blinded them with surprise. Because she never spoke much, she no longer knew up to what point words were likely to reveal thought, and her heart was pounding in horror. Could the man have understood? And the worst of it, she thought in reaction, is that it was a lie; it wasn't love that she wanted!

Fortunately the expression on Martim's silent face was vacant. She had been afraid that he would show that he had understood. And then right away, for an instant, she wished precisely that it might have happened: that he would have said he had understood and that everything would finally have crumbled. In the next instant she would have killed him if he had dared to understand. She could not tolerate the idea that he found it obvious that she loved him—above all she reacted because it was not true.

"All right. I'm going," Martim said.

He left, and his boots were already beginning to make a hollow sound on the wooden plank.

"Wait," she said with a harsh voice. "I'm not through."

He turned around obediently, his steps in the rhythm with which he had started to go away.

"I want to tell you," she said, pale, "that I was not asking you questions about your life as you seemed to think. Your life doesn't interest me. You work, you earn your pay, and that's all I need or want to know. Is that understood?"

He laughed. For the first time, he laughed.

"It is."

He turned to go away again.

"Wait," she called. "When I've finished speaking you can leave. I'm not used to having people turn their backs on me."

Again he stopped. And again he went back over to her. But this time he stopped farther away from the woman, as if he knew that in a little while he would start to go and in a little while she would call him back: Therefore he stopped halfway.

She remained standing stiffly. She was paler.

"I still want to tell you that you should not think that you can judge by appearances. You don't want to say anything about your life, but I know very well that you also don't want to be judged merely by what is apparent because you are vain and deceitful. So don't you judge in your turn when you see an older woman taking care of a farm and think that the woman is just an older woman taking care of a farm," she said with great authority, as if she had said something intelligible.

When she had said "older" he had not reacted at all, but she thought she had noted a certain surprise in his eyes; and her heart contracted with joy.

"What I mean to say," she continued with pride, "is that

(274)

this is not my whole life"—and she pointed with a shaking hand at the sunny fields on the farm.

"You don't talk about those things," he murmured heavily, fleeing with his eyes.

"But I want to talk about them!" she shouted quickly, as if he might physically stop her from going on. "Listen," she said, somewhere between an order and a request, accustomed as she was to giving him orders. "Listen."

"I'm not a priest," he said brutally.

"But listen!" she repeated with the same violence.

"I don't want to hear your secrets," he said then, very severely.

"You're afraid," Vitória said illogically.

"Afraid? Not that either." He had realized in time that she was trying to drag him through her life. "No, that's going too far. I'm not afraid. It's just that it's useless to talk about things like that."

"But listen! I want to tell you that my life is not just this."

"But why me?" he exclaimed furiously.

"Because I need a witness!" she replied in the desperation of rage. "Don't think that my life is just this. What would you say—I wonder, what would you say, with that way you have of sneering at other people's lives—what would you say if I were to tell you that I'm something of a poetess?" she shouted.

Martim looked at her with such surprise that she became paralyzed. A reddish color spread out over the woman's startled face.

"Well," he said, laughing suddenly and shrugging his shoulders, "I wouldn't say a word."

"I'm something of a poetess," she repeated as if she had not heard his interruption, "I don't write because I don't have time. But I do collect proverbs and thoughts. I have a huge collection," she was surprised and she knew that she had just destroyed the secret of her collection forever and that she would never again copy down a single proverb, because not being

(2 7 5)

understood by the man had disoriented her. "I collect thoughts," she said very restlessly. "I have a lot of life inside. I'm very curious about life," she exclaimed in an outburst of frankness. "Everything in the world interests me and I study the open book of life. And my inner life is very rich," she said, and she shook her imprisoned hair as if it had been turned loose in curls.

Martim took a quick look at the tree, as if he and the tree were exchanging a furtive glance.

"I even started a poem once," she said, frightened, forcing herself to go on because she thought that talking consisted in saying everything, and at the same time she saw herself slipping into nothingness with her shame being sacrificed uselessly. "The poem began like this: 'The queens who ruled in Europe in the year 1790 were four.'"—He was going to know everything, and she would not have anything left . . . "But the poem wasn't going to be about queens, you understand?"—but she knew that he did not understand, she knew that there was only success and failure, and that between them nothing existed, and that because of that she would never come out of her limbo to prove that through the phrase about the queens the poem would take its subtle drive; and since she knew that she would never prove to other people the infinite beauty that can take flight with a simple phrase, then she, who believed only in success, did not believe in the very truth of what she felt; and there she was, all tangled up in the inexplicable phrase of the poem, and after she had said it she had been left with four queens in her clumsy hand. "It was just for the sake of beauty!" she said with violence.

They remained silent. The woman was breathing heavily. But what she could not tell him, what she could not say, was that she was a saint. Opening her mouth several times in agony, she tried to, but she could not. That, that could not be told to anyone.

"You need to fall in love," he said with a grave air, and he found it so funny that he had to put on a mask to stop himself from laughing.

She looked at him unbelieving, with her mouth open.

(2 7 6)

"What do you know about me or anything else?" she finally said, and she was so surprised at his boldness that she did not quite know what to say in return.

"That's right, I don't know anything," he agreed softly. "But I can try. You, for example, just asked me why I came here. And you," he inquired, half amused and half cynical—"why did you come here?"

"That's stupid," she said furiously. "What a stupid question! Just plain stupid! It's as if I—as if I were to ask you something like, as if I were to ask you: why are you alive!"

"Because I have a certain instant in mind," he said with soft rapidity.

She faced him, perplexed and affronted. The man, satisfied with himself, looked at her, smiling brazenly. But something on the woman's face made him blink with an uncomfortable feeling. Like addicts who recognize each other, he had just seen himself in her. Which was disagreeable. There was in her that thing which also existed in him, and which he did not accuse her of because it also hurt within himself, and because a person who had it suffered with it. Martim averted his eyes.

"In any case," she said, recovering, "if it's going to be a question of 'who,' and of 'why' someone came here, I'm the one who should be asking the questions and not you. You're in no position at all to ask questions; you're in a position to answer them."

Martim made a tired gesture of assent that revealed how near his patience was to an end. And because he had opened his mouth at the same time, the woman judged with surprise that the man was at last going to answer her and say why he had come to the place . . . It was then that she made an energetic movement with her hand, stopping him from going on. As Martim had not had the slightest intention of giving an answer, he did not understand what she had meant by such a sudden movement, and he looked at her intrigued.

She had also been startled at the unexpected automatism of her own arm. The gesture had come before her understanding of the gesture. She looked at Martim, surprised and attentive, as if

(2 7 7)

in his face their might be an explanation for what had only just now been revealed: that she did not want to know his reasons for coming to the place. It was as if by learning facts she might only at that instant lose the direct knowledge that she realized she had of the man—because with surprise she discovered that she knew him deeply. It was only on the surface that she did not know him. But deep inside his skin she knew him, and had known him from the moment she had seen him for the first time. The way in which she had known him had been the way she had preened herself when she saw him; one of the most profound ways of knowing was in the way one responded to what was being seen. And now, looking at Martim, the woman was afraid of losing that irreplaceable contact which was telling her all about the most inner nature of that man standing there; and about whom, not knowing anything, she possessed the limitless knowledge that comes from watching and seeing. Facts so often disguise a person; if she knew the facts, she might lose the whole man.

Oh, it was a blind knowledge, hers was. So blind that while knowing him, she still did not understand him. It was one step before really knowing, as if she were passing over everything that she did not know about him and going directly to the patient throbs of that heart. "I know you in my skin," she thought with an uncomfortable shiver, and her body drew back, resentful at the intimacy she was using it for. It was just that she was making someone else out of herself. That other person . . . Suddenly she was afraid that she would never know herself, because in her flesh she understood in silence that the night of the rainstorm had been more than a nightmare. That Sunday night had been the dark opening to a world of which we can barely guess the first joy; and she knew that a person dies without knowing it, and that there were hells to which she had not descended, and ways of holding that her hand still had not guessed, and ways of being that we ignore with great courage—and that she herself was the other person who had never been used. In over fifty years of life she had learned nothing essential that could be added to what she already knew and what had been kept intact during those years had been exactly what she had not learned.

And one of the things that nobody had taught her was that strange way of hers of knowing a man.

"And you, why did you come here?" Martim repeated, resigned to wasting time now that she had held him back. His tame tone came from the fact that he knew that if he repeated the question several times that woman who was only waiting for an imitation of insistence would end up talking.

Vitória made an impatient gesture, her face got ready to answer the insolence. But suddenly she calmed herself and said:

"There was nothing for me to do in Rio. I came here to build a life, to make my life."

"And did you build it?" he asked, irritated.

"But I do know one thing!" she exploded. "That only saint-hood can save someone! That you have to be a saint through passion or a saint through action or through purity—that only sainthood can save you!"

White with rage, trembling without knowing why, Martim looked at her.

"What's it all about?" she asked vigorously. "I'm only taking advantage of your freedom! What's it all about, can't you tell?" she asked with great severity.

She did not know exactly what she was referring to, and he understood without knowing exactly what she was referring to. But if it were not that way, how poor our mutual understanding would be, our comprehension made with words that are lost and words that have no meaning; and it is so hard to explain why one person was happy and why the other one despaired—we do not keep in mind the miracle of words that are lost; and for that reason it has always been so worthwhile living, because many have the words been that were spoken and that we scarcely heard, but they had been spoken.

For an instant neither hesitated to understand the other within their incomprehension.

"I can see that, yes," he replied then, entering for a brief second a world more nearly perfect in understanding; we who have a keenness of understanding that escapes us. From there Martim immediately emerged to look with puzzlement at that woman who had said nothing and yet with whom he had just agreed. He looked at her, and as always, it seemed to him that he was not grasping her essential part or that of other people—even though it was with that essential part that he was blindly fighting.

"Well, then," the woman said, "don't be surprised at what you yourself brought out: my freedom," and then she was puzzled because she realized that she did not know what she was saying and that she had become lost, playing with words.

Then they remained silent as if to give that thing, which had the fragility of an undiscernible mistake, time to be reabsorbed into forgetfulness.

But when she saw the man's somber face, the lady did not know how to interpret it and she was afraid that she had startled him. Even though she was cruel she had always managed to have the mindful pity not to startle other people with the truth.

"No, no," she then said quickly and imploringly. "You mustn't think that I meant that I was pure or a saint," she explained to him the way a mother assures a child that she is nothing but a mother so that he will not feel that he is the child of a stranger and become a stranger himself. "You didn't get what I meant when I mentioned sainthood. Don't think I meant by that that I was good," she continued, because more than anything she did not want him to judge her as "superior" and then admire her with contempt.

"I didn't mean that I was good," she repeated, forcing herself into a frankness that was painful but which almost immediately gave her relief and resignation. "I never did anything for the poor people in Vila Baixa, all I do is feel for them. Don't think that I'm saying I'm a saint . . ." Her chest pained with joy because at least, in a negative way, she was telling the truth—and what other way was there to tell the truth except by gracefully denying it? What other way was there to tell the truth

(280)

without running the risk of giving the emphasis that destroys it? And how can we tell the truth if we feel sorry because of it? More than being afraid, we feel sorry.

The woman felt tranquil, knowing that she had not confessed simply because the man had not received her confession—because nothing had been said. She needed to talk, yes; but she was tactfully avoiding being understood. From the moment in which she would be understood, she would no longer be that deeply untransmissable thing which she was and which made every person be that very person he was—because Vitória thought that this was what was happening in the communication. Could it be that surrender of herself was making her hold back? Or was it fear of the imperfection with which souls touch each other? But it was not only that of which she was afraid. The fact was, that lacking any training in communication, she had the instinctive delicacy to abstain.

"I did not mean by that that I'm pure"—she tried to pacify the man. "My soul is dirty, my life is quarrelsome. I'm not good, I'm . . ." Sainthood was a violence for which she would not have the courage; in a certain way a bad person was more charitable than a saint, sainthood was a scandal for which she did not have the courage. "I'm no good, you understand? I'm no good like . . . I'm no good like a disappointed woman!" she suddenly said with a certain coquetry.

"Disappointed?" he said, bowing like a gentleman, and accepting but not feeling the dignity that the woman wanted to give to her confession.

"With myself," she finished gloriously, shaking her imprisoned hair.

"Oh God, how you bore me," Martim thought.

"Can't you see," Vitória thought then trying to communicate with her eyes; Martim could only perceive the effort and not the meaning. "Can't you see that if I wanted to be ready for everything my life would have to be pure? And I did want to be ready for everything and I got ready every day. Not for moral purity!" she thought. And at that moment Vitória realized that

by mistake she had ended up falling into moral purity and that
she would never attain purity as a way of life . . . That was
more or less what she was thinking; and then, a little startled,
she said to him,

"I'm not pure . . ."

"How you bore me," Martim thought. "That complexity of
a woman who's afraid to die—could that be it?" he wondered,
because Ermelinda was so very alive the way a flower is alive,
and the duality confused him. "And the complexity of a woman
who's afraid to live—could that be it?" he also wondered, confused, because in her gray wrinkles that woman had more of
death than life about her, and yet it was life that she was afraid
of; "and the confusion of a man who . . . of a man who did not
want to be afraid?" Yes, and all the while the sacred cows. Was
that it? But having given words to facts that were not even facts
was unsatisfactory for the man. Then, unable to define what was
happening to them, and because Martim wished, even without
her hearing it, that there would not be the least doubt about his
feelings, he thought quite clearly: "You bore me. I know all this
and it doesn't interest me. It may be that there isn't anything
behind that anxiety, but I've had enough. I just simply want you
to go to hell," he concluded somberly. "It doesn't interest me
any more." He looked at her. An impoverished body that probably was trying to take refuge in thoughts? A body that when it
became exicted could turn into spirit.

The confused woman was being so sincere that the veins on
her neck were bulging from the effort of telling the truth—or of
lying, Martim did not care which. He did not have anything to
do with all of this. And he was tempted to tell her absurdly: "I
know that you're telling the truth, but to be frank with you, I
don't have any faith in it." Oh, the boring female. At times he
could get so sick of women that the feeling strengthened his
whole being in his own clean masculinity. And now, because he
had had all he could take, if that woman was at one extreme, he
wanted to be exactly at the opposite extreme.

With sudden fatigue, entrapped by the woman, all that

Martim asked of men and women at that moment was that they be unconscious of themselves, with just that little light necessary for them not to be in the dark, the light of a dog's eyes in a dog's darkness: that was all he wanted now, tired as he was. "You tire me," he thought heavily, rudely. Indifference made him look at her with the raw precision with which one might watch an ant twisting about. "At the point I'm at now, silent and tired, I'm sick of the twistings of the soul and I'm sick of words," he thought. At the point he was at, he was large and his hands were covered with calluses, and the soul is large, the trees are large. The sun was large and the land extensive. All that was lacking was a different race of men and women—the race that he would create if he could. With sudden brutality, the man thought that living was the only thought that one should have, and that the rest was just the words of women like Vitória, and living was the maximum conquest and was the only way to give a worthy answer to a tall tree. Because, remembering the noble decency there had been in his Tertiary plot of land, that very moment was what Martim wanted to have.

And there was the woman . . . He looked at her as if she were a stranger. Mouth, teeth, stomach, arms, all the things that had had the opportunity to be a clean plant. But all of it corroded and damaged and elevated by the spirit. "You bore me, you're a mistake, you're the mistake a plant made." "From now on," he discovered with a weariness that immediately took the fascination out of the discovery that one day he would feel it when he found out how much love there was in it—"from now on I want things that are equal to each other, and not different from each other. You talk too much about things that shine; and yet there's a core that doesn't shine. And that's what I want. I want the extreme beauty of monotony. There's something that's dark and doesn't glow—and that's what counts. You bore me with your fear, because even that shines. From now on I want things that are equal to one another." And she still came around to say that she was disappointed . . .

"You're afraid," he said, uselessly using some sort of dignity and trying, with definite courtesy, to maintain the tone of the woman's abstract polemic which, in the sunlight, had trouble being sharp.

The lady had trouble believing what she had heard:

"Afraid?!"

Afraid? Her? Her impulse was to laugh, as if laughter could have answered the absurd. Afraid? She shook her head in disbelief. She, who ran that farm with the strength of a man? She, who gave orders to that man standing there, afraid neither of herself nor of him? She, who had quietly fought against the drought and had conquered it! She, who knew how to wait for it to rain. Afraid? She, who walked about in her dirty boots and with her face exposed without being afraid of never being loved. She, who courageously went through the inheritance from her father to keep that farm functioning, without even knowing why, courageously waiting for the day when that place would be the best in the region, and then she would be able to extend her fences. Afraid?

Her whole body revolted against the man's lack of understanding and the insult of the word; her whole being got ready for a gesture that would make her own indignation explode, but none seemed strong enough to her. Afraid! She looked at him surprised, bitter. What did he know about her, that man? How could that man who was looking into her face now without any fear ever understand her great courage. She perceived for the first time how stupid his face was. From the taut forehead one could guess at the difficulty of thought; there was a painful effort showing in the face of that man. And she shook her head, bitter, ironically. Since she had known that he was an engineer, she had never really thought about his intelligence. But when one looked at him nakedly, how stubborn and crude he was! The man's face had that sleepwalking perseverance of stupid people.

"Afraid? Yes." he said patiently as if he were talking to a child.

The repeated insult made her tremble, and this time her whole being got ready to strike back with an insult. Afraid, her . . . her mouth twisted with sarcasm.

(2 8 4)

But instead of that, the features of her face suddenly gave way. She could not take any more. Afraid? Yes. Afraid? Yes. She remembered how being afraid had been the solution. She remembered how once she had humbly accepted fear like someone kneeling with his head lowered to receive baptism, and how her courage from then on had been one of living with fear. Afraid, her? And suddenly, as if she were regurgitating her soul, she shouted with the pride of her fifty mute years:

"Afraid, yes! What do you think that means? Afraid, yes. Listen then and take it if you can; take it if you're not afraid. I've already been afraid. I took care of my old father over the years, and when he died I was all alone . . ." The woman stopped herself. When her father had died she had suddenly been all by herself and on her own, and with the clumsy impulse of those who start late and no longer have the skill for it, she had wanted for the first time to try what she called "living,"—which, in a first and uncertain step toward glory, would be to go by herself to a hotel and stay there all alone and concentrate on herself and have the highest idea of herself, like a monk in his cell; and that would be the furtive way that she would make her first obeisance to . . . to what? "I went to be by myself and to concentrate;" she said with pride, "and I left everybody and I took a ferry with my suitcase. But once on the boat, once I was on the boat I began to become that awful person I had recognized, that ordeal, that almost good but dangerous feeling. As soon as I had stepped on that boat that was rocking wildly everything touched me and made me sad, curious, alive, full of curiosity—but wasn't that just what I had wanted? Wasn't that just what I'd gone to look for? It was, but why was it that I refused to realize that it was happening? Why did I look at everything with my head held high, making believe? It was still afternoon when I got to the island—my heart contracted with fright when I saw the big old hotel with high-ceilinged rooms and flies in the dining room, and people relaxing on the terrace and looking at me as I passed among them and begged their pardon; what was lacking there was the protection there is in the smallness of a cell, and I had made a great mistake. I didn't

know anyone on the terrace and I didn't let any of them guess
that it made my heart beat faster. I left my bag in my room, but
my impulse was to get on the ferry and go back; but that would
have been failure! Had I gone there for some reason to endure
what was happening to me, since that was not the life that I had
wanted? And if I couldn't accept it, was it just because it was
more naked than I had expected—it would be defeat and deser-
tion. But very much stronger than the shame of running away
was the anticipation of what a night all alone in that room
would be. Then I went downstairs and without any shame I
inquired about the schedule of the ferries going back, and my
horror was confirmed: they told me, 'Only the next morning.'
Then I calmly went out of the hotel, but outside the air was
bright and clear; it was afternoon, and the blue sea made the
most delicate line against the horizon that I have ever seen. The
beauty was so painful, and I was so alive; and the only way that I
had learned to be alive was to feel myself so helpless. I was alive,
but it was as if there were no answer to being alive. Then I
quickly went back to the hotel, driven away by the light of the
beach, and among strangers I gobbled down my meal with great
courage. After dinner I tried to take a walk at night outside the
hotel, because hadn't that been what I had planned? Wasn't
that an encounter with day itself and with night itself? But
outside the hotel the whole beach was glowing in the dark.
Beautiful, all white with so much sand, with the dark sea—but
the foam, I remember that the foam was white in the dark, and
I thought that the foam looked like a piece of lace, there was no
moon, but the foam was white like a piece of lace in the dark.
Then I hurried back to my room and quickly turned into the
daughter of an aged father because it was only as a daughter that
had I known calm and composure, and only then did I realize
the security I had lost with the death of my father; and I resolved that from then on I wanted to be only what I had always
been before, only that. I put on a clean starched nightgown
because that was a pleasure I was accustomed to, and I combed
my hair for a long time because those were the habits through

which I understood myself and knew myself, and I smoothed my hair so much with the brush that I managed to make myself a thing that was neither raw nor exposed. I was full of flattery for myself; I was treating myself with ceremony and trying to see if I could reach some level where I would feel comradeship with the frightened coward I was being, and for whom I had such repugnance, but I pretended that everything was perfect. I even sighed comfortably in bed with the book in my hand, the book that I had never thought I would open on the island. I knew that I was not reading, but I never let myself be convinced that I was making believe; and it had not been reading on an island that I had come to find there. I tried to ignore the fact that God was giving me exactly what I had asked Him for and that I—I was saying 'No.' I was pretending that I did not understand that I had built up a whole hope in what was happening to me at last, but that there I was with my glasses on and the open book, as if I were so much in love that I could only shout 'No.' But I also knew that if in that very moment I did not pick up the calm thread of my previous life, my balance would never come back and my things would never be recognized by me. And that's why I pretended to be reading. But I could hear the ocean waves; I could hear, I could hear! It was then that all at once all the lights in the hotel went out. Just like that, all at once, without any sound, without any warning, nothing. Only the next day did I learn that at nine o'clock at night the lights were turned off to save electricity. The lights had all gone out, and I was left with the open book in my hand; I was left in the dark as I had never been before. Only last night was I left in that dark for the second time in my life—like that, with that simple way of being in the dark. I had never been in it, and I had never been in the dark by the sea. It was very dark as if I was trying to find the hotel and did not know where it was; the only thing I could touch was the book in my hand. The fear, the fear that you accuse me of, would not let me make one single movement, but afterwards it became surprise—then there burst forth what I had only barely kept back until that instant—the beauty of the beach, the fine line of the horizon, the solitude to which I had come of my own free will, the rocking of the boat that I had thought was pleasant, and also the fear of the intensity of joy that I can reach—and unable to lie any more, I cried as I prayed in the dark, praying as I said 'Never this again, oh Lord, never let me be so bold, never let me be so happy. Take away my courage for living forever; don't ever let me allow myself to go so deep into myself, don't ever let me give myself grace, so pitilessly, because I don't want grace, because I'd rather die without ever having seen it rather than see it just once! Because God in His goodness allows, you know. He allows and He counsels people to be cowards and protect themselves. His favorite children are those who dare; but He's strict with someone who dares, and He's benevolent with someone who doesn't have the courage to look straight ahead and He blesses those abject people who are careful not to go too far into rejoicing and into the search for joy. Disappointed, He blesses those who don't have the courage. He knows that there are people who can't live with the happiness there is inside of them, and then He gives them a surface to live on, and He gives them a sadness. He knows that there are people who have to pretend, because beauty is arid. Why is beauty so arid? And then I said to myself, 'Be afraid, Vitória, because being afraid is salvation.' Because things can't be looked at face on, nobody's that strong, only people who damn themselves are that strong. But for us joy has to be like a smothered star in our hearts, joy has to be just a secret, joy has to be something like a glow that people never, never should let escape. You feel a splinter and you don't know where it came from; that's the way joy should be. You shouldn't know why, you should feel something like: 'But what's the matter with me?'— and not know. Even when it touches something, that thing will glow because of the great secret that was snuffed out—I was afraid, because who am I without contention? When I was sitting in the ferry the next day I thought that I had died. But as if before I had died I had received communion."

Martim was pale. Oh, what he would have given to insult that naked and shameless face.

(2 8 8)

"I don't believe a word you said," he said.

But as if both of them had understood each other beyond the words, the woman was not offended by what he had said. Nor did he repeat it, as if he really had not opened his mouth. He turned his eyes away only because he did not wish to look at that pained face. And she, she only sighed. They were tired as if they had been doing some kind of violent exercise. In some way the woman's stupid outburst had been good for them, because inexplicably, besides being tired, the two of them were now tranquil.

Besides, nothing seemed to have happened. There is nothing so destructive for spoken words as a sun that keeps on burning. They remained silent, giving themselves time to forget. By a tacit pact they would forget that rather ugly thing which had happened. Neither of them was young and they had had some experience. A person has the nobility not to notice certain things, and has pity on us and forgets, and has the tact not to have noticed—if one wanted to stop a moment of comprehension from crystalizing us and making our life something else. Neither of them was young, and they were prudent. So then, after the outburst they remained silent, as if nothing had happened, because no one can live in fright and no one could live on the basis of having vomited or of having seen someone vomit; those were things that one does not think too much about, those were the facts of a life.

The lady wiped the sweat from her face and took a quick look at that narrow head, that curly hair. There had been restored once more to his face the calm human stupidity, that opaque and obtuse stolidity which is our great strength. They both looked into the emptiness of each other's eyes. Without pain, one seemed to be asking the other: "Who are you?" As they looked at each other, the basic one-to-the-otherness was not caught by them, and yet it was once more with that principal thing that they were fighting. Until, out of emptiness, their eyes began to fill up and become individual, and the one was now no longer imprisoned by absorption in the other. Then they looked at each other frankly, with nothing to say—only that; extreme frankness. Then they averted their eyes without any pain, in common agreement, knowingly; and again they waited an instant for the frankness which never has any words, to have time to go away, so they could go on living.

Without insisting she said calmly, as if they had just had a friendly conversation, "Naturally, if that night on the island I had known everything that was going to happen, I would have taken a chance on being more unhappy. But at such a time, one always thinks it's forever. And it happened too that at that moment I didn't understand that I was experiencing exactly what I'd gone to look for; I didn't recognize it completely, and I thought I was mistaken. Naturally, after that, I became more careful. I knew then that you can't approach things directly the way I had. Never directly," she said, as if it were a formula. "I also want to tell you that I was afraid, yes, but not because I was sorry for myself. I'm never sorry for myself," she said without vanity.

And, by God, she wasn't.

"It was only a matter of finding out that one doesn't approach things directly," she said then in a conciliatory way. "And I learned that all by myself. All by myself," she added with a certain simplicity.

"Why didn't you ever think to ask for somebody's help?" he asked, bored, without really knowing what he was saying.

"Don't you understand," she said, irritated again, "that I'm not capable of asking? That I need so much that nobody can give it to me? In that case, you probably don't see that I would ask for more than they could give me." In her excitement she forgot that she had no right to be annoyed, because if the man was listening to her, it was only because he was doing her the favor or because she had obliged him to listen; and she forgot that after all, he had nothing to do with any of this.

"Nobody," Martim said, unexpectedly emphatic—"nobody can ask for more than he can receive from someone else! Human nature," he said very self-satisfied, "is always the same. Nobody can ask for more than someone else can give him because asking and giving is the same act, and one doesn't exist without the other. Besides, nobody can invent what doesn't exist, my dear lady. If asking was invented it's because the answer exists in giving!" he said quite firm and contented.

"But asking whom?" she yelled.

"Well," Martim said, stumbling and already losing interest —"that's the question. But then there's also this"—he added, suddenly serious and sensual—"there's also this, there's a definite technique in asking! Because, my dear lady, things are not like that. No, my dear lady! You can't just say 'Give me!' and let it go at that! Lots of times you have to deceive the one you're asking," he said, intimate, sensual. "To be exact, you have to ask in some disguised sort of way. You're an intelligent and well-read woman, you must have learned that too. Let's imagine, for example, that you were married and needed a pair of shoes," he said, suddenly most interested in the problem, while the woman looked at him, her eyes silly with surprise. "If you needed a pair of shoes, the wisest thing would never be to say to your husband, 'Give me some shoes!' The wise thing would be to say a little by little every day, 'My shoes are getting old.' 'My shoes are getting old.' 'My shoes are getting old,' " Martim said and could not help laughing. "You understand?" he said— "and one fine day your husband will wake up in the morning and without knowing why he'll say: 'Vitória, my love, I'm going to buy you a pair of shoes!' Because in asking for help there's a definite technique! Receiving a request frightens people a lot, while on the other hand, dear lady, they're really itching to give you something. You understand, a definite technique! For everything else too there's a definite technique! For example," he continued with enthusiasm—"for example, you can only express what you want to say, when you express it well! There's a definite technique. You've got to know how to live in order to live, because the other side, dear lady, is spying on us at every step. One wrong step, and suddenly a walking man looks like a monkey! Just one wrong step, and instead of being perplexed, people laugh! One moment of weakness, dear lady, and love is perdition. It takes skill, dear lady, lots of skill, because without it life goes wrong. And lots of wisdom: because time is short, you have to pick a fraction of a second between one word and another, between remembering and forgetting; there's a definite technique!"

"Technique?" she repeated, stupefied.

"That's right," he said, bored with the wisdom she had forced on him.

The lady looked at him, completely stupid. The man smiled in a constrained way, without knowing how to get out of the predicament to which he had brought himself.

"I'm going to the cowshed," he then said in a low voice, with discreet modesty, as if he were asking permission to go to the bathroom.

But she suddenly came to: "Listen."

The insistence put into the word began to tear at the man's fibers and make him give in. He stopped again. He felt that he was being used by that woman as if she were emasculating him little by little: there were women like that, who break everything they touch. With the mouth of a leech, she was sucking something out of him, something that was not valuable, but which after all still belonged to him. What she was doing with what she sucked out he did not know. He looked at her without pleasure, without curiosity. He no longer seemed to have the strength to resist the word "listen," which finally made him bow down, resigned. Slowly, without any defense at all, he prepared to hear her out.

"Listen," she repeated then, gentle, like a mother who had surprised her child with an involuntary shout. "Listen: before you came here I was different," she then said, as if she were going back to the beginning of beginnings. And she gave the man the fatigue he had felt before and put a heroic readiness for sacrifice on his face. "Not that I was really different," the lady added with certain kindness, "but the fact was that I hadn't always owned this place."

She paused. Because—busy at showing consideration for the

man whom she was nullifying in some way—the meaning of what she had wanted to say escaped her. The heat had left them wet and salty.

"I used to live in Rio," she continued, and her tone tried to be unpretentious, as if having lived in the city would make her too big in the man's eyes. "But I came here of my own volition. I know, I know it was a mistake; you don't have to tell me," the lady added with that vanity of hers which offended so easily. "But I'd made a mistake. What was I going to do? To err is human; I made a mistake like a woman who had been deceived by a man's promises—oh, there wasn't any man, if that's what you mean or at least what you're thinking," she interrupted, flattered by the possibility that it might have occurred to Martim. "But how can I explain it?" she asked, as if he were anxious to understand, even though there was no question on the man's complying face. "I thought that here I could find . . ."

What had she really come to find? The passion of living? Yes, she had come in search of the passion of life, the woman discovered disappointedly; and a drop of sweat ran sadly down her nose.

"I'll tell you what happened," she said then with effort, and probably that woman had already had her speech prepared for years. "This is how it all started. Once, some relatives had come to visit us in Rio, and I left Ermelinda to take care of my father. I took them around to show them the city—my relatives I mean. We always drove: my uncle had rented a car. It was already getting chilly . . . I never saw such long roads, it was getting cold, every day I wore a blue dress that I had never had a good chance to wear. And we ate in restaurants so many times, enjoying ourselves and getting to know the restaurants. It was the first time that I had ever done anything like that . . . eating juicy steaks. I have to admit"—she informed him—"that I had always shied away from big meals. I always liked dry things; my meals had always been so simple! Because until then I had ended up adopting my father's diet . . .

"But at that time," the woman continued, her face suddenly cleared by pleasure and by the unexpected attack of an unattainable ideal, "at that time they would come with huge plates filled with stuffed pork chops; and when I left the restaurant, I could see that the fruit in the pushcarts was squashed and then . . ." She was quiet. By interrupting herself, however, all she did was make herself smell, as if the breeze had brought in the smell that came from inside the pushcarts, the whiff of rotten pineapples and warm chicken feathers—and then she smiled with a face that was clear, mysterious.

"When I left the restaurant, I tossed my coat, which was also new, over my shoulders; but it wasn't because it was cold, it was only because it seemed that something was happening to me. I don't know," she said, having trouble wiping away the perspiration, "but it was as if I saw that things are much more than the dry shell, you understand me maybe? It was as if I could see that even though I had felt sick before, it was because I knew then that the danger was beneath the dryness—I don't know why, but driving around those days, it seemed to me that everything that existed was, was horribly ripe, you know how it is? And I felt so tired that it almost hurt. To tell you the truth, it didn't even seem like wintertime. It's hard to believe, but it didn't seem like it; the cars blowing their horns, the pushcarts so full of fruit . . . fruit that was almost rotten, almost—almost I don't know what," Vitória said softly, lovingly, and out of pure intimacy with the man she did not try to explain it any better.

Martim took his dirty handkerchief out of his pocket and wiped his face. The woman saw that he had not understood. But now it was nice and too late to stop, it did not matter now even if he did not understand. She stayed there for a moment with an unraveled look, reduced to remembering herself alone as in the restaurant and how her mouth glowed at the sauce as it poured out, giving her a touch of repugnance; how in those days it had seemed to her that one had to exult in what was ugly; and then, with a feeling of nausea that she suddenly had not been able to separate from love, she had admitted that things are ugly. The smell of the pushcart seemed to be a warm smell of dirty people, and one had to get emotional over things that were so imperfect that they seemed to ask for her understanding, her support, her pardon, and her love; happiness weighed upon her stomach in those days. Yes, and she had felt that she was capable of loving all of that. It was surprising, it was horrible, as if it had been a wedding.

At that instant the woman trembled, as she remembered that it was precisely those strange days of happiness that later on had led her to dare go to the island all alone—to look for something more. And that she had failed nevertheless.

She looked thoughtfully at the man without seeing him. It did not even pain her any more whether Martim understood her or not. A woman has the right to speak out once in her life.

"Driving around that time," she informed him humbly, "it was as if I had become ill . . ."

"Maybe the food was too heavy?" he suggested with his head boiling in the sun and his hair crackling itself dry.

"A man without a calling at least ought to have the advantage of being free," Martim mused, absorbed in his thoughts. But everybody calls it following a duty. And truthfully, in the sun, he was just as completely mixed up as he had been before; wherever a man goes, a city grows up, all that is needed are streetcars and movies. Ermelinda wanted him . . . what did Ermelinda want? And Vitória was forcing him to take her confession. It was difficult not to collaborate. Then in some vague way there grew in Martim a new explanation for his crime—that crime which was becoming more and more elastic and amorphous—and the man had already got so far away from it that he really seemed to have committed an abstract crime; and his crime now really seemed more like a sin of the spirit, just that. Therefore, in the sun, persecuted by the presence of Vitória, he thought like this: that the only way to be free, as a man without any calling has the right to be, had been to commit a crime, and make other people stop recognizing him as someone like themselves and not ask anything of him. But if that explanation was

(295)

the right one then his crime had been useless. As long as he himself survived, other people would call on him. Burning there in the sun, that man, tired out by a sleepless Sunday night, thought that this was the most reasonable explanation for his crime. Restless, he knew also that he was only wandering.

It was then that it occurred to him that he was about to be arrested. So that they could tell him at last what his crime had been. He was about to be arrested and so other people could judge him, because he, he had already made up a legend about himself.

"It's quite possible," Vitória said in anguish—"it's quite possible that the meat was very heavy indeed, and I had been eating my father's diet for so long!" she added distractedly.

They remained silent, and the man scratched himself.

"Why didn't you go to a stomach specialist?" Martim asked, not exactly because he did not understand her, but because he was trying to see if, honestly reducing what she was saying to a question of a medical cure, everything would come out in its real proportions.

"The fact is that it was partly because of those days driving around that years later I found that I ought not sell the place I had inherited from my aunt, and I decided to live here," she concluded suddenly, startled as if she had come to the tape much more quickly than she had calculated, and without even being ready to have arrived there.

"Oh," he said as if he had understood.

They remained silent again. The woman had finally stopped wringing her hands.

"I think," she said with a final sigh, "I think that I thought I would be able to find here in this place what had happened to me during the days I was driving around. I mean those things I saw when I came out of restaurants. Of course, not in the impossible way I wanted to find them on the island—find them here, yes, but within my reach, every day and little by little within my reach," she said, feeling herself that she was irremediably obscure and foundering in the inexplicable.

(296)

And suddenly everything seemed really inexplicable to her. It was true that living in the country had come to give a passion to her purity; it was true that for the first few months she had been touched by the laziness with which the plants grew erect, and for the first few months nature had given an ardor to her confusion. Yes, that was true. . . . But it was also true that because of paths that could no longer be retraced she had ended up falling into the truculent brutality of moral purity; and her arteries had hardened like those of a judge.

But all the same, that wasn't the only truth! She justified herself, because there she was, a hard woman, unburdening herself so simply in front of a man who was not even listening to her, the way a drop of water can no longer bear its own weight and falls where it falls; the thing had had enough strength of self-direction to do it all alone. And it was also true that at the same time in which a moral code could harden that she herself did not understand; she had approached inside, without knowing in the slightest, through despoilment upon despoilment, something that was alive.

"I suppose," she said to the man, "that I was imagining I would find all of that on the farm. But later on"—she added surprised, as if only then she had realized—"later on I got a little confused . . ." she said and smiled, constrained, pardonable, with the enchantment of unprotection on her face.

What Martim had least expected had been a smile. And he agreed, interested. Going back over it all in a more alert way, he managed to reproduce in his ears the last words of the woman, "I got a little confused." It was, therefore, those words which, even though they said no more than any others, seemed to transmit to the man a kind of total understanding, as if out of tenderness he could no longer ignore anything about that woman. With his effort of looking at her and understanding her, the material that made up the man's face finally melted, and on the surface a kind of expression arose, the shadow of a thought perhaps.

Vitória noticed it, emotional, sad, modest:

"As I was saying, it was because of that that I came here. It was a mistake. But I've done so many other things for the same reason that I can't explain it!" she said simply, perplexed. "It's as if something that should happen is waiting for me; and then I try to go after it, and I keep on trying, trying. It's something that happens that keeps on encircling me—it's something that owes itself to me, it looks like me, it's almost myself. But it never gets close. You can call it fate if you want. Because I've tried to go out and meet it. I sense this happening as if it were some kind of affliction. And it's as if, after it happened, I would become someone else," she added peacefully. "Sometimes I have the feeling that my fate is just having a thought I didn't have before. I get anxious over what will happen, yes, but at the same time I've done everything I could to put it off; I don't know how to explain it. I've even yearned for times like now, when I could live without it—because I got used to it in such a way that I would see it in everything, for better or for worse, in some place. Lots of times I felt that if I let myself go, really let myself go, what was going to happen would come close. But since I'm afraid, I avoid it. Even before I go to sleep I read a little so that it won't be able to happen . . . But once"—she said serenely—"once, while I was waiting for a streetcar, I got so distracted that when I came to, there was wind on the street and in the trees and the people were passing by, and I saw that the years were passing by; and the policeman signaled to a woman that she could cross. Then, do you understand? Then I felt that I, I was there—and it's the same as if what was going to happen had been there . . . I don't even know what was going to happen, because almost before I felt it, I had already recognized it—and without even giving me time to know what it was called, I had somehow fallen down on my knees before it, like a slave. I swear I don't know what had happened to me, but my heart was beating, I was I, and what had to happen was happening. Oh, I know that I was very frightened, because being on the street had nothing to do with my father, or with my life, or even with myself; it was something as isolated as if it had been something that had

happened—and all the while, in spite of that, there I was surrounded by the wind, the streetcar passing by, with my heart
beating as if it had just had a thought. That was one of the times
when I had come closest to what I'm used to calling 'my fate.' I
could feel it the way a person feels something in his hand."

The man looked at her austerely, seriously, without understanding, because there was beauty in the woman's face.

"What you probably needed was somebody next to you to
give you some kind of guarantee," he said like a priest. "Everything people don't understand is resolved by love. You probably
needed to find some kind of love."

But instead of getting annoyed she answered with a hoarse
voice. "I've already had plenty," she said hoarsely. "When I was
a girl I had plenty."

They both looked at each other with interest, but a little
tired.

"Once," she said with sudden recklessness, "once I was
spending the holidays with my aunt—funny, right here! It was
right here!" she said, feigning surprise only to make the story
interesting. "It was right here, when my aunt was alive! What a
strange coincidence. God, life is full of all sorts of things."

Since the woman had stopped, he said in a show of impatience, "And then?"

"It was the first time I'd been here, and I never thought that
one day it would be mine," she continued, insisting on the
coincidence. "I was on vacation, and I watched a boy lighting a
bonfire in the field. I stood there looking at him; there was a
little boy watching him too!" she exclaimed so as to guarantee
the truth of what she was saying. "The little boy died sometime
after," she said hoarsely. "I watched the boy lighting the bonfire,
the warm dust from the leaves was flying about, making things
warm—making people warm. The little boy who died said something, if I'm not mistaken he said something like, 'Look at the
bonfire.' The boy was quiet, and he was feeding the fire; his face
kept getting darker and darker, darker with the flames, also
because it was almost night already. And I—there I was—me,

still very much a child, a girl, very pretty, crazy, oh so crazy; no
one knew how crazy I was. When I think what was going
through my head, I was such an idealist! I was standing there,
just like that, and I—I was in love with that boy, I was in love
with that boy and with the bonfire he was lighting. He didn't say
a word ! not a single word."

Since she had spoken about love, almost to her distaste and
overcoming a sudden discretion, the man took a quick look at
her body; he looked at her openly, without pity, without evil. To
tell the truth, she wasn't bad at all. Martim suddenly looked at
her attentively, mistrustful, as if they had been hoodwinking
him until now. The fact was that she was "O.K." She wasn't a
"dog." Then he turned his eyes away with caution:

"And he must have been in love with you," he said, covering
up his discomfort.

"Of course he knew I was there," she defended. "I was
young, I didn't have a touch of make-up on my face; I was
beautiful, idealistic. I was there with my new red jacket on; he
knew I was there."

"And that was your love, then?" Martim asked with a delicacy that he did not think himself capable of.

"Yes," she said a little disappointed, wiping away her perspiration. "That was my love too."

"It lasted as long as the bonfire," Martim said in a silly way,
perhaps trying to copy situations in the past or things he had
read; but his tone came out uncertain, he did not know how to
build her up to face up to the poverty of her love-story.

"It lasted as long as the bonfire," she repeated, surprised,
looking at him. "But if you could have seen it," she said,
suddenly taken up with sweetness—"if you could have seen how
there was—how there was a little aurora—and a small horizon
because of the bonfire. It was all there. The two of us," she
added suddenly, imploring, as if she were asking Martim also to
take such a soft detail into consideration—"the two of us were
standing there, he with his back to me almost all the time. Oh,"
she shouted then without being understood—"you have to re-

member that I was different from what I am now; I was slow to answer everything. When a leaf would fall, I would just watch it. It wasn't happiness the way they talk about happiness today. Times change everything; today people ask much more of other people."

She became quiet, a little stupefied. A greedy love for her own story had taken possession of her. There she was standing at that moment, rich, crazy, boring, even making up there, while she had been speaking, a past for herself that she had never suspected . . . "But I still have a whole past in back of me!" she shouted suddenly in a burst of surprise. She had even been beautiful, she had even been young—things that she would never be in the future. She trembled when she thought that if she had not told Martim about the boy at the bonfire, perhaps she would have never known what had been happening to her, happenings that belonged to her, that she had a right to. Because only when she told about them had she remembered . . . as if only then did she know that a boy and a bonfire were also feelings, and that that too had been her life. Oh, who can tell if the vehemence resulted from her coming out with what she had forgotten, who knows.

The woman then wondered, absorbed, whether there might not be a thousand other things that had happened to her . . . and which she simply had not learned about yet. She wondered, with the gravity of a discovery, whether she had not really chosen to live off a few past facts, when would she be able to live off others that had happened just the same way—and she had every right to them—just as at that moment she was reliving the boy by the bonfire. There she was, stupid and heavy; here the past was revealing itself to be as full of possibilities as the future. Because the past had the richness of what has already happened.

"And naturally you will never enjoy anyone else," Martim said with irony.

"Why?" she replied distractedly. "But that was love."

"And where is the bonfire boy?" he asked in a polished way.

"How should I know?" she said startled, because with that

(301)

question the man had shown that he had not understood any-thing.

She had been reduced, my Martim's incomprehension, to remembering all by herself. Besides, at that moment she asked nothing except this: to think alone, like a person who has received a letter and is impatiently waiting for a chance to read it. In her first cautious steps toward an unexplored past, Vitória was trying to remember more about the boy at the bonfire. In that inferno of fire, in that soft evening, that boy who moved with the dark delicacy of an animal . . . That was how Vitória saw the boy in her own past. And telling herself that the boy had always been there! That young man, big, dark, moving about the fire, moving about in his own autonomous existence and irradiat-ing his own warmth. And life was big in him; life had space in him. He was not nervous—oh not the least. There were people like that: life was big in them, but that did not make them nervous. Oh, how many memories she had, and she had never touched upon them! Avid as she was to live, when—when she really had already lived. When really what was to happen had already happened. What was to happen had already happened to her a thousand times. And she had not known.

She unexpectedly remembered another man, so similar to the one by the bonfire that she was surprised. Happenings repeating themselves and persisting—and blind as she was, she had not noticed. "But I was always alive!" She remembered that other boy who was playing ping-pong and who had repeated for her the existence of the boy by the bonfire. She had seen him playing in a club where she had taken her father to let him enjoy himself. It was twenty years ago! It was twenty years ago that it had happened. Oh, the richness of getting old. The older one gets the more unknown the past is. The woman blinked in surprise; twenty years ago a boy had been playing ping-pong, agile and calm, and—while the world had continued on its way—she, Vitória, had stopped at the door of the game-room and, twenty years ago, she had watched him. And watching him, she had known that that was the way one could love because she had seen, once and for always, that boy playing ping-pong.

(3 0 2)

"And did he love you?" Martim would have asked if she had told him that fact too, that fact which from then on, yes, from then on would be her future.

"How do I know?" she would have answered. Because afterwards she had left the club, passing through the rooms on the lower floor. And she had taken with her the impression that today, now, at that moment, was finally being revealed to her. As if she had kept it hidden in herself for so long that what had finally happened gave off a ripe smell of fruit, and the wine that had been new had taken on body and the quality that make it shine in a glass.

The man, who at that moment was waiting on the sun, did not understand anything; he knew it all. But Vitória did not seem to need him any more—as if she had chosen to live the great freedom that can be lived when everything that has happened has happened. She looked at Martim with a deep and tired sigh. He did not understand anything. But she could not even blame him. Because looking, absorbed now by everything around her, not even she herself could know how to make logical and rational the fact that one's own deep love had been scattered away, the fact that the mystery had been kept, the fact that one time or another the sign of richness had pointed toward a warning, the fact that she had always tried in her humble calling to look for some kind of intimate glory. And how could one make rational the fact that all of this mixed-up business was the source of the austere beauty and goodness of a saint, and that all the while it was also the source of the suffering of a woman? And how could one make rational the fact that a boy in front of a bonfire was there warming her face today? And how could one explain that she, all by herself on the farm, she was the queen of a world where at night one could look into her own entrails and no longer be surprised—oh, no more surprises, because a person is not herself; a person is somebody else? And how could one make rational the fact that all alone she was walking along that thought which a person should have at the most only once in a lifetime? And how could one explain that love is not just love; love was all of that—and how heavy it was on her, oh, how heavy it weighed. How could she blame Martim for not understanding, if she herself did not understand . . .

"Why didn't you ever get married?" Martim asked without having noticed that the conversation was over.

"I never found a man who was honest enough and who could understand," she replied simply. "I could see when I looked closely that everyone I've met up until now was too free. I never found anyone who came close to my needs of order and respectability."

"You're terribly conventional!" he said half gallantly, and trying to do homage to her rectitude of character, he was judging her in a quite conventional way, as people expect to be judged. That is why they work their whole lives through. "You are conventional," he said with a degree of respect.

"Conventional?" she repeated. "No," she explained slowly— "it's just that I've always needed some shape out of life because I'm also the kind of person who is so free that I look for some kind of order where I can use my freedom."

"In that respect," she thought—"I'm a saint." She did not tell the man, because so many mistakes can be made about saints.

And Martim did not really understand what she had said— because not only did the lives of others seem quite abstract to him, but also he was more alert to his own thoughts than to those of others—nor did she herself entirely understand what she had said. But, if she had not spoken the truth in all the words of truth, she had said something that could be recognized. And the woman assumed a vaguely satisfied air. Both of them, further-more, had the tranquil impression that something had finally been justified.

The heat of the sun was unbearable: it was noontime. The man looked with speculating eyes at the blouse of the woman which was wet around the armpits. He tried to turn his eyes away, but something in that dark dampness held his fascinated eye. Vitória, not realizing that there had been silence for a time and that her own thoughts were very confused, closed her mouth then, and became even more silent.

"So?" the man said, tired.

"So what?" she asked, waking up surprised.

As if she had shown him in a mixed-up sort of way everything she had to show, the lady had nothing more for him. What had she wanted from Martim? Because everything she had told him had had nothing to do with the purified and useless life that she had chosen one day back everything that she had told him had had nothing to do with the night of frogs that she had gone through. And it had nothing to do with the fact that she had just discovered that, without having known it, she had been alive. And if until now the knowledge of herself had not brought her anywhere except to a rocky gorge out of which she could not climb it now seemed as if the rocks had become crumbly and had allowed her to pass, pass at last into a past. Oh, she deserved that: to experience at last what she had been through. And that man? What had she wanted of him? She looked at him without surprise, and he was a stranger. She had even forgotten that she had turned him in; she had forgotten again. Now that she had a whole past in front of her again he was a familiar stranger.

And he, the stranger? The stranger was looking at her with a polite and curious attention. As he was looking at that woman, he thought, "Bad people are so ingenuous!" Because Vitória's face was only soft and tired. In a contradictory way he was thinking, "The danger is only in what bad people can do because they can make some effect. They themselves are not dangerous, they're infantile; they're tired, they need a little sleep." And he looked at her with curiosity, with a cordial smile. It was then that their looks met and there was no way to escape: we all know the same things. The man then became a bit emotional, and, letting himself go in a kind of generalized love, he said very suddenly, very young:

"What the hell, life can't be that serious!"

Vitória was a little shocked. For a moment, true, an almost shrewd look passed across her face as if she had found in herself a new way of seeing things, unsuspected opportunities and freedoms that were not dangerous. But it was just a moment, and immediately she lost Martim's meaning. There she was with only his smile.

He was smiling . . . And—and she felt that he understood her so well she drew back rigidly, as if the man had done something obscene. She was startled. She, who now wanted to be alone with her past, was startled. Any gesture of kindness in her direction was still dangerous! She did not want his smile! It was still too soon for her to be tempted; she was still not old enough! A quick shudder ran through her: "Don't understand me. Otherwise, if you don't . . . because if you don't, I'll be free again." And, oh God, never again did she want to have again the experience that freedom had brought her over and over again, and never again did she want to shout that all was past. She was startled, because she knew that she was dangerously ready to receive charity. "Don't break down my power!" she thought— because she had just built up a whole life behind her—"Don't be polite to me, don't smile at me; it was always dangerous for someone to be nice to me!" Innocently he was tossing her a bone. "Don't destroy me with your understanding," she inwardly implored him. She knew that, forgetting fear, she would again go directly to get what belonged to a person, if that person . . .

The lady looked at that man, that man who was so crudely today, the present's impossible now. And how can we who are today touch today immediately? She had a horror of the man, just as she had had a horror of the great lonely beach shining in grace and the expectation of happiness. Everything is yours if you just have the courage—but she only had the courage to look at something clearly when it was already impossible to see clearly. Only now had she been able to look at the lost boy by the bonfire, and the past must have been full of things that she could finally see without fear. But, but suddenly, from that man there, time would come from so far away it would destroy today: today, the urgent instant of now. "Don't understand me," she thought a little less convulsively now, and fortunately for herself, a little sadder. "Don't love me, not for a second. I don't know how to be loved any more and it's too late. Good-bye." She did not know how to be loved. To be loved was something much more serious than loving. That woman was not certain of anything. From a mistake in life—and one mistake was all that was needed in that fragile thing called "aim" for someone not to arrive—from one mistake in life she had never used the silent request that people use and that makes other people love us. And, despoiled, she had become so, so proud. And now—now she no longer knew how to be loved.

However—however, who could tell it . . .

Then Vitória turned her eyes away from the man's smiling, kind eyes. "No," her soul said again, just as it had said one night on the island. "No."

And her self-contempt left her bent and small among the large trees, because again she had said no.

What did she feel, then? What she felt was this: "Oh God, what shall I do with this happiness around me that is eternal, eternal, eternal, and which will leave at any moment because the body only teaches us to be mortal?" That was what she felt because by saying "no" again, wounded as she was, she had also seen the trees, and from the simple recognition of beauty, she had loved the beauty that was not hers; and she had loved the sadness that was hers, and proud as she was, she had felt very, very happy for an instant—only from pride, only from insolence.

The impression Martim had of Vitória was made up of superimposed and unclear images. Sometimes it was the image of a confused woman who was sweating under her arms—and then he wondered if maybe he had not simply invented danger in order to stay on the place, because a sweating woman was not dangerous. Sometimes the image of a face would appear to him all by itself—and he could no longer say that he knew it. Coming up against the peculiar mystery of a face, and then the woman would become dangerously unpredictable with her two hollow eyes. But then the image he had of the woman would become in some way as familiar as if he had touched her whole body, or as if both of them there in the sun had not realized that several years of intimacy had passed. But then, as if they really had been living together for several years in common love, with familiarity, again he suddenly did not know her.

When, however, he remembered her telling him that she was a poetess—then something like ridicule covered the memory of the boney woman, and the poetess was no longer dangerous any more, she and her four queens. Who, really, had proved that Vitória had reported him? Nobody. What had happened, probably, was that the mistress of the place, fascinated had mentioned his presence to the professor, because the latter apparently had made himself the spiritual guide of those uncertain and menstruous women. Therefore there was no reason to be afraid.

Chapter 5

A*ND* as if everything had come to an end before its appointed time, and as if everybody had got whatever it was they had wanted from the man, they suddenly left him alone. The air was soft and full, and in the morning the cow gave birth to a calf.

Ermelinda would disappear for hours on end. Martim heard her tell the mulatto woman that she was going to cut out a new dress. Francisco was working silently, not in any hurry. As for Vitória, she no longer followed Martim around giving orders; she no longer seemed to get any pleasure out of laying out chores for him, or she had suddenly admitted that, left to himself, he knew what ought to be done. Merely curious, Martim would watch her pass by, dressed in feminine clothes now—clothes that seemed even odder to him because, besides being out of style, their wrinkles showed the mark of the trunk out of which they must have come. She seemed even less dangerous wearing those clothes. One day he saw a most extraordinary thing: he saw her trying on a hat that was so ancient and dusty that only the unexpectedness of the situation kept him from smiling. And the woman was paying such deep attention to what she saw in the living room mirror that she did not even notice the man. He interpreted the fact that she did not even see him—she, who had always followed him about with her staring eyes—as a sign that he was finally free. Besides, after the big rain, every peaceful thing was in its place, and Martim even thought it plausible that instead of running away, he would simply give Vitória notice that he was leaving. But he no longer even had to leave.

There followed a period of great calm. Life revealed obvious progress the way one suddenly perceives that a child has grown. With the heavy rain, nature ripening, headed toward a maximum point that could be sensed in the leafier way the trees were

(3 0 9)

swaying. And the few days that followed mounted up without incident, like one single day.

They were clear and tall days, woven into the air by the birds. Wings, stones, flowers, and deep shadows formed the new damp heat. The clouds gathered white in the sky and gracefully broke up, letting the immaterial depth that surrounded the house be seen, the work of each one, and the large nights. In the morning, high up in the sky the first shreds of clouds would serve as a resting place so that the eyes could reach off into the distance. In the early morning things were peacefully shining. And in spite of the distance, the clear air brought the mountain within the range of a shout.

They had all lost contact with each other; each one had withdrawn into an individual life that was already preparing them for the life with which they would be left after the man had gone. Absorbed, they were already living in the future, the way one can count on a vacant room as soon as its dying occupant has gone. Even the woodshed had an air of being clean and swept out. And in the cowshed, after the birth of the calf, serenity reigned.

Somewhat disoriented by the peace, Martim tried at times to plan a flight. But the buzzing of the bees seemed more real than the future. And the man now had so much work ahead of him—work no longer interrupted by Vitória's contradictory orders—that only his chores seemed real. No one had ever told him that there could be a threat in the sad figure of a primary school teacher. In a short while Martim was no longer able to work up even a simple suspicion because of the reality that was emerging more and more, in the ditches that he was opening with his own hands, in the golden heat full of short-lived mosquitoes, in the blade of the plow as it turned up a darker soil. Perhaps only men should be able to feel a bit of sadness. But the sky was so high and beautiful that Martim, in spite of himself, joined in with the light and went over to the side of the victors.

And taking advantage of the crest of a wave to raise himself up, he let himself be carried along without any worries on the surge of fullness. Through consideration and docility, he had transformed himself into an instrument of his own work. Never, for example, would he dig a ditch where the ground was too hard. And when the cow refused, he would not milk her. That called for a dedicated patience on his part; he felt the pleasure of one who has discovered a more delicate mode of expression.

The farm benefited greatly from that new condition, as if a long, productive Sunday had been established there. For there was a Sunday air about the indolence upon which the land was growing fat. The corn was getting heavy; the apple tree was breaking out in new shoots, as if its wound had alerted some impulse in it; the wind urged the creek along. That same wind sometimes carried the heavy, fertile smell of ripeness—which Martim, interrupting his work with surprise, recognized as if he were now sleeping with wheat and corn, recognized from the depth of centuries the smell of fertility. The world had never been so large. Birds, active as children, partook of the soil that had been turned over for planting; with closed wings they dived into the waves of the air, and out of the infinite returned with a flutter of wings to watch over the effort of the seeds. Now that the drought was over the trees were full and covered the house with shade, giving its interior the coolness of a siesta. The cows were lowing in the pasture. The world was doing Martim's thinking for him; and he accepted it.

Moreover, the women of the house seemed paler, calmer, carrying out their duties. With mating time now over, the dogs were thin and happy. They barked at the clouds. And the mulatto woman sang so loud that even by the well an occasional sharper, single note echoed. The whole farm was buzzing.

Chapter 6

IT WAS A LITTLE WHILE before the detectives arrived with the professor and the mayor that Vitória sent for him.

It was in the afternoon, and Francisco brought the message to Martim in the cowshed. A little later Martim appeared before Vitória, his face still showing the concentration that he had been putting into his work, his sleeves rolled up, his boots muddy.

The woman examined him in silence. She herself was back in her black slacks and her old blouse. Martim looked at her in fascination; his image of her was still the one of the past few days—tranquil, dreamy, dressed like a woman. Now she seemed chilly to him somehow. And he did not like it. What could have happened? Had he missed some important link? It seemed to him, illogically, that the woman had failed somewhere. And he did not like it: it had been his experience that when a person failed he became a menace to other people; he feared the tyranny of those who are in need. And he did not like what he was seeing at all.

But he was also used to women "not having a thing to wear," and he wondered if what had happened was that she had just ended up not finding anything better to wear than the old slacks; he even wondered whether the condition of the farm had reached the point at which the lady could not afford to make any new clothes, because she had tried on her old ones and they had not been right for her. Who could tell? Who knows? maybe it was just a problem of clothes. He remembered the sad face of a woman who did not have anything to wear. But what he really did not like was the tired, chilly air of that woman, who looked as if she had returned from a long and fruitless journey.

"You sent for me," he finally remembered to say.

She was silent for an instant, as if she had not heard. Then

(3 1 2)

she gave a sigh that was softer than her breathing. She closed her eyes, opened them again. And she said:

"Francisco has piled up some branches and leaves in the back of the yard, near the fence. They have to be burned."

It was the first order for some days, and he looked at her with curiosity. He was also feeling a bit of vanity: at any rate, she had needed him again. Then he looked at her contentedly, with disdain.

"So?" she said, seeing him standing there.

"When I get through in the cowshed," he retorted with the soft insolence of a servant.

"No. Right now!"

"What do you mean 'right now'?" the man asked, surprised.

"They have to be burned right now," she said more calmly.

The leaves were thrown on top of the branches in a high pile which the man felt had been put together too loosely: the force of the fire when it got going would scatter the little pieces. Martim shook his head, disagreeing with pleasure. He undid everything and carefully began to build a tripod with the short, thick branches. That took some time.

Then he skillfully intermingled the leaves and small pieces; he put the green branches to one side, they were damp and would not catch fire. And he lit the fire.

At first a wisp of dirty yellow smoke arose with no visible sign of a flame. But soon little tongues of flame, quicker than could be seen, were escaping from the grid of branches, and right away they came into sight among the leaves. And soon the fire was finally burning, the branches twisting under the surprise attack, the hot leaves rapidly shriveling along their edges; and everything suddenly began to crackle as if branches and leaves had been reached all at the same time.

And soon with suffocating smoke and charred leaves dancing in the air the air in the yard was unbreathable; the man was working surely and precisely with his pitchfork. With mounting skill and just at the right moment he pushed the things that were trying to escape the heat back into the fire, removing the unburned bark. There was an odor of smoked spices, and his nostrils could smell cinnamon and pepper; at the same time there was an intimate smell of something animal that was burning, something like the smell a bird's feathers have underneath its wing, but what was most distinct was a deep fragrance of hard bark turning into embers. The smoke was so heavy that it took on the thick form of a spiral, even though the spiral scattered in confusion six feet above the fire, hesitating, pushed from one side to the other by the wind, which was also disoriented by the impulse of the smoke.

For a moment Martim turned away from the heat to wipe his face, and he saw Vitória among the thick clouds of smoke.

She was staring at the bonfire, her arms were crossed and her hands were clutching at her shoulders coldly. It was a quick look the man gave, and it had no expression. And then he went back to poking the fire, as if he had not seen the woman. She kept on standing there; he could almost guess the rhythm of her breathing. The afternoon was clear, but there was no sun. Yet next to the bonfire it was just as if night had come on, dark and reddish.

Now the activity of the leaves and sticks of wood had become intense and, carried by the wind and the frightened force of the fire, the burning smell reached up beyond the treetops. Now that the fire was completely in the open, the flames were quick like joy and fear, the coals trembled with illumination. Martim poked the fire with his pitchfork, quick and skillfully, and there was no question about his skill, his firmness had no pity. He was sweating, his attentive, reddened eyes would not let the burning stop for an instant. The glare, which sometimes rose up in a sudden larger impulse, was putting the air of the yard to flame.

The woman was behind him, and he could sense her with his back, his neck, his legs, no moment of truce, pushing him, pushing him, asking for more as in the arena. Martim was obeying as he concentrated his violence; the fire was climbing higher and higher, crackling and obeying. Until the man unexpectedly spun around and turned his fury on her.

(3 1 4)

Her eyes were opened very wide, she was gasping as if she had been running, looking horrified at the beauty of the world.

Then, without taking his eyes off her and without looking at the pitchfork, he threw it far away with an effortless and brutish gesture. And so, with empty hands, his arms hanging away from his body, it was as if he had thrown away his last weapon and was ready to fight with his bare hands. He would have offered her his own death as an offense. But still he had not moved and he was looking at the woman, breathing with difficulty, with rage.

The woman did not look at him. Even had someone shaken her by the shoulders, she would not have taken her eyes off the fire.

But when the man's brute look made her look at him—not at the other one, but at him—she stepped back a pace, as if she had finally perceived that she had gone too far. The man was leaning over frontwards, his naked arms open to the air like those of a black and happy ape. She took another step backward, terrified.

As unexpectedly as he had turned to face her, he turned back to the bonfire—without the woman's even being able to determine in what moment the transition had taken place. And with fury the man poked the fire, the lowest flames began to rise again—without being afraid of using his own life, Martim created the fire; he worked with those hands that had become quicker than the flame he challenged, and he could feel the heat singe the hair on his arms.

Then, there was almost nothing left to do.

Like the first smoke, the final smoke was dirty and thick and malignant; and it curled away in a twisting thread. The coals were still blinking, for brief instants they would turn gold with a show of life. Then one could sense that they flamed up because there was no more light left, and they quietly went black.

The man watched them as he panted, his neck shining with sweat. His mouth, still snarling from the effort, showed its teeth.

Finally, forced to admit that there was nothing more to be

done, he dropped his shoulders, relaxed his arms, let his brow rest. Covered by their lids once more, his eyes became calm, intense. Without surprise he saw that Vitória was no longer there. Then he looked foolishly around, as if he had just shown what a man is capable of.

The afternoon was clear again. The great softness of the air that enveloped his wet body made him scrutinize the sky with infantile surprise, squinting up at it as if it had given him something. He stretched his burned arms out to the breeze; he leaned his lips against his scorched hands. Standing there, he was complete, with an air that was mysterious, magnanimous, bestial. Fighting with the fire had been the work of a man, and he was proud and calm. And a woman had been terrorized and satisfied; and because of that too he was calm and proud. Everything was so round and realized that there was even a touch of sad dignity in Martim. And the promise that was made to us— the promise was there. He could feel it there; he would only have to extend his hand that had finally been burned in the exercise of his function as a man.

Even though now, older and wiser, he did not extend it.

But at least he had the gift of sight, and there was no implication of mutual offense in that. At least he could look in a grand way, and as one equal to another. Having nobly burned his hand in combat, Martim looked. The countryside had become vast and the light had the religious grace that comes to a man who is no longer ashamed of himself and looks face to face at human nature that has already been redeemed in him.

Unexpectedly, the first step of his great general rebuilding had been accomplished. If he had created himself a while back, now he was inaugurating himself. He had just reformed the man. The world is vast, but so am I. With the obscure satisfaction of having worked at the fire and of having frightened what had to be frightened him in the shape of a word. He had attained it with the innocence of strength. Just like that—he had attained it. And then, with the smugness necessary for creation, the whole time was being reborn for him, and he knew

(316)

that he had the strength to begin again. Because—because finally having fully reached himself, he would reach men; and, throwing away the pitchfork and working nakedly, exposed and naked, he would guide himself even to "transform men."

How he would transform men, Martim was wise enough not to know—and wise enough not to question, because he was a wise man now.

But not knowing was of no importance. His future had now become so vast that it was rising dizzily up into his head. The time was ripe and the moment had arrived. That was all that his calm heart and the patient breeze were telling him, and the deep love that was peacefully spreading itself out from him was like something that was finally taking root. It was because until that moment he would not have been able to do it—as long as he had not recovered in himself the respect for his own body and for his own life, which was the first way of respecting the life there is in other people. But when a man respected himself, then he had finally created himself in his own image. And then he would be able to look other people in the eye. Without the constraint of our great mistake, and without mutual shame.

And as for not understanding other people . . . Well, in a woman, his first honor had been remade. It seemed to him that from now on he would only need to have the voice of a man and try to act like a man: that was what he was. Never had his thoughts been as lofty as the work he had just done.

And deep inside himself he then began to despise people who did not love what they were doing, or who did not have the courage to do what they loved. Having forgotten that only a few minutes before he had found a symbol of work, and that he ought to be merciful toward those who had not found it, he was fatuously admiring himself. That man was loving himself for the first time, which meant that he was ready to love others, to love us, who are given ourselves as a sample of what the world is capable of; and himself, who had just proved it.

"How could I have imagined that the time was coming to an end?" His heart was pounding hard. Because it just, it just

(3 1 7)

began . . . As if time had been created for a deeper freedom, now suddenly the future was being reborn. And he who had been sure that he had hesitated in its reconstruction saw that it had only been the great patience of an artisan, and he saw with pleasure that he had known how to sleep, which is the hardest part of a piece of work. Because—as if the pause had only been the preparation for the leap—his first objective step had unexpectedly ripened: for the first time Martim had made a complete advance, like someone who says a word. So the word that he had been waiting for had not come to him in the shape of a word. He had attained it with the innocence of strength. Just like that: he had attained it. And then, with the smugness necessary for creation, the whole time was being reborn for him, and he knew that he had the strength to begin again. Because—because finally having fully reached himself, he would reach men; and, throwing away the pitchfork and working nakedly, exposed and naked, he would guide himself even to "transform men."

How he would transform men, Martim was wise enough not to know. And wise enough not to question it, because he was a wise man now.

But not knowing was of no importance: his future had now become so vast that it was rising dizzily up into his head. The time was ripe and the moment had arrived: that was all that his calm heart and the patient breeze were telling him, and the deep love that was peacefully spreading itself out from him like something that was finally taking root. It was because until that moment he would not have been able to do it—as long as he had not recovered in himself the respect for his own body and for his own life, which was the first way of respecting the life there is in other people. But when a man respected himself, then he had finally created himself in his own image. And then he would be able to look other people in the eye. Without the constraint of our great mistake, and without mutual shame.

And as for not understanding other people . . . Well, that would not even be important any more. Because there was a way of understanding that did not need any explanation, and which came from the final and irreducible fact of standing there, and from the fact that another man too has the possibility of standing there—because with that minimum of being alive, everything was already possible. No one so far has ever had a greater advantage than that.

"Besides"—Martim thought, feeling that he was going beyond himself a little bit, but no longer able to hold back—"besides, it was foolish not to understand." "A person doesn't understand just because he doesn't want to!" he thought boldly. Because understanding is a way of looking. Because understanding is, besides, an attitude. Martim, very satisfied, had that attitude, as if now, stretching out his hand in the dark and picking up an apple, he would recognize, with fingers that love had made so clumsy, that it was an apple. Martim no longer asked for the name of things. It was enough for him to recognize them in the dark—And rejoice, clumsily.

And afterwards? Afterwards, when he went out into the light, he would see the things his hand had felt before, and he would see those things with their false names. Yes, but he would have known them already in the dark, like a man who has slept with a woman.

Chapter 7

A LITTLE WHILE after that Martim was sent for.

The mayor of Vila Baixa was a clean little man whose hair was slicked down, and he had an Argentine look about him. The two detectives were short and calm. The professor was moving about with intensity, his flabby jowls vibrating, as if he had to take care of everything all at the same time. Martim was the only tall person among them, as if he were surrounded by a band of armed midgets. He looked around stupefied. It was because there was no logic at all in what was happening. From the very beginning, the fact that he was tall among so many short people left him physically clumsy, incomplete, and at a disadvantage.

The others were waiting patiently. It was obvious that the man had still not understood what was happening, and so they were giving him time. Vitória, very pale, had put on the dress she wore to receive visitors. The professor was talking on and on. Martim kept nodding his head in agreement without hearing, and he smiled as if that perhaps was what they expected of him; until he found his footing, the best thing would be to move cautiously in accordance with what the others expected.

". . . you must understand! We have to take our punishment, you know why? If not, everything would lose all meaning!" the professor was saying agitatedly, and Martim, too confused to think about himself, wasted valuable moments in understanding finally why the two women called the professor kind; he was; even if he was not; a man who passes judgment makes a sacrifice. "We have to take our punishment!" the professor repeated sadly. "You're an intelligent man, you must understand! I'm calling on an engineer! I'm talking to a superior man; you must understand why I did this! And I swear to you that it's not for me that you must understand! Because I, I understand what I did. God gave me the inspiration to make me understand myself! Because if you don't understand, you're doomed! If you don't understand, everything I did will be doomed, and you won't finish what you started out to do with your crime! You must understand that if there were no punishment, the work of millions of people would be doomed to uselessness!" he shouted imploringly. "There are periods of human history that have . . ."

"Yes, yes," Martim said stupidly, calming him down.

"You're an engineer, a superior man, you must understand!" the professor ordered.

"I'm not an engineer," Martim said then. "I'm a statistician," he said very absent-mindedly, passing his hand over his head and losing a precious moment.

No one knew what to answer. The professor, a little unwillingly, made a gesture of sudden annoyance, as if he could have spared them the disagreeable news. But the tension had been broken. For an instant the situation had been thrown off its previous track which had been leading to what was still going to happen—which left them all indecisive.

"What did he do?" Vitória finally asked the detective.

"I killed my wife," Martim said.

And he looked at her, deeply surprised. Could he have forgotten?

"I killed my wife," he repeated then, testing what he said with great care.

Was that all? Was that all? But then, why had he not said it way back? He blinked his eyes, dazed. Vitória was looking at him open-mouthed.

"But why?" she finally shouted, crushed. "But why? Why?!" she became enraged.

"Because I was almost certain that my wife had a lover," Martim said.

It was surprising how easy it had become to talk, and it was surprising what he himself had said. The detective with a piece of black tobacco on his lapel cleared his throat. "He'd come back from a poker game and he started a row."

There was silence. Martim had not understood anything. He smiled stupidly, he seemed a little embarrassed. "So much attention," he thought, "being paid to me." He was overcome by a crisis of timidity. He was not understanding any of it, he only felt that he was losing time, which gave him an urgency that was uncomfortable and physical. If there was some recognizable feeling in him, it was one of curiosity. He was looking about curiously. That was all that he could recognize. Because from the moment he had said the surprising phrase to Vitória he had become a stranger to himself. He had nothing more to do with the man who had just lit a bonfire. Up to the point of having the dizzy impression that before he had said the simple revealing phrase he had been lying all the time.

Had he been lying all the time? Then he began to sweat a little. There he was with a crystalized smile. In one minute he had recovered the polish of one person among others, the civility of a man who had discreetly perspired. But his upset was giving him a feeling of weight upon his chest. He began to sweat a little more, and he mopped himself with gentility, with light taps of his handkerchief on his forehead, even though he had only managed to breathe just now. The cold sweat moistened his face again, he passed his trembling hand across his mouth. But his upset grew larger. Then he smiled carefully, with ironic abstention. He still had nothing to do with what was happening to him. It suddenly seemed to him that the physical location of a soul was in the chest, imprisoned there the way a dog's soul is imprisoned in the body of a dog. He opened his mouth in a smile, and he had that total muteness; if he had wanted his soul to speak it would have barked. He stood there startled, smiling.

But he had spoken! He had spoken at last. The phrase about his wife had been one of the most ancient phrases, slowly recovered the way a paralytic takes a step. And there were even other words waiting for him, if his tongue could only get up . . . he had discovered that with curiosity when he had said so simply that he had suspected a lover. Which, if it were not the best of truths, was at least a truth that had the value of exchange for something. With curiosity, with the weight on his chest, he was exchanging once more, buying and selling. It had been that, then, that had happened to him: he had suspected a lover. Only that? And everything else that he had figured out, thought about, or wanted—everything else began to become so unreal that he passed a soft hand across his mouth. Could a man's fate be invented? He passed his hand across his dry mouth, fascinated.

"Because of jealousy," Vitória said, demolished. "You loved her so much that you were capable of . . ." The woman went quietly back into her depths, looking at that deep man.

Martim trembled in his great surprise. "He had loved her so much . . ." Vitória had said. That must have been it, then! Intrigued, Martim looked at her.

And among the four men whom he was now examining one by one, the long interregnum of his dream suddenly expired. "He had loved her so much," Vitória had said in explanation. Perhaps it did not even matter that he had never really loved his wife. But, reduced to its own proportions, that was how he could understand it: "He had loved her so much."

"He had loved her so much?" he was startled again, still not stable on those legs which were being given to him. He looked startled at the four men and the woman who were waiting. "It must have been true, then. The truth of others had to be his truth, then." The truth of others had to be his truth, or the work of millions of people would be doomed. Wouldn't that be the great place that everybody had in common? His eyes blinked from liveliness and sharpness and curiosity. Even if he knew that he had not loved her, he tried with some degree of caution to make the words of others his words, because after all, they couldn't be empty words: "Because a man does love his wife."

With a certain avidity, he was clinging to the wisdom of four little men—and suddenly, suddenly even if it had been possible, he had no desire to run away.

(3 2 3)

And then, as if he had not seen people for a long time, he looked with curiosity and some emotion at the messengers. He had forgotten what they were like.

"He had loved her so much?" he insisted, surprised again, forcing himself with some impatience now to recover the outside truth. Yes, it had been because of love. Martim still wanted to see if he could hit the mark in establishing a compromise between his truth and the truth of others, trying to make out of both of the two sides one single truth: "Yes, it had been because of love, not for his life, but because of love," he thought, blinking his eyes. "A crime of love . . . for the world," he chanced, disconcerted, clumsily making a try at presumption. "What nonsense am I thinking?" he startled himself with, because the faces of the four men, which were becoming more and more objective, would not allow him the slightest compromise. They only asked him for the hard choice. "A crime of love for the world?" Martim was ashamed: things like that did not exist! Only acts existed! Only people's faces existed!

But once more he tried in a timid way to build a bridge between himself and the four men. "A crime of extreme love, yes, which he had not been able to bear except in perfection; a crime of pity; of pity and disillusion? And of heroism. In a gesture of rage, repugnance, disdain, and love he had done a beautiful job of violence."

Martim wanted to go on thinking like that because he had even been getting close to the mark. But the faces of the men had begun to be an obstacle that was growing larger and larger. If he wanted to go on thinking like that the solution would be to avoid those faces with their open eyes. Then he turned his eyes away, as he had done once in a restaurant when he had been eating a steak and a child had stationed himself behind the window to contemplate him.

Perturbed, he turned his eyes away. "Yes, a crime of love." In a world of silence, he had spoken. Oh, what silliness was going through his head? Martim was ashamed, even though he had not been ashamed before of things that were much worse. But this time he was really embarrassed because in spite of his not looking at the men, the four men were undeniably standing there. "What was my crime, really?" he wondered, still not looking at them out of fear. "What was my crime? I substituted the real, unknown, and impossible act for a shout of denial." Perhaps that had been the sense of his crime.

"But denial?" How could he understand the meaning of that word, if denial, his blow, suddenly seemed to him now the most obstinate tremor of hope, and the hand stretched out as far as it would go to the four men. Had his crime been a shout of negation—or of appeal? "Answer me."

"What did you say, exactly, about my loving. What was it exactly?" he implored, extremely confused, because he was a man who never should have sought the depths. He was basically a person to be led.

"I said . . ." Vitória, after automatically starting to obey him, looked at him in silence, unable to express herself. Now that she knew the facts about Martim, now that she was finally looking at him with open eyes, now she did not know him. And like a blind person who has got his vision back and cannot recognize with his eyes what his sensitive hands know by heart, she closed her eyes for an instant then, trying to get back her previously complete recognition; she opened them again and tried to make the two images into one. "I said . . ." again she looked at him quietly; but because she no longer needed him for anything she could also look at him with pity and disdain. "I said," she repeated then, bitter and untouchable, "that you loved her so much that, out of jealousy—"

"Yes, yes, now I remember!" he interrupted quickly, his eyes moved.

Had he been jealous of her? Oh, Lord, but I'd forgotten one of the capital truths!

The men were talking quietly among themselves.

"You might be sorry to know it," the detective with the dark tobacco on his lapel then said ironically, "but she didn't die. The ambulance got there in time, and they were able to save your wife's life."

They all looked at Martim with curiosity.

"Wonderful," Martim said finally, and his eyes glistened wet for a moment.

So she had not even died.

And that was the way everything was snuffed out. There wasn't even any crime.

What had happened then? To be honest, a man would probably have to say that he had tried to kill his wife because he was jealous of her, because, as any person could guess, he had loved that sleepy wife of his so much. Clinging to that immediately, Martim then asked himself in his affliction, "Will she forgive me? How long will I spend in jail? Will I still have time to begin to love her, so that what will happen in the end will be that I loved her all the time?" He was making an effort to construct a retrospective truth.

"And my son?!" he shouted with a jump, like a man who has woken up too late. Using words again, he shivered. He had always been crazy about that boy of his—and now those words were fitting him perfectly and he accepted them with greed. "What about my son!"

"Your wife," the mayor said severely, "deserved a much better fate than being married to you. She hid everything from the boy. Your son thinks you're off on a trip."

And now that? Martin's eyes were shiny with tears. And now that? What would he be able to make out of that, for example? So that was his wife! A great woman. He saw her again while she yawned in front of the mirror and actively scratched her armpit. Brave and good—everything he had known about her was now becoming dim in the presence of the four men, and all that was left was that she was brave and good. The other truth—a truth that was completely useless in the presence of the four men whose strength simplified them and gave them size—the other truth had become just as nonexistent as the crime that had never come to be. Martim got an unexpected pleasure out of using words that had some value in the world: brave and good. They were beautiful words—because the existence of hollow words like that had saved his son's soul.

(3 2 6)

That sentimentalizing of decency captured Martim with a painful assault.

"Brave and good," he said aloud then, so that the men could see that he was one of them.

The four quiet men looked at him, the four representatives. Representing, mute and beyond appeal, the harsh struggle that is joined every day against greatness, our moral greatness; representing the struggle that is courageously joined every day against our kindness, because real kindness is a violence; representing the struggle that we make every day against our own freedom, which is too big and which we diminish with careful effort. We, who are so objective that we end up being only that part of ourselves which is useful; with application we make of ourselves the man that another man can recognize and use, and through discretion we are unaware of the ferocity of our love; and through delicacy we pass by the saint and the criminal at a distance; and when someone speaks about kindness and suffering, we lower our ignorant eyes without saying a word in our favor; we apply ourselves to give of ourselves only what will not be frightening, and when someone speaks of heroism we do not understand. The four men standing there, representing . . .

Then, suddenly—oh, hell, oh, hell! Suddenly, with a quick look at the impassive faces of the men, which had noses, mouths, eyes, birthmarks, and heads, Martim realized, startled, they know! He realized that everybody knows the truth. And that was precisely the game: act as if you did not know . . . Those were the rules of the game. How stupid he had been, he thought, appalled, shaking his head in disbelief. How ridiculous had been his idea of wanting to save something that was already being saved. They all know the truth, nobody is ignorant of it! Startled as he faced the noses and mouths with which we are born, Martim looked at the four men: they all knew the truth. And even if they did not know it, the people's faces knew it. Besides, everybody knows everything. And one time or another somebody rediscovers gunpowder, and his heart pounds. People get mixed up when they try to speak, but everybody knows everything. That silent face with which we are stubbornly born.

The men were conversing in low voices. And during that time Martim was trying to grasp his mistake. His previous mistake had been trying to understand by means of thought. And when he had tried to rebuild the construction he had fallen irremediably into the same error. But if a person does not become perverted by thought, an intact person would know the truth. What a fiasco his had been he discovered with shame and sentimentality. As if he had gone to tell a mother how to love her child, and the mother had lowered her eyes and let him rant on—and suddenly he would understand that without any words and even without understanding, the mother was loving her child. And then, vexed—in one of those shames through which very ardent people pass—he would tiptoe away, promising himself that never again, oh never again would he make so much noise. Because millions of people were working without cease, day and night, saving. Only impatient people did not understand the rules of the game. He had thought that the bushes were sleeping untouched, and suddenly he discovered from the faces with noses that people have, he discovered that the ants were silently gnawing all over the bushes. "Hell! we're interminable!" What he had not understood was that there was a pact of silence. And, ridiculously heroic, he had come along with his words. Others before him had already tried to break the silence. No one had succeeded. Because long before those who have the gift of speech, the four men and all the others already knew.

Martim passed his hand across his head, confused. The men were talking, studying the map. The truth was that, infected by the quiet faces of the men who were talking over the map, Martim, as if he too had lost his speech, could no longer think now in terms of words, he was metamorphosing himself into the four men, and transfiguring himself into himself at last—and penetrating that step beyond, whose maximum point consists in having a face that knows. And that was why he no longer knew how to express, not even to himself, the belief that everything was certain.

(3 2 8)

Miraculously certain. Oh, Martim knew that in the face of intelligence it would be very foolish to say that. But what was happening was that, supported at last by the four, he was not afraid of being foolish. Oh, how could one explain that everything was certain? Initiated into silence now—no longer the silence of the plants, no longer the silence of the cows, but into the silence of other men—he no longer knew how to explain himself; he only knew that he was feeling more and more like a man, he was feeling more and more like the others. Which, while seeming to him at the same time like a great decadence and the fall of an angel, also seemed to him like an ascension. But that can only be understood by a person who, with impalpable effort, has already metamorphosed himself into himself. Martim probably could not even manage to explain why a man would have the urgency to be a man as an ideal. Oh, Martim at that point did not know anything else at all. Unless it was that combination of fatigue, cowardice, and gratitude in which he was finally wallowing around with the rather ignoble and delighted pleasure of a lizard in the mud. Oh, but something had been created.

Worn-out, but it had been created.

Above all Martim was very tired. A man all by himself could get that tired. He himself had wanted to bend under a weight— "bend under a weight" was one of the ancient symbols that he had needed to verify by himself the remains of processions and athletic matches that he had watched. He himself had wanted to bend with the weight and carry it forward. But the ones who were carrying it forward were the four tranquil men who with their patience were protecting whatever it was they were carrying forward. He himself, except for grasping at symbols, had not been able to do anything. But the four men were protecting the weight with their ignorance. Oh hell, it wasn't really a weight, it was a "torch" that was generally carried! They would protect the weight with their ignorance, without opening up its mystery, carrying it intact and like that, forward, etc. Every so often, someone would invent a vaccine that would cure diseases. Every so often the government would fall. Sometimes a woman would stop screaming and a baby would be born. "What the hell!" Martim thought with goose flesh, as if they had raised his country's flag, a thing he had never been able to resist.

"Oh, but I didn't even have the right to try!" He suddenly revolted. "I wanted the symbol because the symbol is the true reality! I had the right to be heroic! Because I was the hero, in me, which made a man out of me!"

What was that man really thinking about?

Nothing. Transfigured remains of patriotism and the granting of degrees, milkmen who never fail to deliver their milk every day—things like that which do not seem to teach, but which do teach so much—a letter that one thought would never arrive and it arrives, processions that slowly turn the corner, military parades during which a whole multitude lives off the arrow it has shot into the air. That man was recuperating helter-skelter. Memory ends up by coming back.

What was he really thinking about? Nothing beyond that. The sun was still turning gold, reddish, tranquil. The world was beautiful, no question about that. Through the window the sun was gilding the man that the men were studying. Oh the world was so beautiful! And everything was certain. Certain in a future sort of way.

"What is being certain really like?" Martim was trapped. His tired brain was confused, he did not really know what being certain was. Then he made a superhuman effort to continue. But it seemed that he could not.

It seemed that he could not, and that his good will was not enough; that was where the problem lay. And now that he was almost at the end of the trail, having almost grasped a certain word or certain feeling, now he did not have the strength to reach out his tired arm and attain it. He had to stop where he had stopped and transfer the organizing of the march to other people. And remain there humbly, and once again accept guessing as the maximum ideal.

Confused, in a manner of speaking, Martim was only guessing. But who knows? No force could ever get beyond the maximum extension of a man's arm—and then, with more urging, attain that ultimate and impossible thing which could fill his hand with life. Because a man's arm is a definite measure. And it has something about it that we will never know. It has something about it that we will never know, can you feel that, don't you feel it? The man was embarrassed, wrought up as if that antithetically meant risking himself in the first step of a strange hope.

"She was brave and good," he said, interrupting the men so he could look at their faces, because he felt that once again he was getting lost and away from them.

The men, who were concentrating on the map, lifted up their eyes, looked at him for a second, and, annoyed, went back to the map.

"Brave and good," Martim repeated, interpreting their expression as a sign that they had not heard him. And they had to hear him! It was an open-and-shut question of reducing everything that had happened to him to something comprehensible to millions of men who live by the slow certainty with which things go forward, because those men were risking themselves too. And they could not be disturbed in the work of their sleep, and they ought never to have their certainty shaken up—because that would be the greatest crime.

Thank God that Martim perceived that once more he was slipping into discourse, and that the reality of the four men had nothing to do with that. Then he got a little off his course: nothing that he had to offer seemed to be of any use. He wanted to join the party at any cost, but everything that he did was always so blatant, no matter how discreet he was. He was a little off his course then.

"I want to be face to face with the person who is man enough to tell me that I don't love my wife!" he suddenly said to himself, remaking himself. He had got emotional over his own generosity, he who was offering to sell his own soul, as long as someone would buy it from him. It pained him to lie, but the bravado made him feel very good. With brute good will, Martim wanted to buy everybody a drink today, and he wanted them all to drink as much as they wanted to, and then he would not think of confessing that he didn't have any money—and then he too would have a secret to be sacrificed, the way the others had.

Martim wanted to sacrifice his disbelief. And with that heroic amputation he would accept in himself only what men could understand and without, being understood, their stride faltered. He accepted the fact that he had committed a crime of passion.

He accepted the fact that he had committed a crime of passion, not only because, remembering his wife's breasts at that moment, he was overcome with a retrospective rage, but because it seemed to him that if he had merely committed a crime of passion, he would have avoided the greater crime: that of doubting. And after all, truth is a secondary thing—if you want a symbol. And now he had a new symbol to pursue.

"I'm one of you," he thought then, still with the remains of a gravity that was becoming proud of itself. "I'm one of you," he thought, capitulating, attentive, conscious. And the truth was that by giving away his own consciousness, he was only giving away, after all, a consciousness that had failed; it wasn't much. A consciousness that had let itself be pulled along by beauty. "Is that really the way I should make my act of surrender?" he asked himself, trying to find the maximum through concentration. And by handing the key over to the small, strong men, he was voluntarily standing up against the wall, waiting to be shot.

Oh, but was he perhaps exaggerating his own importance, and the importance he was handing over to them? He was, yes. But how could one live without exaggeration? How could one reach things without exaggerating? Exaggeration was the only possible size for someone who was small; I have to exaggerate myself—if I don't, what can I do with the little thing I am?

And that was why, with all the good will he might have had, he still did not know how to be a different man. And he was handing himself over enormous, clumsy as an inflated rubber doll. He was aware of that; and he tried to correct it or at least disguise it. Because that way of handing himself over was as if he were offending some poor man by showing off the charity of his wealth, it was as if he were scandalizing the modesty of four men. It was as if he had thought that "the thing would become quite certain" if he suddenly exposed himself in the nude—and the others turned their eyes away without a single sign of reprobation, simply showing by silence that this was not the way either, and that nakedness is a purely personal thing.

All right, I made a mistake then. But how can a man become the other man then? How? By an act of love, it occurred vaguely to Martim, a thought that, at the same time, seemed terribly foolish to him.

And since he was now up a blind alley, he rapidly tried to cover up his complete lack of tact. "It'll all be over soon enough! Let's not talk about it any more, O.K.? Let's forget what happened; let's not even touch on the subject! I killed someone, didn't I? So I killed someone! Even without killing I killed! But nobody has to grieve over me either. What happened happened! Let's look ahead!" His eyes were moist with the desire to be accepted.

The four men were still leaning over the map.

They had the great practical advantage of being numbered in the millions; for every million that made a mistake, another million rose up. And something was happening through them—happening too slowly for impatience, but happening. Only the impatience of a desire had given the illusion that the time of one lifetime was enough. "For my own personal life, I must ask for help from someone who has already died and from someone who is yet to be born. Only in that way will I be able to have a life of my own," and only in that way did the word time have the meaning that he had guessed one day.

"I am nothing," Matim said to himself then, out of sheer perverseness this time, blinking with pleasure. The fact was that by means of some very complicated reasoning, he had come to the conclusion that it had been a blessing for him to have made a mistake, because if he had not, he would have proved to himself that life's task was up to a man all by himself—which, contradictorily, would have meant that the task would surely not be done . . . A man, all by himself, could reach only a superficial beauty, like a line of poetry, which, after all, is not transmitted through the blood. (Lie! He knew that he had gone way beyond that). A man all by himself had the impatience of a child; and like a child he would commit a crime, and then he would look at his hands and would see that he did not even have any blood on his hands, just red ink, and then he would say: "I am nothing."

That was what he thought. And he also thought, "Actually I can rest. Those men don't know that they know, that's all that's happening to them." The four little men were carrying something forward—jackasses, small, stupid jackasses? "I'm the jackass!—they're going forward. With what? God damn it," Martim thought, quite worked up, "it doesn't matter what. In the last analysis they're carrying something forward. And in order to carry it forward, they are protecting themselves by being small and empty—empty like anything!—and stupid; and if they get all broken up by doubt, thousands of other little people will burst up out of the ground and continue on with the job of certainty."

It was then that Martim, for the first time, found certainty.

Exhausted, as if he had already found it some time before, he recognized it. The only way to discover it was, besides, through recognition. That was how it was.

And that was how it happened, nothing more, nothing less: he had found certainty. How? Oh, let's say that a person has a mathematical mind, but that it doesn't know that there are such things as numbers—how would a person like that think, then? By being certain! Oh, hope too is a jump forward. Martim then put everything he had on certainty. And he was very quiet.

He was very quiet. From the place from where he had stuck out his foot, life was very beautiful. He had reached a place that was not divisible, not even by the number one. And then he remained there, quiet, fatigued. If he had left home "to find out if it was true," now he knew that it was. Besides, he knew what truth was. Even though he might never have dared say so, not even to himself, because, as they say, he had become a wise man. And truth, when one thinks about it, is impossible. Hell! truth was made to exist! and not for us to know. All that's left to us is for us to invent it. "Truth . . . well, the truth was that which was," Martim thought with a depth that put him precisely in the middle of the emptiness. Truth is never terrifying, we are the ones who are terrifying. And also, "What will truth be like?" Just let someone who does not believe that truth happens look at a chicken walking around with the strength of the unknown. "Besides, truth has happened lots of times." At that point Martim had already become lost in what he had been ironically waiting for. Those depths from which, from which a great wave of love was born inside his chest.

Not knowing at first what to do with love, his soul staggered a little in the face of so much crudeness. Then he was quiet, stoical, firmly bearing up under it all.

A few hours before, beside the bonfire, he had attained an impersonality inside of himself. He had been so profoundly himself that he had become the "himself" of any other person, the way a cow is the cow of all cows. But if beside the bonfire he had made himself, right then he was using himself. Right then he had just attained the impersonality that makes for the fact that as one man falls another rises up—the impersonality of dying while others are being born, the altruism that makes other people exist. We, who are you. "What a strange thing. Even now I seem to be wanting to reach the tip of my finger with the tip of my own finger—it's true that with that extreme effort I grew, but the tip of my finger is still unreachable. I went as far as I could. But why didn't I understand that the thing that I could not reach in me was already other people? Other people, who are our deepest plunge! We who are you just as you yourselves are not you." In that way, concentrating very hard on the birth of others, in a task that only he could carry out, Martim was there trying to give body to those who would be born.

Slowly, he finally came out of his quietness. "I can count on you," he said to himself, groping, "I can count on you," he thought gravely; and that was the most personal form in which a person can exist. We who only have any value as long as we are whole, like money. Martim was even ashamed of having been personal in a different way. It was a dirty past, his; it had been an individual life, his. But it also seemed to him, as he forgave himself, that he had had no choice, that it had been the only way in which he had learned to be other people. Underneath we are all so much alike and the children of the same mother.

Then, when he thought about "children of the same mother," he became all sentimental, he became tender and soft—which was terrible in a practical way because it made him lose track of his thoughts. "Now I have to start all over again from the beginning," he thought, very perturbed. But it was too late to go back with any degree of coldness, because he was so upset by problems of motherhood and love. For that was what it was—making a perfect circle within his own limits, and his luck was rare in being able to return by obscure means to his own starting-point—in a perfect circle within his scant limits, he wanted to be good then. Because in the end, postponing the mystery *sine die*, that was the immediate moment of a man. And especially because, after all, "the other man" is the most objective thought that a person can have! he who had so much wanted to be objective.

He looked. And without the least shadow of a doubt he saw the four concrete men. They were undeniable. If Martim had wanted to have objectivity one day, those men were the clearest thought that Martim had ever had. And to be "good" was in the last analysis the only way to be other people.

Then, as many promises had been made to us, one of them was being fulfilled right there: other people existed. They existed as if he, Martim, had given them to themselves. Martim looked, intrigued, at the detective with the dark tobacco. "I return your greatness," he thought with effort and some solemnity. One of the promises was being fulfilled: the four men. And he, Martim, was ready to feel alien hunger as if his own stomach were transmitting to him the absolute and imperious command to live. And if, like every person, he was a preconceived idea, and if he had left home to find out if what had been preconceived was true—it was true, yes. In some way the world was saved. There was at least a fraction of a second in which each one was saving the world.

Martim's heart was confused. "The difference between them and me, is that they have a soul and I had to create mine. I had to create for them and for myself the place where they and I could walk. Since the process is always mysterious, I don't even know how to tell how I did it; but those men, I stood them up inside of me. To be truthful, I'm not the least bit ashamed that, being nothing, I am so powerful. The fact is that we are modestly our own process. I belonged to my steps, one by one, in the same proportion as these people advanced and made a road and built the world. It was a long road. And it's true that I lied a lot; I lied as much as I needed to. But perhaps lying is our most acute way of thinking; perhaps lying is our way of grasping; and I did a lot of grasping. My hands have a past. It was a long road, and I had to invent my steps; but this innocence I feel inside of me is the purpose, because I can also feel, inside of me, the innocence and silence of other people. Oh, maybe just for an instant! And then?—then I turn over to all of us the job of living. We are our own witnesses, it does no good to turn our faces aside. The consolation is that not everybody has to testify and stammer, and only some feel the damnation of trying to understand understanding." By the grace of God, the world that he had been ready to construct would never have the force of gravity, and the man that he had invented had fallen short . . . indeed, he had fallen short of what he himself was!

Could he be discovering gunpowder, perhaps? But maybe that's the way it is: every man has to discover gunpowder someday. Or else there would be no experience. And his failure?

(337)

How could he become reconciled to his own failure? Well, every personal history is the story of a failure. By means of which . . . Besides, he had not failed completely. "Because I did create the others," he said to himself looking at the four men. And love rose up from out of the depths of the inferno. We who are sick from love. But would anyone ever accept the way in which he had come to love? Oh, people are so demanding! They eat bread and they are repelled by those who pound raw dough; they devour meat but do not invite the butcher to sit down at the table; people ask for the process to be hidden from them. Only God would not be disgusted by his twisted love.

Emotional and generous as he felt, Martim would have become overbearing in his luxury of kindness—the way his own mother, kind and annoying, would insist with great feeling that visitors eat and drink. So, just like his mother, he looked at the four representatives. And without knowing what to give them, he considered patting the detective with the tobacco on his lapel on the back. He opened his mouth to say with malicious complicity, "There, eh, you old devil!"—but he became embarrassed in the middle, because his mother had also been a moderate woman.

Then, without knowing that he had been thinking about his mama, what happened to him, in a perfect circle, was the fact that our parents are not dead. At least not completely dead.

"What was it? What was I thinking just now?" Martim became surprised and startled. Again that man had thought too quickly in relation to his own slowness. Every time he hit upon something, he did not understand himself. "We're too intelligent for our slowness." So, without understanding why on earth he had thought about his mother, he only could realize at that moment that he had been thinking; and he grunted approval of his filial sentiments, with that tendency he had to pay homage. He was a little intrigued at having thought about his mother. Even though he agreed; in a general way he agreed. He did not know with what, but he agreed. What would become of us, in the end, if we did not, like God, use obscurity? Then, without really following the thread of his thoughts, he discovered—all alone and without the help of anyone—that God and people write along crooked lines! I have no way to judge "if they write honestly. Who am I to judge?" he conceded with magnaminity, "but along crooked lines." And that—that he had discovered all by himself.

Another symbol had been touched, then.

Excited by his success, Martim immediately got to work and thought, "Shoemakers' children go barefoot!" and he stopped to see if he had hit upon it again. But he could not make any sense out of it. Martim had fallen into plain babbling, like a happy and tired man. Ever since childhood, whenever he had been successful, he had ended up by coming off badly. When he used to play soccer and made a happy goal, his next kick always ended up by sending the ball out of bounds: he was a man of good will. No, the shoemaker's children hadn't got him anywhere—and the man felt in time that he was abusing his own state of grace and forcing his own hand a little. Oh, everything's so dull, he thought, exhausted, disillusioned.

How many minutes had gone by? What had passed by was the kind of minutes in which thought is time.

"We've already wasted ten minutes over that map," said the detective whom Martim had created and who was functioning for the first time since Martim had thought him up—and functioning perfectly too. "We're going to end up driving at night," the detective said annoyed.

"Brave and good," Martim said to himself, recuperated, ancient, recuperated a little too much even, and almost back in the Middle Ages: his armor was shining.

He was anxious to please them. And for some time now he had been dying to ask them if his wife really had had a lover. Then, for the first time, that was of the greatest importance. And they had to know; those who were strong and good. He wanted to be judged by them, who, secure and armed, must also be charitable—because in Martim's new system of life a person was fated to be perfect as soon as he had arrived at the point of living where a thing came to be born because it was already complete. With moist eyes, he would ask them humbly, as a child would—he wanted to be the man's child and to learn everything all over again. He wanted to obey and to be severely punished if he did not obey. And he wanted to enter that world which had the eminently practical advantage of existing. What am I saying—an advantage that was irreplaceable besides? And he wanted to ask them, "Did my wife really have a lover?" And if they said "no," he would believe them. He would believe whatever they said.

He remembered in despair the contempt that people, especially those who are armed, had for a deceived husband. He was a deceived husband! Feeling that he had been classified filled him with emotion and thanks.

"Did my wife really have a lover?" he asked them, his eyes blinking greedily, because now Martim wanted everything that had happened to be very much his.

The two detectives saw his tears and exchanged ironical looks.

"He's crying," the one with tobacco on his lapel said, nodding at him. "Besides being a . . ." he was going to say the word, but he remembered the presence of a lady in time—"besides that, he cries like a coward."

And that was how, with a new term of classification, Martim re-entered the world of other people, the world he had left in order to rebuild. And he recognized with a sniveling humility, like a dog who has a master but no teeth, the old world where he was once something, the old world where we who need to be something other people can see—otherwise, other people will run the risk of not being themselves any more; and what a complication that would be! He was the word that the detective had not dared pronounce in front of Vitória, a coward. "They must be right," Martim thought avidly, generously skipping over his own disbelief. "They must be right, they know what they're doing," he thought, contented as a woman. He was very impressed by everybody's kindness. They were so kind that they accepted him back. They even had a designated spot where there were two names waiting for him. Were they accepting his return? Oh, but much more than that: they actually demanded his return. They even came looking for him! No man could be lost; the advance of millions needed every man! And they were even ready to erase—not the crime itself, never that, fortunately!—but what he had done that was worse: his attempt to break the silence that man needed in order to advance while they slept."

"What's that music?" he suddenly asked, for he had never heard a phonograph in that house.

"Ermelinda didn't want to hear what was going on in here and she put a record on. But she told me to tell you that she'll wave good-bye from the window," Vitória said.

The unexpected interruption confused them all a little. For an instant they stood there looking at one another, each trying to discover the other's particular importance in the fact of the phonograph. Until that moment, one or another of those present had been in charge of the situation. But now it seemed to be happening all by itself; the meeting had no chairman, events were going on by themselves.

"That's it," the mayor said insecurely, but with severity, because he was there within his own circumscription and it was up to him to make everything clear.

And all of them, without realizing it, seemed to have forgotten some objective, or for a moment they had lost the thing that they stood for. Things become disarrayed so easily with a certain lazy kindness and with a certain empty meditation, that often everybody goes back home and, having awakened from a mirage finally, begins again to do what really matters. And what does really matter? I don't know. Maybe it is to feel with ironic kindness the way that things that are most real and that what we want most suddenly seems to be a dream—that we simply know quite well that . . . that what?

"Will he go to jail?" Vitória asked foolishly, passing her hand across her dry mouth.

"But of course!" Martim said quickly, looking at her resentfully, as if she had clumsily offended the men. "Of course!" he said, flattering them; his voice was soft and not very virile.

Vitória looked at him perplexed.

"Is he all right, Mayor?" she whispered as if she were in a sickroom.

Like a bashful hermaphrodite, Martim lowered his eyes, hiding the fact that he was so complete and perfect. Oh, he was becoming aware of so many things: that he must have seemed so stupid in the eyes of other people; that he himself was making himself stupid; that so many times the feelings he had were not real; that he was pretending truth as a way to reach it. And that he was on the brink of a disaster, and that he might suddenly start trembling with fever or suddenly feel in his own flesh the reality that was happening to him. "Please don't notice," he thought, "that I'm exhausted."

The mayor nodded his head, looking at him and speaking about him as if he were not present.

"That's the way it is, ma'am. When the time comes they break down like that. Before that they think they're something," the mayor said, examining Martim with a curiosity that was already tired from so much practice. "But when the time to be arrested comes, they turn into women; they're afraid."

"Afraid? Oh no," Martim thought, really frightened and upset. "They don't understand me! They have the advantage of arresting me, and they don't even know why!" He lowered his head, annihilated, solitary. Would he be arrested for no special reason?

But as that man was damnably difficult to knock down, he thought, "It's all right. Who can tell whether jail might not be just the place where I'll find what I want?" Because, like a person who has already eaten the cake and still keeps on looking for the cake, he was still enthralled by the idea of "reform." It's all right. For example, in the peace and quiet of jail he could write his confused message. "My own story," he thought, made over again with the fatuousness that he needed to keep a minimum of personal dignity, the dignity which the mayor had snatched away from him. Because there's a lot left for me to do! Because after all, what the hell! He suddenly remembered "I used everything I could, except, except imagination! I just forgot!" And imagining was a legitimate means of arriving. Because there was no way of escaping the truth, one could use a lie without any scruples. Martim remembered when he had tried to write in the woodshed; and how, out of baseness, he had not used any lies; and how he had been dully honest with something that was too big for us to be honest with, we who have the idea that dishonest people have of honesty.

But in jail, with imagination, he could write that very twisted story of a man who had . . . Had what? Let's say—a regret and a fright?

"Above all," he thought, "I swear that in my book I will have the courage to leave unexplained what cannot be explained."

"Besides," he then thought—"the difficulty of it doesn't have any importance at all." Because it's difficult to tell things again, he would use lots of words—so many that it would end up being a book of words. And that pleased him, right from the start. Because he liked quantity too, not just quality, the way they talk about guava jelly. And if he were only tired, he was also greedy, because, after all, what is bigger is always better than what is smaller, even if not always. A fat book, then. He would write the following dedication: "To our crimes." Or, who knows, maybe: "To our inexplicable crimes."

Martim was contented, attentive, thinking up the story he would write. "In some way each of us offers up his life to an impossibility. But it is also true that the impossibility ends up by being closer to our fingers than we are ourselves, because reality belongs to God." Martim then thought that we have a body and a soul and a wishing and our children—and that, nevertheless, what we really are is what the impossible creates in us. And, who knows, his might be the story of an impossibility that had been touched, of the way in which it could be touched, when fingers

(343)

feel the vein in our pulse in the silence. So, that man who once had not even known how to write down a list of "things to know" wanted to write—with his eyes closed in a daydream like the one an old woman has when she remembers the past and seems to transpose it into a hope for the future. Again his armor was shining. He knew only superficially what that book dedicated to our crimes would be. Of one thing, however, he was serenely almost certain, even though cautiously vague: he would end the book with an apotheosis. Ever since he had been a child he had always had a certain tendency toward celebration, which was the most generous part of his nature, that tendency toward the grand. But in the end everything that people strive for is nothing but a preparation for a perfect finale. In which, it is true, one runs the risk of starting to talk out loud, and, finally, only softness is powerful, Martim was beginning to be aware of that. But the temptation of an apotheosis was too strong: he had always been a man who had wanted to buy everybody a drink; he had always become upset when he had been the patsy, and he had never had a chance because of his skill and stinginess; he had always yearned for a generous apotheosis, without any economy, the way musicals end, with the whole cast coming on stage.

"Oh God, God." He was exhausted. He didn't want any apotheosis at all.

Serious now, exhausted, he was looking with drooping hands. Up till then he had been playing out of pure excitement. But now what he wanted was poverty and sweetness. He was soft, tired, he wanted . . . what did he want? "What do I want?" Oh God, help him, he does not know what he wants.

He did not know. And with a superhuman effort to give it to himself, he made an expression on his face which if they had been able to read they would have known what he wanted, even if they could not have said what it was. What did he really want? He did not know. A person substitutes so much that he ends up not knowing.

Oh, let's not get too complicated. After all, in the last

analysis everything is reduced to yes or no. He wanted a "yes." Which could be given with his head bowed or along with all of the rest of the cast on stage; it is a small matter of personal preference, and *de gustibus non disputandum.*

And the truth was that Martim was about to collapse from fatigue. For months he had been working beyond his capacity because it was a question of an inferior person. His breath was short, and the capacity of his stomach small. The crime itself had been a performance that had drained him. "In jail I'll see if I can get some vitamin pills," he thought vaguely, he who had always had the secret desire to be fat. His breath was short and he was becoming nauseated over being a person; he had swallowed more than he could digest.

Out of fatigue then, with the quick balm of a vision, he took refuge among the thick plants of his plot of ground, which must now be peacefully getting ready for night among the running of the rats. "I'm going to the devil," he then said to himself, looking at the men, nauseated at being a man. The peaceful plants were calling him. "Not to be," that was a man's vast night. "Even if it's not even the intelligence with which one goes to bed with a woman," he thought, deceiving himself, and so deep that he really did not understand what he had meant by it. His desirous thoughts went back to the plants of his Tertiary plot, with a longing for the black rats. A softness made up out of sensuality dragged him out of the struggle; it gave him a nostalgic shamelessness, a wandering melancholy. He still tried vaguely to stand up straight and make himself over: "I'm a Brazilian, after all, what the hell!" But he could not make it. That man was sated; he wanted refuge and peace.

But in order to find that peace he would have to forget about other people.

To find that refuge he would have to be himself, that himself that has nothing to do with anybody else. "But I have a right to that!" he justified himself in a tired way. "What the hell! What do I have to do with other people? There's a place where, before order and before names, I am I! And who can tell if that's not the real place in common with what I set out to find? That place which is our common and solitary land, and where we just feel around like blind men. Isn't that all we ask for? I accept you: place of horror where cats meow contentedly, where angels have nighttime space to flap their beautiful wings, where the innards of a woman are a future child, and where God rules that grave disorder of which we are the happy offspring.

Then why fight? Inside a man there was a place which was pure light, but it did not show itself in the eyes or cloud them over. It was a place where, all tricks aside, one exists; a place where, without the least pretension, one exists; or will we be, from the fact of just being, warhorses! Let's not complicate life; we have a right to this tranquil pleasure! And it isn't even a matter for discussion; we don't have the capacity for argument. To be honest, long before we were aware of it, dogs were already loving each other; in short, by the right of having been born, we have the right to be what we are. So let's take advantage of it, let's not exaggerate the importance of other people! Because there exists in a man a point that is just as sacred as the existence of other people. Let other people take care of themselves! From birth a man has the right to be able to go to sleep peacefully— because things are not as dangerous as all that, and the world won't come to an end tomorrow. Fear may have confused reality with desire a little bit, but the dog in us knows the way. "What the hell! What blame do I have for the silent faces of men? You have to trust a little too, because thank God we have strong instincts and sharp teeth, not to mention intuition. After all is said and done, from birth we have that capacity to sit down quietly beside the door of a house at night. And there are ideas that come out of that . . ."

Yes, that was the way it had happened to him. Some ideas and fright. Fright, rage, love, and then the door of the house becomes small, and those feelings and those rights are not enough. You have to be born to something greater . . . What's missing? When the house itself becomes small, the man leaves at dawn to bring something back.

Martim came to rapidly. His softness had passed. That was his chance! He could not lose it out of mere fatigue, he who had gone through a whole life without knowing what to do with his small self, and who now at last had found what to do with himself, small as he was. Join up with the small ones. He came to rapidly, now that he had finally reached a small apotheosis.

"O.K., let's get going," the detective said, folding up the map.

"I hope, ma'am," the mayor said, "that he hasn't caused you any trouble. You were very brave, there aren't many women who could have had a criminal in their house without being afraid. Many ladies like you, that is. Those of us in the town hall hope that it hasn't been any trouble for you."

"No, no," Vitória said rapidly, blushing because she was confused.

Trouble? No, no. Hadn't she got what she wanted out of him, hadn't she?

"Let's go then," the detective said, looking at Martim in a way that was feigned a little, he being really quite used to prisoners. "You don't seem to be the kind of person who would try to make an escape, but I'd better tell you that I'll shoot you at the first sign."

Large and unarmed, Martim was quick to say:

"No, I'll behave!" He said it with pleasure and attention, trying with pleasure to repeat some previous situation, by means of which this one would become understandable. "And don't forget that I didn't do anything, see? Don't forget to tell that to the judge: I didn't do anything! Don't forget that I could have tried to run away," he said in his wisdom.

"Try it and see."

"Oh, I don't mean that I could run away now!" Martim corrected him respectfully. "I meant that I could have run away before! Because before you got here, don't forget, I had months in which to run away!"

What passed rapidly through his head was this: it would have been in his favor if he had lied, saying that he had not run away because he had planned to give himself up . . . But—thinking well and on new terms—how could anyone understand why he had not run away unless he had planned to give himself up? That he had not run away for other reasons was a truth that no longer existed. For an instant Martim remembered the sheet of paper on which he had written his plans, and he remembered that he had not run away because he had wanted to have enough time to carry them out—but that had now become so incomprehensible and was so far removed from the thinking of the four men that it only had one real and final meaning: it had stopped him from running away. Which could be called a lack of resistance. Which could be an extenuating circumstance. How perfect everything had turned out! He blinked.

"You couldn't have run away if you'd wanted to," the detective answered. "After this lady told the professor about her suspicions, we began investigating; and you were under surveillance. If we didn't move sooner it was because our method is to be sure of what we're doing," he added with dignity.

Martim nodded his head with surprise and curiosity; he had completely forgotten how, in a general way, people are stupid.

"But I couldn't have guessed that I was being watched, could I?" he argued with patience. "I didn't know that I was being watched, and yet I still didn't try to run away, did I?"

"No, that's right," the detective agreed reluctantly, looking at him a little fascinated: there was something wrong with it all, but the detective couldn't say what.

"Sure he knew he couldn't get away," dared the one with tobacco on his lapel, who was one of the liveliest people that Martim had created. "He knew he couldn't get to run away," he said, trying to clear up the confusion into which the prisoner had plunged them—"and knowing he was surrounded, he decided not to run away so he could look like a person who's sorry and wants to surrender!" he suggested with sagacity.

Martim looked at him, surprised. He was going to have to experience everything! Even innocence. Unjustly accused, for the first time Martim was experiencing innocence. His eyes blinked damply, gratefully. Another symbol had been reached.

(348)

The Apple in the Dark

And Martim understood then why his father, already near the end of his life, would say stubbornly, inexplicably, "I always got what I wanted." Yes, in some way, one always got it. "And I, what did I get? I got experience, which is the thing that people are born for; and there is deep freedom in experience. But experiencing what? Experiencing that thing which we are and you are? It's true that the most we experience comes with pain, but it's also true that that is the inescapable way of reaching the one maximum point, and everything has one moment, and then we get ready for the other moment, which will be the first one— and if all of this is confusing, we are completely protected in all of this by what we are, we who are desire."

"But in the end, what did I get from all of that? A lot. And so many times our freedom is so intense that we turn our faces away. Yes, but in everything I got, what can I do with the evil? Oh, but it's as if evil were the same thing as good, except that it has different practical results. It comes from the same blind desire, as if evil were the lack of organization of good; so many times a very intense goodness overflows into evil. The natural fact is that evil is a more rapid means of communication. But from now on I'm going to organize my evil into good, now that I no longer have the same hunger to be good. Now that I'm ready for my own soul, now that I love other people. Will I still be able to get something? But I did manage to give the world existence! Which means that now I should be ready to take part in a war of vengeance or of goodness or of error or of glory, and that I'm ready to make mistakes or be right, now that I am at last common."

With a bit of fright, Martim understood that he had not been looking for freedom. He had been trying to free himself, yes, but only so that he could go on without any barriers to meet his fate. He had wanted to be unencumbered; the truth was that he had unencumbered himself of a crime. He did not want to invent a destiny, but he wanted to copy some important thing which was fateful in the sense that it was something that already existed, and of whose existence he had always known, like one who has the word on the tip of his tongue and cannot remember it. He had wanted to be free to go out and meet what existed and what was not any more attainable. It was as unattainable as inventing. No matter how much freedom he might have, he would only be able to create what already had existed. The great prison! The great prison! But it had the beauty of difficulty. Finally he had got what he wanted. I have created what already exists. And he had added something more to what had existed: the immaterial addition of himself.

"Let's go," Martim said, going over to the four men and the security they were offering him. "Let's go," he said with the dignity of a fireman. "Good-bye, Dona Vitória—"

Remembering with sudden pleasure a very ancient and humble phrase, gospel words, he then added, almost marvelling, slowly, little by little:

"Forgive me for anything I may have done that I did not mean to do."

What bothered Martim then was the fact that he had not quoted the phrase exactly. No, that was not how the phrase he vaguely remembered went!—and it became important for him to reproduce it without the slightest error, as if a simple change in syllables would change its ancient meaning and take away the perfection of a perfect way to say good-bye—any transformation in ritual makes a man individual, which leaves in danger all the construction and work of millions; any mistake in the phrase would make it personal. And, frankly, there was no need to be personal. If it were not for that stubbornness, a person could discover that perfect formulas already exist for everything he wants to say, that everything he had wanted to come into existence had already really existed; that the word itself came before man—and those four representatives knew that. They knew that the whole question is a matter of knowing how to imitate, because when the imitation is original, it is our experience. Martim had come to understand why people imitated.

And suddenly, just like that, Martim remembered what the phrase was!

"Forgive me for any thoughtless remark!" he corrected himself then with vanity, because that was the ritual phrase!

"Come now," Vitória said, blushing, turning her eyes away.

"All of us," Martim said, suddenly illogical, "all of us were very happy!"

"Come now," Vitória repeated.

Martim stuck out his hand impulsively. But because the woman had not expected the gesture, she drew back frightened as she put out her own. In that fraction of a second, the man withdrew his own hand without offense—and Vitória, who now had hers outstretched, stood there with her arm uselessly and painfully extended, as if hers had been the initiative of reaching out—with a gesture that suddenly had become one of appeal— for the hand of the man. Martim, perceiving in time the thin outstretched arm, ran forward emotionally with both of his hands uplifted, and he warmly squeezed the icy fingers of the woman, who could not restrain a movement of retreat and fear.

"Did I hurt you?!" he shouted.

"No, no!" she protested, terrified.

Then they were silent. The woman did not say anything else. Something had ended definitively. Martim looked at that empty, tremulous female face, that shapeless, human thing that had two eyes.

And then the mercy that he had been waiting for all of his life broke out inside his chest heavily and impotently, the exposed heart of Jesus, mercy attacked him like a pain. The man's eyes became glassy, his features filled up with a beauty that only God would not be repelled by, he seemed about to have had an attack of paralysis. He babbled:

"Please forgive me for not having . . ." —and the worst part of what he said was happily inaudible, as if the paralysis had already reached that mouth, which was twisted with mercy.

Vitória raised her heard. Her insulted face became white, tragic, and hard. But her look did not tremble, and the face that had been slapped stayed haughty and empty. Martim had the feeling that his very kindness had been a terrible blow—did he have the right to be good?

"Please forgive me for not having . . ." he murmured as he excused himself like someone who was impotent.

(351)

THE APPLE IN THE DARK

But she would never forgive him. Why had he asked for
pardon? She would never forgive him. If until then there had
been no question of accusing him, at that moment in which he
begged forgiveness he had opened up a wound that could not be
healed. And he saw that, that she would not forgive him. He saw
that, even if it were something that he had thought of or spoken
about. But he knew; she would never forgive him. That was not
a thing that could be spoken; it was a thing that was happening,
and it was not the absence of words that makes something that
was existing stop existing, and a plant feels when the wind is
dark because it trembles, and a horse in the middle of the road
seems to have had a thought, and when the branches of a tree
wave, there is still never a single word, and someday one must
discover what we are: he knew that she would never forgive him.
Then Martim kneeled down in front of her and said:

"Forgive me."

From the height of her raised head, she looked down at him,
beyond appeal, like a terrible queen, her severe wings opened
up.

"What the devil am I doing?" the kneeling man wondered,
interested, and he could almost hear her telling someone years
later: he went so far as to kneel down.

But the woman with a sudden irrepressible movement
clasped her stomach with her hands, there where a woman pains,
her mouth trembled as it was touched by it, the future was a
difficult birth: with the movement of an animal, she clasped her
stomach, where fate makes a woman pain, and the joy was such
a misery, her mouth trembled, poor, afflicted.

"What are you doing?" she shouted at him.

But he was waiting with an imploring look, he was insisting
imploringly, he now wanted more than just the woman's gesture, that gesture with which she had finally conceded pity for
herself—he also wanted her pity for him. And, involuntarily,
against her own strength, tortured, feeling as best she could—
she could not help obeying in the end as she lowered her dry
eyes, and, fascinated, dragged along, with the taste of blood

(3 5 2)

filling her whole mouth, she looked at him with stern mercy—tortured and obeying, glorified and obeying, in pain and obeying. Oh, it was something impossible to escape from—sculptors had already done images of women and kneeling men, there was a whole long past of forgiveness and love and sacrifice, it was something from which it was impossible to escape. And if she had been free, she would have somehow stretched her hand out over the head of the kneeling man; there are gestures that can be made, there still are gestures that can be made:

"What are you doing?" she said to him austerely, as if she had raised him up.

The man got up, dusted off his pants. The woman raised her head higher. And it was only then that they were surprised.

But then fortunately it was too late; some essential thing had been done. What had really happened was not known; most of all, neither of them knew, people make a lot of substitutions. Some essential thing had happened which they did not understand, and they were surprised; it may have been something not meant to be understood. Who knows but what the essential thing was destined not to be understood? If we are blind, why do we insist on seeing with our eyes, why do we try to use these hands of ours, which are twisted into fingers? Why do we try to hear with our ears things that are not sound? And why do we try, over and over again, the door of comprehension? The essential thing is destined only to be fulfilled. Glory to God, Glory to God. Amen. And one of the indirect ways of understanding is to find things beautiful. From where I am standing, life is very beautiful. A man, impotent as a person, had knelt down. A woman, offended in her destiny, had raised her head which had been sacrificed by forgiveness. And, by God, something had happened. Something had happened in a careful way, so that our modesty would not be wounded.

They both avoided looking at one another, overwrought with themselves, as if they finally had become part of that greater thing which sometimes manages to express itself in tragedy. As if there are acts that are done totally or else cannot be achieved, something is realized that thought could not attain, we who are created with such atrocious perfection—and the pain is in the fact that we are not at the level of our perfection; as for our beauty, we can barely stand it. Martim, for example, looked at his shoes at that moment. Oh why do we disguise ourselves so much? Embarrassed by the moment of his death, he would be capable of covering up by whistling, as if they had just again realized the miracle of forgiveness; embarrassed by that miserable scene, they avoided looking at each other, uneasy, there are so many unaesthetic things to forgive. But, even covered with ridicule and rags, the mimicry of the resurrection had been done. Those things which seem not to happen, but do happen.

Because how could it be explained otherwise—without the resurrection and its glory. That that woman right there had been born for a daily life; that she, standing there, after all, after all, born for the mystery of daily life, would be the one who tomorrow would give Francisco orders. How could it be explained that that wounded woman, and perhaps only because she had been mortally wounded, would be the same one who tomorrow would go out into the fields again, whole again like a woman who has had a child and whose body has closed up again? Otherwise, how could it be explained that that man, frayed, unprotected, would still continue to be that thing and look at himself and be recognized even by the eyes of a child: a man, a man with a future? The resurrection, as had been promised, had been made. As unimportant as any other miracle. Carefully discreet, so as not to scandalize us. Exactly as we promise ourselves; and you can leave us to our task, and God is our task, we are not God's task. You can leave life to us. Oh, we know quite well what we are doing, with the same impassivity with which the dead who are laid out know so well what they are doing.

The man brushed off his pants again, passed the back of his hand across his nose. He did not look at the woman because he was ashamed of his own exhibitionism, that business of kneeling down; still it is also true that a person has to explain himself. His eyes blinked several times because he realized that in the whole

scene there was something that had escaped him. He felt half-
confused, he was not understanding very well nor did he have
the time, or, better yet, the will to understand any more. But at
least he sniffed again, and once more he passed his hand across
his wet nose. But he felt that, besides having "raised the curtain," he had just fulfilled another commonplace which he had
been searching for since childhood: that story about kneeling
down had always pursued him.

One could say that at last he was realizing everything that he
had planned, even if he had not been able to write down what
he wanted on paper. It was also true that many times that man
had forced his own hand. But it had been necessary. It could not
have been any other way. Then, uncertain, anxious, unprotected,
he thought, "I got what I wanted. It wasn't much. But when you
come right down to it, it's the whole thing, isn't it? Say that it is.
Say it. Make that gesture, the one that's hardest to make, the
most difficult one, and say: yes."

Then, with superhuman effort, he said "yes." And then—
beaten down, tired—another promise to him had been fulfilled.
Because "yes" is after all the content of "no." He had just
touched the objective part of no. He had at last touched the
content of his crime.

Nausea came over him, that soft pleasure as if one had got
over to the other side of death, that minimum point which is the
living point of life, the vein in the pulse. In agony, Martim
turned his face away from himself and sought the compensating
faces of the others.

The others were waiting curiously after having witnessed the
melodrama of the genuflection. Martim fluttered his eyelids
several times, indecisive, tired—those faces. Those faces. And
looking at the four men and the woman, such an absurd hope
came over him that it could only have been a faith. And it had
nothing to do with what was happening, nor with the men who
were waiting, nor with himself. Again he had had in a nauseating
flash the following: certainty. Which was a hope that was
impersonal to the point of tears. As if hope did not mean hoping

for, but getting. With that absurd hope, Martim was reaching something, like a man who was holding a child by the hand.

Stupefied, not knowing whom to speak to, under the weight of fatigue, he looked at them one by one. And more and more he was coming closer to a truth that was imposing itself in such a way that, even without his understanding it, it still kept on imposing itself. Without understanding it? But yes, he did understand it in some way! He understood the way one understands a number: it's impossible to think about a number in terms of words, it's only possible to think about a number as that very number. And it was in that inescapable way that he understood—and if he were to attempt to know any more, then—then the truth would become impossible.

"But in what? What did he have hope in?" he asked himself, suddenly bothered again. A certain pity for the world made him avoid carrying his thoughts to the end.

Then, without answering his question, for by doing so he would make it all absurd; without even trying to answer, he thought that it was in his very extreme lack that he had hope. As if a man were so poor that—that "it cannot be so." There was a secret logic in that absurd thought, except that he had not managed to sound and locate that impalpable logic. If Martim knew that he had been right, it was because he was in pain. But he would never be able to explain, and there is something that we will never know. But our lack sustains us, he said to himself, now that he had finally lost the limits of comprehension and was admitting what is not known.

It was then that the man suddenly really perked up, and he snuffed. There's no doubt, I agree too: the thing is illogical, and hoping is illogical, he thought very animatedly, buying everybody a drink. It's as illogical, he thought knowingly, as two-and-two-is-four, which no one so far has ever proved. But if on the basis of two-and-two-is-four you can build your own reality, then for God's sake why have any scruples? Yeah, if that's how it is, let's take advantage of it, people! life is short! Martim looked at the men in a kind of immoral way; there was cynicism on his face. But he was not being cynical, he was, he was trying to amuse them and make them happy, and impossibility makes the clown. He was giving out of love, out of pure love. Love!—a handspring to amuse them. Oh, amusing other people is one of the most emotional ways of existing; it's true that sometimes radio stars get all worked up and commit suicide, but the fact is that sometimes they come in contact with the difficulty of love.

His cynicism, or whatever it was, did not sustain him for very long.

Oh God, how tired and uncertain that man was! That man did not know too well what hope was. Even though he tried to rationalize hope—oh, even though he tried. But instead of thinking about what he planned to think about, he was thinking like a busy woman. "Explaining never got anybody anywhere, and understanding is futility," he said like a woman busy nursing her child.

But no! But no! He had to think. He simply could not sail off like that—just like that! Then, losing his footing, he argued with himself and justified himself. "Having no hope is the most stupid thing that could happen to a man." It would be the failure of a man's life. Just as not loving was a sin of frivolity, so not having hope was superficiality. Not loving was nature going astray. And what about the perversion there was in not having any hope? Well—that, that he understood with his body. Furthermore—in the name of other people!—it's a sin not to have any hope. There's no right for anyone not to have any. Not having any hope is a luxury. Oh, Martim knew that his hope would scandalize optimists. He knew that optimists would stand him up and shoot him if they heard him because hope is startling. One has to be a man to have the courage to be struck by hope.

And then Martim was really startled.

"Do you know what you're doing, son?"

"Yes, I do, father."

"Do you know that with hope you will never have any more rest, son?"

"Yes, I do, father."

"Do you know that with hope all your other weapons will be lost, son?"

"Yes, I do, father."

"And that unless you're cynical you'll be naked?"

"Yes, I do, father."

"Do you know that hope also means not believing, son?"

"Yes, I do, father."

"Do you know that believing is as hard to bear as a mother's curse?"

"Yes, I do, father."

"Do you know that our likeness is just a lot of filth?"

"Yes, I do, father."

"And do you know that you too are just a lot of filth?"

"Yes, I do, father."

"But do you know that I'm not referring to the baseness that attracts us so much and which we admire and desire, but to the fact that our likeness, besides everything else, is so dull?"

"Yes, I do, father."

"Do you know that hope sometimes consists simply of a question that has no answer?"

"Yes, I do, father."

"Do you know that in the end none of that ever gets beyond being love? a great love?"

"Yes, I do, father."

"But do you know that a person can get tangled up in one word and lose years out of his life? And that hope can become a word, a dogma and a net and a shameful thing? Are you prepared to know that if things are looked at closely they have no shape, and that if things are looked at from a distance they cannot be seen? And that there is only one instant for everything? And that it is not easy to live just by the memory of an instant?"

"That instant . . ."

"Be quiet. Do you know what life's muscle is? If you say that you know you're no good; if you say that you don't know you're no good." (His father was beginning to lose the thread.)

(358)

"I don't know," he replied without conviction, but because he knew that it was the answer that should be given.

"Have you 'drawn back the curtain' a lot lately, son?"

"Yes, I have, father," he said, resentful at the intrusion on his privacy; whenever his father had wanted to "understand him," he had always left him tense.

"How are your sexual relations going, son?"

"Fine," he answered with a wish to tell his father to go back to the hell he had taken him out of.

"Do you know that love is blind, that someone who loves something ugly thinks that it's pretty, and that it could even be yellow for that matter, even if it's in bad taste? and that the shoemaker's children go barefoot, and that you make do with what you have, and that there's a grain of truth in everything?" his father said, losing the thread a little more. Before long he would start telling him what he used to do with women, before he married your mother, naturally. "Do you know that hope is hard to beat, for the weak defeat and for the strong, etc.?"

"Yes, I do, father."

"My boy. Do you know that from now on, wherever you go, you will be pursued by hope?"

"Yes, I do, father."

"Are you prepared to accept the heavy burden of joy?"

"Yes, I am, father."

"But, my boy! do you know that it's practically impossible to do?"

"Yes, I do, father."

"Do you know, at least, that hope is a great big absurdity, my boy?"

"Yes, I do, father."

"Do you know that you have to be grown-up to have hope!!!"

"I do, I do, I do!"

"Then go ahead, son. My order is for you to suffer with hope."

But already with this first nostalgia, the last one, like the first one, based on nevermore, Martim shouted for protection.

"What's that light, Dad?" he shouted, alone now in his

hope, walking on all fours to make his father laugh, asking a very old and silly little question so as to postpone the moment when he would have to take on the world. "What's that light, Daddy!" he asked playfully, with his heart pounding from the loneliness.

His father hesitated, severe and sad in his grave.

"It's the end of the day," he said, only out of pity.

And that was what it was.

It was almost night, and the beauty of it weighed upon his chest. Martim disguised it as best he could, he whistled something vague and tuneless, looking at the ceiling.

From where, slowly and cautiously, he lowered his eyes to the others—and he looked at his fellows, one by one. Who are you? They were faces with noses. Should he invest all of his small fortune in a gesture of confidence? And yet it was a life that could not be repeated, his, the one they would give him. Who are you? It was difficult giving to them. Loving was a sacrifice. And yet—and yet there was a discontinuity. He had barely begun and there was already a discontinuity. Would he have to accept that too, the discontinuity with which he looked at them and—who were those men? Who are you? What doubtful thing are you? As if in some absurd way I had already seen better times and knew a different race of people I can not accept you, but only love you? Really, who are you? And up to what point? And—and will I be able to love that thing you are?

He looked at them, tired, incredulous. He did not know them. A person was sporadic; he no longer knew them. Humble, he still tried to force himself to accept that too: not knowing them.

But he could not bear it; he could not bear it. "How can I go on lying? I don't believe! I don't believe!" And looking at the four men and the woman, he wanted only plants, the plants, the silence of plants. But with his attention slightly roused, he repeated slowly: "I don't believe." Slowly dazed, "I don't believe . . ." Dazed, yes. Because, "Halleluia, Halleluia, I'm hungry again. So hungry that I need to be more than one. I need to

(360)

be two—two? No! Three, five, thirty, millions. One is hard to bear. I need millions of men and women, and the tragedy of Halleluia." "I don't believe!" and the great lack had been born again. His extreme penury had brought him to a vertigo of ecstasy. "I don't believe," he said hungrily, looking at the faces of the men for the thing a man looks for. "I'm hungry," he repeated, abandoned. Should he thank God for his hunger? Because need was sustaining him.

Stupefied, without knowing whom to speak to, he examined them one by one. And he—he simply did not believe. *Eppur, si muove*, he said with the obstinacy of a jackass.

"Let's go," he said then, going uncertainly over to the four small and confused men. "Let's go," he said. Because they must have known what they were doing. They certainly knew what they were doing. In the name of God, I command you to be sure. Because a whole precious and putrescent weight was being given into their hands, a weight to be thrown into the sea, and a very heavy one too. And it was not a simple thing—because there had to be mercy when that burden of guilt was thrown overboard too. Because we are not so guilty after all; we are more stupid than guilty. So with mercy too, then. "In the name of God, I'm only waiting for you to know what you're doing. Because I, my son, I am only hungry. And I have that clumsy way of reaching for an apple in the dark—and trying not to drop it."

A NOTE ON THE TYPE

The text of this book is set in ELECTRA, a typeface designed by W(illiam) A(ddison) Dwiggins for the Mergenthaler Linotype Company and first made available in 1935. Electra cannot be classified as either "modern" or "old style." It is not based on any historical model, and hence does not echo any particular period or style of type design. It avoids the extreme contrast between "thick" and "thin" elements that marks most modern faces, and is without eccentricities which catch the eye and interfere with reading. In general, Electra is a simple, readable typeface which attempts to give a feeling of fluidity, power, and speed.

W. A. Dwiggins (1880–1956) was born in Martinsville, Ohio, and studied art in Chicago. In 1904 he moved to Hingham, Massachusetts, where he built a solid reputation as a designer of advertisements and as a calligrapher. He began an association with the Mergenthaler Linotype Company in 1929, and over the next twenty-seven years designed a number of book types, of which Metro, Electra, and Caledonia have been used very widely. In 1930 Dwiggins became interested in marionettes, and through the years made many important contributions to the art of puppetry and the design of marionettes.